Blaming
the Wind

ALESSANDRA
HARRIS

Blaming the Wind
A Red Adept Publishing Book

Red Adept Publishing, LLC
104 Bugenfield Court
Garner, NC 27529
http://RedAdeptPublishing.com/

Print ISBN-13: 978-1-940215-70-9
Print ISBN-10: 1-940215-70-6

First Print Edition: April 2016

Cover and Formatting: Streetlight Graphics

For all those with secrets.

"If you reveal your secrets to the wind you should not blame the wind for revealing them to the trees."

- *Sand and Foam*, by Kahlil Gibran

PART ONE

CHAPTER ONE

HALLOWEEN

SOPHIA

S OPHIA HAD ACED MOST TESTS she'd taken in her life; but once, just
this once, she hoped for a negative result. She drew a long breath,
and her russet-brown hands shook as she picked up the pregnancy test
from the marble vanity. Like a fortuneteller looking into a crystal ball,
she peered through the plastic cover. She grabbed the box and reread
the instructions: "A (+) sign in the round window indicates a 'pregnant'
result. A (−) sign in the round window indicates a 'not pregnant' result."
A huge plus sign stared back at her from the stick.

Tears filled her eyes, blurring her vision. Wiping them away with one
hand, she opened a plastic bag and shoved the pregnancy test and empty
box into it. As she jammed the bag into the garbage bin underneath the
sink, she felt more like a teenager hiding a pregnancy test from her parents
than the married woman she'd been for over a year and a half. But she
wasn't ready to tell Terrence. She knew what his reaction would be.

Sophia left the master bathroom and shut the door as if to quarantine
the newly acquired information. The nausea and intense fatigue over the
past few weeks now made sense. She closed the blinds, blocking out the
blackness of night. Her king-sized bed, with its soft pillows and comfy
blankets, had never been so appealing, so she pulled back the black-and-
white embroidered bedspread and slid underneath it. Luckily, Terrence
wouldn't be home until late, so she had plenty of time to let the news
sink in without him questioning why she was in bed. She'd agreed to
go to The Spot with Tara that night, but maybe she could get out of it.

Shutting her eyes, she did what she did best when life was too stressful—she hid. It was a coping mechanism she had developed two decades before, in the sixth grade, the year she had been labeled "gifted." Honors courses, scholastic activities, and tests, tests, tests had followed. Usually just lying in bed and resting her body helped her escape stress. But now her heart thumped and she struggled to breathe. Throwing off the blanket, she sat up. She inhaled through her nose, held her breath for a moment, then blew out the air, repeating the exercise until her heart steadied.

Her phone rang, and she grabbed it from the nightstand. It was her mom. She put the phone back down. Seconds later, it rang again. *This better be important.*

"Hello, Mom," Sophia answered.

"So how'd the interview go?" her mom asked.

"It went." She'd gone on a job interview a few hours earlier for an entry-level sales job but had received the same response she got at the majority of the interviews she went on—she was overqualified and in a higher salary bracket than the position provided. She'd known that going into the interview, but at this rate, any job would do to help pay the mortgage.

"Based on your tone, I'm assuming they didn't schedule a second interview?"

"Nope. But they said they'd be in contact."

"Well, keep applying."

Sophia had been applying for at least ten jobs a week ever since she'd been laid off from her sales job nine months earlier. At this point, she'd rather throw her laptop out the window than send another resume, rather pluck every hair from her body than interview for another position. But she didn't voice her frustration. Her mom hadn't held a job since Sophia was a child and had no idea what it was like to invest one hundred percent into a career just to be "let go."

"Of course I'll keep applying. So what's up, Mom?"

"I called to ask you for a favor. You know Carl's been having those heart palpitations, and I think part of the problem is Desiree. Your father up and left, and the last thing I need is this husband dying on me."

Here we go again. It had been over a quarter of a century since her father had left her mother for another woman. Sure, scar tissue still lined Sophia's heart from his departure, but she wished her mother would heal and move on, especially since she'd remarried Carl twenty-three years ago. When her mom wasn't harping on Sophia's dad, then she was complaining about Sophia's half-sister, Desiree. Her mom's second husband, Carl, spoiled their only child rotten, one reason Sophia preferred distance from Desiree.

"What's Desiree doing now?" Sophia asked.

"Doing?" Her mom's voice rose. "That's the problem. She dropped out of college and moved back home. Now she doesn't do anything but party, drink, and spend our money. Carl invested over one hundred thousand dollars in a private university just for her to drop out her senior year because she wants to be an actress. An actress! As if wannabe actresses aren't already overpopulating Los Angeles."

"Mom, give her a break."

"No, I'm the one who needs a break. I was hoping she could stay with you for a while. Maybe you can rub off on her a little bit."

Sophia sighed. "All she'll get from me is a case of the unemployment blues." *While I'll get a headache from her.*

"Now stop talking like that. You didn't graduate top of your class at Stanford to sit around and mope."

"And I didn't ask for Cisco to lay me off either. Anyways, I'll have to talk to Terrence about Desiree."

"Oh, yes. The stranger you ran off with. How's that going?"

"It's been over a year since we eloped, so he's not a stranger. And it's great." Sophia couldn't help but smile when thinking about Terrence. "We're getting into a nice married rhythm."

"Newlywed phase. Let's see how long that lasts. Just think about Desiree, please? I know you two aren't close, so this could be an opportunity to bond."

"That's a nice way to spin it, but you're right. I wish we had a closer relationship. I'm willing to help, but like I said, I have to run it by Terrence."

Sophia ended the call and glanced at the time. *How is it seven already?* She was supposed to be getting dressed for the Halloween party Tara was dragging her to. Sophia had bought a skimpy referee costume from Goodwill the day before, imagining she'd wear it with leggings for the party and on its own for Terrence later that night. Since he was an NBA sports agent, he'd get a kick out of it. But now, her desire to party had completely disappeared.

She pulled the covers back over her head. She'd prefer to stream a romantic movie and get lost in another world. Ever since the layoff, she'd been using Netflix to catch up on all the classic flicks she'd missed over the years as she studied or worked overtime. She'd finished *Love Jones* earlier in the day and couldn't wait to watch *Notting Hill*.

"Sophia?"

Her husband's voice startled her, and Sophia removed the blanket, finger-combing her pressed hair. "Terrence?"

Though impeccably dressed in a gray suit, he wore a sullen expression.

She hurried to him, stood on her tiptoes, and pressed her lips against his. "What are you doing home? Shouldn't you be prepping Eric Richards for the season opener with the Warriors tomorrow?"

Terrence's muscular arms enveloped her body. She inhaled his familiar after-work scent of musk cologne mixed with perspiration. "It's a long story, and it's been a long day. I wanted to come home and unwind. Why are you in bed?"

Sophia forced a yawn. "Oh, just resting."

"You and that bed. If it weren't an inanimate object, I'd be jealous of it."

"But I do need to get ready for the Halloween party." Sophia cupped her hands on his umber cheeks and peered into his large dark-brown eyes. "Will you change your mind and come with me?"

Terrence pecked her on the lips. "I would, but I had a helluva day. How was yours?"

The failed interview and the positive pregnancy test were both topics that required more energy and time than she currently had, and getting out of the conversation took precedence over her desire not to go out. "I'm running late. Can we talk later?"

Terrence pulled her toward the bed with a playful grin. "Just how late are you?"

"Late, late," Sophia said. *In more ways than one.*

Terrence pretended to pout, so Sophia stroked his black, slightly receding hair. She kissed his lips.

After, the corners of his mouth turned upward. "I'll wait up."

Sophia beamed at the gorgeous specimen that was her husband. As she padded to the bathroom, she tried to imprint that moment in her head. She wished she could freeze time and seal their marriage in a special time capsule. But she couldn't. Like an unwelcome guest, change was knocking at their door. Sooner or later, she would have to answer it.

⚬⚭⚬

JOSH

Josh unplugged the drain in the bathtub then gathered the discarded Halloween costumes off the floor. Opening the medicine cabinet, he scanned the orange-tinged bottles, grabbed the Vicodin, and popped one in his mouth. Beyond relieved that his dad duties were over for the day, all he wanted was a beer and to veg.

Tara stormed into the bathroom, a bath towel wrapped around her slender frame. "Josh, I'm running late for the Halloween party. Can you put the girls to bed?" she asked, drying her long blond hair with another towel.

Josh hesitated, envisioning his couch. Since he stayed home all day with the girls, he eagerly awaited Tara taking over at bedtime.

Tara rolled her eyes. "Forget it."

"No, no, I'll take care of it," Josh said.

"Take care of this mess of hair at some point too," Tara said.

Josh made a mental note to get his hair trimmed the next time he took the girls to Supercuts. After leaving the bathroom, he headed down the hallway lined with family pictures then entered the room Teeni and Michelle shared.

"Hey, hey, hey," he called to Teeni, who ran around in circles, flapping her arms like a bird. "It's bedtime." He groaned as he picked her up and placed her in her toddler bed.

"Snow Wipe," Teeni said, arms outstretched to her costume, which Josh fitted on a metal hanger.

"Michelle, get in bed already," he said to his four-year-old.

She lay on the rainbow rug, flipping the pages of her Disney Princesses book. Josh considered himself a patient person and he loved his girls, but after a long day and an even longer week, he just needed the day to be over. But Tara worked hard too, so she deserved a little fun of her own. Josh had to admit he wasn't exactly the life of the party lately.

"I'm Cinderella, Daddy, not Michelle." She crossed her arms, bottom lip stuck out.

He pulled back her pink comforter. "Get in bed, Cinderella."

Smiling, Michelle hopped under the pink sheets, and Josh tucked her in. He hung both costumes in the closet before turning off the light.

Next door, Josh found his eldest daughter in bed, scrolling through pictures on her overpriced iPod touch that Tara had bought against his protest. "I had the ba-est costume in second grade, Dad."

"Great," he said unenthusiastically. He wasn't happy about Chelsea's Elsa costume from *Frozen*. There had been plenty of reasonably priced costumes to pick from—like the other girls had chosen—but Tara had had to buy Chelsea the most expensive, though the dress would most likely only be worn once before spending the rest of its days in clothing purgatory with all the mismatched socks. "Lights out, Chelsea. I love you." Josh switched off her light.

The doorbell chimed, so Josh hurried to the kitchen, grabbed the bucket of candy, and opened the front door. Three boys in their early teens, wearing wrinkled jeans and hooded sweatshirts, extended their paper bags.

"And what are you three supposed to be?" Josh asked, putting a handful of candy in each bag.

"Teenagers," one of the boys said. "My mom said that's scary enough."

Chuckling, Josh shut the door on what was hopefully the last batch of trick-or-treaters. He grabbed a beer from the fridge. A murmur of music came from his and Tara's bedroom, but Josh headed for the couch. Suddenly the murmur morphed into loud music. The last thing he needed was the girls waking up.

"Jo-o-o-o-osh?" Tara yelled from the bedroom doorway. "Can you come zip up my dress? It's a little stuck."

"I'm just about to sit." He tried to hide the irritation in his voice. "Can you come here?"

Tara stormed toward Josh with an exasperated huff. He winced at her white, skintight nurse's costume as he inhaled the floral perfume cloaking her.

"I told you I'm late. All you want to do is watch that damn TV, Josh."

Josh wanted to say that this was the first time today he had flipped on the TV to watch a channel other than PBS Kids and that he was just about to sit down after a very long day of Halloween parades and trick-or-treating. Instead, he held his tongue.

Gathering her hair atop her head, Tara shoved her back toward him. "Zip."

"Tara, I don't think you can call this a dress," he said with a laugh as he struggled with the costume, which was so tight that the two sides refused to join. He noticed that the tag read size four, and he remembered she was a six. "Honey, this dress isn't even your size."

Tara pushed his hand away. She tugged and squirmed until the dress finally zipped, then she spun around to face him. "It fits, thank you very much."

Though her thin lips were pursed and her close-set, heavily made-up blue eyes glared at him, Josh couldn't help but admire his wife's beauty. "Okay. But do you have to go out? We could have a nice evening at home tonight... together." He gestured to the couch.

"I told Sophia I would go."

"Oh, she wouldn't mind." He was actually surprised Sophia wanted to go to a party since she was a more serious type. "It feels like it's been a while since we've spent time together, just the two of us."

Shaking her head, Tara returned to the bedroom.

Josh stared at the empty space Tara had just occupied. Between working late, girls' nights out, and parties at The Spot, it seemed as though Tara was never home. He missed how things were only a few years ago. He missed his wife. Though he didn't like to admit it, Tara's attitude toward him seemed to have changed. But then again, ever since his accident, everything had changed.

Lowering his body onto the couch, Josh exhaled. He popped a bite-sized Snickers into his mouth. Before he could turn on the TV, the doorbell rang. *Seriously?* He heaved himself to his feet and opened the door.

"Trick or treat," Sophia said.

Josh eyed Sophia's referee outfit and black leggings, wishing she'd taken Tara shopping with her. Though he liked Tara's sexy outfit, he didn't like the idea of other men appreciating it also. He gave Sophia a hug. "You look nice."

"Thanks." Sophia shrugged, pushing her shoulder-length hair behind an ear.

Tara whizzed through the room then gave him a quick hug. "Don't wait up, Josh."

Tara's straight nose and high cheekbones gave her oval face a delicate appearance. He embraced her warm, soft body, breathing in her vanilla bean-scented hair. "Have a good night, honey."

Tara pulled away then went out the door. "I'll be back late."

"Don't you want a jacket or something?" he called after her.

Tara shot him a stare as icy as the wind rustling the leaves overhead, then she hurried out into the darkness with Sophia.

Once Tara's car drove away, Josh shut the door, grabbed his laptop, and settled on the couch. With their anniversary fast approaching, Josh had a lot to do to make sure he planned a perfect celebration.

<hr>

TARA

Tara flipped down the visor to check her makeup in the mirror. She reapplied her red lipstick. "Ready, Sophia?"

Sophia shrugged. "I guess. I don't know how you talked me into going to this party."

Tara wasn't sure if it was just the car's dim lighting, but Sophia's face seemed pale. Even so, her friend looked great. Unlike Tara, Sophia wore little makeup, usually just mascara to coat her unfairly long eyelashes, which accentuated her deep-set, brown, almond-shaped eyes. She had thin, perfectly arched eyebrows, a regal nose, and full lips.

"It'll be fun, Sophia. Plus, I'm worried about you. I know being out of work has been hard on you, and I hate seeing you all depressed and stuff lately. Seems like all you do is sit around watching movies."

"What's wrong with movies? I mean, have you seen *Ghost* lately? It's incredible!"

Tara laughed. "See? You really need to get out."

Sophia chuckled. "Probably true."

They left the car, and Tara's three-inch stiletto heels rhythmically struck the sidewalk as they strutted toward the club. She didn't care what Josh thought about her costume. She looked good, and his comments about her nurse outfit highlighted yet another one of his insecurities. At The Spot, an eager line of costumed adults wrapped around the building.

Tara grabbed Sophia's hand and headed to the front of the line. She presented them to the bouncer and yelled over the music thumping through the doors, "Hi, Damian."

"Nurse? Nice." He eyed Tara up and down. "You know, I haven't been feeling well tonight. I might need a shot here." He pointed at his flexed bicep that threatened to burst through his black T-shirt.

Tara squeezed his tanned bicep and thanked him when he opened the door, ignoring the grumbling of the people who waited in line.

"Wow," she said when they stepped into the building.

"Is this our neighborhood bar?" Sophia asked.

When the restaurant turned into a club on Friday and Saturday nights, the usual tables and chairs were removed to create a dance floor. But tonight, it had been transformed completely with Halloween decorations. They ducked to avoid the cotton cobwebs hanging from the ceiling.

"My feet! My feet!" Tara joked as dry-ice mist crawled along the floor.

Tara and Sophia navigated through the packed club to the bar.

"Shall we drink?" Tara asked Sophia.

"I'm not," Sophia said. "Go ahead and get yourself one though."

"Okay, party pooper." Tara pointed at an empty spot at the bar next to a caped figure with red blood painted near his mouth.

Tara signaled for Keith, the bar manager dressed in a cop costume, then ordered a vodka cranberry with an extra shot of vodka on the side.

Sophia ordered a ginger ale then yawned as she smoothed down her hair, pushing it away from her face.

"You sure you don't want anything else?" Tara asked.

Both women shared the love of a good drink. Tara had invited Sophia over for cocktails shortly after she and Terrence moved into the house next door a year ago, and they'd become fast friends.

"Not now," Sophia said.

Tara stepped back and posed. "Tell me the truth. Do you think this costume is too tight?"

Sophia eyed Tara. "The costume's great, but Terrence would barricade the door before he'd let me out dressed like that."

"Give it some time. You two have barely been married a year."

"You mean Terrence will care less what I wear the longer we're married?"

Tara grinned. "No, I mean you'll care less about his opinion."

Sophia looked as if she was trying not to smile. "You're bad."

Keith danced toward Tara and Sophia. Though he pointed his finger up and down like John Travolta in *Saturday Night Fever*, his costume favored one of the Village People. He made their drinks then placed them on the bar.

Tara took a deep breath then threw back the shot, which burned on its way down. She slammed the empty glass on the bar. "One more!"

Sophia nudged her. "Are you sure? You should take it easy."

"Easy?" Tara raised her eyebrows at Sophia. "Nothing's easy about my life these days." She downed the second shot from Keith, then she sipped the perfect blend of cranberry and vodka.

As Tara bobbed her head to the music, she felt alive—a sensation she chased more and more ever since Josh's work injury had ended his construction career. Being the sole breadwinner was tough and too similar to the days when her mom took care of her dad. A time she liked to forget.

A man dressed in a toga and built like a linebacker approached Tara. Flipping back his long blond hair, he bent toward her. "Let's dance." He held out his hand.

Tara stared at his dark-brown eyes and tried to decide if his aggressiveness was a turn-on or a turn-off. She glanced at Sophia, who subtly shook her head no, but then Tara placed her hand in his. After all, Halloween parties only happened once a year.

"Just one dance," Tara said to Sophia.

They squeezed onto the crowded dance floor. An amalgam of body odor, perfume, and cologne clung in the air, and they carved out a couple feet of space. Tara swung her hips from side to side, bounced her shoulders, and snapped her fingers to the hip-hop beat. She couldn't remember the last time she'd danced with Josh.

Toga-man leaned in close to Tara. "So what's your name?"

"Tara. What's yours?"

"Chris." He put his arms around her waist. "You're so sexy."

"Thank you," Tara said, though if he thought this was going somewhere, he was mistaken.

As the song ended, a voice shouted, "Excuse me, Mrs. Fisher with an M-R-S!"

Tara recognized the Spanish accent, and she spun around. Mariana, dressed in a cougar bodysuit and eared headband, stared at her.

"Excuse me?" Tara put her hands on her hips, feigning anger.

The stare-down broke as Mariana and Tara laughed.

"Let's get a drink," Mariana said.

"Okay. Thanks for the dance," Tara said to Chris, who scowled.

Tara and Mariana headed to where Sophia had sat, but Sophia had disappeared. Though she'd probably just gone to the bathroom, Tara regretted leaving her friend after dragging Sophia to the party.

"So I know people are in costume, but I'm pretty sure that wasn't Josh you were grinding on," Mariana said.

Tara smirked. "I was dancing, and no, it wasn't Josh. I think his name was Chris or something."

"Chris, huh?" Mariana raised her eyebrows.

"Yes, Chris," Tara said, searching the club for Sophia.

The strobe light illuminated a man entering the bar. Whether it was the light or the drinks, Tara thought the man was gorgeous. Clothed in a suit, he stood out from the crowd. As he headed for the bar, he must have sensed her eyes on him because he looked at her and smiled.

Startled, Tara's gaze darted away as she pretended to listen to Mariana rambling on about her ex-husband's latest transgressions. Tara could only resist the urge to glance in the man's direction for a few seconds, and when her eyes drifted toward him again, his intense eyes stared at her. As the strobe light stopped, Tara lost sight of him in the crowd.

"Tara? Did you hear what I said?" Mariana asked.

"Of course," she lied. "But I need a drink. I'll buy a round."

"Then make mine a double," Mariana said.

Tara left the table and squeezed through the crowd. The man was ordering a drink from Keith, and against her better judgment, she slipped into the opening next to him, resting her hand on the wooden bar's surface.

"Can I buy you a drink?" the man asked Tara.

"No, thank you," she said, avoiding eye contact.

Keith approached, and she ordered two cosmopolitans. As he made the drinks, Tara felt the man's eyes on her. She turned her head and discovered she was right. The man was stunning up close. His salt-and-pepper hair and the fine lines around his gray eyes gave away that he was at least a decade older than Tara, but he had a twinkle in his eyes that made him seem years younger.

"Can I help you?" Tara asked.

The man shook his head. When Keith placed the cocktails on the bar in front of Tara, the man pulled out a one-hundred-dollar bill and handed it to Keith.

"I told you I didn't want you to buy me a drink," Tara said, though the idea of a man buying her something was a nice reversal from her situation with Josh.

"You'll find that I don't really take no for an answer," the man said.

"Really?" Tara laughed, something she hadn't done very often since Josh's accident.

"See, I got a laugh out of you," he said.

Tara raised her brows. "That's all you'll get out of me."

The man put his hands to his heart, and Tara noticed his wedding band. She relaxed her shoulders, figuring that since he was married also, he was probably a harmless flirt.

"Then I can die a happy man. But before then, can you at least tell me your name?"

"Tara. Mrs. Tara Fisher."

The man grabbed her pale hand and gave it a firm kiss. An electric current ran through Tara's body.

"Pleased to make your acquaintance, Ms. Fisher. I'm Louis Steinman, attorney-at-law, and I will be prosecuting you for stealing my heart."

Tara laughed again, pulling her hand away from him. "Are you serious? Does that work for you when you're hitting on women who aren't your wife?"

"Ouch!" he said.

"Tara, are those our drinks getting warm?"

Tara startled at Mariana's voice. "Oh, uh—"

"I'm Louis." He held his hand out formally to Mariana.

Mariana took his hand. "I'm Mariana. I work with Tara."

"Oh, do you now? And what do you all do?" Louis asked.

Tara subtly shook her head, but Mariana didn't seem to notice, her gaze fixed on Louis. *Those damn gray eyes.*

"We work at Williams and Stansky, not far from here," Mariana said.

A mischievous grin played on Louis's face. "Oh really? I happen to know that firm."

"Well, it's time for us to go," Tara said abruptly, hoping he wouldn't remember her firm's name. "I don't want to lose our table." She grabbed her drink.

Tara scanned the bar, and her heart stood still as her dad's worn and intense face stared back at her. She blinked, and his face morphed into that of another patron. Her dad couldn't possibly be there. The shots must have been affecting her already. Since she still didn't see Sophia, she worried something had to be wrong with her.

"What was that all about with that man?" Mariana asked, placing her drink on their table.

"That was nothing. I'm going to find Sophia. Keep our spot." Tara headed into the women's restroom. "Sophia?"

A toilet flushed, and a stall door opened to the ghost of Sophia. All color had drained from her face, and with red and watery eyes, she said, "Oh, Tara."

"Oh my god, are you okay?" Tara rushed to Sophia.

Sophia's shoulders slumped. "Yeah."

"Have you been in here this whole time?" Tara put her hand to Sophia's clammy forehead.

"Yeah," Sophia repeated.

"Well, are you feeling sick?" Tara felt so selfish, dancing and drinking while her friend was sick in the bathroom.

"I'm feeling… pregnant," Sophia said.

Tara's jaw dropped. "You're pregnant? Oh my god!" She hugged Sophia but couldn't detect a trace of happiness in her. "What's wrong?"

"I'm just not sure if I'm ready for this. I'm unemployed and broke."

Tara waved dismissively. "Small details. What'd Terrence say?"

"I found out earlier today, and Terrence doesn't know yet. I'll tell him tomorrow, so please don't tell Josh."

"My lips are sealed." Tara stuck out her pinkie finger. "Pinkie promise, as my girls say."

Sophia hooked her pinkie around Tara's. "Pinkie promise."

Tara clasped her arm through Sophia's, and they left the bathroom. Though happy for her friend, Tara was so glad she was over the whole pregnancy-and-baby stage. She'd enjoyed it while it lasted, but there was nothing like having her body back and getting a good night's sleep.

When they got to the table where Mariana sat, Tara scanned the bar. *Damn.* Louis the mystery man had disappeared as quickly as he'd materialized. She wouldn't have minded one more glimpse into those eyes. But Tara refocused on Mariana and Sophia. His disappearance was probably for the best.

TERRENCE

Terrence clicked delete. He wished the news could disappear like the email from his inbox. But it couldn't. "Shit!"

He slammed his laptop shut. As he chugged his beer, his gaze drifted to the framed pictures next to his computer. He picked up the one of Sophia, him, and the Elvis lookalike who had officiated their wedding. His lips edged upward then faltered. He still had to tell Sophia what was going down. He couldn't stand to disappoint her.

He put the picture back in its place beside the frame of him and his parents at his graduation. It was the last photo they had all taken together before that damn drunk driver had killed the two most important people in his life. It had fractured Terrence's heart, but his only consolation was that they'd passed on together. Terrence had always considered his parents' marriage pretty close to perfect. Sure, they had fought every now and then, but ultimately, they had each other's back and didn't let each other down. He closed his eyes then shook his head, forcing away the self-pity. Sophia now assumed the highest priority in his life; he *couldn't* let her down.

Terrence drained his second beer and immediately wanted another one, so he abandoned his home office that doubled as a guest room. Stumbling down the pitch-black hall, he replayed the day's events.

"Shit," he mumbled, thinking about the news. Though he loved kids, tonight he wasn't up for trick-or-treaters. So he'd left a tub full of Halloween candy on the porch and shut off the house lights.

He flung open the fridge, squinting as the light pierced the darkness. He reached for a single beer on the door shelf, but he took the unopened six-pack instead. After slipping on a jacket and shoes, he slipped out the front door. *Misery loves company.*

The cold night air raised goose bumps on his arms. He stepped through the hedges adjoining their lawns then rang Josh's doorbell.

Josh opened the door. "Bro, how goes it?"

"Trick or treat." Terrence lifted the six-pack.

"Beer? You're the kind of trick-or-treater I like," Josh said. "Come in."

After grabbing two beers, Terrence handed the pack to Josh, who put them in the fridge plastered with pictures, flyers, and magnetic letters. Terrence followed Josh out of the kitchen and to the living room. Stepping over a laundry basket full of clothes, they plopped on the couch. Though his house's layout was identical to Josh's, his neighbors' home was much more lived in. Toys were always strewn all over the place, the matching floral couch and loveseat showed signs of wear and tear, and family pictures decorated the walls. Terrence stared at the Home and Garden channel on the TV.

Josh grabbed the remote. "You want to watch sports or something?"

"No!" Terrence clenched his beer. "I mean, no," he said softer.

"Sensitive much?"

Terrence gulped his beer. "I don't want to talk about it."

Josh put up his hands innocently. "Talk about what?"

"Fine. You beat it out of me." Terrence ran his hand over his head. "My star client broke the news today that he's gotten another agent. After doing so well during his rookie year, agents were all over him."

Josh's eyes grew wide. "No way."

"Yep. He's leaving and going with someone else." Terrence's heart sank. Saying the news aloud made it somehow worse.

Josh stood.

"Where you going? I know it's bad, but not end-our-friendship bad," Terrence joked.

"Bro, I'm getting you another beer."

Staring at the television, Terrence zoned out. He'd gotten into sports management to help athletes—people who often had no idea how to protect their assets and asses when multi-million-dollar contracts were on the line. What he hadn't expected was needing to protect himself from client-stealing agents.

Josh returned, put two more beers on the coffee table, and grabbed a handful of candy from the bucket. "Want some?"

"Naw, man, I really shouldn't. It's not like I'm in my twenties, when I could eat whatever I wanted and not gain weight."

Josh popped a bite-sized Butterfinger into his mouth. "I wish I could say no." He laughed. "I don't even want to know how much I've gained since the accident."

Terrence had noticed that Josh had gained quite a few pounds over the past year. Extra weight wouldn't be as noticeable on Terrence's six-foot-three-inch frame, but since Josh was barely five ten, it seemed to go straight to his gut. Terrence couldn't blame him though. Having a steel beam fall on your back and being alive and well to talk about it was more than anyone could ask for.

"You should hit the gym with me, man," Terrence said.

"I know. I know. I used to live in the gym when I played football in high school. But back to your situation." Josh pointed his beer at Terrence.

Terrence didn't want to go back to his situation. "Did you know some estimates figure that sixty percent of NBA players file for bankruptcy within five years of retirement? I'm wondering if I'm going to end up like them."

"What do you mean?" Josh asked.

"It's a small agency where every client counts, so they're not happy with me. The worst part is—"

"It gets worse?" Josh asked.

Terrence nodded. "Sophia and I bought our house while Sophia was working and I was doing really well at the agency. We got an adjustable-rate mortgage, and our payments are set to adjust to be higher than we can afford now. Worst-case scenario is we lose the house."

Josh's mouth hung open.

"Say something," Terrence said.

Josh's lips moved but no words came out for a moment. "What does Sophia say?"

"Sophia doesn't know." That sounded worse aloud also.

"You're wrong then," Josh said.

Terrence raised his eyebrows. "About what?"

"Telling Sophia is going to be the worst part."

Terrence put a bite-sized Snickers into his mouth. The melting chocolate somehow eased the pain. "Yeah. I'm going to tell her tomorrow, and I'm dreading it. We practically just got married, she's out of work, and now this happens. She's pretty level-headed, so hopefully she'll understand. It's just... my dad never got into a mess like this. How am I gonna break the news?"

"I don't know." Josh gulped his beer. "But good luck."

Terrence scoffed. "I need more than luck."

"You'll figure this out. I hate to sound like a bumper sticker, but shit happens. You just need to adjust."

"Yeah, like you've adjusted since the accident." Terrence admired the way Josh had gotten back on his feet both literally and figuratively.

"You could say that. But if you'd asked me ten years ago if I would be a stay-at-home dad, I would have laughed in your face. As a site foreman, I was running the show. But right after the accident, I couldn't do anything but be laid up. As time passed and I got better, paying the nanny was almost ridiculous since I was home," Josh said while chewing candy.

"So that's how you became a stay-at-home dad?" Terrence had always wondered but never had the guts to ask about their arrangement.

"Yep. Once I was mobile again, Tara and I decided I would temporarily stay at home with Michelle and Teeni during the day while she worked and Chelsea was at school. But temporarily turned into one year and counting. Since I can't go back to construction, I'm screwed. I don't have experience doing anything else, and I've been out of work for so long, no one will want to hire me. But to be honest, I love being with the girls." Josh held up his hand. "Don't get me wrong. It's tough work. People who think stay-at-home parents don't do anything are crazy. But being able to watch my girls grow up is worth more than a paycheck right now."

"That's cool, man. That's a real good attitude to have. You're a great dad too." Hopefully Terrence would feel the same way when his time came to be a dad.

Josh shrugged. "You know, it probably feels like the end of the world losing that client, but you'll bounce back. And if you need anything, I got your back."

"Got fifty thousand dollars?" Terrence pretended to be serious.

Josh chuckled. "Not even close."

"Know an awesome up-and-coming basketball player in need of an agent?"

"Nope," Josh said.

"Then forget you. I need to find some new friends." Terrence laughed. He was lucky to have a friend like Josh. "I'll get us another round of beers."

As Terrence stood, his house keys fell out of his pocket onto the couch. He scooped them up and squeezed them, determined to do whatever it took to keep his and Sophia's house.

CHAPTER TWO

BRICK

Sophia

S OPHIA STRETCHED HER LEFT ARM across the bed, reaching for Terrence, but her fingers only traced the soft sheet. She'd slept restlessly all night. Though the clock read almost noon, she needed a few more hours—or even days—to come to terms with the pregnancy.

She couldn't say she was surprised by the positive test though. It had been nine months since "the talk" she and Terrence had had on a chilly Saturday evening in March.

Terrence had made reservations at their favorite seafood restaurant in Oakland's Jack London Square, which meant he had big news. As she sat across from him in the dimly lit restaurant, the corners of his eyes wrinkled as he smiled.

"So… what's up?" she asked, ready to get to it after their small talk on the drive there.

Terrence laughed, reaching across the white linen-covered table. "You know me too well."

Sophia interlaced her fingers through his. "Go ahead."

"I wanted to talk to you." His eyes danced with excitement. "Because I'm ready."

Sophia searched her memory, trying to think of a previous conversation about starting something. She stared at him blankly. "For…?"

"A baby. You know I lost my parents suddenly, and I don't know how much time I'll have. I don't mean to sound morbid, but I'm not getting any younger. So… I want us to have a baby. I'd love for you to have my child." Terrence squeezed Sophia's hand, his gleaming white teeth illuminated by the candlelight.

Sophia opened her mouth. Then closed it. Terrence's eyes twinkled as if he were a schoolboy who'd found the toy he wanted and had saved every nickel and dime until he could afford it. This was the dream supposedly. A husband. A family. She couldn't reject the love of her life's request after less than six months of marriage.

"Okay," she finally said.

"Okay? I say I want you to have my child, and that's it?" Terrence asked.

Sophia didn't want to spoil the moment. "I meant, let's do it!" Sophia leaned across the table and kissed Terrence.

On the ride home, Terrence said he wanted to start trying and suggested she stop taking her birth control.

And she'd had every intention of doing just that. Until Monday morning when she arrived at work and got her pink slip. She hadn't exactly *told* Terrence that she continued taking birth control, but she decided it was in everyone's best interest. She needed time: time to get another job, time to get healthy and do all the right things like take folic acid and lay off the wine, and time to *want* a baby the way most women *wanted* babies. Sure, they were cute, but Sophia's focus had always been on starting a career, not a family. After all, she'd learned at an early age that family life was complicated, and she didn't want to complicate what was perfect between her and Terrence.

About seven months of trying later, time ran out when Terrence told her they should consult a fertility doctor since they weren't having any luck getting pregnant. He didn't want to wait too long if there was some sort of problem. "Let's just give it another month or so," she had told him. She'd been so careful to get the birth control and hide it from Terrence, and she couldn't take the chance of Terrence finding out the truth after he had been so excited for a baby. So that same night, she threw out her birth control.

She'd expected it to take several months for her to get pregnant once she stopped the pill. But lo and behold, here she was—pregnant. Fighting the urge to bury herself deeper under the covers like a groundhog in its burrow, she forced herself out of bed and to the bathroom. Keeping this news to herself for so long while knowing that Terrence would be thrilled was selfish. She was uncertain about the timing of the pregnancy, but it was too late to worry about that.

She splashed water on her face to try to wake up. She needed to be lively and excited when she told Terrence the news he'd been waiting for nearly a year to hear. Patting her face dry, she stared into the mirror.

"Terrence, we're having a baby," she practiced. *More enthusiasm.* She smiled wide. "Put on the timer because I got a bun in the oven." *Too cheesy.* "Aunt Flo was a no show this month." *Terrible!*

She abandoned the bathroom. In the living room, Terrence, clad in a white undershirt and basketball shorts, sat on their black leather couch. Though he held a *Sports Illustrated* magazine, he gazed through the sliding glass door to their backyard. Unlike the Fishers' backyard, which was littered with toys and bicycles, Sophia's backyard cried "childless" with just a patio set and barbeque grill. Sophia liked it neat and manageable.

"Morning," Sophia said.

Terrence startled. "Oh, hey. Coffee's been sitting a while since you slept in so long. Did you know that caffeine is the most popular and widely used drug in the world?"

"Never thought of it like that, but sounds about right," Sophia said, amused by Terrence's random fact.

She went into their kitchen. She loved her white cabinets and stainless steel countertops and appliances that made the kitchen look fresh and modern. She grabbed a banana from the fruit bowl on the island, and since the aroma of coffee was making her stomach churn, she opted for a glass of water instead.

Back in the living room, she sat next to Terrence. She pecked his cheek; the stubble on his face tickled her lips.

Terrence draped his arm around her and kissed her cheek in return. Sophia loved being in her husband's arms, and she'd be beyond relieved when she could quit hiding the truth from Terrence.

"How was the party?" he asked.

"Okay." She faced him. "But we need to talk about something else."

"You're right. We do," Terrence said as all light drained from his face.

Sophia drew a breath. "Terrence, I'm—"

"Sophia, we—" Terrence said at the same time.

Sophia laughed. "Go first."

It was Terrence's turn to take a breath. "I lost Eric Richards."

Sophia gasped. "What?"

Terrence rubbed his head. "He was being courted by this asshole behind my back. I had a feeling something was up, and he confirmed to me yesterday that he's switching agents."

"Shit," Sophia said.

"And..."

Sophia narrowed her eyes at Terrence. "And what?"

"Our attempts to refinance failed. Our payments are going to adjust, and the mortgage will be four thousand a month."

As if an electrical bolt struck Sophia, her hand shook as she took a sip of water, trying to drown the fear welling up in her. "Four thousand a month? Our payments are going to go from twenty-five hundred to four thousand dollars a month? We've spent all the money from my severance package, and my unemployment's almost up. And *now* you choose to lose your star client?"

"Come on, Sophia." Terrence narrowed his eyes. "That's not fair."

Sophia glared at Terrence. "Fair? You're the one who insisted we buy this house. I told you it was too expensive, but you promised you'd make it work."

"Well, I didn't factor in you losing your job."

Sophia's face burned. "Oh, so it's my fault then?"

Terrence ran his hand over his head. "No, of course not. But—"

"But nothing." Sophia wasn't sure if it was Terrence's news or the pregnancy, but bile rose in her throat. She stood and stepped away from the couch.

Terrence reached for her. "Where are you going?"

Sophia stormed into the bedroom. The nausea had subsided, so she climbed back into bed.

Moments later, Terrence came to the bedside. "I don't want you to be mad at me."

Sophia kept her back to him. "I invested twenty thousand dollars into this house. Now you're telling me we might lose it. Don't you dare tell me how to feel."

"I'm sorry, baby."

Sophia turned over and raised her eyebrows at him. "Yeah, you are sorry." She regretted the words as soon as they left her mouth. She'd never spoken to Terrence like that before, and it sounded more like something her mother would say.

Terrence bit his bottom lip. He started to speak but instead left the room and shut the door.

Though sweat lined her forehead, Sophia pulled the blankets over her head. *Breathe in. Breathe out.* She'd postponed becoming pregnant because she'd been unprepared. Now she was terrified. *What if we lose our house? What if Terrence loses his job? What if I never find a job?*

She should have told Terrence about the baby. But she wanted the moment to be perfect, not dropped in the midst of bad news. She had to get to a place where she could tell Terrence and genuinely be happy. Because right time or not, a baby was on the way.

TERRENCE

Terrence shot the basketball, and it clanked against the rim. "Shit."

His coworker, Lance, jumped into the air and rebounded the ball. "Next point wins," he yelled as he dribbled down the court.

Terrence chased him.

Lance stopped and shot the ball. *Swish.* "And it's good!" Lance raised his arms like a goal post.

"Aww, man!" Terrence said.

Lance patted Terrence on the back. "That's the game, old man."

Terrence grabbed his Gatorade. "I can't win today." He chugged the drink and left the court.

"Where you going, T?" Lance asked, sweat dripping down his brown face.

"Home." It'd been almost two hours since the fight, and Terrence would have to head back sooner or later.

"You don't want to get whooped again?"

"I'll see you next time."

In the locker room, Terrence checked his cell phone. No missed calls. He might have been one of the smartest students in his law program at U.C. Berkeley, but in that moment, he had to be one of the biggest idiots. He'd worked his ass off to get ahead, but swamped in student loan, home loan, and credit card debt, he'd never felt so behind. Some of what Sophia had said was true, but their current situation wasn't completely his fault, and he was working his butt off to provide for them. He wished he could call his dad and ask for advice. His dad had always known what to do. But he couldn't, so Terrence dialed Josh.

"Bro, what's up?" Josh answered.

"Just finished ballin' at the gym." Terrence ran his towel over his sweaty head. "I need to head home, but I kind of messed up with Sophia."

"I know." Josh's voice lowered. "Sophia came over not too long ago. She and Tara have been having a quiet-voice, eyes-rolling, head-shaking conversation."

Terrence wiped the sweat from his forehead. "Oh, man, this isn't good."

"So I'm assuming the talk didn't go well?"

"Horribly," Terrence said, though that was an understatement. "I knew she'd be mad, but she took it to a whole other level."

"Why don't you swing by? Try to fix things?"

Terrence paused. "Yeah, that's a good idea. I can try to show her how much I love her. Plus, she won't kill me if there are witnesses."

Thirty minutes later, Terrence rang the Fishers' doorbell.

"Who is it?" a girl's voice asked.

"T.M.," Terrence said.

The door crept open, and Chelsea peeked her head out. "Who?"

Terrence jumped. "Tickle Monster!"

Chelsea squealed in delight as Terrence tickled her with his free hand, his other hand holding a paper bag.

When he'd finished tickling her, Terrence said, "But you shouldn't be opening the door without your parents' permission."

Josh came to the front door. "Exactly, Chelsea. Strange people like this wander in when you do."

"Uncle Terrence!" Michelle and Teeni yelled, charging down the hall.

Terrence bent down and opened his arms wide, inviting the girls' embraces. He stood with Teeni and Michelle wrapped around each leg, Terrence ventured into the living room with his human shields.

Sophia's eyes brightened. "Terrence? What are you doing here?"

"I'm bringing you this." Terrence pulled a bouquet of red roses from the bag and handed it to her. "And this." He held out a box of Sophia's favorite See's candy.

Sophia accepted the presents. "Thank you."

"Josh!" Tara yelled. "Did you invite him over?"

Josh entered the living room. "Me? Invite him? Over?" His voice rose an octave with each word.

Tara dismissed him with a wave. "Whatever, Josh. Is dinner ready?"

"Yes. I'm just slicing the garlic bread, honey," Josh said.

"And I assume you want to eat?" Tara asked Terrence with a raised eyebrow.

"Well, that garlic bread does smell good. But only if it's okay." He glanced at Sophia.

Sophia half smiled. "Of course."

"I'm sorry about earlier," Terrence said.

"I am too," Sophia said.

"Well, before we start singing 'Kumbaya,' why don't we go eat?" Tara said.

Terrence laced his fingers between Sophia's, relieved that she seemed to accept his apology and grateful for hers. They didn't usually argue, so the sooner they could put the past behind them, the better. They followed Tara into the dining room; the girls trailed behind them, arguing about who would sit next to Terrence.

In the kitchen, Tara uncorked a bottle of white wine. "Josh, want some?"

"Just beer for me," Josh said.

"Isn't that sophisticated of you," Tara said.

"I'll just have a beer too," Terrence said. "It's a man's drink. You wouldn't know about that, Tara. Right, Josh?"

"You two suck! I'll just drink this wine by myself," Tara said.

"Ooh, Mommy! You said suck," Chelsea scolded.

"Oops!" Tara laughed and covered her mouth with her hand.

"Bad Mommy." Terrence shot Tara a look of faux disapproval. "I'm sure Sophia will join you in a glass."

"Actually, I'll just have water for now," Sophia said as she found a vase to put the flowers in. "But thanks."

Terrence was happy that Sophia was turning down wine. Though their efforts hadn't paid off yet, it was good she was preparing for the possibility of a baby.

"You wanna hear a song?" Teeni asked once they were all seated at the dining table.

"Sure, sweetie," Tara said.

As Teeni broke into her rendition of "Itsy Bitsy Spider"—complete with hand motions—Terrence's mind wandered to what life would be like for him and Sophia and a baby. The two of them ate most of their meals in front of the television. That would have to change. Terrence used four-letter words from time to time. He wouldn't be able to do that anymore. Sophia spent copious amounts of time in bed. That would be over. As a matter of fact, a lot of things they did would have to change once they had a baby.

And though he wanted that, with everything going on financially, he was glad she wasn't pregnant yet.

CHAPTER THREE

HAPPY BIRTHDAY

TARA

TARA SQUEEZED HER ELDEST DAUGHTER tight then pecked her cheek. "Happy birthday, sweet cakes."

Chelsea sucked in a breath. With one long blow, the flames on all eight candles lining the smiley-face pancake vanished. A faint smell of smoke lingered in the air.

"Eat fast. Five minutes 'til takeoff." Arms outstretched like a plane, Josh made zooming noises as he moved around the kitchen.

"Ready for your birthday surprise?" Tara asked Chelsea. She didn't know who was more excited about this present: her or Chelsea.

Chelsea squealed. "What's the surprise?"

Michelle crossed her arms with a pout. "Where's my surprise, Mommy?"

"Me too?" Teeni asked.

Tara wrapped her arms around her precious daughters, still in their pajamas since their day started later. "Just wait," she whispered. "It's Chelsea's birthday."

"Back to my surprise. Is it big?" Chelsea asked.

Tara shook her head. "No."

"Is it furry?" Chelsea bounced up and down.

"No. We're still not getting a dog," Tara said.

Chelsea frowned. "Oh, come on, Mommy."

"Yeah, a dog," Michelle pleaded.

Tara chuckled. "You'll still like it, Chelsea."

"Don't tell me it's another sister. The last time you said you had a surprise, we got Teeni," Chelsea said.

"Me?" Teeni asked, apparently confused.

Tara laughed, wondering where her girls came up with these things. "It's definitely not another baby." She'd be even more apprehensive than Sophia if she ever became pregnant again. She opened a cabinet and pulled out three wrapped presents. She placed a box in front of Chelsea and handed the other two to Teeni and Michelle. "Surprise!"

The three girls tore off the wrapping paper.

"An iPhone! Cool! You're the best, Mom!" Chelsea stood and planted a kiss on Tara's cheek.

"I got a princess purse!" Michelle said, beaming.

"Bubbles!" Teeni yelled.

Josh glared at Tara. He hadn't been happy when she bought Chelsea an iPod Touch. But Tara had never gotten presents she actually *wanted* when she was a child, and she worked hard now to ensure she could spoil her girls a little. *Of course Josh didn't get it.* His parents had given him everything he had ever asked for and more.

Tara went to the bedroom to grab her purse.

Josh followed her. "I told you that eight is too young for a smartphone."

"Oh, come on. Don't ruin this," Tara said.

"I care about what's best for Chelsea. We're taking back the phone."

"Don't tell me what I can and can't do with my money." She couldn't believe Josh's nerve. She left the bedroom. "Let's go, birthday girl."

<hr />

Rushing past the man-made waterfall in the lobby, Tara ran to the elevator and pressed the button until the bell dinged. She wasn't ready for Monday. The night before, she had single-handedly finished the bottle of wine and hadn't crept into bed until after two in the morning. Josh had tried to get her to go to bed around eleven, telling her she'd regret it in the morning, but she'd ignored him. She hated when he acted as though he was her dad. She yawned, making a mental note to take a couple Tylenol for her pounding head.

Monday or not, she loved her job. Working at Williams and Stansky was one of the best things that had ever happened to her. She had started as a receptionist, making seven dollars an hour. Now, as a paralegal, she was making seventy-five thousand a year. Though she hadn't graduated from college, she had earned her paralegal certificate through classes the firm sponsored at a community college.

When the elevator doors opened on her floor, Tara tried not to roll her eyes at the sight of Corinne. Tara liked the receptionist, but Corinne never appeared less than perfectly manicured, and she had a smile that seemed tattooed on her face. Tara would give anything to arrive at work and see Corinne with red eyes, disheveled hair, and a hickey on her neck. *No one should be that perfect.*

"Morning, Tara," Corinne said.

"Morning, Corinne." Tara strutted down the hall.

Once in her office, Tara opened her Outlook calendar. A reminder alerted her to an appointment with a client at ten. *Perfect.* She had forty-five minutes to finish reviewing the discovery responses that had to be out before five. Sophia wanted to meet at The Spot after work, so Tara didn't want to have to stay late.

With his arms full of files, Peter, Tara's supervising attorney, entered the office. "I need you to read the intake notes and the client's chronology then draft a complaint. I know you have a client coming in at ten, so try to keep it short and have this back to me ASAP."

"Okay. I also have those discovery responses due today for the Drymeir case."

"So I guess that means getting straight to work, right?" Peter said as he headed out of Tara's office.

"Right." She didn't know why Peter had to be such a hardass all the time, but considering she was the only working member of the family, she didn't have much room to complain. She'd just have to work faster to ensure she got out at a reasonable time.

As she scanned the file, there was another knock at the door.

"Come in," she said.

Corinne popped her head into Tara's office. Her smile was larger than usual, something Tara hadn't thought was possible without some type of mouth enhancement surgery.

"Yes, Corinne?"

"Someone's husband loves her," Corinne sang as she held out a huge vase containing fuchsia roses and lush greens.

Tara's eyes widened as the stress from a moment before vanished. She brought the flowers to her face and inhaled their aroma.

"Oh, there's a card!" Corinne reached for the tiny envelope attached to a plastic stick.

"It's my daughter's birthday. I didn't expect Josh to get me these." Tara accepted the card. Too bad the morning had ended on an ugly note. "Thanks for bringing them in, Corinne."

"Yep. I hope I meet a guy like Josh," Corinne said before leaving.

Tara set the flowers on her desk. She couldn't even remember the last time Josh had bought her flowers. She grinned and slid out the card. "Guess who?" it read. Tara examined the card then read it again. *Odd thing for Josh to write.*

She strode toward the phone to call Josh and thank him for the flowers and apologize for being so stern. But there was another knock on the door. Opening it, she startled. Louis stood in front of her.

"Like the flowers?" He wore a smirk as he brushed past her, closing the door.

Tara's jaw dropped. "They were from you?"

"You're welcome."

Willing her expression to become neutral, Tara asked, "And how'd you get in here?"

"You'd be surprised what a man in a suit has access to." He went to the credenza where Tara's glass chess set rested, picked up a queen, and inspected it.

Tara should have put her foot down and let this Louis guy know his behavior was intrusive and unacceptable. She glanced at him, surprised that his chiseled jawline was even more pronounced in daylight. Then she focused on his gray eyes. Bad idea. Her resistance faded. "You play?"

Louis nodded. "I do."

But Tara couldn't entertain having this stranger in her office any longer. "Look, what exactly are you doing here?"

"I have something else I've wanted to give you since we met." Louis approached Tara, entering her personal bubble.

She held out her hand just as Louis leaned forward and planted the softest kiss on her lips.

Tara jerked back. "How dare you!"

He held up his hands. "I have your card. I'll be in touch." He strolled out of her office as casually as he'd strolled in.

Tara leaned against the wall, fingers on her lips.

<hr>

With the wind picking up and the slight drizzle threatening to burst into a downpour, Tara rushed from her car to The Spot. Once inside, she grabbed a seat next to Sophia at the bar. "Hi there. How are you?"

Sophia shrugged. "Okay. Thanks for meeting up."

"Of course. Is everything all right?" Tara asked, though her friend's sullen expression revealed it wasn't.

"I just needed to talk. How's your day?"

Louis came to mind. Luckily, he'd come and gone so quickly that no one seemed to have seen him. But Tara felt as if his kiss were imprinted on her lips. If it wasn't for the flowers, she would have thought she'd made up the whole thing. Though she wanted to tell Sophia all about it, she could tell her friend was the one who needed to talk. *It was nothing anyways.*

"What'd you want to talk about?" Tara asked.

Sophia bit her lip. "I still haven't told Terrence about the baby."

"Really?" Tara was surprised. It had been three days since Sophia had told her. When Tara had found out about her pregnancies, Josh was always the first person she told.

Sophia drummed her fingers on the bar. "You know how much I love Terrence. And I want nothing more than for us to be happy. But like I told you yesterday, financially, things have gotten really bad since he told me he was ready for a baby months ago. I wasn't sure I was ready then. Now I'm even more unsure."

"Sophia, your feelings are really important, but I don't think I'm the right person for you to talk to about this. When I read my horoscope today, I read your sign's also. It said that now is the time to come clean with a loved one. You need to talk to Terrence. You two are beginning a long journey together, and now's not the time to start hiding things."

Sophia's face fell. "You're right."

"So you're going to tell him?"

"Yeah. He's working late in the city tonight. But I'll tell him first thing tomorrow morning. I just have to come up with the perfect way to tell him. Hopefully he'll still be thrilled in spite of the setbacks."

Tara patted Sophia's hand. "Good choice. I'm always here to talk though."

"I know," Sophia said.

Tara's phone rang. She glanced at it then silenced the call.

"Do you need to get that?" Sophia asked.

"It's just Josh."

Sophia laughed. "He's probably had a long day with the girls. I won't keep you."

"I can stay," Tara said. "This is huge for you."

"I'm actually tired and not feeling so hot. Let's get going." Sophia rose from the stool. "Thanks again."

Tara gave her a hug. "Don't thank me. This is what friends are for."

Once in her car, Tara's phone rang again. At least now she could truthfully tell Josh she was on her way home. She grabbed her phone from her purse, but the call was from an unfamiliar number.

"Hello," she answered.

"It's Louis. I can't stop thinking about you."

"Excuse me, but how'd you get my cell phone number?"

"I told your receptionist I'm a friend from college visiting for the week."

Tara shook her head. She'd have to talk to Corinne. "Well, you can't do this. No more flowers, no more visits, no more calls."

"You don't sound very certain. I have to see you to believe that's what you want."

Tara chuckled. "No chance in hell."

"Remember me and that no word?" Louis asked. "I'd like to see you one more time. Convince me you want nothing to do with me, and I'll disappear."

"You promise?" she asked.

"Yes."

"Then tomorrow. I'll text you the location." She hung up the phone. *Unbelievable.*

CHAPTER FOUR

WHAT BABY?

Sophia

"No!" Sophia screamed.

"Sophia," Terrence said.

Sophia squinted as light from the lamp hit her eyes.

"You had a bad dream." He caressed her arm.

Sophia struggled to make sense of her surroundings. Her pelvis throbbed with pain.

"You okay?" Terrence asked.

Sophia pulled back the bedspread. "Oh my god!" Blood soaked her pajama bottoms and the sheet.

Terrence followed her gaze then jumped as though he'd discovered a snake in the bed. "Are you on your period?"

Oh god! The baby! "No," Sophia whispered. She swung her legs to the side of the bed and stood, but her knees buckled when her feet touched the ground. She fell, staining the cream carpet. "Call 9-1-1," Sophia said, fearing the worst for the baby.

"I'll be right back." Terrence jumped out of bed and disappeared down the hall.

Sophia struggled to her feet. Her heart jumped, and she wrapped her arms around her stomach as if she could hold onto the baby. She didn't want to lose it.

Terrence ran back to her side. "The ambulance is on the way."

He doesn't know... "Terrence, I'm—" A stabbing pain in her pelvis stole her breath.

"Don't try to talk, baby." Terrence smoothed her hair. "We'll be at the hospital before you know it. We'll figure out what's going on."

Sophia shut her eyes tight. *Shit! That's what I'm afraid of.* It was only a matter of time before Terrence found out she had been hiding the pregnancy from him.

Within minutes, the faint sound of a siren wailed. It grew closer and closer.

Terrence released Sophia's hand. "That's them now. I'll let them in."

Two paramedics rushed into the room with a gurney. After asking her a dozen questions that she could only half-answer through the pain, they were ready to transport her to the hospital.

"Lie down on this," one of the men instructed.

"Okay," Sophia said.

"I'll grab your purse and phone," Terrence said.

The men pushed the gurney through the bedroom, down the hall, and out of the house. She shivered as rain pummeled her skin.

Tara ran toward her. "Sophia! Oh my god, what happened? We heard the ambulance."

Sophia winced. "Please come."

Tara turned to the paramedic. "Can I go with her?"

"We can't take anyone but her in the ambulance, but you can meet us at Valley Medical Hospital's emergency room," he said as he and his colleague rolled Sophia into the ambulance.

Terrence ran to the ambulance. "Can I go with her? I'm her husband."

"No, but you can meet us there also."

"Sophia, I love you." Terrence's trembling hand squeezed Sophia's hand.

"I love you too," Sophia said.

Terrence ran to his car.

"I'm pregnant," Sophia said when the paramedic shut the door to the ambulance.

The paramedic's face softened. "We'll get you to the hospital as soon as possible. Now I'm going to take your blood pressure."

"But it's not looking good... is it? For the baby?"

"Try not to think about that right now. We'll get you examined as soon as we get to the hospital." He wrapped the blood pressure cuff around Sophia's upper arm.

Sophia closed her eyes. She wasn't used to lying or hiding important information, especially from her husband. Given the fact that they had been supposedly trying for a baby for months, Terrence would be furious and heartbroken.

Maybe this will be it. In the recesses of her heart, she feared her marriage would come to an end as her parents' had. She just hadn't expected she'd be the one to blame.

Pain radiated through Sophia's pelvis as the paramedics rushed her through the double doors into the emergency room. They had a brief conversation with the staff, then she was transferred to a wheelchair.

"Good luck," the paramedic said as he left.

"Thanks." Sophia needed all the luck she could get.

A smiling, fifty-something nurse approached Sophia. "I'm going to take you to a hospital room, and an ultrasound will be done. How far along are you?"

"I'm not sure. It's almost time for my period, and I didn't have it last month."

"Okay, honey." The nurse pushed Sophia's wheelchair through the hospital and into a room.

Sophia climbed onto the bed and closed her eyes, trying to shut out the pain and fear. "My husband should be here any second."

The nurse patted her hand. "We'll bring him right in. And once we know what's going on, we'll get you some pain meds."

"Thank you."

Within minutes, there was a knock, and a slim man with a receding hairline entered the room. "I'm Dr. Malone, the on-call OB-GYN. I'm here to do an ultrasound." Dr. Malone sat next to the machine in the left-hand corner of the room, an arm's length away from Sophia's bed. "The paramedics let me know that you're experiencing bleeding, and that you believe you're in your first trimester. Let's take a look and try to figure out what's going on. I'm going to put a warm jelly-like substance on your stomach." He gently lifted Sophia's shirt, put a warm and thick goo on her stomach, then he ran the ultrasound wand over it.

Dr. Malone raised his eyebrows. He moved the wand over different parts of Sophia's stomach then paused to type on his keyboard. "Well—"

There was another knock at the door. A nurse stuck her head in. "The husband's here with a friend."

Dr. Malone raised his eyebrow at Sophia.

"They can come in." Sophia's heart rate increased.

The nurse opened the door, and Terrence and Tara entered the room.

Dr. Malone cleared his throat. "Well, there's your baby. See that right there? That's the baby's heart beating."

Sophia faced the ultrasound screen for the first time. Tears filled her eyes when she saw the small dot pulsing on the screen. Letting out a breath, she relaxed a little. She had been so sure she was losing the baby, but she was getting a second chance. In that moment, she said a silent prayer. *Thank you. I won't take this baby for granted. I'm going to be one hundred percent devoted to this pregnancy.* After all, she was carrying the baby she had made with the man she loved. Nothing was as important as that.

Her relief morphed into dread when she turned to Terrence. His face had gone pale, and his eyes were wide.

"What baby?" he asked. "Did you know you were pregnant?"

Sophia nodded.

"And you didn't tell me?" He glared at Sophia then left the room, shutting the door.

⧼⧽

TERRENCE

Terrence jogged down the hall. His head spun. He stopped running and reached out to the wall to steady himself. Once he could see straight, he found a waiting area and slumped into a chair. He brought his hands to his head. Though he thought he'd moved past the events from almost two years earlier, all the memories came rushing back.

He had only been dating Sophia for about six months, and things were going… okay. She was unlike any woman he had ever met. And he'd met a lot of women in his thirty-two years. He and Sophia could talk for hours about anything and everything. Their interactions felt so natural—as if they'd known each other all their lives. And though Sophia's extreme intelligence and natural beauty appealed to him, what stood out to Terrence was how unattached she was. Unlike the girls who latched on to him after the first date, Sophia kept her distance. Despite their chemistry, Sophia acted as though she couldn't care less if things were to end. So to Terrence, she was the classic challenge. And like a moth to a flame, he couldn't help but be drawn to her. What he hadn't expected was the burn.

On a Friday evening, they had plans to meet for dinner at seven at a pizza place in downtown San Jose. Though Terrence had parked around the block fifteen minutes before seven, he strolled into the restaurant ten minutes late, eager to prove he was as detached from their budding relationship as she seemed to be. It had turned physical months before, and again, they had amazing chemistry in the bedroom. Yet Sophia remained emotionally closed. She could talk about politics, religion, and her aspirations, but she rarely talked about anything like her family or friends or the possibility of a future for them. Understanding her could be likened to deciphering Morse code, and he was dying to learn the language of her heart.

He glanced around the restaurant but didn't spot Sophia. The waitress led him to a table draped in a red-and-white-checkered cloth. He ordered a beer while he waited. Seven ten turned to seven thirty; seven thirty turned to seven forty-five. When she hadn't shown up by eight, Terrence grew worried. Sophia wasn't the type to be late, let alone not show up altogether. He finished his third beer and dialed her number for what must have been the tenth time that night. It went straight to voicemail. Sophia lived in a luxury condominium building within walking distance of the restaurant, so he decided to go check on her. He had to make sure she was all right.

Upon arriving at the high-rise condominium, Terrence went straight to the parking garage and punched in the code Sophia had given him. He checked Sophia's parking space, where her gleaming silver Prius was parked. *She must be home.* His heart pounded. *Something's wrong.* He ran up the dimly lit stairs. At the fifth floor, he stopped. Catching his breath, he wiped sweat from his brow.

When he reached Sophia's door, his knock turned into pounding. "Sophia!"

He paced back and forth. While she hadn't seemed attached, she'd given no indication of wanting to break off the relationship, so he didn't think she was avoiding him. She hadn't mentioned she was going out of town, so that probably wasn't it either. Nothing at all had seemed out of the ordinary the last time he saw her. He glanced at his watch then took a few steps back toward the stairwell. Then he stopped. The same uneasy feeling welled up in his stomach. Something was wrong.

He hurried down the hall and banged on door 527. Sophia's neighbor opened the door. *Thank you.*

"Deborah," he said, "I'm worried about Sophia."

Deborah adjusted the belt around her bathrobe. Her jet-black hair was wrapped in a towel. She opened the door wider. "What's wrong?"

"We were supposed to meet for dinner, and she didn't show. She isn't answering her phone. Her car's downstairs, but she isn't coming to the door."

Deborah scrunched up her face. "That doesn't sound like Sophia."

"I know you have her key. Do you think you can just check on her?"

Deborah shifted her weight from one foot to the other as if she were a scale weighing the pros and cons. "Well, the key's kind of for her, like if she locked herself out. I don't really feel comfortable."

"I won't go in. I'll wait outside. I'm just really worried."

Deborah blew out a loud breath. "Okay, I'll get the key and be right back."

Deborah reappeared minutes later, fully clothed and key in hand. They rushed down the hall, and after knocking on the door several times, Deborah jammed the key into the lock.

She narrowed her eyes at Terrence. "Stay right here." Deborah disappeared into the room.

"Sophia?" Deborah called. Minutes later, Deborah emerged. "She's not here. Let's go." She avoided making eye contact with Terrence and pulled the door closed.

Terrence pushed against it and entered the condo.

"No, Terrence!" Deborah yelled after him. "I said she's not there."

He raced through the neatly kept living room, past the ivory leather couches, heading for Sophia's bedroom. The door to her room was open. He stopped in his tracks. Sophia lay curled in a ball under a lavender comforter, only her head visible. A box of Kleenex and crumpled tissues were strewn on the bed.

"Sophia?"

Sophia eased herself into a sitting position. Her eyes were red and puffy.

"What's going on?" His eyes traveled to her nightstand where four pill bottles rested. Something was definitely off. She was either sick or hurt, but he was at a loss when it came to her behavior.

"I'm sorry. He just charged in," Deborah said.

Sophia shrugged. "It's okay. Let me talk to him. Alone."

Deborah scowled at Terrence. "You asshole."

Terrence waited for her to leave before he sat next to Sophia. "Are you okay? You had me worried."

"I'm okay... now."

"Well, what's up? We had dinner plans. You sick or something?"

"Oh, Terrence, I forgot. I had a procedure... I was..."

"You were what?" If she was sick, Terrence didn't understand what the big deal was. The least she could have done was answer her phone. He'd been worried sick.

"The procedure was at Planned Parenthood. I was pregnant."

"Pregnant?" Terrence stood. "Why didn't you tell me?" All his concern for Sophia disappeared. He couldn't believe she could drop a bomb like that so nonchalantly.

Sophia furrowed her brows. "Why would you have cared?"

Terrence's face burned. "Why would I have cared?"

"I took care of it," Sophia whispered.

"You took *care* of it?" Terrence's voice rose.

"Stop repeating everything I say."

"I'm trying to wrap my mind around this. We aren't teenagers. I'm thirty-two years old. I had every right to know that you were pregnant. It was *our* baby. Unless the baby wasn't mine." Terrence glanced sideways at Sophia.

Sophia glared at Terrence. "Don't be an asshole. Of course it was yours."

Terrence threw up his hands. "Then why didn't you tell me?"

"This wasn't planned," Sophia said.

"You said you were on the pill."

"I am. But the doctor explained that some antibiotics can weaken the effect of birth control, and I was on amoxicillin." Sophia shrugged.

"Okay, but how could you abort our baby without a second thought?" Terrence didn't even want to hear her answer. All of the great attributes he had assigned to Sophia had been wrong apparently, if she could be this heartless.

"Are you kidding me? No woman has an abortion without a second thought. This was the hardest thing I've ever done in my life! And I don't need you standing on some pedestal"—Sophia's voice broke—"looking down at me."

Terrence's heart softened when tears trickled down her cheeks. "All I'm saying is that we could have made it work. I love kids. Sure, we're not the Huxtables, but—"

"It wouldn't have worked," Sophia said curtly. "As a matter of fact, this isn't working anymore."

Terrence put up his palms. "What isn't?"

"You and me. It's over. So let yourself out, just like you let yourself in." Sophia pointed toward the door.

"Are you serious?"

"Yes. Now get out!" Sophia yelled for the first time since he'd met her.

"Sophia, come on—"

"I said get out." Sophia lay on the bed, her back to him.

Terrence had just stared at her in disbelief. He'd lost his girlfriend and unborn baby in a manner of minutes. But he wasn't going to lose his temper too. So he left and planned to never return.

Terrence opened his eyes and adjusted to the fluorescent hospital lights. His mom would never have kept a secret of this magnitude from his dad. And Sophia had done it to him... twice. "Fool me once, shame on you. Fool me twice, shame on me," his dad had often quoted. Terrence hated being a fool. He stood, unwilling to sit around the hospital looking like one.

TARA

Tara eased the hospital room door closed. Sophia had said she needed to be alone, so Tara had squeezed her friend's hand and left. She leaned against the wall, trying to absorb what had just happened. Regardless of whatever past Sophia had, she didn't deserve to be treated that way. She was pregnant, for god's sake. Tara needed to find Terrence.

Hurrying down the hospital corridors, she searched for him. When she arrived in the waiting area, she sighed. It was nearly empty, holding just a weary, worried family of four. Near the vending machine area was a doctor in scrubs getting a cup of coffee.

She pulled her phone out of her purse and dialed Terrence. It rang and went to voicemail. Of course he probably didn't want to talk to Tara. She had no idea how she would handle the situation if she were in his position.

Glancing at her wristwatch, she learned it was almost four in the morning. Though she didn't want to leave, Sophia had made it clear she needed time alone. Tara could sleep in the waiting area, but then again, she had two large projects that needed to go out first thing when she got to the office. So she made one last loop around the hospital, searching for Terrence, then left.

Tara tiptoed to her bedroom and ignored the clock on the nightstand. She removed her clothes then climbed into bed, desperate to get some sleep.

Josh turned toward Tara. "How's Sophia?"

"Sophia is... pregnant."

"Pregnant, huh? Is everything okay?"

Tara let out a loud yawn. "I guess there were complications or something. I'm exhausted, and I have to be up in two hours."

"Okay." Silence filled the air. "Terrence excited?"

"Josh..." Tara whined.

"Well, is he? Just answer, and I'll let you go to sleep."

"I guess he didn't know about the pregnancy?"

49

"What do you mean he didn't know?"

"What I said. Sophia hadn't told him yet." The situation sounded a lot worse than she hoped it would for Sophia's sake.

"Well, hell. That's a big thing to hide from your husband. Are you hiding any secrets from me?" Josh asked.

Louis's kiss came to mind. "Of course not."

Tara closed her eyes. If tonight had taught her anything, it was that secrets were like ticking bombs that had a way of exploding at the worst time. She'd have to be very firm with Louis that his behavior was unacceptable and had to end. But right now, Tara wanted nothing more than to cross the line between consciousness and sleep.

CHAPTER FIVE

GOING HOME

SOPHIA

SOPHIA'S LEGS DANGLED FROM THE side of the hospital bed where she sat... waiting. After an evaluation by another on-call OB-GYN—a short Indian woman wearing a gray hijab who spoke in a low, soothing tone—Sophia was told that the pain and bleeding she was experiencing was a "threatened miscarriage." So Sophia needed to be on bed rest indefinitely. Though relieved that the baby was okay for now, Sophia hated her precarious situation.

Sophia's gaze returned to the clock on the bare wall. She watched the second hand tick, tick, tick. It had been almost six hours since she had last seen Terrence, and based on his reaction to finding out about the pregnancy, she was certain she should call a cab to get home. The two of them had never spoken about the abortion after they got back together, but Sophia was certain that was all that occupied his thoughts now. She would never have another abortion. She desperately needed to tell Terrence that. But she doubted he would believe her.

"I'll go find him," the nurse had said almost half an hour earlier.

"He's not here," Sophia said, deflated.

"I'll make one round, and if I can't find him, we'll call you a taxi," the nurse said before exiting the room.

Sophia's heart skipped a beat when there was a knock on the hospital door.

"We found him. He was wandering around, a little bit lost," the nurse said proudly.

ʼothed down her tangled hair. *Maybe it will all work out.*

.ry. It's just me." Josh ran his hands through his curly dirty-
_ nair.

Sophia forced herself to clear her throat, a trick she'd learned to stop from crying. "He sent you?" she whispered.

"Terrence called me this morning. Said he has a hectic day at work, so yeah, he sent me," he said warmly.

"Where are your girls?"

"Chelsea and Michelle are at school, and Teeni is with my mom. I'll pick her up after we get you all nice and tucked into bed. That's what the nurse told me. Bed rest, right?"

Sophia gulped down her fear. "Right."

Josh and Sophia padded silently down the corridor to the exit. Though her pain had subsided considerably, she still held her hand to her stomach, which ached. The reality of her situation hit her, and a heavy cloak of fear descended on her. Terrence wasn't mad at her; he was furious. The only thing worse than him being furious was that he had every right to be.

She needed to explain to Terrence that she had been waiting for the perfect time to tell him about the pregnancy, but she wasn't convinced that that would help. Plenty of women would jump at the opportunity to be with Terrence, and after everything that had happened, one of those women could possibly snag him. This could be the beginning of the end of their marriage.

This was why she'd remained unattached to Terrence in the beginning. He'd had all the characteristics of the man she wanted to marry: funny, brilliant, hardworking, earnest. But she'd never wanted to give her heart to him, because she'd seen how easily hearts break. She'd expected him to hate her after he found out about the abortion, so she'd ended their relationship. What she hadn't expected was that he'd come back.

Now, on the drive to their neighboring houses, Josh tried to fill the awkward silence by rambling about the girls: the funny things they'd said lately, Teeni's various potty training fiascos, and Michelle's obsession with Disney princesses. Though Sophia feigned interest by asking a question or two and forcing a laugh from time to time, her mind might as well have been in a different galaxy as she planned the best way to talk to Terrence. Putting off telling him about the pregnancy had caused this problem, so she'd have to speak to him as soon as he came home.

"Sophia. Sophia, we're here." Josh gently shook her shoulder. "Let me see you in and make you something to eat. I'm sure you're starving." Josh got out of the car then jogged to Sophia's side and opened her door.

"Oh no, Josh, I couldn't ask you to do that."

Josh helped her out of the car. "It would be my pleasure. I loved spoiling Tara when she was pregnant."

"I'm absolutely exhausted. I think I should go lie down and just try to get some sleep."

"Yes. The doctor said bed rest, but Doctor Josh Fisher says that baby needs some nourishment. So you get comfortable in bed, and I'll make something from the BRAT menu."

"First, you're not a doctor, Josh. And second, brat?" Sophia raised her brows. She had acted immaturely by not telling Terrence about the pregnancy, but Josh didn't really need to call her a brat.

"Yes, B-R-A-T. Bananas, rice, applesauce, and toast. It's one of those things the pediatricians tell you about, and it works like a charm when the girls are vomiting or have diarrhea. You know one time, Chelsea was really sick and she had this projectile vomit that—"

"I got it." Nauseated already, the last thing she wanted to hear were stories about projectile vomit. Once she stepped inside her house, her shoulders dropped and her breathing normalized. Tara was awfully lucky to have a husband like Josh. "Josh, I'm grateful for your friendship, but I just need to sleep a little. I'll pop a piece of bread into the toaster on my way to bed."

"All right. Let's get you back to bed. I'll fluff your pillows."

"Really, I'm fine. Oh, I have something I didn't get to show Terrence." Sophia retrieved the white-and-gray ultrasound picture from her purse. She handed it to Josh, happy she had someone to show it to. "The baby."

"Aw, I remember these pictures. Amazing." Josh handed the picture back to Sophia. "So you're sure you're okay?"

"Positive."

"Then I'll go so you can get some rest. But I'm right next door."

"Okay, thanks. But did Terrence happen to mention when he'd be back?"

"No, he didn't, but I'm sure he won't want to stay at work long today. Get to bed. I'll let myself out."

Sophia gave Josh a quick hug before going to the guest room. She closed the door and crashed onto the bed. A deep sense of loss sank into her gut like an anchor pulling her dreams for her marriage down to the bottom of an ocean. Sophia had a habit of exaggerating the negative, but if Terrence didn't even want to come home and face her, the situation must have been as dire as she feared.

And who could blame him? He really wanted a baby, and he'd been devastated by her abortion. She closed her eyes but couldn't quiet her mind. She needed to talk to someone.

Sophia grabbed her phone and dialed. "Hi, Mom."

"Sophia, hello. You sound strange. Everything okay?" her mom asked.

Sophia exhaled. "I'm pregnant."

Palpable silence filled the phone line.

"Mom, did you hear what I said?"

"Yes, Sophia, I heard what you said." Her voice had grown rigid. "How exactly do you plan on getting your career back on track if you have a baby? I didn't sacrifice to put you through private school for you to become some barefoot and pregnant housewife."

Sophia sniggered. "I never said anything about being barefoot or a housewife."

"You know what I mean. What's your plan?"

"The plan... the plan—"

"Yes, the plan. I fell head over heels for your dad. I loved him with everything that I had. But what I didn't have was a plan. Your career should be your goal. Marriage is secondary, not necessary."

Sophia had heard this all before. "Mom, I'm married. Come on."

"No, you come on. What's the plan for getting your career back on track?" her mom demanded.

Sophia's mind was blank. "I don't know."

"That's not acceptable. Why didn't you tell me sooner that you wanted to have a baby? First you run off and elope, and now all of a sudden you want a baby? I'm just the last person to know everything these days, aren't I?"

"I didn't mention it to you because I knew you would react like this, just like I knew you would think I was crazy if I told you I fell in love and was getting married."

"So will you continue searching for work?"

Sophia sighed. "The doctor put me on bed rest, probably until the end of the first trimester, so I'll take it easy for a while."

"Wait, wait, wait. Bed rest? Why?"

"I had some bleeding, so it's just a precaution."

"Oh, my god! That doesn't sound good. Are you in pain?"

The concern in her mother's voice surprised her. "I was in pretty bad pain last night. But I just have a little cramping now."

"Well, prepare yourself for the worst. Don't you go getting attached to the fetus, because it'll be just that much worse if you miscarry."

"Mom, are you serious?"

"I've known women who were just beside themselves when they miscarried. It's absolutely devastating. It can take years to recover emotionally. I'm trying to warn you because in your case, it might happen. How far along are you? You aren't even supposed to tell people until you're finished with the first trimester. It's bad luck, you know."

Sophia couldn't believe her mom. "I'm only ten weeks, and I'm not telling people. I just for some ridiculous reason thought *my mother* might care to know." Sophia didn't want to even think about miscarrying. That would be devastating for her and Terrence.

"Oh, don't take that tone. You can be so sensitive. I do care, of course. What did Terrence say?"

"He's thrilled," Sophia said, though there was no enthusiasm in her voice.

"Why do I feel like you're not telling me everything?" her mom asked.

God, she's good. "Short story is that we got into a huge fight. Our mortgage payments are going up, and I don't know if we can keep the house."

"Oh, how terrible! You know what? Since you seem to have gotten yourself in a predicament, I think it's best that Desiree not come out there. I don't want you under additional stress, and if you end up miscarrying while she's there, you'll somehow blame me for it, like you blame me for all your shortcomings."

Sophia had totally forgotten their conversation about Desiree. "Are you sure?"

"Yes, that's probably best. But you know what? I feel like giving my son-in-law a call. What's his number again?"

"Mom, please. Terrence has been wanting a baby for a very long time. Please don't mention a miscarriage to him."

Her mother humphed. "How about this. Not only will I not mention the bleeding or the possibility of a miscarriage or the fact that his wife is unemployed, but I'll congratulate him."

"You just had to throw the unemployment thing in, didn't you? Bye, Mom. I'm hanging up now. I'll text you Terrence's number."

Sophia closed her eyes, and tears streamed down her cheeks onto the pillow. She had been foolish to think her mom could possibly make her feel better. She pulled the covers over her head. Her whole life had changed in a matter of days, and fear threatened to smother her. And poor Terrence. Dread settled in her stomach. She'd fallen deeply— possibly too deeply—in love with him. She didn't have a plan. Now she couldn't work, was pregnant with a baby she might miscarry, had blown through most of her savings, and her marriage might be ending. All she could do was hope the one person she needed the most wouldn't abandon her now.

* * *

Josh

"Girls, it's time for bed. Ouch!" Josh lifted his foot and discovered the culprit: a lone pink Lego in the middle of the carpeted floor. Bending to retrieve it, he groaned as a sharp pain shot down his lower back. "This is not my night." He limped to the bathroom.

Inside the medicine cabinet, he fumbled through the prescription bottles that contained what had been his salvation after the accident. He swallowed a Vicodin and grabbed the thermometer from the bottom shelf. "Teeni, let's take your temperature."

Teeni didn't raise her head from the couch, where she lay staring at the bright cartoons dancing across the television screen.

Michelle's eyes were wide. "Teeni's not feeling good, Daddy."

"I know, sweetie." He sat next to Teeni and lifted her chin so that her glum gaze met his. "Open up."

Teeni opened her tiny mouth. "Aaaaaah."

Josh put the thermometer in her mouth, and seconds later, it beeped. A large 1-0-3 blinked at him. Anything over one hundred was bad. This was worse.

"Am I betta, Daddy?" Teeni's voice was as soft as the hum of the heater.

Josh stroked Teeni's strawberry-blond hair, and his rough hand came away wet with her perspiration. "Getting there, Teeni. I'll be right back."

He laid her back on the couch and stood, a knot forming in his stomach. *Think, Josh, think.* He returned to the medicine cabinet and pulled out the Children's Tylenol. Empty. *Of course.*

Walking into the kitchen, he cursed under his breath. He should have taken her to the doctor when he'd first noticed her lethargy when he picked her up from his mom's. Instead, between getting the older girls from school, cooking dinner, and doing laundry, he had forgotten to take her temperature. And of course now it was too late since the pediatrician's office was long closed.

Tara had called two hours ago to say she and Mariana were going out for a "girls' night" after work, and though he didn't want to bother her, it was necessary. He picked up his phone and dialed her.

"Damn." Voicemail. Josh hated how Tara made a habit of not answering his calls.

He didn't want to drag Teeni out of the house so late with such a high fever. He contemplated his options then dialed his mom's number. Relief washed over him when her voice answered.

"I'll be right over," she said after Josh explained Teeni's condition.

Fifteen minutes later, the doorbell chimed.

"Thanks for coming, Mom," Josh said as he let her in.

His mom gave him a quick hug, and her unruly mass of curly brown hair swept his face. "And where are my granddaughters?"

"Grandma, Grandma!" Michelle yelled as she skipped to the door.

She tugged on the hem of her grandma's heavy brown coat. "Teeni's sick."

Josh's mom bent down and kissed Michelle's cheek. "Let's try to make her feel better then. Will you be my helper?"

"Yeah, yeah!" Michelle jumped up and down.

Josh's mom handed Josh a box of Children's Tylenol and her coat.

He grabbed a towel from under the bathroom sink, wet it with cold water, and handed it to Michelle. "Can you carry this to Teeni and put it on her forehead?"

"Yep." Michelle took the towel and skipped out of the kitchen.

"Where's Tara?" Josh's mom asked.

Josh yawned. "Girls' night."

"Didn't she just have one of those? I could have sworn she was out a few nights ago when I was helping Chelsea with her diorama for that book report."

Josh shrugged. "I'm not really keeping tabs." Of course Tara had just been out on Halloween and a few days before that.

"I never hear about you taking a boys' night. Maybe that would do you some good. Why don't you call some of your old friends from work and go out?"

Josh stretched his upper body, turning to the left then the right. "Probably not a good idea."

The truth was that it was hard for him to go out with his friends who still worked construction. He didn't fit in anymore, and they were always cracking jokes about him being a stay-at-home dad. The last time he'd gone out with them, it was as if he was the guest of honor in a comedy special roast, and he'd promised himself it would be the last time.

"But I should take Terrence up on his offer to go to the gym," he said.

"Do you think that's okay for your back?" his mom asked.

"Mom, I'm fine," Josh said, although it had been sore lately.

"And you and Tara. How's that going?"

"I'm worried about Teeni. What's with all the questions?"

His mom's face dropped. "I'm sorry, Joshie. But just like Teeni's your baby, you're my baby, and I worry about you too."

"I'm not your baby anymore. I'm an adult. Come on already." He shook his head as he left the bathroom.

Josh and his mom stopped in their tracks in the living room. Michelle held the wet towel to Teeni's head, and Chelsea rubbed Teeni's back.

"Just look at you two," his mom said. "You're such good helpers. And you deserve a treat! Who wants cookies?"

"Come on, Mom, it's bedtime," Josh said.

Teeni raised her head slightly. "Coo-kies, Gamma."

Josh's mom laughed. "Give Teeni the medicine. She's going to be just fine."

Josh lifted Teeni onto his lap and dispensed the thick purple Tylenol. His mom's presence was like a lifesaver in the rapids, and the knot in his stomach loosened. Still, he couldn't help but wonder where Tara was and what she was doing that was so important she couldn't answer her phone. She'd rush home if she knew Teeni was sick, but still, Josh was irked.

After putting all three girls to bed, Josh and his mom settled into the living room.

"So I'm planning a surprise tenth wedding anniversary date for Tara. Can you babysit the girls?" he asked.

"Of course. How exciting!" His mom eyed her watch and raised her eyebrows. "Ten fifteen. Hmm. I wanted to say hello to Tara. Any word from her?"

"Not yet." Josh nonchalantly flipped from channel to channel on the television.

Josh's phone rang. "That must be her now." Terrence's number displayed on the screen. *Damn.* "Mom, I've got to take this. Can we talk later?"

"Sure, sure. I'll clean up the kitchen." Josh's mom rose and left the room.

"Bro, what's up?" Josh answered. "How goes it?"

Terrence cleared his voice. "It's going."

"How's Sophia?"

"She's… good, I guess."

"Are there more complications?" Josh asked.

"I actually don't know how she's doing. I haven't been home yet, and I haven't spoken to her."

"Really? Tara mentioned Sophia hadn't told you about the pregnancy yet, but is it that bad?" Josh didn't understand how Terrence could be so cold to his pregnant wife.

"I don't really want to get into it, but yes. It is that bad. Do you have an empty couch?"

"Terrence, are you serious? You just found out your wife is pregnant." Josh tried to keep his voice down so as not to wake the girls. "She was in the hospital. She needs you, bro."

"I hear you, but I got to figure this shit out. I mean, Sophia and I have been trying for a baby for a while, so I don't get why she wouldn't have told me she was pregnant. Unless she was planning on having an abortion like last time."

"Whoa… okay. Yes, the couch is free." Hearing that Sophia had had a previous abortion was the last thing Josh expected.

"Thanks, man. Do you need to clear it with Tara?"

"She'll be fine with it. Just head over when you're ready," Josh said.

"Knock, knock."

"Are you telling me a joke?" Josh asked.

"No, I'm outside your door."

Josh laughed. "Mom, can you open the door? Terrence is outside."

Josh headed to the front door where Terrence greeted his mom. Bags hung under Terrence's eyes, and he wore a sullen expression.

"How have you and that pretty wife of yours been, Terry?" his mom asked.

Terrence shrugged. "Good."

"And he's going to be a dad," Josh added.

"Oh my goodness! Well, congratulations, young man!" Josh's mom put her hands on her hips and tilted her head. "But may I ask why you're here and not home? What is going on with you young married people these days?"

Josh cleared his throat, giving her a warning glance. Sure, he agreed that Terrence should be at home, but he didn't want Terrence to feel worse when he was already stressed out.

"Oh, never mind then, Terry," Josh's mom said.

Terrence held up a six-pack of Heinekens. "I come bearing gifts."

"Much needed. Just put them in the fridge and make yourself comfortable," Josh said.

"I'm going to take off," Josh's mom said. "But send Sophie my love, Terry."

"It's Sophia and Terrence," Josh said.

Josh's mom hugged him tightly. "Okay, Joshie. Have a good night."

In the doorway with his arms crossed, Josh rubbed his biceps as he watched his mom drive away. The wind whipped his skin, but he stood in the cold and rain for a few minutes longer, hoping to see Tara's car pull up. But it didn't come.

Josh finally joined Terrence in the living room, but a knock on the door stopped him. *Mom must have forgotten something.* He went back and opened the door.

"Hi, Josh," Sophia said.

Josh's heart broke for Sophia, whose eyes were red and worried. "Sophia, you should be in bed, not out in the rain."

"Is he here? He won't answer my calls. He hasn't been home, but his car's in our driveway."

"Yeah, he's here." It wasn't his business, but this situation had to be resolved. "Come in. You and Terrence need to talk."

Sophia took a step then stopped. "Actually, I don't want to force him to talk. Can you just tell him I'm sorry about everything?"

"Please just come in." Josh gestured inside.

"I can't." Sophia left, heading toward her home.

Josh lingered in the hallway before heading back to the living room. He hated getting in the middle of other people's problems. Actually, he just hated problems. He liked life to be steady, continuous, peaceful.

He strutted into the living room. "Terrence, that was Sophia. She's worried about you."

"Oh," Terrence said as if Josh had told him the weather forecast. "I need another beer."

Josh gaped while Terrence disappeared into the kitchen. He returned with two beers and resumed his position on the couch.

"I'm not used to it being this quiet here," Terrence said, ignoring Josh's bewilderment. "Usually the girls are laughing and running around, and you and Tara are yelling at them to calm down. Hey, where is Tara?"

Josh threw up his hands. "Tara, Tara, Tara. Forget Waldo—all she needs is a red-striped shirt and hat and we can play 'Where's Tara?'"

Terrence raised his eyebrows. "Did I hit a sore spot?"

"No, I'm sorry. My mom was just giving me a hard time about it earlier. Tara's out with her girlfriend." A thick silence filled the air. Josh had to say something. "Terrence, you're welcome here. You know that. But... I think you should go home. Sophia needs you."

"And I need a wife who's honest with me."

"I hear you, but you can't just ignore her or the situation. She's carrying your baby."

"The truth is, I love Sophia too much to find out that she was planning on aborting our baby again. If she admits that, I can't act like everything is okay. If she admits that, I'm gone."

Josh nodded. "I hear you. But I was with Sophia today, and I don't think that's the case. She showed me the ultrasound picture, and I could see in her eyes that she loves this baby with everything she has. Can you just hear her out?"

Terrence hung his head. "I guess."

"Just talk it out, bro."

Terrence stood. "I will."

Josh walked him to the door and watched Terrence follow the pathway to his house.

"Hey, Terrence," Josh called. "Congratulations!"

"Thanks, man."

Josh went to the kitchen to get a snack. Tara had never kept secrets from him the way Sophia had with Terrence, and he was thankful for that. He didn't know what he would do if he ever found out Tara was hiding something from him.

Josh wanted to tell Tara how much she meant to him, so he picked up his phone and called her again. Ringing, ringing, ringing, then voicemail. *She must be having a good time wherever she is.*

※

TARA

Tara's phone rang as she entered the small diner. The bells attached to the heavy glass door jingled as the door closed behind her and Louis. The lady at the host station looked up.

Louis held two fingers in the air. "Two, please."

Tara had stumbled upon the diner a few months earlier, after she and Mariana had drunk too much and needed to sober up before going home. Tara had been back on several occasions, and every time, the diner barely had any customers. Though that would probably concern its owners, it made the diner the perfect place to meet Louis.

The woman, whose name tag read "Roberta," had gray hair tied back in a bun and deep wrinkles. Yawning, she glanced at her wristwatch then grabbed two menus. Tara followed the woman's dull brown eyes as they scanned the dozen tables, each identically adorned with a white-and-blue-checkered tablecloth, salt and pepper shakers, sugar container, and a fake carnation in a dark-blue vase. Tara glanced at Louis, and when her eyes met his gray ones, she smiled and averted her gaze quickly. They were both on the verge of erupting into full-scale laughter at the woman's annoyance.

The only other patron was an older man wearing a red-and-black plaid flannel shirt, seated at the counter. His shoulders slouched; he sipped a cup of coffee, a half-eaten piece of pie at his elbow. Tara strained to hear the familiar melody playing softly, but the clank of pots in the kitchen made it impossible.

"Follow me," the woman said, her voice as dull as her appearance. She led Tara and Louis to a table in the middle of the diner.

"Can we have that one instead?" Louis pointed at a secluded table in the corner.

Though the table's location was safer as far as being seen, Tara didn't like the intimacy being isolated would create. Still, better to be safe.

The woman grunted and led them to the table. Louis pulled out a wooden chair for Tara to slide into. *So this is chivalry.* She couldn't remember the last time Josh had pulled out a chair for her.

"Are you two eating?" The woman wiped the table with a wet cloth.

"We'll browse the menu," Louis said. "But just two cups of coffee for now."

After the woman placed the menus on the table and headed back to the host station, Louis pushed the salt shaker, pepper shaker, sugar container, and vase to the edge of the table, then he set a traveling chess set in front of her. "Help me set up."

He meticulously removed the chess pieces from their nooks within the case and placed them on the chessboard.

"Louis, I don't have time for games. I only met you to tell you that this has got to stop."

Louis arranged the pieces on the board. "I'll play you for it."

Tara stared at Louis. "For what?"

"Your friendship. If you win, I'll never bother you again. But if I win, we can be friends."

Tara couldn't help being impressed by Louis's persistence. "No—"

"One game," Louis said as the woman came back to pour their coffee.

Tara's phone rang, and when she pulled it out of her purse, the screen showed Josh's picture. She stared at the photo.

"Everything okay?" Louis asked.

Tara looked at Louis then back at the phone. Josh's image had an unsettling effect on her. She'd hidden every interaction she'd had with Louis from Josh, and she'd lied to him about where she was going tonight. The dishonesty transported her to when she was ten years old and attending summer camp. Her father had come with her mother to pick her up, and his thinning gray hair was disheveled. He wore a neon-green shirt and soiled, stonewashed denim jeans. To Tara's horror, he was so medicated that drool formed at the corner of his mouth. The new friends she had made at camp eyed her father in disgust, so she'd lied and told them that her mom was a nurse and her father's caretaker.

"Everything okay?" Louis repeated.

"I'm sorry." Tara began to rise. "I lied to my husband and said I was meeting my friend Mariana. I should go."

Louis gently grabbed Tara's hand. "One game. Then you're free to go."

Her body tingled at Louis's touch. She put away the phone with Josh's picture. "Okay. One game."

As they moved their pieces, Tara and Louis completely focused on the game. For Tara, it was a nice vacation from her usual worries of work, home, finances, and kids. She got lost in the game, which was one reason why she'd started playing in junior high. It had helped her get her mind off her worries and garner control in an unpredictable world.

Louis seemed to be having the time of his life as he interspersed comedic commentary with every move. His humor surprised Tara.

Finally Louis smacked his hands on the table. "Checkmate!"

Tara cursed under her breath. He had her cornered. She conceded defeat and quickly helped put the pieces away. Louis left a twenty on the table before Tara led them out of the diner.

"Bye, Roberta," Louis said with a smirk.

The woman at the host station glanced up from her book, glared at Louis, then continued reading.

"She's warming to me," Louis said as they walked through the empty parking lot in the rain.

Though they'd just met, she would miss Louis's sense of humor. Tara shivered and wrapped her arms around her chest.

"You can't be cold. It's fifty-five degrees."

"Exactly. It's freezing!"

Louis chuckled. "You Californians are so spoiled. Live through a winter in Minnesota and then have the nerve to shiver in front of me on a beautiful night like tonight. Let's get in my car and out of the rain. I'll even turn the heat on."

Louis headed to his black Mercedes-Benz, but Tara didn't follow.

"I'm not getting in your car. You said one game. We played it, and now I need to get on with my life. Without you." Tara hurried to her car, eager to put the night behind her.

Just as she reached for the door handle, Louis's body pressed against hers. She turned toward him, and he brought his lips to hers. He wrapped his hand behind her head, easing her closer to him. His fingers ran up her scalp, and electricity pulsed through her body. She parted her lips. His tongue entered her mouth, caressing hers. Then she kissed him back.

She couldn't remember the last time she had been kissed like this. If ever. Louis took total control, and he knew what he was doing. But Tara didn't know what she was doing, making out with a man in a diner parking lot as if she had completely lost her mind.

Tara pulled away. "I can't do this." She pushed Louis away and opened the car door.

"Tara—" Louis called.

But she slammed the door. Her tires screeched as she peeled out of the parking lot, and she looked in the rearview mirror at Louis. It would have to be the last time she ever saw him, because Josh could never find out about this.

TERRENCE

Terrence yawned as he entered his house. Plopping down in his recliner, he laced his fingers together behind his head and leaned back. The faint murmur of the television came from their bedroom, but since Sophia hadn't met him at the door, she probably had fallen asleep. He was glad, because he couldn't bear to see her.

Terrence wished he could talk to his parents, though he'd be too embarrassed to tell them what was going on. They had always been open and honest with each other and would probably be appalled by Sophia's behavior.

His mind raced back to right before the car accident that killed them. The three of them had attended the Bay Area rival game of the Oakland A's versus the San Francisco Giants. The sun beamed down on them in the bleachers as they ate popcorn and hot dogs, cheering on the teams and swapping jokes. His dad had a laugh so loud, Terrence swore it could have woken the dormant San Andreas Fault.

When the conversation turned to Terrence, his dad's voice grew serious. "You know, Terrence, I don't think I've told you how proud I am of you. It's not easy being a black man in America. I know that firsthand. And I see the grief some of my friends' kids give them. Getting girls pregnant then leaving them. Doing drugs. Going to jail. You've never done that to us. I've made mistakes, plenty of mistakes, but I will go to my grave knowing I got you right."

As Terrence reclined in the chair, drifting nearer and nearer to sleep, he could hear his mother's voice.

"Get you a good wife, have you some good kids, and don't ever let anyone tell you you can't succeed at whatever you put your mind to. You got that?"

After his parents' deaths, he vowed he'd never let them down.

Granted, it had taken him a while to find someone he could spend the rest of his life with. But after he met Sophia, the time had come for him to get serious. When he found out about the abortion, he felt as though he'd failed. His father had drilled into him the importance of fatherhood and responsibility, and if Sophia didn't even feel as though she could confide in him that she was pregnant, he must have done something wrong. He knew how hard dating was for women. Before his parents' deaths, he'd been reckless with a woman's heart many times. But after things ended with Sophia, he knew he had to make it up to his parents, Sophia, and his baby he'd never meet.

And he had. He'd gone back and married Sophia. He'd told her he wanted a baby. He'd chased success as if it had stolen something from him. But there he sat in a house he might lose, facing setbacks at work, and married to a woman who wouldn't open up to him. It all seemed like a waste of effort.

Terrence's cell phone beeped, drawing him from the edge of sleep. A text from Josh that simply read, *Talk to her, bro.*

Terrence chuckled. He checked his phone and found a voicemail from Sophia and another from a number he didn't recognize. He listened to Sophia's first.

"Terrence, I'm so sorry that you had to find out about the baby the way you did. Please come home. I need you to know that I had every intention of telling you about the baby. I had started to on Saturday, but then the shit hit the fan. Please. Let's just talk. I love you."

Terrence's jaw dropped. Shit. That's what she had wanted to tell him? He stood as he played the second voicemail, heading toward the bedroom. He'd have to apologize to Sophia.

"Terrence, this is Rachel, your mother-in-law. Sophia gave me your number, and I'm calling with my congratulations," her voice said.

Reaching the doorway, a huge smile played on Terrence's lips. Maybe Sophia was happy about the baby if she had immediately told her mom.

"And Sophia told me about the financial mess you seem to have gotten yourself into," Rachel continued.

Terrence clenched his jaw. He couldn't believe Sophia would embarrass him by telling her mom about their financial trouble. Sophia knew how he prided himself on taking care of them financially.

"I don't want Sophia more stressed out then she already is, so Carl and I will lend you enough money to cover the mortgage for a few months. Have a good evening. And congratulations again."

If Rachel thought he'd accept her handouts like a man begging on the streets, she was wrong.

"Terrence?" Sophia asked, stirring in bed. "Is that you?"

Terrence tried to speak over the pounding of his heart. "You called your mom and told her about our finances?"

Sophia sat up straight. "Not exactly."

"She left me a message. Said she'd cover the mortgage a few months. How could you embarrass me like that?"

Sophia reached out to Terrence. "I didn't mean to—"

Anger pulsed through Terrence's veins. "I cannot believe you."

"Please, Terrence, hear me out," Sophia said.

Terrence glared at her. "So this is what you do, right? You just take care of things, huh?"

"No, Terrence, no," Sophia said firmly.

"I won't take nobody's charity. I'm outta here." Terrence grabbed his gym bag, stuffed it with clothes, then stormed out of the room. The last thing he would do was look like a fool.

CHAPTER SIX

HE SAVED ME

Sophia

Sophia sat up when the front door creaked open. She hadn't expected Terrence to come home in the late afternoon, if ever. She paused *Sleepless in Seattle,* wishing she'd changed out of her white T-shirt and gray sweat pants, then rushed to the front door.

"Oh, Tara," she said when she stopped.

"I hope you don't mind that I used the spare key. I didn't want you to get out of bed. Am I interrupting anything? Scratch that, you're on bed rest." Tara tossed her keys on the credenza near the door.

Sophia grinned. "I was doing extremely important things, thank you very much."

"Which movie are you watching?" Tara asked with a smirk.

"*Sleepless in Seattle.* Have you seen it lately? It's a classic."

"Yeah, yeah," Tara said sarcastically. She placed a reusable bag on the kitchen counter and proceeded to remove the contents. "I was thinking about my favorite pregnant friend and decided that I should bring some nourishing food for the both of you. It might cheer you up. I Googled healthy foods for pregnancy, so *voilà*: orange juice, yogurt, broccoli, lentils, and figs."

"Thanks." Sophia didn't want to hurt Tara's feelings, but all she really wanted was a bacon cheeseburger smothered in peanut butter. "I'll help myself later."

Tara pulled out a quarter-empty bottle of wine.

"Wine?" Sophia asked.

"Oh, that's for me." Tara reached into the cabinet, grabbed a wine glass, then filled it.

"Shouldn't you be at work?"

"It's Josh's and my anniversary today. I skipped lunch so I could take off early. Let's get you back in bed." Tara grabbed Sophia's hand and led her down the hall toward the bedroom.

Tara kicked off her shoes before joining Sophia on the bed, and Sophia eyed Tara's glass with envy.

Tara frowned. "Oh, I'm sorry. I should have brought you something to drink, like chamomile tea."

"I'm on bed rest, not in an infirmary. What are the plans for tonight? Shouldn't you make dinner for the girls?"

"Not sure what the plans are. Josh is planning a surprise. And dinner is Josh's job. That's the least he can do since he's not working."

Sophia coughed. "Tara, are you serious? He stays at home with the girls—"

"Because he can't find a job."

"He takes care of your house—"

"Which he lives in." Tara took a long sip of the wine.

"He loves you unconditionally—"

"Because he knows he can't do any better than me."

Sophia put a hand to her hip. "Will you stop cutting me off! Josh is a good husband and father. He deserves credit for that."

"Tell me—*please* tell me—what is so good about a man who sits at home all day and lets himself go?"

A lump rose in Sophia's throat. Before she could contain it, she burst into tears.

"Oh my god! What's wrong?" Tara asked.

"You just described me," Sophia wailed. "I have no job, and now that I'm on bed rest, my days will be relegated to searching the web, watching movies, and eating. Terrence stormed out last night, and he may never forgive me. He resents me just like you resent Josh!"

"Shh, Sophia." Tara smoothed Sophia's hair down. "Everything will work out with Terrence. You'll get a job. You'll be back on your feet. You'll be happy again."

Sophia wasn't so easily convinced. "What if none of those things happen?"

Tara squeezed Sophia's hand. "They will. And I don't resent Josh. It's just… complicated, you know? Part of me loves Josh more than anything. He helped me through a tough time in my life."

Sophia peered into Tara's eyes. "I knew you met in high school, but what was the tough time?"

"I moved from Sacramento to Cupertino to live with my aunt, after some… well, you could say problems at home. I enrolled at Cupertino High School. I didn't know a soul, and no one cared to know me.

"One day, about six months after starting school, I still hadn't really made friends and was wandering aimlessly when Josh came up to me, introduced himself, and said he'd seen me around the past few months. He said I always looked so sad, and he just wanted to see a smile on my face. He was one of the"—Tara hooked her fingers into air quotes—"'popular kids' since he was a star football player. As soon as the other girls saw me with him, they started introducing themselves left and right, sitting with me at lunch, inviting me to parties, sharing homework. Things really started looking up. It was another month before we were officially 'going out,' but he made a really bad situation better. He saved me. He saw someone who needed help, and he took it upon himself to do it."

"So what changed with you and Josh?" Sophia asked.

"He changed after the accident. It's like he's lost his zest for life. He just wants to hang out and not *do* anything. He doesn't work, barely goes out with friends, and we almost never have dates."

Sophia tried to understand Tara's perspective, but she could also see Josh's side. "Coming from someone who got laid off, I can say that *everything* changes when you find yourself out of work. It's like a divorce. You spend years going to work, socializing with coworkers, being a part of a business or corporation or whatever. And then it's all gone. Your identity is stolen from you. I'm not Sophia, Director of Sales for Cisco, anymore. I'm just Sophia. I'm still trying to figure out who I am now that I'm separated from work. And though my plan was to find a new job, now I'm not so sure what to do."

Tara took another long sip. "I didn't think about Josh's work situation like that. Josh has been through a lot—I've been right there with him—but I'm ready for him to get out of the quicksand and move forward. I tell him to take some classes so he can learn a new trade, but he won't do it. I tell him we can afford to put Michelle and Teeni in daycare so he can focus on his job search, but he won't do it. I tell him to come to the gym with me so he can get in better shape, but he won't do it. I mean, come on!"

"But that's what *you* tell him to do. Have you asked what *he* wants to do?"

Tara shrugged. "I haven't."

"Maybe you should start. He does so much, but you only focus on what he's not doing."

Tara hesitated then hugged Sophia. "You're right. Whatever Josh has planned for us tonight, I'm going to spend that time appreciating him."

Sophia patted her friend's back. "Good for you. And while you do that, I have to figure out how the hell to get my marriage and life back on track."

"Josh mentioned you'd had an abortion before. Why didn't you ever tell me?"

Tears filled Sophia's eyes. "I didn't want anyone else to ever look at me the way Terrence did when I told him. Like I was a monster."

Tara patted Sophia's hand. "You're not a monster. I would never judge you."

"I judge myself though. I was always so careful, and I just didn't know what to do back then when I found out. I thought having an abortion was the responsible thing to do, but I never knew how hard it would be after. It hurt. I just need Terrence to hear me out and believe that I wasn't going to do that again. I can't lose him again. When I broke things off with him the first time, my heart ached in a way I didn't know was possible."

Tara squeezed Sophia's hand. "Be honest with him, and it will work out."

Sophia didn't think it would be that easy, and when she looked at Tara's hand on hers, she noticed the time. "I hope so. Tara, you should get home for your anniversary surprise."

Tara drained her wine glass. "Okay. But if you need anything at all, I'm right next door."

"I know. Have fun tonight," Sophia said.

Sophia took a deep breath as Tara left the room. While her best friend was going out for her tenth anniversary, Sophia wasn't even sure she'd make it to her second.

JOSH

Josh rushed to Tara when she pushed open the door, juggling her purse, laptop bag, and groceries.

"Whoa, let me help you." He took the grocery bags and peeked inside.

"Mommy!" the girls screamed from the living room before they stampeded to the door.

As Tara knelt and embraced them, smothering their tiny faces with wet kisses, Josh couldn't help but wish the girls acted that excited to see him once in a while.

"What's in the bag you brought, Mommy?" Chelsea asked.

"Oh, just some graham crackers, chocolate, and marshmallows," Tara said.

"S'mores!" the girls screamed, jumping up and down.

Josh handed the bag to Chelsea. "Take this into the kitchen, please." Josh followed Tara into their bedroom. "How's Sophia? I assume you were there since your car was here but you weren't."

Tara removed her earrings and placed them in the jewelry box on her dresser. "She's pregnant, so she's insecure, unhappy, sensitive, and emotional."

"Ah, yes, I remember those days." Josh laughed.

Tara glared at Josh. "I was not that bad."

"You don't remember when you were pregnant with Chelsea and cried for fifteen minutes because your bamboo plant died? Didn't you even name it?"

"Bambi?" Tara said. "I invested a lot in that plant. Water. Sun. Soothing words. I was devastated and petrified that if I couldn't even keep a plant alive, I was doomed as a mother."

Josh went to Tara. "Then and now, you are a great mother."

"You too. I don't say it enough, but you're a great dad."

Josh opened his mouth then closed it. He couldn't remember the last time Tara had complimented him. "Thanks."

The doorbell rang, and Josh rushed out of the bedroom to open it.

"Why, aren't you handsome, Joshie?" his mom said.

"Hey, son," his dad said in his gruff voice, taking off his hat and revealing his bald head.

Josh patted his dad on the back. "Thanks for coming over."

"We just love getting to spend time with our granddaughters. Where are you two lovebirds going to celebrate the big one-oh anniversary?" his mom asked.

"It's a surprise," Josh said.

"Well, have fun, and stay out as long as you like. Your father and I will be just fine with the girls. Right, girls?"

"Right," Michelle and Chelsea said, exchanging glances as if they knew a good spoiling was on the way.

"Wight," Teeni echoed.

Tara came out of the bedroom and grabbed the car keys. "Thank you so much for babysitting," Tara said to Josh's parents. She turned to her husband. "I'll drive. Just tell me where?"

"Unh-unh-unh." Josh wagged his finger and reached for the keys. "Like I said, it's a surprise."

Tara released the keys into Josh's hand and walked to the car.

Once they were on their way, Josh broke the silence. "Pop quiz. What was our official first song?"

"What?" Tara asked, fiddling with her iPhone.

Josh wanted her to put the phone away. "When we first got together, do you remember what our first song was?"

"Jo-osh," Tara whined.

Josh gripped the wheel tightly. "It's okay if you don't remember. I'm just playing with you."

She put the phone in her purse and turned toward him. "Our first song was 'Hold My Hand' by Hootie and the Blowfish. I had to basically put on a football uniform and tackle you to even get a kiss. Playing 'Hold My Hand' for me was the most risqué move you made."

Josh laughed. "Was I that bad?"

Tara had a wide, mischievous smile. "The opposite. You were that good. Your mother really succeeded in instilling the fear of God in you."

Josh's body grew warm. He was sure his cheeks were turning red. "Not many people can say that, right? That they're with their first and only love. You were my first and will be my last. I'm not ashamed of that." Josh glanced at Tara.

Tara met his gaze. "That sure is something."

"I remember the first time I laid my eyes on you. I told my friend Rich—you remember Rich, right? Well, I told him, 'That's the girl I'm going to marry.' I still feel the same way about you now that I did then."

"You know what I remember?" she asked.

"What?" Josh asked eagerly.

"I remember those tight pants you used to wear when you played football."

"Really? You have to bring up the pants." Josh chuckled.

"Not only were you the most athletic, but you had the most heart. I admired that about you. No matter how many times you got knocked down, you always got back up."

Josh exited the freeway and made a right to head downtown. He parked and stopped Tara before she could open the door.

"Wait a second." He pulled a handkerchief from his pocket.

"Oh, please," Tara said.

"It's still a surprise." Josh leaned forward and tied the blindfold on Tara. He rushed out of the car, grabbed a blanket from the trunk, then opened Tara's door. "Give me your hand."

Tara outstretched her arm, and Josh interlaced his fingers with hers.

"You're not going to make me do a trust fall or anything like on the high school retreats, are you?" Tara asked.

"Only if you want me to." Josh squeezed Tara's hand.

Josh guided Tara past the laughter and murmur of activity from downtown. The longer they walked, the quieter it became, save for the crickets chirping.

"Okay, stop," Josh said. He untied the blindfold. Standing in front of them was a horse and a Cinderella-inspired white open carriage with gold trim. He faced Tara, whose eyes were wide and glimmering.

"Josh, how much did this—"

"Nope. We are not going there. It's covered, and I didn't spend a dime of your money."

The stoic carriage driver opened the door. "Welcome. Happy anniversary." He took Tara's hand and helped her up the three steps.

Josh followed then took a seat next to Tara. He spread the blanket to cover their legs.

"Ready?" the driver asked once he was settled in his seat, reins in hand.

"Ready," Josh said.

As they rode, the wind nipped at their faces. Josh put his arm around Tara, and the warmth of their bodies negated the cold.

"How did you even think of this?" Tara asked.

"I wanted to do something to show you I can still sweep you off your feet."

"It's working," Tara said.

In the carriage was a basket filled with wine, wine glasses, cheese, crackers, and an assortment of fruit. They helped themselves, and though the sun had already set, they enjoyed the view of the park. Josh felt as if they were transported back to another time, before the accident. They were happy. Talkative. Playful.

After the hour-long ride, Josh and Tara headed back to the car, their hands clasped together.

After dinner at their favorite Italian restaurant, they arrived home; Josh's mom and dad met them at the door.

"I hope you enjoyed your surprise," Josh's mom said with a yawn. "The girls are asleep."

"It was magical," Tara said.

"Thanks again," Josh added, anxious to be alone with his wife.

Josh shut the door behind his parents. Tara stumbled down the hall, resting against the wall. Josh went to her, and she brought her lips to his, kissing him with a passion he hadn't experienced in what seemed like years. She grabbed for his belt, freeing it from the buckle, then unbuttoned his pants.

Josh reached for Tara's jeans and slid them down. He removed her shirt then unhooked her bra. He bent down, and his lips traced her breasts. When his tongue found her nipple, Tara moaned.

Josh had longed for this moment: to want and be wanted, to kiss and be kissed back, to make love and be made love to. It'd been several months since the last time they'd been intimate. They abandoned their clothes at the front door, and Josh took Tara's hand, again leading the way, though it was so dark they both seemed to be blindfolded this time. He laid Tara on the couch, pulled off her panties, and rushed to take off his boxers.

"I've missed this so—" he breathed.

Tara grabbed the back of his head and interrupted him with a kiss. He lay on top of her, only their breathing piercing the silent room. He spread her legs, anxious to enter the place that belonged to him.

"Mommy! Daddy!" Michelle cried.

Josh and Tara froze.

"Mommy! Daddy!" Michelle cried again.

"I'll be right there," Josh called. He looked at Tara. "It's probably a bad dream. Meet me in bed, and we'll continue this."

Damn it. He jogged to their bedroom, put on his robe, then went to Michelle's room. "What's wrong, Michelle?"

"I had a bad dream that I was Gretel and an old lady was trying to eat me," Michelle sobbed.

"That was just a bad dream. It's not real. No one will eat you. Now, just try to go back to sleep."

"But I don't want to go back to sleep. Can I come into bed with you and Mommy?"

"Oh, no. You stay right here."

"Can you stay for a little while with me?"

Josh groaned as he lowered himself onto the floor next to Michelle's bed. "Sure, Michelle. Close your eyes. I'll be right here."

Josh tried to keep his eyes open, but he didn't usually drink wine, and it seemed to have gone straight to his head. Knowing sleep was on the way, he struggled to his feet.

"No, Daddy, no," Michelle cried.

Josh sat again. Though he tried with all his might, he fell fast asleep.

TERRENCE

Terrence grimaced as he pushed the bar in the air with a grunt. Lance grabbed it, and the bar clanked back onto the rack.

"Man, my biceps are screaming." Terrence sat up. Grabbing his towel, he wiped the sweat that dripped down his neck and onto his black muscle shirt.

A woman with a long brown ponytail, spandex shorts, and sports bra stood near Terrence and Lance. She stopped in front of Terrence. "Terrence? Oh my god! You dropped off the face of the earth."

"Oh, hey... girl." Terrence racked his brain to place the woman.

"What are you up to these days?" the brunette asked, scanning Terrence's body.

Terrence shrugged. "Working hard. How about you...?"

"Trisha," the girl said.

And then Terrence remembered her and the night they'd spent together a couple years ago. "Right, Trisha."

Trisha leaned in close. "Maybe we can, uh, get together again sometime."

"That sounds..." Terrence glanced at Lance, who looked amused. "Nice, but I can't." Terrence held up his left hand. "Married now."

"Too bad," Trisha said with a lift of her eyebrow before sauntering away.

Terrence twisted the top off the Gatorade bottle and chugged the remaining blue liquid. From what he remembered about Trisha, her offer was a tempting proposition.

Lance nudged Terrence. "'Married now'? That chick was fine! How are you going to let a body that tight just get away?"

Terrence chuckled. "I'm just not focused on that. You'll get it one day."

"Shoot, don't curse me like that. Whatever *it* is you got, I want no part of that. Trying to act like you wouldn't have had that number and that piece of ass all in one night B.S."

"B.S.?" Terrence asked.

"Before Sophia." Lance laughed. "You were notorious. While most of us mortal men have to chase women, your biggest problem was brainstorming the politest way to ask the stranger in your bed to leave the next morning."

"I wasn't that bad," Terrence said.

"I said you were notorious—in a good way. Like Notorious B.I.G.," Lance said. "And if everything's so great at home, why did you crash on my couch last night?"

"Shut up, Lance. You need to grow up."

"Call me Peter Pan because I never, ever want to grow up if it means having to pass on an opportunity like that." He gestured in the direction Trisha had headed.

"Whatever, Peter. You wanna get a beer?"

"Look, I'm not like you. I'm not into the whole marriage thing. But I know your wife is pregnant now, and you're mad at her. So go home. Make up."

Terrence patted Lance's back. "Good advice, man. I'll hit the shower then head out."

<hr />

Tiptoeing through the dark house, Terrence didn't hear a sound. He went to the kitchen and turned on the light above the sink. An ultrasound picture was taped to the refrigerator door.

Tears filled his eyes. Though he knew Sophia was pregnant, the ultrasound picture hit him like cold water splashed in his face. The way he treated Sophia directly affected his baby now.

He went to the bedroom and eased open the door. Sophia appeared to be fast asleep since she didn't move. Terrence took off his shoes, changed into a pair of shorts, and took off his shirt. He lay next to Sophia and wrapped his arms around her, inhaling her coconut-scented hair.

Sophia turned to him. "I'm so sorry, Terrence."

Terrence pecked her on the cheek. "I know, baby."

"I love you more than anything. I love this baby that much too. I don't want anything to come between our family."

And though Terrence didn't know what to believe, he said, "I love you too." He was certain of that.

"I'm not good at this," Sophia whispered.

Terrence leaned in closer. "Good at what?"

"Opening up and relying on anyone else. I'm scared about our future, and I didn't know how to just tell you that. I was scared that if I don't have it all together, you might not want to be with me."

"I don't have it all together either. No one does. But I want you to know that I'll always be here. For you. For our baby."

"Thank you, Terrence."

Terrence placed his hand on Sophia's stomach. "No, thank you."

———————— ❦ ————————

TARA

Tara stared out of the deli window at the gray noon sky. "I know we aren't officially there yet, but I hate winter," she said to Mariana.

"Who doesn't?" Mariana asked.

"No, like, I really despise the cold, and the rain, and the overcast skies. It's depressing as hell." Tara sipped her Diet Coke.

"Are you okay? You seem a little down." Mariana said it more as an accusation than a concern.

Tara wished she could just be honest and tell Mariana that everything was messed up. After spending last night alone, she was disappointed in Josh. He'd let her down. Yet again. And even more than that, ever since ending things with Louis, she felt like a fruit that had been drained of all its juice. Louis had awakened something in Tara that she hadn't even known she had. He'd filled her up with excitement and passion and life. She missed the soft sensation of his lips on hers and feeling as if fireworks were exploding in her body.

But she couldn't tell anyone. Especially not Mariana. "Everything's fine. But I'm super swamped with discovery in the Drymeir case. How are you?"

"Xavier is absolutely driving me crazy. He and that little tramp want to take the boys to Tahoe for Christmas, but he knows he has them for Thanksgiving and I have them for Christmas."

"Can you just switch this year?"

Mariana narrowed her eyes at Tara as if that was the most absurd suggestion she had ever heard. "And let him win? Hell no! He's the one who left me. Why should he get Christmas too?"

"Mariana, I'm sorry. I can't even imagine what it must be like."

"Of course you can't imagine it. Josh would never leave you. When he looks at you, it's as if he's laying his eyes on you for the first time and falling in love with you all over again. You don't see it because you're too busy fussing at him, but that man loves you more than he loves himself."

Tara leaned forward. "Can I tell you something?"

"Of course."

"I love Josh, but I met him when I was just a teenager. We're both all grown up now, and sometimes I wonder if the person I am now is still compatible with the person he is. I wonder if he can satisfy me the way I need." Tara took another bite of her sandwich, giving Mariana a chance to digest her words.

"I've known the two of you for—what—like, seven years? You've added a couple of kids, and he got injured, but he still seems like the same old Josh... in a good way. Sometimes you just have to remember what attracted you to him in the first place. Try to remember the main thing that made you want to marry him," Mariana said.

Tara looked out the window again. An image of blood on the basement floor of her parents' house flashed through her mind. She could almost hear the screaming. "He made me feel safe. I knew he would never hurt me. That was the first time in my life that I felt that way."

Mariana sat back in her chair. "Safe from what?"

Tara wished she could take back her words. "I mean, uh... my heart. I knew my heart was safe with him."

———◦✕◦———

Tara yawned as she packed up to leave work at the end of the day. Besides her quick lunch with Mariana, she had spent the entire day gathering the documents she needed to produce for opposing counsel. It was a quarter to eight, and she was definitely one of the last employees in the office.

Her phone vibrated on her desk. A text from Louis. Her heart raced. She hadn't heard from him since the diner, so she assumed he was respecting her decision not to see him anymore. But now he was texting her.

She opened the message and couldn't help but smile. *I'm trying really hard to respect your wishes, but I can't get you out of my mind. Can I see you one last time?*

She put the phone in her purse, then took it out and read the message again. She knew what she should do: delete the text, go home to her husband and children, and resume her normal life. After the kiss in the parking lot, there was no way she could cling to the story that he wanted to be just friends; friends didn't make out with each other. So responding to the text would mean she wanted more than friendship, something she couldn't give him.

Home it had to be.

She startled when she opened her office door. "Louis?"

"I'm sorry, but I had to see you." He looked gorgeous in a white business shirt—partly unbuttoned—and black trousers, a matching suit coat slung around his arm.

"How'd you get in here?"

"I spotted your car in the garage in the basement. I told the janitor I left something in my office, and he let me in."

"Louis, I can't—"

He pressed his index finger to her lips.

"Someone could see you here."

Louis walked in, closed the door, and locked it. "Problem solved."

"What are you doing here?"

Louis pulled out his iPhone and placed it on the desk. Music flooded the small office. Bob Marley's voice followed.

"You shouldn't be—"

"Shh. Just listen."

Louis held out his hand, and Tara took it, allowing him to pull her to him. They swayed as Bob Marley sang about giving good loving.

Louis leaned forward and kissed her. She kissed him back. When his mouth ventured to her neck, a moan escaped her. Their bodies moved in unison toward Tara's desk. Louis hiked up her skirt then picked her up and eased her onto the desk. He parted her legs and moved forward.

His mouth was on hers, smothering her with kisses. Tara found herself enjoying that he tasted like spearmint gum.

Louis pulled back then cupped Tara's face. He looked her in the eyes, his gaze penetrating her. "I want you in my life. But we don't have to do this. I will take no for an answer. Do you want to stop?"

Tara's mind screamed yes. There was Josh, her husband, the father of her children, the only man she had ever been with. There were her daughters, the example she wanted to set, the devastation they'd go through if Josh ever found out. There was Mariana, whose life had been torn apart by Xavier's infidelity. There was her reputation. But all those things faded when Louis's fingers slipped into her. She arched her back, and Louis unbuttoned her shirt.

He kissed her neck again. "Tara, do you want me to stop?"

She closed her eyes tightly. "No," she whispered.

PART TWO

CHAPTER SEVEN

FREE AT LAST

Sophia

"Sophia Douglas," a short Filipina in pale-pink scrubs called from the door.

"That's me." Sophia rose to her feet, placing the *Pregnancy* magazine on the coffee table.

The nurse held the door open for her, and they went to the next room.

"If you wouldn't mind stepping on the scale," the nurse said.

Sophia stepped on the scale then gasped. "Impossible. Don't write that down." Sophia got off the scale, removed her jacket and shoes, then got back on the scale. It was a pound and a half less. It'd been ten weeks since she found out she was pregnant. There was no way she could have gained eleven pounds. "Is that scale right?"

The nurse nodded. "Mrs. Douglas, you were on bed rest, so you probably weren't burning many calories. The weight gain is a little high, but nothing to be worried about. You want to aim for about twenty-five to forty pounds by the end of the pregnancy. I need a urine sample, then you can go wait in the examining room. Dr. Smith will be right in."

Sophia took the plastic cup to the bathroom. She closed the door and *really* looked at her reflection—something she'd been avoiding. Roundness filled the mirror: her face, her belly, her hips. And to her, it wasn't the cute everything-is-skinny-except-the-stomach way that pregnant women appeared in movies. She just felt fat.

After giving the urine sample, she waited for the doctor in the examining room.

There was a tap on the door, then it opened. "Mrs. Douglas, nice to see you. How have you been?" Dr. Smith asked.

Sophia smiled at her doctor, a lanky woman whose silver hair was bound in a low ponytail. "I've been well."

Dr. Smith rolled a stool near the examining table and took a seat. "Any bleeding or abdominal pain?"

"Nope."

"How's the nausea?"

"It's actually been subsiding." Sophia was ever so grateful for that.

"Good. That's normal. Lie down, please."

Dr. Smith pressed on Sophia's round stomach then took out a fetal Doppler and positioned it on her abdomen. A sound like galloping hooves—her baby's heartbeat—filled the room. Sophia loved that sound. It meant everything was all right.

"You and the baby are checking out well." Dr. Smith helped Sophia sit up.

Sophia folded her hands. "So does that mean I'm off bed rest? I've gained eleven pounds! Don't get me wrong, I don't mind lying in bed and watching movies. This is the longest in my life I've just relaxed. But I need to get on with my life. Find a job, start exercising a little, clean my house, and—"

"Whoa, whoa, whoa." Dr. Smith put up her hand. "Sophia, bleeding and abdominal pain are very serious. Once you're off bed rest, you still need to take things slowly. I don't want to scare you, but you're not out of the woods yet."

"I get where you're coming from, but I don't have the luxury of putting my life on hold indefinitely."

Dr. Smith laughed. "Let me break this to you now so you're not surprised later. Life as you know it will never be the same once you have a baby."

Sophia didn't laugh. Truth was, that was her main fear. She didn't mean to be selfish, but she liked her life as it was.

Dr. Smith tapped her pen on the clipboard. "You're twenty weeks along and you've had no additional bleeding, no pain, baby's heartbeat sounds good, so... yes. You are free to spend more time out of bed. But take it slowly. We'll see you in two weeks."

Sophia lowered herself off the table and gathered her things. She left the office, squinting at the gray clouds in the late January sky. Once she was in the car, she dialed Terrence.

"Hey, baby," he answered. "How'd the doctor's visit go?"

"Other than the fact that I'm getting fat, it went really good."

"Remember we don't use that F-word. You're absolutely gorgeous, and regardless of how thin all the celebrities look when they're pregnant, pregnant women are supposed to look pregnant. What else did the doctor say?"

Sophia appreciated Terrence's opinion so much. Though the extra weight bothered her, he seemed to love every inch of her body. "She also said I'm off bed rest."

"Is she sure about that? I think rest is really good for you and our baby."

"Yep, we have a clean bill of health."

"That's wonderful! But at least put your feet up when you're sitting."

Sophia laughed. "Want to celebrate tonight?"

"Sure. I'll surprise you with something."

Since she was close to Tara's office, Sophia made a detour in the hope that Tara could go to lunch. When she got to Tara's floor, Corinne, the receptionist, greeted her.

"Hi, Sophia. Wow! You sure are getting big. How are you?"

"I'm good." *Better when people don't comment on my weight.* "Is Tara here?"

"Yep." Corinne smiled as if she was waiting for someone to take her picture. "I'll buzz her now."

Minutes later, Tara strolled down the hall. Though she looked very serious dressed in a black skirt suit, she beamed at Sophia. "Hi, there. What are you up to?"

"I just left my doctor's appointment, and I'm officially off bed rest. I wanted to see if you could do lunch."

"I'd love to. Let me just wrap up a couple of things. Come on back."

"Look at those," Sophia said in Tara's office, spying a dozen red roses on the credenza. "Josh give you those?"

Tara sat at her desk, her eyebrows raised above wide eyes. "Uh, no.

I bought them. I like keeping fresh flowers in my office. Signs of life in a profession that often sucks all the life out of me."

Sophia remembered that feeling all too well. But she actually missed it a bit after being on bed rest. "Aww, have you been feeling stressed?"

"It's just the same case we've been working on for a while. Peter was hoping to settle it, but that's probably not going to happen. Let me just send a quick email, and I'll be ready to go."

"Take your time." Sophia wandered to the chess set on the credenza, which had a few pieces on the board while others were lined up on the side. "Are you in the middle of a game?"

Tara looked up from the computer, a sly half-smile on her lips. "You could say that." She stood and grabbed her overcoat. "What are you in the mood for?"

"Anything I can sprinkle crushed red pepper on."

"Like pizza?" Tara asked.

"No, more like Chinese food."

"I don't know if they have red pepper in Chinese restaurants."

Sophia put her hand in her purse and pulled out a packet of red pepper. "Terrence bought me a box. I have a bunch in my purse for emergencies."

Tara laughed until tears formed in her eyes. "Oh, the pregnant days."

After ordering at the Chinese restaurant, Sophia lowered the decaffeinated green tea bag she'd brought with her into the teacup. She gazed around the tiny restaurant packed with people in suits and ties. "Do they sell maternity business suits? Now that I'm off bed rest, my first goal is to get a job. It's either that or lose the house. I've drained all my savings."

"I hear you, but you're already working on the most important thing right now." Tara raised her eyebrows.

Sophia tilted her head. "I am?"

"Your baby."

"Oh, yes, yes. The baby." Sophia rubbed her stomach and smiled. "But the baby needs a roof over his or her head."

"How are you two?"

"Great, actually. Things have been going really well with Terrence and me, and the doctor said everything looks good. I've just gained a ton," Sophia said.

Tara patted Sophia's hand. "It's hard since you went months without being able to work out. Let me tell you one secret. You aren't really eating for two. Most times, pregnant women only need an extra three hundred calories a day. I didn't know that when I was pregnant with Chelsea, and I gained over forty pounds. After she was born, I looked pregnant for months. You should watch out for that. I walked a lot with the girls for exercise."

"I've been working out all right." Sophia made a gesture of scooping food and putting it into her mouth. "Terrence says he loves how I look, but he hasn't shown any interest in me sexually since he found out I was pregnant. It's too awkward to bring up, but pregnant or not, we both have our needs."

"It's new to him. Don't worry about it."

"Well, what's new with you? You look great. I mean, no one could tell you've had three kids. And though I'm the pregnant one, you seem to have this glow." Sophia leaned in close. "What's the secret?"

Tara glanced to the side then looked at Sophia. "I don't know what you're talking about."

"What was that?" Sophia asked. "You looked away."

"Okay, Sherlock, you caught me."

Sophia lowered her voice. "What is it? Don't tell me you're pregnant."

Tara laughed. "Not a chance in hell. But I got a promotion. I'm now the senior paralegal. That's part of the reason I'm stressed—more money means more work."

Sophia clapped. "Tara, that's great! Why didn't you tell me?"

"With you out of work and having financial problems, I didn't want it to seem like I was rubbing it in."

"Do you, Josh, and the girls want to come over and celebrate tonight? It would be fun. I barely see you anymore since you're always so busy."

"That sounds great, but I have a project I'll be working on late tonight, and then I'll probably hit the gym. But let's plan on doing that soon."

Sophia raised her teacup. "Then we'll celebrate right now. To the end of bed rest and me hopefully getting a job and to your new promotion!"

Tara clinked her teacup against Sophia's.

TARA

Tara closed the door to the hotel room that she and Louis had frequented almost every weeknight for the past month and a half. She hated the hotel because it reminded her of her deception, but she couldn't stay away. Her eyes adjusted to the darkness, and her gaze went to Louis, who was illuminated by the television's glow, his fingers interlaced behind his head resting on the headboard. He scooted to the edge of the bed.

Tara stood between his parted legs. "How was your day?" she asked before kissing him.

"My day was tough. I had that individual hearing at Immigration Court. My client's going to be deported to Mexico. He has five kids and a wife—all US citizens—but he has to go back to a country he hasn't been to in fifteen years. I hate when that happens."

"I'm so sorry." Tara climbed on the bed. She knelt behind Louis and massaged his shoulders.

"Mm, that feels good. How was your day?"

"It was okay. My friend Sophia stopped by the office, and we went to lunch. I wish you could meet her. She's the smartest person I've ever—"

"Excuse me?" Louis turned to face Tara.

"I meant, present company excluded, she's one of the brightest people I know."

Louis chuckled. "Better. What does she do?"

Tara laughed. "Let's just say it's complicated, but she worked in sales for Cisco for a long time."

"And how is Ms. Senior Paralegal doing at work?"

"She is doing very well, and she's very thankful for the advice her attorney-friend gave her that got her the promotion."

"Is that all I am to you? An attorney-friend?" Louis raised his eyebrows.

She backed away toward the headboard. "You tell me," she said playfully.

He followed her. "Or I could show you."

Tara closed her eyes, anticipating his kiss. Her body longed for Louis's, and regardless of how much she got, she always wanted more.

When she didn't feel his lips on hers, she opened her eyes. Louis held two pieces of paper in the air.

"What are those?"

"Airplane tickets. For the annual Las Vegas conference for legal professionals this weekend. You'd have to arrive on Friday and leave Sunday. My airline miles are accruing, so I bought you a ticket. Do you think you can find a way to go?"

"I could try to talk to Peter about sending me. But even if he goes for it... well."

"Your husband, right? Must be nice. My wife couldn't care less. She works so much at the hospital, the only person who'll notice I'm gone is our son's nanny."

Tara sat up and ran her fingers through her hair. All the passion and excitement that had consumed her just minutes ago slipped away like bathwater down a drain at the mention of Louis's wife. "Is that why you're here? Because your wife is too busy for you?" She scooted to the edge of the bed and got up.

"Why are you so upset? You're married, and I'm married."

"I hate thinking about you being with someone else."

"I'm not 'with someone else.' I'm with you. Here. Now." Louis cupped Tara's face. "If you ask me, what we have is special. We're not here because of a label that society imposes on us, or a sense of duty we have to one another. We're here because we want to be. What we have exists outside of all that nonsense, in a genuine place."

"Okay." She accepted Louis's kiss.

What we have is special. Though life was fun and exciting with Louis, she hated the lying, the sneaking around, the secrecy. The possibility of the affair ever being exposed terrified her. But those fears took a backseat to her irresistible urge to be with Louis.

<hr />

TERRENCE

Terrence opened the door, and Sophia ran to him.

"Hey. Careful there." He hugged her gently with his free hand. His other hand held their dinner.

"I'm off bed rest, remember?" Sophia said.

"Yeah, but that doesn't mean you should be practicing the hundred-yard dash." He bent and rubbed Sophia's stomach. "Hey, little fella."

Sophia laughed. "Or the female equivalent of fella."

Terrence wrapped his arm around her shoulder and led her into the kitchen. "Close your eyes while I make our plates."

Ever since she'd been put on bed rest, Terrence had brought home or cooked a wide variety of food. They played a game where he fed her the first few bites, and she had to guess its country of origin.

Sophia sat at the table and closed her eyes.

He removed the vegetarian platter from the container and shoveled it onto a plate before bringing it to Sophia. "Open up."

Sophia accepted the forkful. "Mmmm. One more bite."

He gave her another bite.

"It's... Ethiopian?" Sophia asked before opening her eyes.

Terrence kissed her forehead. "Absolutely right."

"Pregnancy taste buds, I tell ya," Sophia said proudly.

Terrence noticed a laptop, a newspaper, and a notebook littered the far end of the table. "What's all this?"

Sophia pointed at the computer. "I'm job searching. I'm off bed rest, so I can work now."

"Wait a second. You just got the okay to get out of bed after serious complications. You can't jump to working all of a sudden." Terrence didn't understand why he needed to be the voice of reason when their unborn baby was involved.

"I feel fine. And more importantly, I don't want to lose our home. You turned down my mom's offer, and money won't materialize out of thin air. Without money, we can't stay here."

"The priority is our baby. I'd rather lose the house than him."

Sophia huffed. She stood and wrapped her arms around Terrence. "I don't want to lose anything. I just want to help out around here. The further along I get, the harder it will be to get hired. Why don't I just apply and see what happens?"

Terrence sighed. He wanted to be able to provide for his wife, as his father had for their family, and he hated that she felt she needed a job while pregnant. "Okay. Apply to a few places, and we'll go from there."

As he and Sophia ate, he just hoped that no company would respond.

After dinner, Terrence took the trash outside. The cold winter air stung his face, and the rolling of garbage bins next door caught his attention.

"Hey, bro," Josh said.

Terrence waved. "Hey, what are you up to?"

"Not much. You want to come over for a beer?"

"Let me ask Sophia if she minds." Terrence jogged back inside. "Hey, baby, is it cool if I grab a beer at Josh's?"

She smiled. "Of course it is. Tell him I said hi."

Terrence pecked Sophia on the lips then headed next door.

"Where are Tara and the girls?" Terrence asked.

Josh grabbed two beers, handed one to Terrence, then leaned against the kitchen counter. "Tara left for the gym, and the girls are in bed. What's up with you?"

Terrence sipped his beer. "Truth is, I need your opinion. Sophia's on a job-hunting kick, and I don't think it's good for her to work right now."

"Well, I know Sophia, and she's extremely responsible. I don't think she'd do anything to jeopardize the baby's health."

Terrence shrugged. "You're probably right. I gotta figure a way to get ahead financially that doesn't include getting bailed out by somebody. I'm busting my ass at work, but we're still behind."

"You two have been through hard times before and made it out. It'll come together. Didn't you break up once?"

"Yep. After the abortion, Sophia told me she didn't want to see me anymore and ignored all my efforts to contact her. I was like, 'Okay. I'm not trippin' off her like that anyways.' And I went back to, you know, messing around with other females and what not. You know how that is."

Josh laughed. "Me? I've only been with Tara. But what made you want to get back together?"

"I couldn't get her out of my head. Being apart from her made it even clearer what I was missing in my life. Regardless of my feelings about the abortion, breaking up made me realize that no one compared to her, and I'd never felt like that before about anyone. My parents' deaths taught me that tomorrow isn't promised, so I didn't want to regret anything."

"Bro, that's deep. How'd you get her back?" Josh asked.

"I bought a ring and some roses, and I went to her place. I knocked on her door, and when she opened, I told her I needed her in my life. I asked her to take a leap of faith with me and give us a chance. And she said yes. We drove to Vegas that night, and the rest is history." Terrence beamed at the memory. Sure, their relationship wasn't perfect, but he still couldn't imagine being with anyone else.

"Wow. That's quite a story."

"It happened so fast though, and Sophia's been out of work for the majority of our marriage, so I'm not sure how life will go when she starts working again."

"I know what you mean. I barely see Tara. Maybe I'm making it up, but I feel like she wants to be with everyone except me. I want our lives back to the way it was before the accident."

Terrence leaned forward, his elbows on the counter. "I hear you. That sucks."

"Sucks? *Sucks*? My back kills me, I spend all day shuttling kids to and from activities, watching the Disney channel, and cooking dinner, which Tara refuses to eat the majority of the time because she wants salad instead. It's like I'm no good to her since the accident."

"At some point, you gotta put that accident behind you."

"Easy for you to say. That accident changed everything. I'm out of work, out of shape, and outta options."

Terrence knew Josh's pity party had to end. "We're fixing this right now. Go get dressed, go the gym, and work out with your wife. Kill all three birds with one stone by taking action, getting healthy, and showing Tara you're the man she fell in love with. I'll stay here with the girls until you get back. I'm sure Sophia won't mind."

Josh laughed. "No way."

Terrence pointed his beer at Josh. "Do it, man."

Josh seemed to ponder the offer. "Okay, I will. Yeah. Thanks, bro."

Terrence went into the living room while Josh disappeared to change in his room. Terrence turned on the TV, happy he could help his friend.

JOSH

As Josh sped to the gym, adrenaline raced through his body. Terrence's pep talk had pumped him up, and he was ready to make changes. He needed to regain control of his life instead of feeling like a victim of circumstance all the time. No wonder Tara didn't want to be with him. Ever since their anniversary night, when he'd fallen asleep on her, things between them had gone from bad to worse. Whenever he tried to touch her, she recoiled, and if he tried to talk about it with her, she stonewalled him. But that was going to change. He was going to change.

He parked then headed into the gym. Sweat made the air moist, and he had no idea how long it had been since he'd worked out. Tara would be surprised to see him, but in a good way. She always encouraged him to work out, but he always made excuses. That was ending today.

On the second floor, he jogged to the cardio equipment since Tara usually ran on the treadmill. The place was packed with bodies, some toned and others closer to Josh's round shape. But there was no sign of Tara. Though he doubted she'd be lifting weights, he went to the weight area and looked around. Nope. He circled the entire gym twice, but still no Tara. He pulled his phone out of his pocket and called her.

No answer. As usual.

"Tara, I'm at the gym. Where are you? Call me back," he left on her voicemail.

He positioned himself in the front of the gym so he'd see Tara come or leave, and he watched the gym-goers mill about. Most people strutted their stuff, heads held high, chests out, sweat glistening on their bodies. Josh longed to be back in shape. With some concerted effort, he could get to where he needed to be. Even if Tara wasn't where she was supposed to be. But after about thirty minutes and another lap around the gym, Josh left.

Josh sat in the dark living room, fuming. He'd gotten no call from Tara, no text, nothing. His worry and frustration grew with every minute that ticked by. The longer he went without hearing from her, the more convinced Josh became that she must have been in some type of an accident. There was simply no other explanation. Just when he was ready to call the police, the front door opened.

Josh rose and jogged down the hall. "Tara, where have you been? I was so worried."

Tara's eyes widened. "I'm so sorry, Josh. I just got your message. Something came up at work, and I had to go back to the office instead of the gym. Sorry I missed you. What were you doing there?"

Josh's shoulders relaxed, and he hugged Tara tight. The worst-case scenario hadn't happened, and she was home safe. He inhaled a strong mix of Tara's floral perfume and unfamiliar cologne. He pulled back and studied her. Her face was tight with a forced smile. Something wasn't right.

"So you all stayed late?" he asked.

Tara rubbed the back of her neck. "Uh, yeah. I should have told you when the plans changed. Now that I'm senior paralegal, there's more work." She looked past Josh and yawned. "I need to hit the shower. I'm exhausted, and I have to do it all again tomorrow." Tara brushed past him and down the hall. She paused at their doorway. "You coming? Or are you going to sit out here in the dark?"

Josh hesitated. His throat had become dry. "I'll be right there."

In the kitchen, he poured a glass of water, going over what had just happened. While it was true that Tara had been promoted, she rarely got called into work late, and when she did, she didn't come home smelling like another man. Josh gulped the water, trying to drown his worry. It was probably nothing. But if something was going on, he would have to find out.

CHAPTER EIGHT

TRAVEL ARRANGEMENTS

SOPHIA

SOPHIA ROLLED OVER IN BED, awakened from her midday nap by her ringing phone. "Hello," she said, eyes still closed.

"Sophia," her mom cried.

Sophia sat up. "What's wrong?"

"It's Carl. He had a heart attack! I'm at the hospital right now."

"Oh god! What happened?"

"He was having some argument with Desiree. She stormed out of the house. Then about thirty minutes later, he collapsed. I called an ambulance, and they rushed him to the hospital. He's in critical condition. The doctors aren't sure if he's going to pull through. I don't know what to do. They performed a coronary angioplasty or something, and they gave him different medications to stabilize him, but I just don't know what to do."

"I'll catch the first flight out there to be with you. Where's Desiree now?"

Her mom sobbed into the phone. "I don't know, and I don't care. I need you to take her home with you for a while. And if she won't go, she'll be cut off financially."

Sophia had to see Carl. It had been too long since she'd seen him, and hopefully it wasn't too late. She'd need to help her mom and Desiree find a middle ground. For as long as Sophia could remember, there had always been a power struggle between them. Usually it came down to Carl to be the judge, and usually by using tears and faux smiles, her sister would win. With Carl in the hospital, Sophia had a feeling she'd end up being their mediator.

"Mom, it's only one in the afternoon. I should be able to get a flight out today."

"Please hurry."

"It's going to be okay. I'll see you soon," Sophia said before hanging up.

Sophia's body trembled as she grabbed her laptop. She needed to plan her trip. And fast.

———— ✦◇✦ ————

Sophia hurried down the long hospital corridor, grateful she'd been able to catch a flight immediately. Though Terrence had wanted to join her, they couldn't afford both tickets. But now she needed him more than ever.

Her stomach swam as she turned the corner to the waiting room and saw her mom. "Oh, Mom."

When her gaze fell on Sophia, her mom's bloodshot eyes closed as if in relief. She stood, dabbing her eyes with a tissue, and hugged Sophia. Seeing her mom so upset transported her back to when she was five years old and her dad broke the news that he was leaving her mom for another woman. Though Sophia hadn't been able to understand exactly what had happened or why her mother wouldn't get out of bed for days on end, she had known it was bad. But this time, Sophia knew what was at stake. This time, it was arguably worse.

Her mom relied on Carl for everything. He was the only one in their home who worked, so he paid the bills and handled all of the money. Carl financed a somewhat lavish life for himself, Sophia's mom, and Desiree.

"Thank you for coming," her mom said. "How is the pregnancy going?"

"Of course." Sophia patted her belly. "The pregnancy is good. Everyone says the second trimester is the best one. How's Carl?"

"Not good, Sophia."

Sophia tried to push her worries aside. *Focus on solutions.* "What'd the doctor say?"

"Carl had a seventy-percent blockage in his artery. The doctor performed a coronary angioplasty to restore blood flow to his heart. He's been moved to a special care unit where they're monitoring him. If it all looks good, we can see him soon. Sophia, I just don't know what I'll do if Carl doesn't—"

"Mom, stop." Sophia grabbed her mom's hand. "It's going to be okay."

"I'm so glad you're here."

"Speaking of here"—Sophia looked around—"I can't believe Desiree hasn't shown up yet."

Sophia's mom closed her eyes again. "She does absolutely nothing but stress Carl out. Always asking for money. Now that she's dropped out of school, she gallivants around with her spoiled friends, and I even found her"—Sophia's mom lowered her voice—"being intimate with some boy in the house. She doesn't know this yet, but our handyman, Alberto, is changing the locks as we speak. Once I got to the hospital, I called him and told him it was an emergency." She reached into her purse and handed Sophia a key. "This is for you only."

Sophia hesitantly accepted the key. "Don't you think that will cause more drama?"

"I no longer care about her drama. I won't put up with it anymore. I absolutely cannot have her in the house and stressing out Carl," her mom said through clenched teeth.

Sophia didn't agree that kicking Desiree out was the best idea, but she also didn't want to upset her mom or get in an argument about it.

A nurse approached them. "Mrs. Henderson, you can visit your husband, but he's still very weak."

Sophia and her mom followed the nurse down the hall. Sophia gasped at the sight of Carl. His pale white skin looked pasty, tubes protruded from his nose, and an IV connected to his forearm. Sophia's mom ran to her husband but stopped short, as if afraid to touch him.

"It's okay, honey. I won't bite," Carl whispered.

Sophia's mom kissed his cheek, her tears wetting his face.

"Hi, Carl." Sophia approached the bed.

"So this is what... I have to do... to get you... to visit, Sophia? I've been wanting to see you ever since your mom told me you were pregnant. Hard to believe you're not the little girl I met all those years ago."

Sophia tried not to cry at Carl's sentimentality. "I'm sorry it's been so long. And I'm sorry you're going—"

"Daddy!" Desiree rushed through the door. Her light-brown cheeks were bright red and glistening with tears. "Daddy, are you okay?" She wrapped her arms around Carl and put her head full of curly locks on his chest.

"I'm... okay... darling."

"Desiree, please remove yourself from his chest," Sophia's mom said.

Desiree stood and grabbed Carl's hand. "I'm so sorry about earlier. This is all my fault."

"No, it's not. These things happen... and I'm not exactly... a spring chicken."

"Daddy, I hate to ask this, but do you know why my key isn't working at home?"

"What?" Carl's eyebrows raised, and he looked at his wife.

Desiree continued. "I'm not sure, but I think Mom changed the locks. I went home to grab some clothes so I could stay here with you, but my key's not working."

Carl's chest heaved. "Desiree, don't worry... it's probably a misunderstanding. Right, honey?" He looked at Sophia's mom.

"Absolutely not." Sophia's mom pointed at Desiree. "She is no longer allowed in our home."

"You can't tell me I can't go into my own house, Mother. Daddy, tell her!"

Sophia was convinced they had lost their minds if they were arguing in Carl's hospital room. "Now, let's stop."

"I... I..." Carl breathed rapidly and clutched his chest. The machines monitoring his heart rate beeped, and a nurse ran into the room.

"Get her out of here, Sophia," Sophia's mom said.

"He's my dad! I have every right to be here!" Desiree yelled.

Sophia's mom pointed at the door. "Just get out!"

Sophia put her arm around Desiree and led her out of the room. "Let's get some air."

"What are you doing here?" Desiree removed Sophia's arm. "And you look huge."

"I am pregnant." Sophia needed to do something to make the situation better. "And I'm here to bring you home with me."

"Home? With you?" Desiree shook her head. "Oh, hell no. I'm not leaving. That house is as much mine as it is hers. My career is here. My friends are here. I'm staying here."

"It's just until things settle down a little. Let your dad recuperate and let Mom calm down. Think of it as a vacation," Sophia said.

Desiree scoffed. "Like, no way. My dad's sick, and I'm not leaving him."

"Mom said you'll be cut off financially if you don't come with me, but it's up to you," Sophia said.

"My dad won't allow that," Desiree said indignantly.

"I don't think he has much of a say right now." Sophia shrugged and headed to the waiting area. The click-clack of high heels followed her.

"Wait," Desiree called.

Sophia turned to face her little sister.

"If I can get my clothes out of the house, I'll go," Desiree said, relenting. "Just for a few days until Mom comes back to reality."

"Let's go now." Sophia wanted to get Desiree and her mom as far from each other as possible.

"I have to tell my dad so he doesn't think I just left him."

"We can call him and do that," Sophia said before Desiree stomped off toward the parking lot.

Sophia leaned against Desiree's door, watching her throw clothes into her Gucci travel bag.

"I cannot freakin' believe this!" Desiree repeated like a mantra.

"Mom's just stressed out about Carl. Try not to let it get to you," Sophia said.

"She hates me. Always has and always will. She only tolerates me because of my dad. But with him in the hospital, she finally has her chance to get rid of me for good."

Sophia yawned. All the drama was exhausting her. "That's not true. Yes, Mom can be hard-nosed, insensitive, and bossy, but love is her motivating factor. She just wants the people she loves to achieve their highest potential." At least that was what Sophia had to believe.

"She hates me," Desiree repeated. "She laughs at my dreams of becoming a model and actress, and she hates my friends. It's like I can't do anything right because I'm not..."

"Not what?"

"Not you. You're perfect in her eyes."

Sophia held up her palms. "Whoa. Now you really need to stop. Do you know how much flack I've gotten over the past few years? Eloping with Terrence. Getting laid off—even though that wasn't my fault. And now getting pregnant? She's probably on me just as much as she's on you. The only difference is the distance. Believe me, stay with me and Terrence for a couple days, give her a little breathing room, and everything will work out."

Desiree paused in her packing. "I don't have a choice, right?"

Sophia shrugged. "Not really."

"Then eff it," Desiree said.

Sophia pulled out her phone. "I'm going to call Terrence to let him know to expect you." Terrence was so easygoing, she could say Santa Claus needed a place to crash and he'd have cookies and milk prepared.

"You aren't driving up with me?"

"I should stay with Mom until Carl's condition has stabilized." Sophia left Desiree's room to make the call.

In the kitchen, she rummaged through the refrigerator and called Terrence. After a few rings, the phone went to voicemail.

"Oh, yes," Sophia said. He'd told her he had a dinner with a potential client scheduled. After the phone beeped, Sophia said, "Terrence, it's crazy down here. Desiree's coming to stay at our place. Call me when you get this. Love you."

Sophia pulled out two slices of bread and lathered each with mayonnaise before adding cheese, turkey, and a sprinkle of red peppers. Sophia wasn't thrilled with Desiree's behavior, but this situation was at a whole other level.

After Sophia finished her sandwich, she went back upstairs. At the top of the staircase, a rancid odor emanated from Desiree's room. She rushed in but didn't see Desiree. The door to her bathroom was shut, and a thin bar of light shone from the crack between the door and floor.

"Desiree?" No answer. Sophia knocked on the bathroom door. "Desiree."

The bathroom door opened, and marijuana smoke escaped. Desiree's eyelids drooped over her bloodshot eyes. "What?"

"What are you doing? Seriously? You're smoking pot?"

Desiree laughed. "You could say that."

"This isn't funny! It's late, and you have a six-hour drive ahead of you. And you're high!"

"I'm not a little girl," Desiree said. "I'm twenty-one, and I can take care of myself. I've been doing it my whole life. I just needed to relax a little, that's all."

"That's all? I can't let you drive in this state."

"I took a couple hits. I'm fine. Stop over-exaggerating."

If this was how Desiree acted regularly, Sophia understood her mom's frustration. "I'm not over-exaggerating. You can't drive impaired."

"Fine. Help me put my bags in the car, then I'll chill a little."

Sophia grabbed one of the three Gucci bags. They walked down to Desiree's car, and Desiree plopped the luggage in the trunk.

"I need to grab something from the car." Desiree opened the door, sat in the driver's seat, then shut the door and popped her head out of the window. "Later."

"What?" Sophia asked.

Desiree turned up the rap music until it was loud enough to wake up every neighbor on the block, then she peeled off.

Sophia's jaw dropped as the car disappeared. *Unbelievable.* She suddenly questioned the decision to take her in. But at this point, it was too late.

TARA

Tara clicked Print on her office computer and waited for the information about the convention in Las Vegas to materialize. After spending over an hour researching, she had collected enough information from the convention's website for talking points about why the firm should send her.

She poked her head into Peter's office. "Can I talk to you for a minute?"

"What is it, Tara?" Peter didn't avert his gaze from his computer screen.

From how messy his curly hair was, she figured he'd left late last night, gotten in early today, and hadn't even combed his hair in between. Maybe she could figure out a way to use him as an alibi for the night before. At any rate, she needed to get away from Josh for a while, and the convention would be a perfect opportunity.

"I have a proposal..." Tara said.

Peter adjusted his thin-rimmed glasses then continued rapidly typing. "What now?"

"First of all, I'm grateful for the promotion to senior paralegal. Thank you. To fully utilize my assets, I did some research and found a really informative and beneficial conference taking place in Las Vegas... this weekend."

"You want me to send you off to Vegas? Not a chance. You can booze and party right here."

"Really, Peter? Is that the faith you have in me?" Tara said, feigning disappointment. "This would be a great opportunity for the firm. Laws are always changing, and we need to stay current."

"We have the Drymeir case to worry about. Look at me. I'm barely sleeping while trying to prepare. Losing you right now is a bad idea."

"I'd just miss Friday, and I can work from there. Look, you didn't promote me to just sit in the office and do the same things I did before. You promoted me to benefit the company. I can go and take copious notes and give a presentation to the staff when I get back. And since it would benefit me also, I'll even pay for my own airfare and hotel room."

Peter stopped typing and peered at Tara over his glasses. "If I say yes, will you stop bugging me?"

"Yes."

"Then yes. Arrange it and go."

"Thank you, thank you, thank—"

"You said you'd stop bugging me."

"I'm gone." Tara grinned as she strolled back to her office. Once there, she texted Louis. *It's a done deal. You, me, and Vegas, baby!*

Tara waited for a response, which came two minutes later.

Perfect! his text read.

"What's that smile for?" a singsong voice asked.

She looked up. Corinne stared at her from the doorway.

"Nothing," Tara said. "I didn't know you doubled as the smile police. Did you need something?"

"Nope, just stopped in to say howdy. But I will get to the bottom of it," Corinne said playfully.

After Corinne left, Tara was even more determined to keep her secret just that.

Naked, Tara lay facedown on the table in her masseuse's house. Though water-flowing-and-birds-chirping music played through the speakers, she couldn't relax. "Ouch!"

"I'm sorry, Tara. I'm trying to get out this new knot. Is everything okay?" Katie asked.

"I'm just under a lot of stress at work." Though that was true, Tara was more stressed about her affair nearly being exposed.

Katie transitioned to Tara's scalp. "You know, I can only do the physical part. But there's this amazing woman named Belinda who's been helping me with my stress."

"Oh, really? How?" Tara needed all the help she could get.

"She works with chakras. It's kind of hard to explain, but I know you're into metaphysical things, and you just need to meet her."

"Okay, maybe I'll do that. I'm always up for trying something different."

Katie finished Tara's scalp massage then said, "Go ahead and get dressed. I'll give you Belinda's card on your way out."

Tara lay on the table for a few minutes before moving. She wasn't ready to leave and face her life yet. Josh expected her home by six, and she was already going to be late since she'd stopped for the massage. Tara had told Louis she couldn't see him tonight, and though it had only been a day, being away from him was like torture.

Groaning, Tara got up, slipped on her gray dress and pumps, and ran her fingers through her hair. She rotated her shoulders, let out a deep breath, and walked into the living room.

Katie opened her arms. "Give me a hug. You look like you need one."

Tara obliged. Afterward, she handed Katie a check in exchange for the business card that read, "Meta Waves."

Tara got in her car, and though it was six forty-five, she still wasn't ready to go home. So she headed to Meta Waves. A bell jingled as she entered the shop, making her think about Louis and the diner. Incense floated in the air.

"Blessings," the girl at the counter said.

"Umm, hi," Tara said.

"Can I help you with anything?"

Tara surveyed the shop. "I was referred to Belinda. Is she here?"

"No, she isn't in. But Miriam's here. She's new in town, and she's great."

Tara shrugged. "Okay."

The girl left the counter and took Tara's hand before leading her through the store, which was filled with books, CDs, DVDs, crystals, wind chimes, statues, Native American clothing, and a kids' section. It was as if Tara had entered another dimension. Whether it was the massage or the ambience, her guard was down, and she breathed a little easier.

When they reached the back of the store, the girl knocked on a door before opening it and popping in her head. "Miriam, do you have time to see this woman? I'm sorry, what's your name?"

"Tara."

A woman wearing a flowing sea-blue-and-yellow tie-dyed dress stepped out. "Of course. Thank you."

"Sure," the girl said before leaving.

Miriam clasped her hands together. "Would you like a reading? I can give you words that might help you right now."

It'd been years since Tara had gotten a psychic reading, but she thought it might be fun. "Sure."

Miriam motioned for Tara to sit. "Just breathe for a minute."

Tara sat on a small wooden stool across from Miriam.

"Place your hands in mine," Miriam said.

Tara placed her hands in Miriam's soft, warm hands.

Miriam exhaled loudly. "I sense that you're caught between two paths. What are their names?"

Tara's eyes widened. "Excuse me?"

Miriam tilted her head. "The two men. What are their names?"

Tara looked around the room, somehow expecting to see something that would explain how this woman knew Tara's secret. But seeing nothing out of the ordinary, she looked at Miriam. "Josh and Louis."

"Josh is your husband, and Louis is your lover?"

The words sounded so formal. "Yes. I don't know what to do."

"It looks like a decision will be made soon."

It was Tara's first time meeting this woman, but for some reason, in that instant, Miriam was exactly who Tara needed in her life.

━━━━◆◇◆━━━━

JOSH

As Josh cleared the dinner plates, Chelsea finished her homework at the kitchen table.

"Dad!" Chelsea whined.

"Yeah?"

"You're not paying attention. I asked what's seventy-six rounded to the nearest ten. Seventy or eighty?"

"Eighty, hon." Josh checked his phone again, but still no calls from Tara. Again. This was getting old.

"I'm home," Tara called, carrying two paper bags into the house. "And I have presents."

Teeni and Michelle charged toward her. "What's that? What's that?" they asked, reaching for the bags.

"Where's Chelsea?" Tara asked.

"In the kitchen," Michelle said.

"Let's go there, and I'll show you what I bought."

"Another shopping spree?" Josh asked, irked that Tara was completely oblivious to his requests to stop spoiling the girls.

Ignoring him, Tara placed the bags on the floor and unloaded the contents onto the kitchen table. "After work, I got a massage and Katie told me about this store, Meta Waves, in downtown Mountain View. I bought some things and had a psychic reading."

Josh scrunched his face. "A what? You're not starting up with that stuff again, are you?"

"It was just for fun," Tara said defensively.

"What's a psychic, Mom?" Chelsea asked.

Tara raised her eyebrows and lowered her voice. "It's someone who can tell the future."

Josh shot Tara a disapproving look. "Chelsea, psychics are people who act like they can tell the future. It's all pretend."

"Sometimes you're no fun," Tara said.

"Oh cool. Look, a crystal necklace," Chelsea said as she rummaged through the gifts.

"I want it!" Michelle said.

"Wait, girls, I have something for everyone. Don't fight." Tara stood and stretched her arms. After divvying up the presents, Tara headed for the bedroom. Josh followed her.

"Oh, Josh, guess what?"

Josh hesitated. Last time Tara had said "guess what," she'd announced her promotion. And though that was good financially, it meant she spent more and more time away from home. "What?"

"Peter wants to send me to a legal professionals' convention," she said.

"Send?" Josh didn't like the sound of that. "Where? San Francisco?"

"No... Las Vegas." Tara's eyes briefly met Josh's.

Josh stared at her. "What? Who else is going?"

"It's only for, like"—Tara shrugged—"Friday through Sunday. I'm going alone."

Josh extended each finger as he counted. "Only three days? Only? Do you know how exhausted I am? Taking care of our daughters is a lot of work, and you aren't really around much to help."

Tara put her hand on her hip. "I'm sorry if I have to work and pay the bills, Josh."

Josh didn't even know why he tried. "You just don't get it."

"I get that you're whining because I'm going away for a second."

"Whining?"

He stormed into the closet. He quickly changed into sweats and a T-shirt, then he headed out of the house.

Tara followed him to the doorway. "Come on, Josh. Where are you going?"

Josh opened the car door and slammed it behind him. He was tired, overworked, and fed up with Tara.

When he arrived at the gym, he headed up the stairs and straight to the treadmill. He started the machine, increasing the speed until he was running as fast as he could. After about three minutes, he was drenched in sweat and slowed to a walk. As he huffed and struggled to catch his breath, a little less anger pulsed through his body. A laugh escaped him. It had been silly of him to storm out of the house. Maybe Tara being gone a few days was the space they needed. After Josh walked for thirty minutes, he headed back home, promising himself the gym would become a regular part of his routine.

<hr/>

TERRENCE

Terrence startled at the sound of the doorbell. Yawning, he stumbled off the couch and down the short hall toward the door. He opened it, and his eyes widened. "Desiree?"

He took in the woman, whom he'd only seen in pictures taken years earlier, standing on his porch. She had light-brown skin and curly brown hair with blond highlights. Rain drizzled behind her.

"Yep, and you're Jerry, right?" Desiree asked.

Terrence was confused.

"You're an agent, right? Jerry McGuire? Show me the money."

"Oh, Jerry McGuire." Terrence chuckled. "I like that. Do you need me to help you get your bags?"

"That would be awesome. I know my dad will be better soon. He'll tell my mom that she's out of her mind, and then I'll be back home. So I packed light."

"Yeah, I'm sure it will all blow over soon enough." Terrence didn't mind getting a chance to hang with Sophia's sister. Because they'd eloped, he'd never gotten to meet any of her family, and Sophia had never been eager to change that. Terrence picked up the umbrella next to the front door and opened it when he stepped outside.

"I'm right there." Desiree pointed at a cherry-red Mustang that looked as if it had just left the lot.

Sophia had mentioned that Desiree's dad spoiled Desiree. If the car was any indication, Sophia was right.

Raindrops splattered on the umbrella. The yellow glow of the street lamps illuminated the street with a dreamlike air.

"Can you take this?" he asked, handing her the umbrella.

"Yeah, of course."

Terrence pulled out her three-piece Gucci luggage set. *Packed light?* He handed one bag to Desiree and carried the other two. They hurried back into the house, and Terrence led her to his office, which was now functioning as the guest room since the guest room was transitioning to the nursery. "It's not exactly the Ritz, but it's a place to crash."

"It's cool." Desiree looked around. "Like I said, I'll probably be here a few days, max."

"Can I get you anything?"

Desiree stretched her arms. "It was a long ride. Do you have anything to drink?"

When they got to the kitchen, Terrence flicked on the light. "We have a couple of sodas, some orange and cranberry juice, and—"

"I meant like a drink-drink." Desiree had an eyebrow cocked.

"Oh, okay. Gotcha," Terrence said. "So we have some Heinekens... and there's an old bottle of Hennessey up in the cabinet."

"Awesome. I'll take the Hennessey."

Terrence looked at Desiree again. "What do you know about Hennessey?"

"Let's just say I know about a lot of things."

Not sure what she meant exactly, Terrence ignored the comment. "Careful now," he said as he handed the bottle to her.

Desiree flashed her sparkling white teeth. "I'm a big girl. You don't have to worry about me."

"Well, enjoy. I'm gonna hit the sack. I have to get up pretty early."

Frowning, Desiree said, "Please have a drink with me. I'm just freaked out about my dad and could use a distraction."

Since his parents had been killed in the car crash, nothing was the same. He could definitely understand where Desiree was coming from, so he ignored the clock on the microwave that said it was after two in the morning.

"Okay, sure." He took the bottle back. "Do you want a mixer?"

"Give it to me straight, Jerry," Desiree said in a Western accent.

Terrence laughed and handed her glass to her. "That sounded good."

"Really? We practice different accents in this drama class I'm taking."

"Do you act?"

"Aspiring model and actress. But who isn't in LA, right?"

"I believe in following your dreams, regardless. Have you gotten any work?"

She shrugged. "I've done a couple of magazine ads. But my mom thinks I'm just wasting my time. She so doesn't get it."

With her large almond-shaped eyes, which were identical to Sophia's, strong features, and thin figure, Terrence could see how she'd be a great model. "So no sales like Sophia?"

"No way! Corporate America is not for me. Sophia always did the school thing, and I was terrible at school. So my mom basically wrote me off, and my dad just bought me off."

Terrence's forehead creased. "I think I hear a symphony."

"No, no, I don't mean it in a bad way. I just meant that we grew up differently. Like, I'm not complaining about anything. I got it good."

"Shoot, driving around in that Mustang, you sure do got it good."

Terrence and Desiree laughed and sipped their drinks.

"You know, you aren't what I expected," Desiree said. "Sophia's so serious and focused, I thought you'd be more uptight. But you seem pretty easygoing."

"Uptight?" Terrence frowned. "Sophia didn't tell you a lot about me?"

"I'm not close to Sophia or my mom, so I didn't really hear about you at all. Are you close to your parents?"

Terrence took a deep breath. "My parents were killed in a car accident right after I graduated from college." Saying that never got easier.

Desiree gasped. "Oh my god, I'm so sorry. I didn't know."

"Don't apologize. It's not your fault."

"I just can't imagine… my dad is my everything. I don't know what I'd do if he died. It's just so scary that—" Desiree burst into tears.

Terrence didn't know what to do or say. He'd been absolutely terrified when he first learned that his parents were in a crash, and he'd never forget the horror of finding out they had died. He couldn't minimize Desiree's feelings, so instead of trying to say anything, he retrieved a paper towel and handed it to her.

She used it to dab her tears away. "I'm sorry."

"Don't apologize. This is a really stressful time for you, your mom, Sophia, and especially your dad."

"Speaking of dads, I can't get how Sophia just refuses to speak to hers. Yeah, he effed up, but that was so long ago. And he's trying to make it up to her now."

Terrence leaned forward. "Hasn't he been out of the picture since she was, like, five?"

"In her mind, yes. But in reality, he's been trying to make amends for years. As long as I can remember, he's sent her birthday cards. He even showed up at the house once when I was, like, little, but my mom cussed him out so bad and threatened to call the police for trespassing. He never came around again."

"No way!"

"Yes way. He drove all the way to the Bay Area to attend her graduation from Stanford, but she wouldn't speak to him."

Terrence was baffled. Other than saying that her dad had left the family for another woman, Sophia had never mentioned him. "Why? I mean, if he's trying…?"

"I totally don't know. It's like Sophia is brainwashed by my mom. She's holding a grudge that isn't even really hers."

"Playing the devil's advocate, I have to ask why he didn't just get visitation. Once our baby is born, nothing and no one could prevent me from seeing him or her."

"Jerry, I was like eight years old when Sophia moved out. I don't know. I just know that he wants a relationship with her."

In disbelief, Terrence said, "That's a shame. I don't think he should forever be held responsible for something that happened decades ago, and if he's trying to make it right… maybe I should try to talk to Sophia about it."

"Huh, good luck. I would just"—Desiree shrugged—"let it go. Sure, it would be great if they could reconnect, but that's not your job."

Terrence nodded but wasn't really in agreement. When he had an idea, it was impossible for him to let it go. "Well, I'm off to bed."

"Night, Jerry."

Heading to his bedroom, Terrence couldn't help but be convinced that Sophia and her mom had Desiree all wrong. He didn't know how, but he felt as though he could help sort out their whole mess.

CHAPTER NINE

SKY HIGH

SOPHIA

"IT LOOKS LIKE YOU TWO are set," Sophia said. "Carl, do you need anything else?"

Her mother and Carl's enormous bedroom suite was messier than normal. An army of pill bottles, with the remote control resting next to them, lined the nightstand next to his side of the bed. Sophia had spent three long days at her mom and Carl's place, and she was ready to get on a plane and head home.

"Well, actually"—Carl turned to Sophia's mom—"Rachel, could you run downstairs? I think I left my reading glasses on the island in the kitchen."

Sophia turned toward the door. "I can get—"

Carl put his hand on Sophia's arm. "Rachel knows what they look like."

"Sure, Carl, I'll get them," Sophia's mom said before leaving.

Carl cleared his throat. "I wanted to talk to you for a second. All this craziness between your mother and Desiree has to stop. I understand that Desiree is strong-willed, but she has a good heart. She just needs a little guidance. I'm hoping she can stay with you a couple of weeks then come back home. Maybe she and your mom just need a little space from each other."

"Desiree's my sister, and I love her. She's welcome as long as she needs to stay."

"You're such a caring person." Carl grabbed his checkbook and a pen from the nightstand drawer. "Now, she has her credit card, but just in case, I want to give you a little extra. You know, if anything comes up with her or you and that bun in your oven." Carl wrote out a check then handed it to Sophia.

Sophia gasped. "Five thousand dollars? I can't accept this." She tried to hand it back, but Carl wouldn't take it.

"Your mom told me that Terrence refused our last offer. I'm a man and I have pride too, but this will at least give you another month or so to figure out your next move while Desiree stays with you."

Her stepdad was always so generous. Sometimes to a fault. "Carl, I can't—"

"You can, and you will, young lady."

Tears of gratitude formed in Sophia's eyes. Hopefully by the month's end she'd have a job, and this would help them immensely in the meantime. She hugged Carl tight. "Thank you so much. You get better. I'll find my mom downstairs to say good-bye."

Sophia ran into her mom at the top of the stairs.

"Are you sure you have to go?" her mom asked.

"Carl's fine. You're fine. It's Friday, and I need to go back home."

"It's not like you're working or anything."

Sophia cringed. Her mom always had to find a way to throw in that fact. "First of all, I am trying to find a job. Secondly, being married, and staying that way, is a full-time job. Fifty percent of Americans ultimately can't do it." Sophia walked down the stairs.

Her mom trailed right behind her. "I hope you put that same energy into finding another job. Don't end up like me—"

"How exactly did you end up? You keep dwelling on what Dad did, but what about everything Carl has done and continues to do? He swept you off your feet and made you queen of his kingdom." Sophia gestured around the expansive home. "He adores the daughter you two have, and he just gave me five thousand dollars. I know what Dad did to you, but don't put that on me or my marriage. And that was so long ago. Focus on Carl for a change." Sophia usually wasn't so assertive with her mother, but whether her courage came from the hormones or the stress, it needed to be said.

Speechless, her mom stared at Sophia.

Sophia picked up the suitcase she had left by the door. "Bye, Mom."

Her mom stood in front of the door. "Is Terrence meeting you at the airport?"

"Actually, he doesn't know I'm flying in today. He's leaving for Vegas tomorrow, so I want to surprise him before he leaves."

Her mom raised her eyebrows. "What's a married man going to do in Vegas?"

"He's meeting with a potential client. No wild bachelor parties or anything like that." Sophia reached around her mom and opened the door. "I love you, and keep me updated on Carl's progress."

"Sophia?"

"Yes, Mom?"

"Thank you," her mom whispered.

"Anytime." Sophia tried not to look too surprised.

The cool night air greeted her outside, and she ducked into the backseat of the private car Carl had arranged for her. On the drive to the airport, Laura—the woman for whom Sophia's dad had left her mom—came to mind. Before she actually saw her, Sophia imagined Laura was the most beautiful woman in the galaxy. She had to have been, because Sophia's mom was the most beautiful woman in the world, with her high cheekbones, bright brown eyes, and hourglass figure.

So Sophia was almost knocked over when she finally laid eyes on her father's mistress. Laura was, in a word, unremarkable. Her dark-brown hair, which Sophia's mother swore was a wig, looked bland. She had stern dark eyes, like an elementary school teacher scanning her classroom for trouble, and she had an extra ten pounds she could lose. Why would her dad break her mom's heart for... her?

Pushing the memory aside, Sophia longed to be back in Terrence's arms, far away from her mom's drama. Her plane would land in San Jose at eight thirty. Hopefully Terrence missed her as much as she missed him.

She closed her eyes and caressed her belly. Both she and the baby needed to be back home and away from the drama. In that moment, she prayed that nothing or no one would ever disrupt her family the way Laura had.

TARA

Tears filled Tara's eyes, but she laughed them away when she entered Caesars Palace. She had never been to Las Vegas, and though Sin City was often showcased on television and in the movies, it awed her in person. The Roman-Greco-inspired hotel had artwork lining the walls of its beautiful, sprawling lobby. A statue of three women stood atop a streaming fountain. Tara admired the dome ceiling.

Louis had booked them a suite in the hotel/casino, but she couldn't help but think it was all a mistake. She couldn't believe that the mysterious man who had materialized from thin air really wanted her with him in Las Vegas.

She strolled through the hotel lobby to the front desk. "I'm checking in. The room is under Louis Steinman." She looked past the lobby desk at the opulent paintings on the wall.

After checking Tara in, the lady handed Tara a room key. "Thank you for choosing Caesars Palace. Have a nice stay."

When she opened the door to the room, her jaw dropped. A dozen red roses sat on a glass table, and she rushed to them. As she inhaled their sweet aroma, she tried to breathe out all her apprehension and guilt. She eagerly read the card. *Can't wait to see you!*

Tara couldn't wait either. Louis was supposed to arrive around the same time as Tara, but he'd texted to say he'd been held up and didn't know when he'd make it.

Tara went to the balcony and shivered as a gust of frigid winter air blew across her. Glittering lights danced on the Strip, but instead of feeling invigorated, she was overwhelmed. She needed to relax. She headed inside and to the bathroom. After running water into the Jacuzzi tub, she took off her clothes. But before she could get into the tub, her phone rang. She ran to it, hoping it was Louis.

It was Josh.

Act normal, act normal, act normal. She took a breath then answered. "Hi, Josh."

"Hi, honey. I was just making sure you got in safely. How's your hotel room?"

Tara looked around at the suite that must have cost Louis a fortune. "It's okay. Can I say hi to the girls?"

"Sure, Chelsea's right here. Hold on."

Tara waited for her oldest daughter to grab the phone.

"Hi, Mommy. What are you doing?"

"Oh, just relaxing a little. How was your day?"

"It was good. Cindy came to school and showed everyone an iPod player she got, but it's not as cool as the iPhone you gave me."

"Mommy, Mommy, Mommy, guess what?" Michelle said, now in control of the phone. "I'm Ariel, and I drew you a picture of me as a mermaid."

"Oh, thank you, Ariel."

"Want to talk to Teeni?"

"Sure. I love you."

"Mommy, listen," Teeni said. "*Tinkle, tinkle, little star. How I wonda what you are.*"

"Very nice, Teeni, now can I—"

"*Up abob the wold so high.*"

"Very nice, can I—"

"*Tinkle, tinkle, little star.* You like dat, Mommy? Wan me to sing again?"

"No, no, once is just fine. Can I talk to Daddy now?"

"Daddy, here."

Tara pictured Teeni handing Josh the phone.

"Hi, Tara," Josh said.

"What do you have planned tonight?"

"My parents are coming over soon to spend time with the girls while I pick up Sophia from the airport," Josh said.

"Okay, well, tell Sophia hello from me and have a good night."

"I will. Night. I love you."

"You too." Tara hung up the phone and lowered herself into the steaming water. Turning on the jets, she closed her eyes, stretched out her legs, and held her breath, letting the water wash over her face. What she was doing was wrong. After all, she'd been married to Josh for a decade, and he was the father of their three beautiful girls.

But Louis made her feel alive in a way she never knew was possible. He was a piece of the puzzle of her life that she didn't know was missing until she found it. He stimulated her body and intrigued her mind in ways that Josh just couldn't.

The longer Tara held her breath, the more focused she became on her body. Her lungs ached for air. Her heartbeat thumped in her ears. Though all the alarms alerted her mind that she needed to breathe, she fought the urge, pushing the limits until she couldn't anymore.

An image of her father flashed through her mind.

"Tara!" his voice screamed.

She jumped up, gasping.

"Tara!"

She opened her eyes, her chest heaving.

Louis hurried toward her. "You scared me half to death. Why were you under the water for so long?"

"Was I?" Tara gasped for air.

She couldn't tell him it was a game she used to play when she was a young girl, hiding from her life in general and her dad specifically. And though she hadn't known what suicide was back then, she did sometimes wish she were strong enough not to come up for air.

She ran her hands over her wet hair and forced the memories to flee. "I saw bags but didn't know what time you'd be here, so I decided to relax. When did you get in?"

Louis's eyebrows relaxed. "A couple hours ago. I dropped my things off with the roses, then I got a call from my old law school buddy. He moved out here about five years ago, and we always get together when I come to Vegas."

Tara smoothed her soaking-wet hair. "Cool. Can you grab me a towel? Or are you coming in?"

"Neither," Louis said. "Get out. I want to see you wet."

Tara bit her bottom lip as she eased out of the tub. Though she'd carried and birthed three children, she knew her body still looked good.

"Beautiful," Louis said. "Now come to me."

Like a yo-yo being yanked back to the finger that controlled it, Tara walked to Louis, water dripping from her body.

"This place is beautiful. I can't believe I've never been to Vegas before," she said.

"I come a few times a year. I like to gamble, so I have a deal with

Caesars Palace where I spend my money here and they give me a free room. It works out for both parties."

"I've never gambled."

"I love the thrill."

A strange feeling welled up in Tara's stomach, and she stopped in her tracks. "Is that all I am to you? A thrill?"

Louis's eyes widened, his brows furrowed. "Tara, how could you ask that?"

"Like I said, I don't gamble. I have no poker face. All my cards are on the table. But if I'm merely entertainment for you, I need to know."

Louis stepped toward Tara and stared into her eyes. "Do you think I would play a game with stakes this high? I know what you're risking to be here, to be with me in general. My marriage and reputation are on the line as well. So no, this is not a game. What we have is real. Right?"

Tara closed the space between them. "Right."

<hr />

TERRENCE

Terrence approached his front door and cursed under his breath. He'd had a hell of a day at the office, and his boss had basically said that Terrence needed to land a new client or look for another job. He opened the door, and the scent of pepperoni pizza wafted to him.

"Hey, Jerry." Desiree had a wide grin. "I hope you didn't eat, because I bought us a pizza. I know you're taking off for Vegas tomorrow, and I wanted to say thank you for letting me stay here the past few days."

"You're welcome." Terrence frowned as he rubbed one of the many knots in his shoulder.

"What's wrong?" Desiree asked.

"Work. Like usual."

"I'll grab you a couple slices of pizza. Go sit in your recliner and put your feet up." Desiree sauntered past him wearing a pair of shorts that barely covered her ample backside and a midriff shirt that showed off her slim abs. He was used to seeing girls like that around the athletes at work, but not in his own house. He always appreciated Sophia's modesty.

Terrence slumped into his chair in the living room.

When Desiree returned, she handed him a plate with a slice of pizza. "You seem uber stressed, Jerry."

Though he wouldn't use the word uber, Terrence had to agree. "Yeah." He bit into the pizza, relishing the oozing cheese and tomato sauce.

"I got something that can help. Be right back."

Terrence finished the pizza then rubbed his temples. The stress was like a sledgehammer to his brain. When Desiree reappeared, she opened a tin box on the coffee table.

Terrence sat up straight, his eyes growing wide. "Desiree, is that a pipe?"

"Calm down, Jerry. I have a four-twenty card because of my anxiety."

Terrence let out a curt laugh. "You can't just light up and get high in here."

"Oh, come on, relax. I know you probably used to smoke."

Terrence chuckled, not because she was right, which she was—he definitely used to take the edge off during law school—but because this twenty-one-year-old was trying to tell him what to do.

Desiree packed the pipe, lit it, took a hit, then exhaled. "Here." She extended the pipe to Terrence.

Terrence waved. "Naw, I shouldn't. Sophia would think I was being immature and irresponsible."

Desiree lowered her voice. "It's just between you and me. Sophia won't have to know. It'll make you feel better. Unless you're too scared." She pulled her hand back.

"Too scared? Shit, you got me confused with someone else." Terrence grabbed the pipe, trying to steady his shaking hand. He brought it to his lips and took a long hit. The smoke caught in his chest, making him cough.

"Easy, Jerry, easy." Desiree laughed as she held out her hand. She took back the pipe and took another hit like a pro before passing it back. "Easy."

Terrence took another hit but choked again. He glared at Desiree convulsing with laughter. He closed his eyes as his head spun, and he could hear his heart pounding.

"Jerry, bro, without the fro, check my flow."

Terrence scrunched his face. "Are you trying to rap? Aw, come on. Just 'cause you're half black does not make you a rapper."

"But they call me Snoop Desiree... like Snoop Dogg." Desiree wore a smirk.

Terrence stared at Desiree. "They don't call you that."

"I know, but bro, I can flow like a pro—"

"You're doing it again."

Desiree laughed. "I like hanging out with you."

"Well, you aren't as bad as Sophia painted you out to be."

"Oh, thanks a lot."

"I'm just playing," Terrence said, though he wasn't. "I mean, I thought you were Miss Stuck-Up-Get-Whatever-I-Want."

"I am," Desiree said, smiling. "And I do." She winked, though Terrence had no idea why.

He reached out, his shoulders starting to relax, and took another hit.

※

JOSH

Josh pulled up to the curb at the airport's arrivals, parked, and struggled to get out. Bright overhead lights negated the darkness of night. He waved his arms. "Sophia, over here."

Sophia waved back and hurried to him. "Thanks for getting me. I wanted to surprise Terrence."

Josh took Sophia's bags and put them in the trunk. "He'll be so happy to see you. How's your stepdad?"

"Good." Sophia crossed her fingers and held them up. "I think he'll be all right." In the car, Sophia glanced in the backseat. "Where are Chelsea, Michelle, and Christine?"

"My parents are watching them. They're trying to help out since Tara's out of town."

"Oh? Out of town? She didn't mention anything on Monday when we went to lunch."

Well, at least Josh wasn't the only one caught off guard by her sudden plans. "A legal professionals' convention in Vegas."

"Really? Terrence will be there too."

Knowing his best friend would be in Sin City at the same time as his wife made him feel better. "I'll tell Terrence to keep an eye out for her. Make sure she's on her best behavior."

Sophia chuckled. "And I'll do the same with Tara."

When Josh pulled into Sophia's driveway, he saw the red Mustang was still parked on the street. "Terrence mentioned your sister came for a visit. Nice car she's got."

"Yeah. She's definitely living the high life."

Sophia sounded a little more sarcastic than he was used to, and he thought her sister might be a sensitive subject. "How long will she stay?"

"I'm not sure. Come in and meet her."

"Okay, cool." Josh retrieved Sophia's luggage and followed her to the house.

After they stepped inside, they exchanged worried glances. The house reeked of pot. Sophia's face grew red, and she stormed into the living room.

Josh followed her. Sophia's sister had some nerve to be smoking marijuana in their house. Though his car was parked in the driveway, Terrence must have been out with friends, because he'd never allow that behavior.

In the living room, Josh's jaw dropped. Terrence and a young woman Josh assumed was Sophia's sister sat on the floor in front of the coffee table, laughing. Terrence's hand held a pipe.

"Terrence!" Sophia yelled. "What the hell is going on?"

Josh took a step backward. *This isn't good.*

Terrence shot to his feet, his bloodshot eyes wide with fear. "Sophia? I didn't know you were coming home."

"So when I'm not here, you smoke weed?"

Sophia's sister stood too. "It's my fault. I wanted to help him relax."

"Shut up, Desiree," Sophia said. "Terrence is a grown man. He can't blame you for his actions."

Josh took another step back. Maybe leaving would be the best thing.

Sophia pointed at Terrence. "You have one of the biggest meetings of your career tomorrow, and instead of preparing, you're getting high?"

Terrence ran his hand over his head. "It's just that—"

Sophia's voice rose. "And the house stinks of pot. You think that's good for the baby?"

"No, I didn't—"

"You're going to Vegas for a few days tomorrow," Sophia continued. "Now I wonder if I can trust you when I'm not around."

Terrence put his hands on his hips. "To tell the truth, I wonder the same thing. You're the one with a history of not telling me important things."

Josh winced. This was getting worse. He cleared his throat. "I should go."

Sophia looked at Josh with tears in her eyes. He'd never seen her so upset. "Please, Josh, take him with you. I'll leave his bags outside the bedroom door." She turned and left the room.

"Bro?" Josh raised his arms in a question.

"I know, man." Terrence hung his head.

"I'm Desiree, by the way," Sophia's sister said with a shrug.

Josh extended his hand, noticing the girl barely had on any clothes. "Josh."

The girl left the room, though she didn't seem bothered by Sophia's explosion, and Josh turned to Terrence.

"You better watch out. That girl's trouble," he whispered.

"You know what, I'm starting to think that's right."

A door down the hall slammed, and Josh followed the noise. He picked up the suitcase Sophia had left outside the bedroom door and carried it back to Terrence. "We should go, I guess."

Terrence took his suitcase. "Lead me to the doghouse."

As Josh left with Terrence, he hoped that Desiree's situation would be resolved. Quickly. The last thing Sophia, Terrence, or their marriage needed was a girl like her around.

CHAPTER TEN

VIVA LAS VEGAS

JOSH

RUSHING FROM THE BATHROOM TO the living room, Josh grabbed his ringing phone off the coffee table. "Oh, Terrence." He tried to catch his breath.

Terrence chuckled. "Man, nice to hear from you too. I was calling to say I landed safely in Vegas and to thank you for letting me crash at your place last night."

"Sorry, bro, I just thought it was Tara. I haven't heard from her yet, but I know she's probably busy in the convention."

"Well, I'll keep an eye out for her. Are you busy?"

"Not really." Josh balanced his phone between his shoulder and ear as he folded laundry. "My parents are coming over in a bit to take the girls to dinner. What's up?"

"I need some advice. How should I make things better with Sophia?"

Given the status of his love life, Josh was probably the last person who should be giving advice. "I don't know. She was pissed."

Terrence exhaled. "I don't even get why she's so mad."

"She was probably just surprised. I'm sure the hormones don't help either. She won't be mad forever."

"Forever? Man, I need a date and a time shit'll be better. But Lance just got to my room, and we're going to go meet with a potential client. I'll talk to you later."

"Later, bro," Josh said.

——— ◦◦◦ ———

The doorbell rang, and Josh rose from the couch. Gulping the remainder of his beer, Josh tossed the bottle into the recycling bin then opened the front door. "Hi, girls. Did you bring me a doggie bag?"

"You're not a doggie, Daddy," Michelle said as she and Chelsea ran past him to the living room.

"Up, Daddy," Teeni said, holding out her arms.

Josh grinned. "Up? But where's the food?"

Teeni patted her stomach. "In here."

Josh tickled her stomach.

"Are you hungry, Joshie?" Josh's mom said.

"No, Mom, I'm just teasing the girls. I had a salad earlier."

Josh's dad followed his wife in. "Salad? What's wrong with you?"

"Just trying to lose a few pounds. I've even hit up the gym a couple times."

"You look fine, Joshie. Don't overdo it with your back," his mom said.

Josh's dad cleared his throat. "Josh, I was wondering if I could talk to you for a minute?" Josh's dad gestured to the backyard. "Let's just go outside."

"Ooh-kay."

Josh's mom took the girls into the living room and turned on the TV while Josh followed his dad out the back door.

Outside, Josh hugged his chest, shivering from the cold. He couldn't wait for winter to be over. "So what did you want to talk about?"

"Now, I don't want to keep bugging you, but Kyle just quit, and I have a position opening up in parts and production at the shop. I'd like you to take it."

Josh stiffened. "Come on, Dad—"

His dad put up his hand. "Just hear me out. I'm not blind. I see the tension between you and Tara. Mom tells me she's out a lot, and it might be a good idea for you two if you got back in the working world."

"Now Dad—"

"Let me put it to you straight. Women want the man to provide. Regardless of all this twenty-first-century bullshit, a woman wants her man to contribute to the household. When he isn't, there are problems. You should listen to me now."

Josh swallowed the lump in his throat. Though he didn't appreciate his parents' intrusion, his dad's words confirmed what Josh had been thinking. But while his dad acted as though he wanted Josh to work for him, Josh knew it wouldn't work out. Josh had had a trade he was good at, but now that that was gone, he was useless in the working world. He wasn't a quick learner, he knew nothing about cars, and he didn't want to let his dad down, which ultimately would happen.

Instead of voicing that, Josh took the easy way out. "Let me think about it, and I'll get back to you."

Josh's dad put his arm around his shoulder. "I'm just concerned for you."

"Okay, Dad. Now can we go back into the house before we catch pneumonia?"

Josh's dad chuckled. "Sure."

Back in the house, the girls were sprawled on the living room floor, watching the Disney channel.

Josh glanced at his watch. "Time for bed, girls."

Chelsea stretched and looked at Josh. "Can we call Mom and say good night?"

"Of course. That's a good idea." Josh grabbed his phone off the coffee table and called Tara. The phone rang before going to voicemail. *Strange.* Josh dialed again. Still no answer. "Sorry, girls, but Mommy isn't picking up. How about we call her first thing in the morning?"

Michelle stomped her foot on the floor. "I want to talk to Mommy."

"We'll talk to her tomorrow." Josh clapped. "Let's go."

Michelle and Teeni sprinted to their room. Without taking her gaze off her phone, Chelsea followed them.

Nothing in Las Vegas could be so important at eight thirty at night that Tara couldn't answer her phone. She didn't have any friends in Las Vegas, and she was the only one sent from the firm. He was fed up with her never being available, and though he hadn't brought it up before because he wanted to avoid a fight, that was going to be the first conversation they had when she got back.

⟶ ◦◇◦ ⟵

TARA

When they got back to their suite, Tara checked her cell phone. "Shit!"

Louis stood behind her, massaging her shoulders. "What's wrong?"

"Josh called twice while we were at dinner. I didn't hear it because it was in my purse. They probably wanted to say good night."

"Just call him now."

Tara looked at her watch. "It's ten thirty. I'm sure the girls are asleep by now. I'll text him."

"I'm going to take off these clothes. Meet me in the Jacuzzi."

"Be right there." Tara sank into the coffee-colored couch. *When did I become such a terrible wife and mother? I can't even remember to call my daughters to say good night.*

She texted Josh. *Sorry I missed your call. Have a good night. I'll call in the morning.*

A text popped up seconds later. *I miss you. Can you talk?*

Too tired. But in the morning.

I love you.

"Tara, are you coming?" Louis yelled from the bathroom.

Tara pressed the "I" then hesitated. Her finger hovered over the "L."

"Be right there," she said, though she made no attempt to move. She stared at the "L."

"Tara?" Louis called.

Tara put her phone back in her purse. "Coming."

Rose petals lined the floor leading to the bathroom. "Louis? When'd you do this?" She opened the door to the bathroom and caught her breath.

Candles flickered around the room. A bottle of champagne and a box of chocolates rested on a table next to the Jacuzzi Louis soaked in. His wet hair was slicked back, and his eyes were closed.

"You never cease to surprise me." Bob Marley flowed from the speakers. "What's this song?"

"'Stir It Up,'" Louis said.

Tara swayed to the music, hypnotized by the melody. "It sounds kind of sad."

Louis opened his eyes. "Is that how you're feeling? Maybe you're projecting it onto the song?"

"What?" she asked, pausing in taking off her shoes.

"You just seemed a little melancholy today."

Tara appreciated that Louis cared enough to notice a shift in her mood. "I am sad."

He raised his eyebrows. "Why?"

"You... this." She gestured to the candles and rose petals. "You can't do this and expect me to be able to go home and act happy."

Louis laughed, a long amused laugh. "Get in here, Tara."

Tara didn't move. "I'm serious."

"So am I. Come in," Louis said.

Tara undressed then lowered herself into the turbulent, heated water. Leaning her back against his chest, she slid between his legs.

Louis massaged her shoulders. "You just need to relax a little. Enjoy this, because I sure as hell am. I don't know much about your home life, but you mentioned your husband doesn't work. Taking financial responsibility for your household must be stressful. So when you're with me, I take care of everything, including you. As a matter of fact, I think you need a drink." Louis grabbed the champagne glasses.

Tara turned around in the tub, leaning her back against the side opposite Louis, and accepted the champagne glass Louis proffered. Once he'd poured the golden liquid into the glass, she took a long sip. She rested her head against the wall of the tub and closed her eyes. She did enjoy Louis spoiling her.

Louis cleared his throat. "I meant for you to relax, not fall asleep."

Tara opened her eyes. "I'm not sleeping. I'm just trying to store this moment in my memory so I'll always have it."

"You don't need a memory, Tara. You have me."

<hr/>

After they made love, Louis fell asleep. Tara lay in the darkness, listening to his breathing. The text she hadn't sent Josh was on her mind: "I love you." She'd heard that different languages, like Greek, had separate words for the different types of love, and now she knew why. She wondered if there was a special word reserved just for people having affairs. Or a word for love for a spouse who was loved less than someone else. She needed to talk to Miriam again. Get some type of help, because it was too tough for her to figure out alone.

The Las Vegas trip was making her more confused than before. She'd met Josh when she was young and scared, and as she'd told Mariana, he had been her savior. She loved him for that—for making her feel safe. He would never hurt her, and that was all that had mattered then, because love could be dangerous. Her mind went back to the night her whole life had changed, her sophomore year in high school.

She didn't allow herself to remember everything that had happened—those memories were locked away in an off-limits segment of her brain—but she did remember her mother instructing her to pack as much as she could and fast. She could almost smell the salty tears that had dripped down her face as she ran to her room, grabbed whatever she could find, and threw it into a duffel bag. Minutes later, her mother told her they had to leave. They rushed to the car, and two and a half hours later, they were at Tara's aunt's house in Cupertino.

Her mom didn't get out of the car. Tara finally realized her mom hadn't brought a bag.

"You're staying too, right?" Tara asked.

"No, I'm going back home," her mom said, her voice barely audible.

"But why?" She held up her mom's bleeding arm. "Look what he did to you. He could kill you! And I don't want to stay here by myself. I don't want you to leave me."

"Tara, you're fifteen and old enough to take care of yourself. You'll be fine here. But your father... he needs me. And I love him."

In that moment, Tara promised herself that she would never love any man that much. She never wanted to open her heart to the point where she was willing to risk everything for love.

And that was what scared her now. Somehow, Louis was forcing open those doors Tara had shut. She couldn't keep the safe distance from him that she had always maintained with Josh. She was doing things she would never have done before, like lying and cheating. She needed to regain control of herself before it was too late.

TERRENCE

Terrence's phone rang. "Sophia?"

"Hey. How was the meeting with James McKay?" Sophia asked.

Relief swept over Terrence when he heard Sophia's voice. In spite of how upset she'd been, she knew how important the meeting was and called him. "It went well, baby. But look, I'm so sorry about last night."

"Won't happen again, right?"

Terrence chuckled. "No chance in hell. I love you."

"Love you too. I'm exhausted, so let's talk tomorrow."

"Okay, baby. Sleep tight."

"Was that a booty call?" Lance asked when he exited Terrence's bathroom.

"Naw, man, just talking to Sophia."

"We're in Vegas, surrounded by beautiful women. We just rocked the hell out of the meeting with James McKay, and you're talking to your wife? I want the old T back."

Terrence put up his hands. "Let's not start that conversation again."

"Okay, okay, but just tell me. What changed?"

Terrence didn't hesitate. "My folks being killed in the accident. My mom always said I needed to stop messing with girls' hearts, find a good woman, and settle down. It took a few years, but once I found Sophia, I knew she was it."

"Yeah, my mom says the same thing about settling down," Lance said.

"I always promised her that I would do it eventually. I felt like I had my whole life. But after they passed, I realized tomorrow isn't guaranteed. I feel like I need to carry on my parents' legacy. And that includes being married and having a family. You'll get it one day."

"Me, I'm immortal." Lance puffed out his chest.

Terrence laughed. His friend was hopeless. "To this day, I wish Sophia could've met my mom. But regardless, I know what I have, and I'm not going to ruin that."

"Dude, I didn't ask you to get all deep on me. But I respect that. Now, enough with all the serious stuff. We need to celebrate."

Lance was always ready to celebrate. But it was too early.

"You know McKay hasn't officially made his decision," Terrence said. "If he changes his mind, I'm basically out of a job."

"McKay basically said that if he goes pro, he's choosing you." Lance pointed at Terrence. "That's enough for me to celebrate."

"*If*, Lance. *If.* It could be months before he decides."

"Shit, I'll take if. Now let's get out of here and party."

Terrence glanced down at his black slacks and blue business shirt. "Let me change, then we can get a drink."

"Go like that. Believe me, the chicks love a man who looks like he has a day job and some money."

"Whatever, man." Terrence couldn't keep the peace with one woman. The last thing he needed was to worry about others.

They left Terrence's suite and took the elevator to the ground level. As they stepped into the lobby, a group of scantily clad women entered.

"Where's the party at?" Lance asked.

"Our suite. Want to join us?" a blonde said with a wink.

Terrence elbowed Lance. "No way."

Lance pulled out a business card and handed it to the woman. "Call me later. I gotta babysit this dude, but I'll be up late."

Terrence pulled him away. "Easy, Lance, we just got here. Where do you want to go?"

"We're in Vegas. Let's hit up The Gentlemen's Club."

"I meant somewhere the women have clothes on."

"Like I said, we're in Vegas, baby. Girls don't have much on. Period."

Terrence laughed. "Why don't we check out a casino, play a little, and get a drink?"

They strutted down the path, recounting the play-by-play of their meeting with McKay. When they approached Caesars Palace, a sign read, "Legal Professionals Convention." Terrence recalled Josh mentioning that Tara would be in Vegas and asking if he'd keep an eye out for her.

"Let's stop in here," he said to Lance. "I'll get us drinks."

Thick cigarette smoke permeated the casino, and Terrence coughed as he walked to the bar. He ordered two double whiskeys and Coke, then he found Lance at a roulette table. Terrence chuckled at two young women, one on each side of him.

"Go, baby, go, baby, no!" Lance hollered as the tiny ball stopped on the red number thirty on the roulette wheel.

The dealer swiped his long stick, removing a stack of Lance's chips. Both of the women looked at Lance, then each other, then darted away.

Terrence put the drinks on the side of the table and patted Lance's back. "It's all good. Try again while I run to the bathroom."

Shaking his head, he laughed at Lance's misfortune as he strolled away. He scanned the crowded room for the restroom, then his gaze fell on a woman who looked just like Tara, though she wore a slinky black dress and had her hair up in a twist.

"Tar—" Terrence froze in his tracks.

A tall, salt-and-pepper-haired man carrying two martini glasses approached her. Tara accepted one of the glasses then leaned forward. Her lips met the man's, lingering for what seemed like an eternity.

Terrence's stomach dropped as if he were headed full speed down a roller coaster. *What the—?* Terrence took a couple steps in Tara's direction, then he stopped. An image of Josh and Tara's three daughters giggling as Josh tickle-wrestled them flashed through his mind. Knowing his decision would affect all of their lives, Terrence turned his back and headed to the bathroom. He needed time to figure out his next move.

❖

TARA

"I don't want to ever leave," Tara said.

Surrounded by rows of brightly lit slot machines, game tables, and people looking to make money, Tara came alive. Trying to be incognito, she'd stayed holed up in the convention or the hotel room since she got to Vegas, but Louis had talked her into going to the casino. All the gambling meant nothing to her. She had already won the jackpot with Louis.

Louis kissed Tara again. "I can't say I'm thrilled to go home either. I could get used to this."

"What's this?" Tara asked seductively.

Louis wrapped his free arm around Tara, pressing her body against his. He whispered in her ear, "Waking up to you in the morning and going to bed with you at night. Making love to you for however long I like and in any way I like."

Tara's face grew warm. "Louis."

"I'm telling the truth. But we still have tonight. Quite frankly, I'd rather be in our room than in this casino right now."

Tara bit her bottom lip and raised her eyebrows. "So would I."

"Let's go after we finish our drinks."

Tara put the martini glass to her lips and chugged her fourth drink. The sweet liquid burned its way down. "Ready."

Louis laughed. "What am I going to do with you?"

Tara winked. "I have a few ideas."

"Let me finish my drink, and then we'll go."

"Okay, I'm going to run to the ladies' room."

Tara stumbled toward the bathroom and froze. Terrence was exiting the men's, a scowl plastered on his face, and he turned his head as if searching for someone in the sea of people. She hurried into the women's room and rushed into a stall, locking the door behind her. *Oh my god! What if Terrence saw Louis and me?* Her heart pounded. *Think, Tara, think!* She grabbed her phone from her clutch and saw a text message from Sophia.

Are you still coming to our Super Bowl party? Desiree wants to buy party supplies, so I'm getting a head count, it read.

Yes. We'll be there, Tara texted back, though in that moment, the future was very uncertain.

She texted Louis. *Meet me in our room. It's an emergency!!!!*

The phone beeped, and a text from Louis read, *K.*

Tara peeked her head out of the bathroom. Step by step, she emerged. She scoured the room but didn't see Terrence, so she hurried through the casino, nearly knocking over a cocktail waitress with a tray full of drinks. By the time Tara made it to the elevator, her nerves were fried.

She ran through the hall and stopped outside their suite. *Damn!* Louis had the key. Leaning against the door, she closed her eyes.

"Please, please, let Terrence have not seen me," she whispered.

A man turned the corner and headed toward her. *Oh, god. It's him!* She tried to think of what she would say, but nothing came. The man approached then passed by—it wasn't Terrence.

Less than two minutes later, Louis ran down the hall wearing a quizzical look. She buried her head in his chest, trying to block out the fear that welled up in her stomach.

"What's wrong?" Louis asked.

"My neighbor Terrence was in the casino. He's a good friend of Josh's. I'm worried he saw us."

Louis swiped the key to open the suite's door. His brows were furrowed and his lips pursed.

Tara ran into the suite. "Say something!"

"I'm thinking."

Tara paced from the living room to the kitchen. "I think he would have said something to me. But what if he did see me but just didn't say anything? What if he did see me, and he called Josh. What if—"

Louis wrapped his arms around Tara when she walked past, like a fisherman catching a fish with his net. "Tara, you will drive yourself crazy doing this. We can't change whether he saw us or not. Either way, I'm here for you."

"But it could ruin everything if Josh finds out," Tara insisted.

"Would that be so bad?" Louis asked, raising his palms. "You're miserable with him."

"I never said that."

"Oh, so you're happily married then?" Louis raised one eyebrow.

"I didn't say that either," Tara admitted. She'd been with Josh for so long, she couldn't imagine her life without him.

"I believe in fate. I believe that fate brought us together. And if your friend saw us, that's fate too, right?"

"I don't believe in fate." Tara stepped back from Louis. "We have free will. We make choices that lay the foundation of a path, and later we have to walk down it."

"We might make decisions, but fate puts people on that path. Fate gave me you." Louis pulled Tara to him.

"So, Mr. Almighty-Knower-of-Fate, what does fate have in store for us then?" Tara asked.

Louis's gray eyes met hers. "Well, Ms. I-Don't-Believe-In-Fate, I guess that's up to us to decide."

He reached for the zipper on the back of Tara's dress and eased it down as far as it could go. As he brought his hands to her shoulders, Tara shivered. The dress slid off her arms, and she allowed it to fall to the floor.

"What I'm deciding right now is that I want to enjoy the last night I have in Vegas with you."

Tara couldn't enjoy anything with Louis now. "But what if—"

Louis pressed his finger against Tara's lips. "Shhhh. Let's let fate handle the what ifs."

He scooped Tara into his arms, making her skip a breath. He carried her to the bedroom and laid her on the bed, and Tara closed her eyes. Louis's lips pressed against hers, firm and tender.

"Tara, I love you," he said.

Tara's resistance melted. "I love you too, Louis."

After Louis fell sleep, Tara lay awake. She had been so careful about hiding the affair, and she scolded herself for letting her guard down, something she'd taught herself never to do.

Tara had mastered the art of duplicity early on in her life. At school, she was "normal Tara." She played with her classmates, listened to her teachers, and learned the material as best she could. She learned to smile instead of cry and always said everything was "okay." Though she didn't know what a "normal" home life was, she knew her family was vastly different from the families on television sitcoms.

But one day in fourth grade, she let her guard down. Instead of going straight to the library, where her mother picked her up after work, she accepted an invitation to go to her classmate's house. That morning, she'd had no clean clothes to wear, which wasn't unusual, so Tara threw on the closest-to-clean shorts she could find, forgetting about the welt on the back of her leg from her father's belt. Beth's mom noticed the welt, asked what happened, and Tara made up a lie, which she hoped satisfied Beth's mom.

But the next day, she'd ended up being called into the principal's office, where she was again questioned about the mark. The principal seemed ancient to Tara, with fluffy white hair and a high-pitched voice that always cracked. Tara was so nervous, she couldn't remember the lie she'd told Beth's mom, so the principal called her home. Unfortunately, Tara's mom was at work, so her dad answered the call.

Tara had heard her father before he appeared, his words slurred as he demanded to know where "the little shit is." Her whole body trembled at the sound. Tara would never forget the principal's reaction when her father stumbled through the office door. The principal had had a look of pure shock.

Her father's face was bright red, and the familiar scent of vodka oozed from his pores. He glared at Tara. "What'd she do?"

"She didn't do anything," Principal White answered.

"Then why the fuck did you call me in here?"

Principal White cleared his throat. "That language is uncalled for. I called you in here because Tara has an unexplained welt on the back of her leg, and we're concerned about it. Would you happen to know how that got there?"

Tara's father looked at Principal White then Tara. A laugh like a rupturing fire hydrant bellowed from him. "You're joking, right? I have no idea how that got there. You hear?"

"I'm going to report you," Principal White said.

"You need to stay the hell out of my business." He glared at Tara. "Get your ass up. We're going home."

Principal White rose. "Mr. Peterson, I will not allow you to take her out of this office."

Tara's father stomped right up to the edge of the principal's desk and leaned so close to him that Tara knew his breath was heating up the principal's face. "Fine! Do what you want with her. I'm out of here." Tara's father stormed out of the office.

Tara had sat in silence, she and Principal White exchanging occasional glances.

Ten minutes later, Tara's mom ran in. "What's going on? The school called my work and said that Tara's hurt."

Tara raised her hand, requesting permission to speak. "I'm okay, Mommy."

Principal White cleared his throat again. "We have reason to suspect that your husband hit Tara, causing a welt on her right leg. If we suspect child abuse, we're mandated to call the police."

"Oh no, no. Please don't. There's no abuse. That is unnecessary. Please."

"I still have to make a report. Tara, go back to class, please."

Shoulders slumped forward, Tara tiptoed back to class. All she could think about was that it was her fault. She shouldn't have gone to Beth's house. Other people always had a way of interfering.

And now it was Terrence. She didn't know what she'd do if Terrence had seen her. She wasn't ready to lose her life with Josh, but she couldn't stop seeing Louis either. She'd have to scope out Terrence, see if his behavior was any different or not. Regardless of whether Terrence did see her, sooner or later, she had to make a decision. But if Louis was right about fate, it might not be her decision to make.

CHAPTER ELEVEN

HOME AGAIN

Sophia

Thirty-two ounces of water weighed down Sophia's steps into Dr. Smith's office. Though eager to have another ultrasound and see her baby's progress, Terrence had called and said his flight was delayed back home. She missed him and desperately wanted to share the appointment with him.

"Mrs. Douglas, how are you?" the nurse asked when Sophia signed in.

Sophia forced herself to smile. After all, pregnant women were supposed to be happy. "I'm good."

"Excellent! Let's get you settled into a room. Come on back."

In the room where the ultrasound would be performed, Sophia closed her eyes with her hands on her belly. When she'd had her last ultrasound, in the emergency room, she'd been so worried about being pregnant. But now, even with their financial trouble, she couldn't imagine anything more precious than her growing baby.

A knock on the door preceded Dr. Smith's entrance. "Sophia, good to see you. How are you and the baby?"

"We're both great."

"That's what I like to hear. And is the baby moving much?"

Sophia furrowed her brows. "No, I haven't felt the baby yet."

Dr. Smith's expression grew concerned. "No movement at all?"

Sophia's heart pounded. "Is that bad?"

"Well, it depends. First-time mothers generally feel fetal movement later than women who've had other children, but we expect the baby to move sometime between sixteen and twenty-five weeks. So we shouldn't worry."

Sophia tried to control her breath to steady her heart. "I'll feel better when we see my little one."

Dr. Smith applied warm lubricant to Sophia's little hill of a stomach, then she ran the transducer over it. A grainy black-and-white image of the baby appeared on the screen. "And there's your baby."

"The baby looks very still," Sophia said, the idea of lack of movement now worrying her.

"The baby might be sleeping." Dr. Smith leaned closer to the screen and moved the wand. "We should be able to see the heart beating though."

Perspiration lined Sophia's forehead. Something wasn't right.

With one hand on the wand and the other hand on the computer, Dr. Smith fell silent. She studied the screen, moving the wand from one position to the next on Sophia's stomach. "Hmm. Sophia—"

Another knock sounded at the door, and the nurse popped her head in. "Her husband's here."

Terrence jogged into the room. "Sorry I'm late."

"And there we go," Dr. Smith said, pointing at the screen. "See that? The baby just kicked."

Sophia grabbed Terrence's hand and couldn't stop the tears of relief from pouring from her eyes. "You're just in time."

Terrence kissed Sophia's lips. "I won't even tell you who I had to bribe to get here on time," he said with a laugh. "Is everything okay?"

Sophia squeezed his hand. "It is now."

Dr. Smith shook Terrence's free hand. "Nice to meet you." She pointed at the screen again. "Now that's what I wanted to see. There's the heart pulsing. There are the legs. Are you two finding out the sex?"

"No," Sophia and Terrence said in unison.

"There are so few surprises left in this world," Sophia added.

Dr. Smith wiped the gel from Sophia's belly with a towel then pulled her shirt down. "Everything looks excellent. I'm going to print out pictures of the baby for you. If you need to use the bathroom, it's right down the hall."

After she left the room, Terrence kissed Sophia's forehead. "We did that. We made a living being. Incredible."

It was unbelievable. "It's kinda freaky knowing a real person is growing in me."

"Yeah, kinda like *Aliens* or something. Maybe we should watch that movie," Terrence joked.

Sophia laughed, content that in that moment, things were okay. "This whole experience gives me a new appreciation for my mom."

"What about your dad? In a perfect world, would you want to reconcile with him for the baby's sake?"

Sophia contemplated the question. Before he left, he'd been such a good dad to her. But that was ages ago, and she had no idea what he was like now. She didn't want to seem negative and ruin this perfect moment though, so she said, "For the baby, in a perfect world, yes."

<hr />

TARA

Tara's fingers flew as she typed the jury instructions for the upcoming Drymeir trial.

Her intercom buzzed, and Peter's voice blared through. "Tara, I'm expecting you to present today at three. Get your stuff ready, and I won't accept any excuses."

Tara straightened her shoulders. "Yes, Peter."

Shit. Though she had spent the days at the convention, all she could remember were the nights with Louis. She shot out of her chair and paced her office. She'd barely slept in Vegas, but now a nervous energy coursed through her body. She went to the credenza, where the bouquet Louis had given her was wilting. She scooped up the fallen petals and put them in the trash. Her thoughts raced between Terrence, work, Josh, and Louis. A walk might help her clear her mind. She picked up the entire arrangement to take them to the Dumpster in the parking garage.

She padded down the hall, and as she turned the corner, she ran into Peter.

He raised his eyebrows. "You're not sneaking off, are you?"

"Nope. Just going to throw these away, then I'll be right back."

Peter took off his glasses, wiped them on his shirt, then replaced them. "Make it quick. We have a lot to get out today."

"Morning again, Tara," Corinne said at the reception desk. "Where are you off to?"

Tara didn't appreciate her every movement being tracked. "Just taking these flowers to the Dumpster."

"Aww, poor flowers." Corinne pretended to pout.

Tara glared at Corinne. *Poor flowers?* Tara wanted to say that her life was unraveling at the seams and she didn't give a damn about flowers. Instead, she jammed her finger into the elevator button. When the doors opened, Tara rushed in, almost running into Mariana.

"*Cuidado*, where's the fire?" Mariana asked.

"Sorry. I'm just going to throw these flowers out downstairs, and Peter wants me to give a report on the convention this afternoon. I'm not ready for it."

Mariana stayed in the elevator. "I'll go down with you. I want to hear all about it. Were you bored out of your mind?"

Tara sank into the elevator's corner. "No, it was great until—"

But Mariana didn't know she had been with Louis. No one knew about Louis... except possibly Terrence. She needed to keep it that way.

"Great until what? I mean, I like the law and all, but I've never heard anyone say that a convention was great," Mariana said.

"I meant being in Las Vegas was great. It was my first time there, and it was great, until I had to come back." Tara forced a laugh.

Mariana slammed her hand against the stop button. "Look, Tara, I've known you for seven years. I'm not buying it. Just tell me what's going on with you."

"I can't talk about it. I just... can't."

"You can tell me anything. You know that."

Tara reached around Mariana and pressed the door open button. "I can't."

She stormed past Mariana and marched through the parking garage, the off-yellow lights casting an eerie glow. When Tara got to the green Dumpster, her hands trembled as she threw away the flowers. She squeezed her eyes shut, and tears spilled out.

"*Tara*," her dad's voice whispered.

Tara opened her eyes and searched the garage, but no one was there. She took a deep breath and wiped away the tears. She needed to get it together and fast. Too much was at stake. She ran back to the elevator. When she got to her floor, Mariana was waiting at Corinne's desk.

"I'm staging a friend-er-vention," Mariana said. "You've been ignoring me lately, and you're acting strange. I'm worried, so I'm forcing you into rehab, which is lunch with me."

"Me too," Corinne added.

The last thing she needed were two more people on her case. "Look, I love you, Mariana, but I'm absolutely swamped with work. Maybe tomorrow."

Mariana exhaled loudly. "Whatever."

"I need to get this presentation ready for Peter, or I'll need to find a new job." As Tara hurried to her office, she tried to collect her jumbled thoughts. She needed to sort things out, but she had no idea how.

After a long day at work, Tara entered Meta Waves for an appointment with Miriam.

"Tara, how have you been? You look flustered or scared." Miriam gestured for Tara to sit.

Tara obliged and sat on the wooden stool. "Do you believe in ghosts?"

Miriam raised an eyebrow as she poured hot water into a mug. "Yes and no. I believe that we're all spirits. During our lives, we have bodies, after our deaths, we leave them behind. Why do you ask?"

Tara exhaled. It was crazy, but it needed to be said. She couldn't confide in anyone else. "I think my father's spirit is haunting me."

Miriam handed the cup to Tara. "Tell me more."

Tara appreciated that Miriam wasn't fazed. She'd made the right decision coming to see her. Miriam understood her. "I sometimes think I see him, and I heard his voice earlier today."

"Oh. How long ago did he die?"

Tara sipped the tea. "I was in high school, so a while ago."

Miriam lit a match. She put the flame to the wick of a blue candle. Placing the candle on the table, she stared into Tara's eyes. "This could be serious."

"That's what I'm afraid of."

Miriam patted Tara's hand. "No need to be afraid of anything, honey."

And though Tara said, "Thank you," she couldn't shake the fear that engulfed her.

JOSH

Josh stretched his arms as he hurried to his front door. He'd assumed Tara would be home by now, but her car wasn't out front. Though his body ached in all the right places after a good gym session, he now had to do something less pleasant. He needed to talk to Tara.

"Hi, Joshie," his mom said when he opened the door. "Dinner's in the oven." She gave him a stern look. "Hope you didn't overdo it at the gym."

"I didn't, but thanks for watching the girls for me." Josh chugged his water as the girls charged down the hall toward him. Amazing what being away from them for a couple of hours could do.

"Hi, Daddy." Michelle wrapped her arms around him then recoiled. "You're all sweaty."

"Girls, give your grandma a good-bye hug. I have to meet Grandpa for dinner," Josh's mom said.

After the girls said their good-byes, Josh fixed a plate of food and ate at the table while the girls watched television in the living room.

The front door opened, and Tara jogged in. "Sorry I'm late. My appointment with Miriam ran over. Where are the girls?"

"In the living room." Josh didn't want to address Tara frivolously spending money on some quack. He didn't even want to know how much it cost. He pushed his plate away. "I lost my appetite. I'm going to take a shower."

Tara followed as he headed to the bedroom. "What's with the attitude?"

Josh turned toward Tara. "Funny, I was going to ask you the same thing. You're the one who doesn't answer calls at night, isn't where she says she'll be, and comes home smelling like another man."

Tara ran her hands through her hair and glared at Josh. "I told you I was working. My boss, who I work with closely, is a man. Do you think I'm having an affair with Peter of all people?"

Josh hesitated. She had a good point. "No, it's just—"

Tara continued. "Do you have any idea what it's like to have four people depend on you? Do you know how hard it is to be a working mother? Do you know how much pressure I'm under every single day to make ends meet in Silicon Valley? Do you?"

Josh's heart sank. He'd never seen Tara so frazzled, and the exhausted look in her eyes concerned him. "I'm sorry, Tara."

Tara closed her eyes, and Josh embraced her shaking body.

"I'm sorry," he repeated. "I just love you so much."

Josh expected her to pull away, but instead she hugged him back.

"I love you too, Josh," she said.

And though her voice quivered when she said it, he believed her.

✦

Terrence

Terrence took a deep breath, forced a smile, and opened his front door to let in their guests. He'd been avoiding Josh and Tara since he arrived home a week ago, and he was still trying to figure out what the hell he should do. Usually he'd talk to Sophia and ask her for advice, but the last thing he wanted was to stress her out. So while he still hadn't decided the best way to handle what he'd uncovered about Tara, the time had come for him to act.

"Bro, let's get this party started," Josh said.

"Paw-tee," Teeni said, following Chelsea and Michelle.

The three girls were dressed in colorful shirts that read "Viva Las Vegas." The older two clobbered Terrence with hugs before racing into the house. Teeni lifted her arms toward Terrence, and he picked her up.

"How's my Teenster?" Terrence asked.

"Good, Tewence." Teeni's gaze traveled to the gold and red balloons that Chelsea and Michelle swatted back and forth in the corner of the living room. Teeni squirmed to get down, and once Terrence had obliged, she ran toward the fun.

Terrence poked his head out the door before asking Josh, "Where's Tara?"

"She's finishing up the seven-layer bean dip. She's not really into football, but she loves watching the Super Bowl commercials. As you can tell, she went overboard with the Vegas souvenirs. That's all we need, right? Get them started on the partying and Vegas lifestyle early," Josh joked.

Terrence closed the front door and lingered there. He exhaled, glad he had a little more time to figure out what to do. He had slept restlessly the night before as he mulled over the situation, and seeing Josh and the girls made him question his strategy. The information he had could potentially change their worlds forever.

"Terrence, everything okay?" Josh asked.

No, it's not, Terrence wanted to say. "Uh, why?"

"Because I asked what you want me to do with these." He held up a case of beer. "But you didn't seem to hear me."

"Oh, sorry. Let's go put them in the fridge."

In the kitchen, Sophia unwrapped the plastic from a ready-made fruit tray.

"Don't do that!" Josh scolded Teeni, who was crouched near the refrigerator and trying to steady a red balloon in order to sit on it.

With an exasperated expression, Sophia said, "It's Desiree's fault, Josh. She had to go all out for this party even though she knew we aren't expecting many people."

"I heard that," Desiree yelled from the living room, hanging the gold and red streamers from the ceiling. "Don't be a hater."

"I meant for you to hear it," Sophia yelled back. She placed the tray on the island then looked at Josh. "It's excessive, isn't it?"

The tension between the two women had been thick since the weed incident, and Terrence wanted to lighten the mood, so he wrapped his arm around Josh's shoulder and said, "Whoa, whoa, whoa. Josh, as an almost-attorney, I advise you not to answer that question. It's a lose-lose situation."

"Come on." Desiree walked into the kitchen. "Let the man speak. It looks great, right?"

"Excessive," Sophia muttered.

Josh looked at Sophia then Desiree with a nervous laugh. "I'm outta here."

The two men left the kitchen and took seats on the couch in front of the television. Terrence fidgeted with the remote, and though he wanted to tell Josh and get it over with, right now was a terrible time. Tara would be there any moment, and who knew what the girls would overhear.

"Bro, my dad asked me again to come work at the shop. One of the guys in production just quit," Josh said.

"Really?" That sounded like a great opportunity. "What'd you say?"

"I told him I would think about it, but only to get him off my back. There's no way I'd take the job. I respect my dad too much to go into his shop and mess things up."

Terrence didn't agree at all. "Come on, man. Don't get down on yourself like—"

"And he likes to play mind games," Josh added.

Terrence cocked an eyebrow. Josh's dad had always seemed straightforward to Terrence. "What do you mean?"

"He gave me some speech about how it's not right for the man to be at home while the wife is working. He acts like Tara's going to run off with some other guy or something." Josh snickered.

Terrence choked, nearly spitting out his beer.

"It's crazy, right?" Josh's eyes searched Terrence's for reassurance.

Terrence pictured Tara kissing the mystery guy. He shuddered, trying to rid himself of the memory.

"Right?" Josh repeated.

The doorbell dinged.

"I'll see who that is." Terrence bolted off the couch, happy to get off the hook. He opened the door and snickered. "Speak of the devil."

"What?" Holding a casserole dish and a bag of tortilla chips, Tara avoided making eye contact as she brushed past him.

He followed Tara into the kitchen and watched her give Sophia a hug and a rub on the belly, kiss her daughters while scolding them for eating cookies before "real" food, then grab a Diet Coke from the fridge. Terrence couldn't believe her. She had the nerve to act... normal.

Terrence retrieved another beer while Chelsea, Michelle, and Teeni danced around the kitchen, nearly knocking over the platters of food. They acted as if instead of eating cookies, they had been attached to an IV pumping pure sugar into their veins.

"Maybe they should run around in the yard a little. Get out some energy or something. Sophia, you're the responsible party. Why don't you take them?" Terrence suggested, hoping for a few minutes alone with Tara.

"Great idea. Let's go, girls." Sophia shooed them out of the kitchen and toward the sliding glass door that led to the backyard.

"I'll come too," Desiree said.

Tara's cell phone beeped, and she examined her phone, her lips edging toward a smile. He waited until Sophia and the girls had cleared the room.

"Who's that?" Terrence asked.

Tara's red-eyed gaze shot up from the phone. "Excuse me?"

"I saw you, Tara."

"What?" Tara whispered.

"In Vegas." Terrence looked Tara dead in the eye. "With him."

Tara narrowed her eyes and glared at Terrence. "I don't know what you *think* you saw, but you're mistaken."

Terrence couldn't believe she was trying to lie. That was the oldest trick in the book, and it sure wouldn't work on him. "Oh, no, I'm absolutely sure. I saw you tonguing some guy who wasn't Josh. Are you really going to stand here and lie to my face?"

Tara's jaw clenched. "Let me just tell you this. If you try to run to Josh with—"

"Did I hear my name?" Josh asked.

Terrence and Tara simultaneously faced Josh as he entered the kitchen.

"Uh, no, I mean, yes, I mean..." Tara looked at Terrence and gently shook her head.

"Tara and I were just talking about Vegas," Terrence said. With everyone else outside, now was the time to tell Josh.

A startling shriek came from backyard, and the trio turned toward the noise.

"Uh oh. The girls!" Josh ran toward the backyard.

Tara and Terrence stared at each other. A new complication had arisen. If Tara denied Terrence's accusations, Josh might not believe Terrence and end their friendship. He needed more time to think everything through, so Terrence ran toward the sobbing emanating from the backyard.

Desiree kneeled on the grass, bawling. Sophia stood next to her, stroking her hair.

"What happened?" Terrence asked.

"Carl died," Sophia whispered.

Terrence patted Desiree's back. "We're here for you." But as the words came out, he flashed back to when his parents had died. Nothing would make the pain better right now. And with Desiree's already tense relationship with her mom, things would probably only get worse.

CHAPTER TWELVE

HE KNOWS

TARA

"Tara," THE VOICE WHISPERED.

Tara sat up in bed. Josh slept soundly beside her.

"*Tara*," the voice called again.

She slipped out of bed, out of her room, and down the pitch-black hall. She couldn't continue to ignore or run away from this. Whatever this was.

"Who are you?" Tara whispered.

"*Follow me.*"

Tara trailed behind the voice until she was in front of the garage door. She took a breath. Placing her hand on the cold knob, she turned it and opened the door. Darkness enveloped her. Her fingers fumbled to find the light switch. When she found it, she flicked it up.

The light went on, and she was in her parents' basement. Her father stood there with a maniacal grin that morphed into a scowl.

"I know what you're doing!" he said.

Tara closed her eyes tight and screamed, "You're dead!"

"Tara, I'm alive."

"No, no, no!" Tara screamed.

"Tara, you're having a nightmare. I'm fine. You're fine." It was Josh's voice now.

She opened her eyes, trying to adjust to the lamp's light. Josh put his arm around her, gently pulling her to him. She rested her head on his chest, the beating of his heart comforting her.

"What was it about?" Josh asked.

"I don't remember," Tara said, though the image of her father's crystal-blue eyes glaring at her was still clear in her mind.

"Want me to turn the light back off? It's only two in the morning."

Tara breathed in his comforting smell. "No. I just want to lie here with you like this."

"He knows!" Tara screamed into the phone as she paced her office.

"Who and what?" Louis asked.

"My neighbor, Terrence. Remember, I was worried he saw us in Vegas?"

"Oh, right. What did he do or say?"

"He damn near told Josh what happened. Luckily—I mean, not luckily because it's sad, but luckily for me—there was an interruption. He's going to be out of town for a few days, but I don't know what to do."

"Tara, this is important, but I can't talk right this minute. I needed to be in a meeting five minutes ago. Let's meet for lunch at the hotel, and we'll go over strategy."

Tara slammed the phone down then rested her head on her desk. She hadn't been able to go back to sleep after the dream about her father. Her life and her nightmares were blurring together.

"Sleeping on the job?" Mariana asked after barging into Tara's office with Corinne.

Tara jerked up. "What?"

"Tara, you look like shit. Let's go to lunch. I think work's stressing you out too much," Mariana said.

Her father's laugh rang in her ears. "I can't," Tara said, trying to ignore it.

"Why not?" Corinne asked.

"I'm uh... meeting Josh and the girls. Tomorrow though." Tara grabbed her purse and stumbled out the door.

SOPHIA

Sophia's fingers clung to the armrests as the plane shook on its touchdown into LAX. "I'm not sure I'm ready for this."

Terrence put his hand on Sophia's stomach and rubbed it. "It won't be that bad."

Sophia disagreed. "Based on the fact that my mom thinks Desiree is responsible for Carl's death, I'd say it's pretty bad."

"She can't really believe that, can she? I mean, Carl was how old?"

"Seventy-five." Though he was definitely up in age, he had always seemed young at heart. Sophia couldn't believe he was gone. "Considering that my mom doesn't believe in God, I think she needs to have someone to blame."

"Poor Desiree," Terrence said.

Yes, poor Desiree. Other than when her father left her mom, Sophia had never seen someone in so much emotional pain. Josh, Tara, and the girls had politely headed home after Desiree received the call, and Terrence had had to almost carry Desiree to her room.

An hour later, Desiree had emerged. With her Gucci duffel bag around her shoulder, sunglasses on her face, and keys in hand, she strode past them to the front door. "I'm going back to LA."

Terrence had tried to talk Desiree into flying with them, but she'd refused, saying she needed to be alone.

Sophia put her hand on Terrence's, holding onto the only stable thing in a world that seemed to be shifting under her feet. "I'm worried about Desiree. I've tried to call her a dozen times, but her phone is going straight to voicemail."

The pilot thanked everyone on the plane for flying Southwest, but while the passengers began to file out, Sophia didn't move. The problem was that her family wasn't a math equation that needed to be solved or an essay question to be answered. It was real life, and if she knew anything about real life, it was that anything could happen.

"Sophia, we kind of need to leave." Terrence nodded toward the flight attendant, who had a smile plastered on her face but glared at Sophia sitting in the empty plane.

Sophia held out her hand, and Terrence helped her up. "Here we go." She tried not to focus on the sensation of butterflies in her chest.

Fingers interlaced, they made their way through the crowded airport terminal. After retrieving their luggage, they were greeted by an overcast sky and Sophia's mom, who had insisted they use one of Carl's cars instead of waste money renting one.

In spite of everything going on, Sophia's mom looked fabulous in a black skirt suit and black Jimmy Choo pumps. Her black sunglasses rested in her dyed auburn hair styled in a French twist. She looked at least ten years younger than her real age of fifty-five.

Sophia held her arms open to her mom. "How are you?"

Her mom hugged her tightly. "I'm awful." She stepped back and studied Sophia. "Well, look at you. You look bigger than the last time I saw you."

"Thanks, Mom," Sophia said sarcastically. "How's Desiree?"

"Desiree?" her mom asked nonchalantly.

"She left yesterday and said she was going to LA," Terrence said.

"She didn't come to my home. She used to treat the house like a hotel, popping in and out at all hours of the night, bringing in vagabonds doing god knows what, and leaving a mess for the housekeepers to clean up. The only time she really talked to Carl was to ask for money, money, and more money. She's so ungrateful, but she's going to learn the hard way what life is all about."

"So where is she then?" Terrence asked, a trace of panic in is voice.

"I have no idea, and quite frankly, I couldn't care less. Let's get going. Are you two hungry? I have no appetite at all. My stomach just twists in knots when I think about the funeral I have to plan."

Sophia rubbed her mom's back. "It's okay, Mom. That's why we're here—to help. I'm going to try to get in touch with Desiree. Maybe she could come over and we can sort this whole mess out."

Sophia understood why her mom didn't want Desiree around; Sophia didn't even want Desiree around. But they were sisters, so Sophia needed to be there for her.

"I'm in no mood to see her."

"Mom, she's your daughter, and I know you love her. That's all that matters."

"It's not that simple, Sophia."

"It is though," Sophia said, though the truth was far from it.

———— ✦ ————

JOSH

Teeni sang as Josh drove cautiously through the wet streets to Michelle's preschool. "Wain, wain, go away, come 'gain 'nother day."

"Very nice, Teeni. I wish this rain would go away."

Josh pulled into the parking lot. He scooped up Teeni and ran to the building, dodging the raindrops. The salty smell of Play-Doh scented the heater-warmed air when he opened the preschool's door. Michelle was in the middle of the room, dressed in a fireman's costume and spraying pretend water on a boy writhing on the alphabet mat while screaming, "I'm on fire."

"Michelle, come on, sweetie," Josh said as he signed her out.

As he drove away, Tara came to mind. He couldn't figure her out. She'd seemed so preoccupied and distant, yet needy and clingy since returning from her trip. And he couldn't forget the scene with her and Terrence. He'd obviously caught them in the middle of a heated conversation, so something must have happened in Vegas.

Either way, he wanted to see Tara. He needed her to know he loved her and that he would do whatever he needed to in order for them to get through this rough spot.

Josh went through the McDonald's drive-through and bought food for him and the girls and a coffee for Tara. The windshield wipers were going full speed as Josh drove to Tara's office. He parked in the underground parking garage as the clock read ten past one, so Tara should have been back from lunch. The girls skipped through the garage, then they took the elevator up to the fifth floor.

"Mommy," Teeni yelled after stepping off the elevator.

Josh put his finger to his lips as they approached the receptionist desk. "Shh."

Corinne put her hands on her cheeks. "Oh my god! They are too cute!"

Josh patted the girls on their backs. "Say hi."

"Hi," they said in unison.

"We were actually going to drop this off for Tara." Josh held up the coffee. "Is she back yet?"

A confused look crossed Corinne's face. "No, I thought she was with—"

Josh raised his eyebrows. The familiar dread settled in his stomach. "Peter. A working lunch with Peter."

"Long lunches and late nights, right? Do you have to work late when everyone else does? Or just Tara and Peter?"

Corinne looked thoughtful. "Peter's the only one who works late. Tara's usually the first one out of here actually. Heads straight home to you guys."

Josh raised his eyebrows. "Right." Josh handed the coffee to Corinne. "Tell Tara that we stopped by."

"Sure thing," Corinne said.

As Josh headed down the elevator with two disappointed girls, he was even more confused. Instead of seeing Tara and reassuring her of his love, he now had proof that she had been lying to him.

TARA

Tara sped recklessly down Highway 101, which was slick with rain. She'd spent over an hour and a half with Louis at the hotel. She'd gone there expecting him to somehow make everything better. After all, that was what the whole affair was about—an escape from the harsh reality that was her life. But instead of solving anything, he nonchalantly said they couldn't control what Terrence did. The dice had been thrown, and they'd have to see how they landed.

That wasn't good enough for Tara, and they'd spent the remaining time arguing about their next steps. Nothing had been resolved, but Tara had to come to one realization. If she was getting out of this mess, it'd take her action, not Louis's apathy. She'd have to figure out something. And fast.

When she exited the elevator, Corinne's face fell. "Oh, Tara, can we talk?"

Tara put up her palm. "Not now."

In her office, a mountain of files crowded her desk, reminding her that she was seriously behind. There was a knock on the door, and Corinne popped her head in.

"Look, Corinne, I'm swamped. What's up?"

"How was lunch?" Corinne asked, entering Tara's office and placing a McDonald's coffee cup on her desk.

"Uh, fine. Why?" Tara asked, though it was none of Corinne's business.

"Well... you said you couldn't go to lunch with me and Mariana because you were meeting Josh and your daughters."

"And...?"

"Josh, Michelle, and Teeni just stopped by. They wanted to surprise you with that coffee."

"Take a seat," Tara said as she crossed the room then closed the door. She went back to her chair and sank down. She felt as if she was back in the principal's office. "Look, Corinne—"

Corinne's face was expressionless. "Why are you lying?"

Tara's sleep-deprived mind tried to think of yet another lie, but it was as if her brain had met its capacity for dishonesty. She exhaled. "I'm having an affair."

Corinne's jaw dropped. "Oh."

"And I think I love him and Josh." Tara's shoulders slumped. Somehow, telling someone about the affair was a sort of release. She'd been holding it in for so long, and at times, she felt as if she'd explode.

"Who is he?" Corinne asked quietly.

"His name is Louis Steinman. He's a lawyer who works at an immigration firm in San Francisco," Tara said.

The two women fell into a long silence that Corinne eventually broke. "Tara, it's not my place to say anything. But you're married to a great man, and you have three beautiful daughters."

"I know. It's just taken me a long time to remember that."

"Your girls are so cute. Don't you care about how this is going to affect them?"

"Of course I care." Tears came to Tara's eyes. If this came out, it would destroy Josh, the girls, their family. "Please don't tell anyone, especially not Mariana. She would be the last person on earth to understand where I'm coming from."

"I won't tell Mariana," Corinne said.

"I have a ton of work to do, so I should be getting back to it." Tara headed for the door. She opened it, and Corinne took the hint and left.

Tara shut the door behind Corinne. She braced herself against it, the gravity of their conversation weighing her down. Tara immediately regretted telling the office gossip. Her affair was getting out of her control. Then again, it might have never been in her control.

CHAPTER THIRTEEN

SURPRISE!

Sophia

"THANKS FOR GETTING ME OUT of Mom's," Sophia said to Terrence as they entered the Brazilian restaurant. Her stomach grumbled when she inhaled the aroma of chicken and plantains. "I hope the baby loves all kinds of food as much as I do."

Terrence approached the host station. "We have a reservation under Douglas."

The hostess scanned the paper. "Right this way. The other member of your party is already seated."

Sophia looked at Terrence. "You didn't mention we were meeting anyone."

Terrence squeezed her hand and led her through the crowded restaurant. "Now, Sophia, with all the sad things going on, it was really important to try to do something positive."

Sophia narrowed her eyes at him. "What? What do you mean?"

Terrence stopped at a table where a black man sat. The man lowered the menu that had covered his face, and Sophia gasped. The man's once-full black hair was gray and receding. Wrinkles lined his eyes. His athletic build had been traded for an extra twenty pounds, but she still recognized him.

Her father rose with a grin and watery dark-brown eyes. "Sophia, my god, look at you. You're absolutely beautiful. And pregnant!" He turned to Terrence and extended his hand. "So great to finally meet you."

Sophia grew hot as if a struck match had lit a fire in her body. All sound was muted, save for the pounding of her heart. She took rapid, short breaths to try to gain her composure. Her throat closed.

"Water," she managed to get out as she wiped the newly formed sweat from her forehead.

"We need some water. Now!" her father said to the hostess.

Terrence pulled out Sophia's chair, which she nearly collapsed onto. "Are you okay?"

The hostess rushed to the table with a glass of water. Sophia gulped it down, glaring at Terrence. She hated her father, and Terrence knew it. Her heart pounded faster, and her head spun. She'd finished the water, but her mouth was dry. She couldn't catch her breath.

"Just breathe in through your nose then out of your mouth," her father said. "Please, more water," he called to the hostess.

Sophia glanced at his concerned eyes. She placed the glass on the table, closed her eyes, and focused on her breath. Her heart steadied. The hostess refilled her glass, and Sophia took a sip, sweat running down her forehead.

"You know what? I can go. If this is too much for you, I can leave. I don't want to upset you or your baby. I just... I just want you to know I'm so sorry," her father said.

Sophia looked up. "What?"

"I'm sorry, Sophia. It's been decades since I've spoken to you, and that's my fault. Regardless of what happened between your mother and me, I should have fought to have you in my life. But I didn't. I want you to know I regret that. You two take care." He began to walk away.

Terrence sighed, and Sophia shot him a glare.

Sophia felt as if she were in an ocean with waves threatening to overtake her. She couldn't decide if seeing her father and having him apologize was a dream or a nightmare. Before he'd abandoned her, she loved her dad more than anything. He used to tell her stories before bed and make her blueberry waffles for breakfast. On the weekends, he always had a new and exciting adventure for her, whether it was a museum, the zoo, or a nature park.

That was why it had hurt so much when he left. At first she'd waited for him to come back. But when she realized he wouldn't return, her hurt turned to anger. Though she grew up hating him, at the same time, she missed him.

Regardless of her mother marrying Carl, her life had always had an empty place that belonged to her father. It was still empty, but she wasn't sure if she wanted him to fill it.

"Wait," Sophia called.

Her father cautiously returned and sat back down. "Are you feeling better?"

Sophia's face burned. She couldn't believe she'd overreacted so severely. "I'm fine."

"I was sorry to hear about Carl's death, and even more sorry to hear about the situation with your mother and Desiree," her dad said.

Sophia raised her eyebrows at Terrence. "How does he know all this? Since when do you talk to my father behind my back?"

Terrence shrugged. "It's not like that. It's just that after I talked with—"

"Talked with who?" Sophia asked. No one who knew her would think this was a good idea.

Terrence ran his hand over his hair. "Remember when you said you'd reconcile with your dad for the baby's sake? I looked him up before we came here. He's a well-known psychiatrist, so it wasn't hard to find him. I thought it was time for you two to at least meet again… to talk."

"I said in a perfect world, Terrence. That meant never." Sophia couldn't believe Terrence would misconstrue her comment so outrageously.

Sophia's father said, "Terrence loves you. And I want you to know that I'm here for you, and I love you too."

That was too much for Sophia to handle. "How can you say you love me? You abandoned me. You walked out on me and Mom and never looked back."

"That's not true. I looked back. I tried. But your mother—"

"Don't you dare blame my mom!" Sophia said. "You're the one who walked out. You left us."

"I'm not blaming your mom. You're right. I did leave her. But I never wanted to leave you. I love you, and I wanted to be there for you. I just didn't go about it the right way. But I want to be there for you now.

I want to be in my grandchild's life. I want to be in your life. Terrence opened that door. Please don't close it."

A waiter approached the table. "Have you had time to look over the menu?"

Sophia handed her menu to the waiter. "I'm sorry, but I lost my appetite. Give me the keys, Terrence. You two can enjoy your dinner, but I'm going." Terrence went to stand, but Sophia put out her hand. "Just give me the keys. You can figure out your own way back to my mom's place."

Terrence handed Sophia the keys.

"I understand. Here, take this." Her father extended a business card. "It's my card. Call me any time for any reason. Please."

Sophia took the card then turned her back to him, knowing the sky would have to fall for her to ever actually call him. Hand to her belly, she raced through the restaurant. Outside, a breeze cooled her body.

"Sophia, wait," Terrence yelled. "I'll go with you."

"After what you just pulled? Not a chance in hell!" She got in the car and slammed the door, trying to catch her breath. Hot tears streamed down her cheeks.

She didn't know if she was more upset because of what Terrence had done or because of her conflicting emotions. Hating her dad was easy—she'd been doing it most of her life. But seeing his earnest eyes, hearing him apologize, watching him plead with her to let him in her life—it was all too much. She had to get away. Gripping the steering wheel, she sped off.

JOSH

Josh was at a stop sign a block from their house when his cell phone rang. Pulling the phone out of his jacket pocket, his heart pounded when he saw Tara's number on the screen. "Tara?"

"Corinne said you stopped by. Sorry I missed you," she said.

"So where were you?" Josh asked, anxious to hear how she'd answer.

"Uh... I was just running late getting back from lunch with Mariana."

"Oh, really? Corinne said you were at a working lunch with Peter."

"Are you sure?"

Josh gripped the wheel tighter. "Yes. She did."

"Are you keeping tabs on me? I just went to lunch, okay?" Tara's voice had grown hostile.

Tired of dancing around Tara's emotions, Josh said, "No, it's not okay. Either you went to lunch with Peter or Mariana or—"

"I went to lunch with Peter. Mariana came later, and we stayed a little longer. This conversation is over," Tara said then hung up.

Josh parked in front of his house. He stared at the steering wheel. Though Teeni and Michelle sang along with the Kidz Bop CD, all he could hear was the silence from Tara hanging up on him. Things were not adding up. His stomach was queasy.

If the definition of insanity was doing the same thing over and over again but expecting a different result, then he was certifiably insane. Arguing with Tara was not going to solve the problem. But based on the way she'd been talking with Terrence, Josh knew he'd be able to give Josh some clarity.

<hr/>

TERRENCE

Terrence opened his eyes. His back ached from spending the night on the hardwood floor at Sophia's mom's house. He had taken a taxi there after dinner, knowing Sophia's dad might be the next dead husband if he'd driven Terrence back.

Terrence knocked on the bedroom door again. "Sophia? Open up."

No answer. His plan to reconcile Sophia and her dad had failed miserably. After his conversation with Desiree, he'd done some research and ended up contacting Darryl, who had been overjoyed to hear from Terrence. After a few conversations, Terrence had decided that Darryl was a great guy who'd made a bad decision when he'd fallen in love with a woman who wasn't his wife. Terrence wasn't immune from making bad decisions, and apparently springing the dinner on Sophia was another one.

Sophia's mom appeared in the hall. "Haven't given it up yet, huh?"

"Morning to you too, Rachel," Terrence replied.

"Well, what did you think would happen? Or did you think? Taking her to see that bastard. Why on earth did you do that?"

Terrence couldn't tell Rachel about his conversation with Desiree, so he said instead, "He's my child's grandfather."

"You'll learn." She stomped down the stairs.

Learn what? he wanted to scream. Regardless of Sophia's anger, Terrence didn't regret what he'd done. There were so many things he wished he could have said to his parents before they were killed, and he didn't want Sophia to regret not making amends with her father. He also wanted his grandchild to know his or her only grandfather. But maybe he'd gone about things all wrong.

Terrence banged on the door again. "Sophia, please open up."

No answer.

The intercom buzzed downstairs. That could be Desiree. He'd been so worried about Sophia, he'd forgotten about her. He hurried down the stairs, where Rachel opened the front door.

Sophia came down the stairs after him. "Mom, who is that?"

"This is Timothy, the family attorney. He's here to go over Carl's will with me," Rachel answered.

A thin, white man dressed in a black suit walked in with a stern expression.

"Timothy, this is my daughter Sophia, and her husband, Terrence," Rachel said. "I just brewed some coffee."

Terrence could really use a cup himself. "I'll go pour some."

"No, thank you," Timothy said.

"Well, let's have a seat." Rachel gestured for him to sit at the oak dining table.

"Would you like to do this in a more private location?" Timothy asked.

Rachel frowned. "Is everything as planned?"

Sophia, whose face had grown worried, sat at the table. From the bags under her eyes, it appeared she hadn't slept much either.

Timothy's expression didn't change. "I would like to discuss this... in private."

"You're worrying me, Timothy. Whatever it is, you can say it in front of my daughter and son-in-law."

Timothy placed his briefcase on the table. "If you insist. Please, take a seat."

Rachel remained standing. "What is it?"

"Carl made a few adjustments to the will after his heart attack." He pulled out a thick folder.

"What adjustments?" Rachel asked.

A knot formed in Terrence's stomach. He wanted to comfort Sophia, whose face was contorted into worry as she rubbed her hands nervously. Terrence had negotiated a lot of contracts, and based on Timothy's tone, the adjustments couldn't be good for Rachel.

Timothy flipped through the folder. "On paragraph three, line—"

"Damn it! Just tell me the bottom line!" Rachel yelled.

"He left everything to Desiree," Timothy said.

Sophia gasped. Terrence dove toward Rachel and caught her as her knees buckled.

"What exactly?" Rachel asked.

"Everything, Rachel, everything," Timothy said.

SOPHIA

"Sophia, it's time to go," her mom called through the door.

"I'll be right out," Sophia said.

Sophia smoothed her black maternity dress over her round stomach. As she combed her hair, she sang quietly to the baby and felt a tiny kick in her stomach. She rubbed her belly. Since she still wasn't talking to Terrence, her mom was beyond stressed, and Desiree was MIA, the baby was the only person giving her joy. She wondered if she'd have a boy or a girl. Secretly, she wished for a boy. Girls seemed to have it so much harder in life. Boy or girl, Sophia would do everything in her power to protect her baby from hardship.

When Sophia left her room, she didn't see her mother, so she went to her mother's room. Though life would have certainly ended for Sophia if she had received the news about Carl's will, her mother had amazed Sophia with her transformation into the quintessential widow. The wake went off without a hitch, and afterward, her mom had gone to dinner with some old friends of hers and Carl's, not returning until almost midnight.

Sophia knocked on the door. "I'm ready, Mom," she said, opening it.

Sophia's mom looked stunning. Her makeup was perfect, and she wore a black dress with silver embroidery along the plunging neckline and another pair of black Jimmy Choos. "Okay, just let me grab my hat."

Sophia ventured into the room. The last time she had been in there a few weeks ago, Carl was still alive. Now it held no trace of him at all. "Where'd all of Carl's stuff go?"

"I had someone pack it and take it to Goodwill. The last thing I want is any reminder of that bastard. I gave that man over twenty years of my life, just for him to leave me high and dry."

"I'm so sorry. Are you okay?" Sophia asked.

Sophia's mom looked at Sophia. "Of course I'm okay."

"I just mean"—Sophia shrugged—"what are you going to do?"

Her mom didn't skip a beat. "I'm going to fight to get the house back in my name."

Sophia wondered if the hard shell was just an act. "It must hurt though."

Sophia's mom shot Sophia a menacing look. "It would only hurt if I still had a heart. Your father ripped mine out decades ago. Now let's get this damn funeral over with."

A chill ran down Sophia's spine. Guess that was the answer. It was a shame her mom had been burned twice by the men she loved.

They drove in silence to the small funeral home. When they got there, Terrence, who had gone ahead to make sure everything was in order, smiled at her.

"Sorry," he mouthed.

Sophia wanted to remain mad. She'd nearly passed out when he'd surprised her at the restaurant two days ago, so in a way, he'd put her and her baby's safety in danger. But she couldn't look into her husband's eyes without melting a little. "I know," she mouthed back.

Terrence walked to her and enveloped her in his arms. She breathed in his scent, which she'd missed. She wouldn't admit it, but she had slept horribly the night before since she wasn't sleeping next to him, his hand protectively placed on her belly.

Sophia and Terrence sat next to Sophia's mom. She admired the white rose bouquets that made the small room beautifully elegant and an oversized picture of Carl resting on an easel next to the casket. A handful of friends and coworkers filed into the room. As the officiator took his place at the podium, loud sobbing emanated from the room's entrance. Desiree walked in wearing a short black dress and black stilettos. Black eye makeup mixed with tears ran down her cheeks.

"Oh, please," Sophia's mom said.

"Mom." Sophia stood and pointed at the empty chair next to her. Though she wasn't exactly thrilled to see her sister, she needed to be the bigger person. "I know this is hard, but we'll get through this," Sophia said after Desiree took the seat.

Throughout the ceremony, sadness crept into Sophia. The fact that Carl was dead was still unbelievable. He'd never tried to be her dad, but Carl had been a constant presence in her life, one that she would miss.

After the officiator said his final words, everyone lined up to view Carl's body. Next to the coffin was a huge floral arrangement. When she got to the casket, Sophia barely recognized Carl. The embalming fluid had darkened his white skin. The finality of the situation hit Sophia, and tears fell.

"Thank you," Sophia whispered. "Thank you for everything."

Sophia congregated with the other guests at the refreshment table in the foyer, where she poured punch into a cup and sipped the sweet pink liquid. Cup in hand, she ventured back into the funeral room to inspect the beautiful floral arrangement. A small card was attached to the flowers. She read it: "With condolences from the Mitchell Family." Sophia's body burned. How dare her dad send flowers! It would only further upset her mom. And how dare he call himself and his mistress a "family." She threw the card in the trash bin and went back to the foyer, where Desiree and Terrence stood talking.

She gave Desiree a hug. "I'm sorry."

"Thanks, it's just—"

Her mom approached them and dug into her purse. She pulled out a manila envelope that she handed to Desiree. "Look this over and sign it."

Desiree pulled a paper out of the envelope. "What is it?"

"The deed to the house. I want you to sign it over to me," her mom said.

Desiree's eyes were wide as she looked at Sophia then at their mom. "What are you talking about?"

"Don't play naïve. Timothy told me he's talked to you about the will. Seems that your last act of manipulation got Carl to change his will and leave everything to you. That's not going to work, and you need to do what's right. Sign the house back to me."

Desiree narrowed her eyes. "I had nothing to do with that."

Sophia didn't believe a word coming out of Desiree's mouth and didn't doubt for a second that Desiree had been in constant contact with Carl since the heart attack, securing her future income.

"Don't bullshit me. I know you. You've had him wrapped around your finger since you were born, and there's no way he would have done this without your intervention." Sophia's mom's voice rose, quieting the other guests.

"Maybe he knew the truth—that you're a gold digger who was only with him for his money," Desiree said.

Sophia's mom slapped Desiree across the face. "Don't you ever speak to me like that again!"

Terrence stepped between Sophia's mom and Desiree. "Let's calm down."

Conscious of the guests' stares, Sophia put her hand on her mom's shoulder. "Mom, we need to go back to the house and figure this out once and for all."

"*We* can go back, but *she* is not to step foot into that house until this is settled," Sophia's mom said.

Desiree put her hand to her cheek. "Mom, you don't get it. I don't want the house. I don't want the money. I just—"

"I don't give a damn what you want anymore. My attorneys are already on it. You won't win this one. I'm not leaving, and you're no longer welcome in *my* home. Sophia, let's go." Sophia's mom stormed outside.

"Desiree's been through enough. I think the three of us should all go back to our home," Terrence said. "Give your mom some space."

Sophia agreed that her mom needed space. She didn't want to be apart from Terrence another night, but her mom needed her. "Go then."

"Sophia, please just come home with us," Terrence said.

"I'll catch a flight out as soon as I can."

Sophia kissed Terrence then hurried to her mom's car and got in. When the car pulled away, her hopes of a resolution to the situation between her mother and sister disappeared.

CHAPTER FOURTEEN

WE NEED TO TALK

TERRENCE

TERRENCE'S FEET MIGHT AS WELL have been weighed down with concrete as he struggled toward Josh's house. He took two steps then stopped. He didn't want to do what he had to do. But Josh had called, saying it was important they talk as soon as Terrence got back in town. He took two more steps. It was time.

He exhaled then knocked on the door.

A minute later, a soft voice asked, "Who is it?"

"Terrence."

The door opened, and Chelsea wrapped her arms around him.

"Now, Chelsea, I've told you that you really shouldn't be opening the door. Let your parents do it, okay?" Terrence said.

Tara appeared in the doorway. Her eyes were red, and dark bags hung underneath them. Her usually picture-perfect blond hair looked stringy. "Chelsea, go inside. I'm going to talk to Terrence." Tara stepped outside in her bare feet, closing the door behind her. "Terrence, hi. Josh mentioned that you two were going out for drinks."

"Yes. Josh is one of my best friends and—"

"Terrence, you were right about Vegas. Please don't hurt Josh by telling him that—"

"You're the only one hurting Josh, not me," Terrence said.

Tara shifted her weight. "I just need to figure it all out."

"What is there to figure out?" Terrence asked. "I can't stand by and let you do this to Josh."

Tara grabbed Terrence's hand and cupped it in between hers. "I'm begging you, Terrence. It will ruin my family."

"So now you're thinking about your family? Then tell me you'll end it." Maybe if Tara gave him her word it would be over, Terrence could withdraw from the situation.

"Just give me a little more time," Tara pleaded.

The door opened, and Tara dropped Terrence's hands and backed away.

Josh stood in the doorway, his face dark and inquisitive. "Oh, Terrence. I didn't know you were here yet."

Terrence waved. "Hey, man."

"So... what are you two talking about?" Josh asked.

"I'm just talking to him about Sophia's baby shower," Tara said.

Terrence glanced at Tara, amazed at how easily she could lie. "You ready to go?" Terrence asked Josh.

"Sure," Josh said.

Tara's gaze bore into him, her eyes silently pleading with him. He looked away.

—————— ►⬥◄ ——————

The Spot was packed with people watching a sporting event on the flat screen TVs.

"Hey, fellas," Keith said.

"Hey, man. Is there an open table?" Terrence asked.

"Yeah, sure. A two-top just opened in the back. Everyone's watching the UFC fight." Keith led them to the table and wiped it down with a cloth from his back pocket before gesturing for them to sit. "What can I get you two?"

Terrence chuckled. "We want the sampler appetizer, a bottle of Hennessy for me, and a case of Heinekens for Josh."

Keith laughed. "Got it."

At the table, Josh cleared his throat and folded his hands together. "Terrence, what the hell has been going on?"

Terrence hesitated. Tara's words had thrown him off. The last thing he wanted was to be a homewrecker or see Josh hurt. But at the same time, he had an obligation as Josh's friend. "That's a helluva way to start the conversation."

Josh shrugged. "Sorry, bro. Something's up with Tara, but I don't know what it is."

Unfortunately, Terrence *did* know. He didn't know if he could tell Josh though. "For real?"

Josh exhaled, his body slumping forward. "Yeah. That's what I wanted to talk to you about. Maybe you have an idea about what's going on with her? I've walked in on the two of you having what seemed like serious conversations after she came back from Vegas."

Cheers erupted from the crowd. Happy to avert his eyes from Josh's gaze, Terrence focused on a TV screen displaying a man pummeling another man in a ring. If he lied, he was an accomplice. If he told the truth, it could ruin Josh's life. It seemed like some type of karmic retribution for his indiscretions before he'd met Sophia. Terrence had been Tara before. He'd been a cheater. As a matter of fact, his marriage was the longest he'd ever been faithful to anyone. Some people believed that the truth always came out, but that wasn't always the case. He'd gotten away with infidelity plenty of times. Now he needed to decide if he should let Tara get away with it in the best interest of everyone.

Josh waved his hand in front of Terrence's face. "Bro, you there? What's going on?"

Keith approached and placed two drinks on the table. "Hennessy and Heineken. The appetizer will be out soon. Anything else I can get you two?"

Terrence wanted to ask if there was a car waiting out back that would take him somewhere, anywhere. "No, we're good."

As Keith left, Josh's eyes were on him.

"What? What were you saying?" Terrence asked, trying to buy more time to figure out what he should do.

"Is something up with you and Tara?"

"With me?" he asked, pointing at his chest. "And Tara?"

"Yeah, Terrence."

"Man…" Terrence's gaze wandered. Then he looked Josh in the eye. This was his best friend. He couldn't be the one to break his heart. "No. Nothing is up at all. Just trying to ask her how I should handle the situation with Sophia, her mom, and Desiree."

"You sure? That's all?"

Terrence ran his hand over his head. "Yes. That's all."

Josh stood abruptly, knocking back his chair. "I don't buy it. Something's going on, and I'm going to find out what it is." Josh jogged away.

Terrence had never seen Josh upset like that. He stood to chase him but stopped and sank back into his chair. He sipped his drink, trying to convince himself that he'd done the right thing. But he wasn't sure whose best interest was on his mind when he'd lied to Josh: Josh's, Tara's, or his own because he was too chicken to get in the middle of it. He'd had his opportunity to come clean with Josh, and he didn't take it. Now he needed Tara to end the affair, because if it ever came out, Terrence would lose a friend.

<hr />

TARA

Tara heard her cell phone beep. She rushed into her bedroom and to the side table where her phone rested. She picked it up. There was a text from Louis.

I need to see you tonight. It's urgent. What time can you get away? it read.

Tara needed to get away. If Terrence came clean to Josh, her marriage would be over. And though she didn't want that, she needed to know where she stood with Louis in the long term.

She dialed Eleanor, who answered on the first ring. "Eleanor, Josh is hanging with Terrence, and my friend is having an emergency. Can you come over for an hour tops?"

"Sure, honey. I'll be right over," Josh's mom said.

After hanging up, Tara texted Louis back. *I'll meet you at 8 at the hotel.*

"*Bad girl,*" the voice said.

"Stop it!" Tara whispered.

She rushed to her drawer and pulled out the bottle of holy water Miriam had given her. Splashing it on her head, she tried to focus, though confusion blanketed her mind. Sleep. She just needed solid sleep, since she'd barely gotten a wink of it over the past week. But it would have to wait. If Louis needed to meet, she had to find out why.

Maybe he missed her desperately since they'd decided to take the week off from each other. Then again, it might be the opposite. Maybe things had become too complicated, and he wanted to end their relationship.

At this point, Tara wasn't sure which she would prefer. She hurried to the bathroom and fumbled through her makeup bag until she found her red lipstick. Her hand trembled as she applied it, and she remembered the sensation like lightning striking whenever Louis's lips met hers. She stepped back from the mirror and frowned at the absolute mess staring back at her.

"*You are a mess.*"

Tara splashed water on her face then jumped when the doorbell dinged. "I'm going out, girls," she called to her daughters, who played with Legos in the living room.

"Where, Mom?" Chelsea asked with an annoyed expression.

Tara didn't answer. "You're a lifesaver. I won't be long," Tara said to Eleanor on her way out.

In the hotel parking lot, Tara reapplied her lipstick then hurried inside. When she entered the lobby doors, like Pavlov's dog, her body tingled, remembering all the liaisons she'd had with Louis over the past few months. At the hotel's bar, she immediately ordered a cocktail as she perched herself on a tan bar stool. She needed to calm her nerves.

Her watch read eight, and she scanned the room for Louis. He was never late. She fished her phone from her purse, but it vibrated in her hand and his number appeared.

Tara's shoulders relaxed as she answered. "Where are you?"

A hard tap on her shoulder made her turn around. A tall woman in a navy dress and matching jacket stood behind her. Appearing to be in her early forties, she had her brunette hair cut in a tight bob. Her perfectly made-up face was distorted into a grimace.

She lowered the cell phone in her hand. "So you're Tara. You're the woman sleeping with my husband."

Tara's heartbeat pounded in her ears. Though a million thoughts bounced around in her head like a ball in a pinball machine, she couldn't say a word.

Louis's wife pulled her hand back and slapped Tara in the face, knocking Tara off the stool.

"Hey!" the bartender yelled.

Tara scrambled to her feet as the bartender stepped between the two women. Tara raised her hand to her cheek, which throbbed.

"You better leave my husband the hell alone!" Louis's wife shouted. "If I ever find out you called him or tried to see him, you will regret the day you were born!"

"Do you want me to call the police?" the bartender asked Tara.

"No, I better go."

The eyes of every bar patron bore into her like a floodlight exposing her transgressions. It was too much. She grabbed her purse and fled the hotel.

Tara opened the door to the car and collapsed into the driver's seat as she sobbed. She didn't know what Louis's wife was capable of. She had to get out of there. And fast. After turning on the engine, she slammed on the gas and sped away.

Once home, Tara pulled down the visor to look in the mirror. She gasped at the large red circle on her cheek and mascara-tinged tears staining her face. She reached into the glove compartment, pulled out a tissue, and tried to clean her face like a criminal concealing the evidence of a crime.

"Really, Tara?" Josh said in the living room when Tara rushed down the hall without addressing him.

"He knows."

Tara ran into their bedroom then to the bathroom, closing the door. Seconds later, there was a knock on the bathroom door.

"Everything okay with Mariana?" Josh called.

"What?" Tara asked.

"Mariana. Didn't you tell my mom there was some emergency with her?"

"Oh, uh, yeah. I mean, yes, it's fine. She was just having drama with Xavier. I'm going to take a quick shower and get ready for bed." She lifted the nozzle to the shower. Water pounded the tub as steam filled the air.

"Drama? What drama?" Josh raised his voice.

"I can't hear you," Tara lied.

Stepping into the shower, Tara's mind ran like a hamster in a wheel. There were too many thoughts, too many voices. She needed to get away. But she had nowhere to go. So she'd have to pull it together.

After her shower, Tara concealed the red mark on her cheek with makeup. She opened the bathroom door and startled. Josh sat on their bed. She leaned against the doorjamb.

"Your eyes are all red," Josh said, more as a question than a statement.

Tara looked away. "How's Terrence?"

Josh ignored her question. "What's really going on?" His stare penetrated Tara, digging for the truth she had buried.

"What are you asking me?"

Josh shrugged. "I'm asking for the truth."

Her husband's eyes looked concerned. They were the same eyes she'd looked into when she'd promised to love him forever at the church's altar. He didn't deserve to be hurt, but she couldn't keep lying.

"The truth is... it's just that... Josh, it's all too much for me right now. I can't be everything to everyone all the time. I'm just tired. Too tired." She slid down to the floor, her body racked with sobs.

"Then get to sleep," Josh said.

Tara looked up. Then Josh did something that amazed Tara. He didn't push her further or call out her lies. Instead, he stood and walked out the door.

Tara threw herself on the bed and punched her pillow. She couldn't go on like this. A decision had to be made. She had to talk to Louis.

A sliver of morning light shone through a crack between the heavy brown curtains, piercing the darkness of Tara and Josh's bedroom. Tara, relieved morning had finally arrived so she could abandon the pretense of sleep, glanced at Josh. The dark-blue comforter covered him from shoulder to toes, his curly, dirty-blond hair rested on the matching blue pillowcase, and his lips were slightly parted. A wave of guilt washed over her as she remembered the way she'd spoken to him the night before. Her thoughts and her father's voice had tormented her all night.

Exchanging the warmth of the bed for the chilly morning air, Tara eased the blanket from her body. "Josh." She tapped his shoulder. "I forgot I have to be at work early. Can you drop Chelsea at school for me?"

"Yep," Josh said groggily.

Tara navigated through the dark room to the bathroom. She dressed quickly, brushed her teeth, and applied her makeup. When she opened the door, sunshine greeted her. She got in the car, stepped on the gas, and sped to San Francisco.

Once she passed the San Francisco airport, clouds filled the sky. She found a parking space a few blocks from Louis's office, and her heart thumped like a drum beat. She marched toward the high-rise building and entered the revolving glass door. She scanned the directory. Louis's firm was on the eleventh floor.

Once she stepped off the elevator, a receptionist greeted her.

"I'm here to see Louis Steinman," Tara said.

"Do you have an appointment?" the woman asked her.

"Just tell him Tara's here."

The receptionist picked up the phone and relayed the message. "He's not available right now."

Tara's mouth grew dry. "Available or here?"

"He's not available," the woman repeated.

Tears welled in Tara's eyes. She started toward the elevator then spun around. She stormed past the receptionist.

"Louis," Tara called throughout the office. "Louis!"

A few people stared at Tara, but she had to speak to him. Farther down the hall, Louis appeared. He looked relaxed and rested but wore an unfamiliar scowl.

"Tara, what are you doing here?" he asked.

"We need to talk." She tried unsuccessfully to hide the panic in her voice.

Louis looked at the people staring at them. "Let's go talk downstairs." He grabbed Tara's arm and led her back toward the lobby. "Lucy, I'll be right back," he told the receptionist.

When they got downstairs, Louis stopped and stared at Tara. "Tara, what the hell has gotten into you, storming into my office like that?"

Tara wanted to know what had gotten into Louis. He'd never treated her like this. "Your wife confronted me last night."

"I know. She found my phone with our text messages." He walked toward a bench that faced a brass elephant statue. Water spewed out of its trunk and collected in a pond littered with sunken pennies.

Louis gestured for her to sit, which she did, but he remained standing. Tara shivered and pulled her coat tighter around her body, unsure if the low temperature or Louis's cold demeanor was giving her a chill.

"Look, Tara, my wife gave me an ultimatum. And... I can't see you anymore."

"You what?" Tara rose to her feet and reached for his hand.

He shoved it into his pants pocket. "Tara, we're both married. We have kids, for god's sake. You've known what this was the whole time." Louis shrugged. "But now it's over."

A deep-seated dread settled in Tara's stomach, like a weight tugging her heart to the bottom of a dark ocean. "I've never known what this was. So tell me. What was it? Why did you do it? You pursued me, remember?"

A woman nearby stalled and glanced at Tara before hurrying past.

Tara didn't care. "You made love to me! You said you loved me! What was all that?"

"I've thought about it, and..." Louis lowered his eyes and his voice. "It was a mistake. I made mistakes. Tara, I'm truly sorry."

Tara wiped away the tears that dampened her cheeks. "You're sorry? Well, it's not okay, damn it! You ruined my marriage."

"Whoa, don't put this all on me."

Tara could barely speak. "You bastard," she whispered.

"I don't want to go there. It is what it is. Good-bye." Louis walked away.

Tara wanted to follow him, to make him pay for the mess he'd turned her life into, but she had already made enough of a fool of herself. Putting one foot in front of the other, she made it to her car. She sank into the driver's seat. Leaning her head against the steering wheel, she sobbed. She started the engine. She couldn't go to work in her condition, but she couldn't go home to Josh.

Forty-five minutes later, she parked in front of Meta Waves. She cursed the jingling bells when she opened the door. Ignoring the girl at the counter, she went directly to Miriam's office. Miriam sat at the table, flipping tarot cards.

"Louis left me," Tara said.

"I know. Have a seat."

CHAPTER FIFTEEN

THE CALL

SOPHIA

SOPHIA SAT IN TERRENCE'S RECLINER with her feet up as she flipped through a pregnancy magazine while Desiree watched a soap opera. Sophia had just flown back into town that morning. She missed Terrence and couldn't wait to see him when he got home from work. Her phone rang, and she grabbed it, sure it was Terrence asking about her flight. Instead, it was an unfamiliar number on the screen.

"Hello?" she answered.

"May I speak with Sophia Douglas?"

"Speaking. Who is this?"

"My name is Maxine Turner. I'm from the human resources department with Micro Analytics, a software company in Mountain View. I received your application for the director of sales position, and I'd like to know if you're available for an interview tomorrow."

Sophia was shocked into silence. It'd been so long since she'd gotten a response from the plethora of jobs she'd been applying to.

"Ms. Douglas? Hello? Ms. Douglas?"

Sophia sat up straight in the chair. "Yes, yes. I'm here."

"Are you still interested?"

Of course she was still interested. "Yes. Definitely. I would appreciate that greatly," Sophia said.

"I'll email you the interview information. Looking forward to meeting you."

Sophia hung up the phone. *Did that just happen?*

"Everything all right?" Desiree asked.

Sophia nodded.

"Why are you smiling like that?"

Sophia didn't know she was smiling. "That was a call about a sales position. I have an interview."

"Cool. But who's gonna hire you when you're almost six months pregnant?"

"I can suck my stomach in," Sophia joked. "I'm going to call Terrence and tell him."

There was a knock on the front door.

"Are you expecting anyone?" Sophia asked.

"Nope. Unless it's Prince Charming with my missing slipper."

Desiree didn't attempt to move, so Sophia rose then opened the front door.

Chelsea, Michelle, and Teeni stormed into the house before Josh.

"Where's Terrence?" Michelle asked Sophia.

"Te-wence," Teeni yelled.

Sophia hated to disappoint the girls. "Sorry, girls. He's not here."

"Aw," Michelle and Teeni whined in unison.

Sophia gave Josh a hug. "I hope my baby likes me more than your girls do."

"They like you," Josh said.

But when Sophia looked at the girls, they were shaking their heads.

"Stop it, girls," Josh said. "Sophia, can we talk for a second... alone?"

"Of course. Desiree, can you watch them?"

Desiree shrugged, and the three girls walked into the living room cautiously then sat themselves as far away from Desiree as possible.

Sophia and Josh headed to the kitchen. "What's up, Josh?"

"I feel like something is going on with Tara. I'm worried about her, but if I say anything, she flips out. I know you're busy with everything going on, but I was wondering if you could just kind of, you know, check on her. I've asked Terrence about it, but he claims not to know anything."

"Of course. I'll call her right after you leave."

"That would be great. Michelle has a dentist appointment, so we have to jet. Girls?" Josh called. "Time to go."

After Josh and the girls left, Sophia made herself some tea then called Tara. The call went to voicemail, so Sophia left her a message. Hopefully Tara was okay, because the last thing Sophia needed was more drama.

⚬⚬⚬

TARA

Tara's phone rang, but she didn't move from Miriam's dining table to answer it. She'd called in earlier to tell Peter she was taking a sick day, and though he was irritated because the Drymeir trial was starting next week and they weren't close to ready, there wasn't much he could say. She had no desire to answer the phone or speak to anyone.

Once Tara had explained that she was experiencing an emotional and spiritual emergency, Miriam asked her to come to her house so they could work more intensely without the interruption of Meta Waves's flow of traffic. Of course it would cost more, but Tara was willing to pay a fortune to put the scattered pieces of her life back in some semblance of order.

Miriam's house was just how Tara imagined it would be: blue front door to welcome visitors; beads hanging in doorways instead of doors; books, statues, candles, and various knickknacks spilling out from every corner. Miriam handed Tara a cup of steaming hot green tea.

Taking a seat in a chair opposite Tara, Miriam placed a huge brown book on the table and thumbed through it. "To start, let me say it will get better. I promise you that. I've been thinking about how to move you forward, and I decided you need to get in touch with your spirit animal."

Tara furrowed her brows. "My what?" Tara had heard the term before, but never knew exactly what it meant.

"Your spirit animal. It will help guide you through this tumultuous path. I'm going to hypnotize you, then you'll tell me what your spirit animal is."

"Okay."

Tara stared at Miriam swinging a pendulum in front of Tara's eyes. She breathed in raspberry incense, listening to the melodic words flowing from Miriam's mouth, peaceful like a babbling brook. Tara didn't know

183

the last time she had slept through the night. She drifted further and further from consciousness. She descended the wooden basement stairs one by one.

"Tara, no!" her mother's voice screamed.

Tara jumped and opened her eyes.

Miriam patted Tara's hand. "It's okay, Tara. You're safe."

"I'm not safe."

Miriam pointed at a page. "Raven. You said your spirit animal is a raven."

"So what do I do now?"

"Nothing. Your spirit animal will soar into your life when you are ready."

"I mean about my life. How do I go on?" Tears formed in Tara's eyes.

"Fate made its choice for you—Josh. Go home to your husband." Miriam closed the book and handed it to Tara. "Here, take this. Read more about the raven. You'll find strength and comfort."

"Thank you," Tara said. This was the right path for her, Josh, and the girls.

"I have to get back to the shop."

Tara wrote Miriam a check. "Thank you for everything."

Once inside her car, her phone rang again. Relief swept over Tara when Sophia's number appeared. She'd been so preoccupied with her own drama that she hadn't spoken to Sophia since the Super Bowl party. The last thing she wanted was for Sophia to find out about the affair, especially after what Sophia's dad had done to Sophia and her mom.

"Hi, Sophia."

"Tara, hi. I'm glad I got a hold of you. I tried calling you at the office, but the receptionist said you were out sick."

"Oh, yes. I'm just feeling a little... tired."

"Really? I didn't see your car at home."

"No offense, but you're sounding like Josh with all these questions."

Sophia laughed. "I'm sorry. Let me back up. I miss you, and soooo much happened in LA. Are you free to meet up for an early dinner?"

Tara looked at her watch. She couldn't believe the day had gone by so fast. If she went home now, she would have to tell Josh she took the day off, which would only lead to more questions. "Sure. Where would you like to meet?"

"That little Chinese restaurant around the corner?"

Her stomach grumbled. She'd barely eaten over the past week. "Sure. See you there in fifteen minutes."

As Tara drove to the restaurant, Miriam's words played through her mind. *Fate made its choice for you—Josh.* She felt as if a light switch had been turned on, illuminating Josh's inner being. He was a good man, a loving husband, and a doting father. Shame washed over her because of her betrayal. She'd never find another man who could live up to Josh. She just needed to figure out how to get their marriage back on track.

Tara opened the door to the tiny Chinese restaurant. It was dim inside, the only light came from hanging Chinese lanterns around the room.

"One?" a petite Chinese lady asked, her pointer finger in the air.

"Two actually. My friend's on the way."

The lady grabbed two menus. "Follow me."

When Tara was seated, she asked the lady to light the candle on the table and opened the book Miriam had given her. The lady returned with tea and a lighter. Tara placed the candle near the book and tried to read, but the words seemed to blur.

"Tara?"

Tara startled.

"What are you reading so intently?" Sophia asked.

Tara stood and gave her a hug. "It's a book my friend let me borrow."

Sophia peered into her eyes. "Have you been crying? And is that a bruise on your cheek?"

Tara smoothed her hair down, feeling self-conscious. "No, I'm just tired."

Sophia sat. "So what's new?"

"I feel like a door to a different realm has been opened for me. Right now I'm reading about my spirit animal. You probably don't know what that is, but it's okay. You don't really need to know, you just need to be open," Tara said in one breath.

"Where'd you say you got that book?" Sophia's eyes narrowed skeptically.

"My friend Miriam, who works at this bookstore Meta Waves in Mountain View, loaned it to me."

"Oh, I've never heard you mention Miriam before. What does she do there?"

"She does a lot of things. But for me, she has opened my eyes to a new existence." Tara would have to buy Miriam a present for saving her marriage.

"Has Josh met her? She sounds... interesting."

"Not yet. He doesn't get the whole psychic thing."

Sophia's eyes grew large. "She's a psychic?"

"Yes, so Josh thinks she's a quack." If only Josh understood how much Miriam really knew.

"How are things with you and Josh? Are you telling him all this stuff?"

Tara peered into Sophia's eyes. "It's not stuff. It's truth. I've been awakened to the truth. And Josh will be also."

"What is your truth?"

A long, loud laugh escaped Tara. "My truth is that being with Josh is my path. I've taken him for granted, but those days are over."

"What do you mean 'being with Josh?' He's your husband. When'd you stop being with him?"

Tara yawned. Fatigue overwhelmed her. "You don't get it either."

Sophia leaned toward Tara. "I'm trying to understand, but—"

"This baby of yours is a blessing." Tara gestured to Sophia's stomach. "Your path is Terrence. My path is Josh, not—"

"Not who?" Sophia sat back, looking concerned.

Tara dismissed the comment with a wave. "Never mind. How was LA?"

Sophia opened her mouth as though she wanted to say something, then she seemed to change her mind. "It was crazy. Terrence had the nerve to arrange a dinner with my dad!"

"My dad?" Tara shot up. "He's dead!"

"No." Sophia stood, reaching out to Tara. "My dad, Tara. Are you okay?"

Tara didn't feel okay. She felt as if she was losing control. Her

186

thoughts were jumbled and unclear. "I'm sorry, Sophia, I need to go home. I'm just not—I can't—"

"Now?" Sophia asked.

"There is only now, Sophia." Tara grabbed the book and ran out of the restaurant.

JOSH

"Sophia, hi," Josh said into the phone.

"You're right. Something is off with Tara," Sophia said.

Josh hurried to his room and shut the door. "What happened?"

"It was kind of hard to follow since she was talking a mile a minute. But she was talking about a spirit pet or something and a psychic, and she just wasn't herself. She didn't even look like herself. Then she jumped up and ran out of the restaurant saying she was heading home."

"Oh, did you stop by her work?"

"No, we met for Chinese since she took the day off."

"Took the day off? She disappeared this morning because she needed to be at work early," he said.

"I don't know what's going on, okay? But like you, I'm worried."

"I think I need to have a serious talk with Tara. I'm going to drop the kids off at my parents' place and then figure this whole thing out."

When Josh returned home, he parked in the driveway next to Tara's car. He sat in the dark for a few minutes. He had dropped the girls off with his parents for the night but didn't head straight home. Instead, he'd made a detour to The Spot, where he'd had a few drinks to relax and figure out his strategy. It was almost nine now, so he had to go inside. Ready or not, he needed to confront Tara.

The door creaked open. Josh took a deep breath then went to the living room.

Tara looked up from her book. "Where have you been? Where are the girls? I've been worried, and you didn't answer my calls."

Josh tried not to laugh at the irony. "They're at my parents'."

"Why are they there?"

"Because we need to talk," Josh said.

Tara closed the book. "We do need to talk. There's something I need to tell you."

Josh sat next to Tara. *Finally.* He didn't know what the truth was, but he was ready for it.

Tara drew a deep breath then exhaled. "Josh, I've known you since I was fifteen. I married you when I was twenty. We have three beautiful girls together. But what you don't know is that when you got hurt, I was so scared that I would lose you. I didn't know how to handle that feeling. So I put up a wall between us, so if I did lose you, it wouldn't hurt as much. I could only do that by making you the bad guy. I told myself that you were unmotivated and lazy, and that made me resent you. But it's not true. You work as much raising the girls as you did in construction, maybe even more so. I love that you're man enough to not care what anyone thinks about you being a stay-at-home dad. I'm just telling you that I love you. I want us to start fresh."

Josh couldn't form words. His wife was back. "Tara, we need to—"

Tara kissed Josh.

He pulled away. "Talk. We need to talk."

"I could say how sorry I am, or I could show you. I prefer the latter." Tara kissed him again.

This time he kissed her back. A lot needed to be said. He needed answers. He needed clarity. But in that moment, he just needed his wife. To smell her, feel her, taste her. It had been too long. He stood and picked up Tara.

She let out a little scream. "Your back, Josh."

"I'm fine." He carried her to their bedroom, kicking open the door, then laid her on their bed.

She turned over so he could unzip her dress, then he pulled it over her head. She fumbled with his belt before taking it off.

He stared into Tara's eyes. "I love you so much."

She peered into his. "I love you too, Louis."

Josh froze. "What?"

"What?"

"Who the hell is Louis?" Josh yelled, pulling away from her.

Tara's cheeks flushed. "What?"

He rose from the bed. "You just called me Louis."

Tara sat up and ran her hands through her hair. "Josh, no, I, uh…"

He'd hoped and prayed his suspicions were wrong, but they hadn't been. He'd been right the whole time. "You're having an affair!"

Tara jumped off the bed and reached for Josh's arm. "Josh, please. It's over."

"It? Tara. It?" His body burned. "You were cheating on me and lied to my face."

"Josh, I love you."

"Love?" he screamed. "You've been fucking someone else, and you have the nerve to say you love me?"

"Josh, please—"

"Please what?" he screamed even louder.

Tara walked toward him. "Let me explain—"

Josh's head spun. Red flashes blurred his vision. He stumbled toward the door and flung it open. "Get out!"

Tara put her hand on his shoulder. He grabbed her hand and pushed her against the wall.

"Don't you ever touch me again! Now get your shit and go!"

Tara collapsed on the floor. "Josh…"

Josh couldn't stand the sight of her nearly naked body. Another man had seen it. He couldn't believe she had done it. He went to her dresser and threw articles of clothing at her. "Get off the floor and get out!"

Tara didn't move.

"I said get out!" he screamed.

She scrambled to her feet, threw a dress over her head, then ran out.

Josh's blood pumped through his body. He slammed his fist against his head as he paced. Someone had to pay for this. Josh punched the wall.

"Shit!" he screamed as his knuckles cracked. He winced and pulled his hand back, blood dripping from his hand. He wasn't going to be the only one hurting. He had to find this Louis guy.

He stormed out of the room, determined to find Tara and demand to know Louis's whereabouts. Where he worked. Where the hell he could be found. But when Josh got to the front door, Tara's taillights were disappearing down the street.

Josh ran next door and banged on the door. "Terrence!"

A minute later, the door opened.

"Josh, what's going on?" Terrence asked.

"You knew, didn't you?"

Terrence put up his hands. "Josh, man, calm down."

"Calm down? You have the nerve to tell me to calm down? You're supposed to be my friend!"

Sophia appeared in the doorway. "What's going on? Josh, you're bleeding!"

"Tell her, Terrence. Tell her you knew my wife was having an affair. Tell her you lied to my face. Tell her you hid it from me."

Sophia frowned at Terrence. "You're having an affair with Tara?"

"No, I'm not. Tara's having an affair with some guy."

Sophia lowered her voice. "How do you know?"

Terrence hung his head. "I saw Tara with him in Las Vegas." He looked at Josh, his eyes pleading for him to understand. "I wanted to tell you. I almost did. But I didn't want you to be hurt."

"You didn't want me to be hurt? Tara tore out my heart, and you just stomped all over it!"

Sophia reached toward Josh. "Josh, come in. Let's talk about—"

"Tell me who he is! Where is he?" Josh said.

Terrence reached toward Josh, but Josh pulled back. "I don't know. I'm so sorry, man, but—"

Josh glared at Terrence. "Save it."

He turned his back and ran back to his house. Josh didn't know how, but he'd make sure Tara and that Louis bastard paid for what they'd done.

CHAPTER SIXTEEN

LOSING IT

TARA

Darkness surrounded Tara as she pounded on Miriam's door. Miriam was the only person who knew the whole truth, and the only person who could help her now.

"Miriam," she called as she beat her fist against the door. "Miriam!"

The door opened. "Tara, my god, what happened?"

"Josh found out about Louis."

Miriam looked at her watch. "Tara, these are not my working hours..."

"Did you hear what I said?" Tara asked frantically. "Josh found out about Louis. I'll pay whatever you want. I don't have anywhere else to go."

Miriam stepped aside. "Come in. Let me make you some tea."

Tara followed Miriam into the kitchen and lowered herself onto the chair at the table. "You said fate was choosing Josh to be with me. After this, he'll probably never want to speak to me again!"

Miriam stared at the kettle, as if willing the water to boil.

"Miriam, I can't lose him!"

Miriam shot a look at Tara filled with contempt. "Were you thinking about that when you were with Louis?"

"Yes. I mean, no. I mean, what does that have to do with anything?"

"You're acting like the victim when your actions got you into this situation. Did you think you could simply have an affair without any repercussions?"

Tara folded her arms on the table and lowered her head. Her stomach was tied in knots. "Can't you just make everything un-happen? Can you help me get my life back?"

Miriam spread out her arms. "Tara, what do you think I am? I'm sorry, but I can't fix this. You wanted Louis; now you say you want Josh. I think you need to take a step back and get in touch with yourself. Figure out what is best for you and your daughters."

Tara shot up and backed away from the table. "Oh my god, the girls. I didn't even think... I need to get them. Before Josh starts telling them horrible things about me. I need to explain that I'm not a bad person. They need to know I wouldn't choose a man over them. They need to know they didn't kill him by leaving. It wasn't their fault, and—"

Miriam slapped Tara on the cheek Louis's wife had slapped the night before. Tara put her hand to the burning skin.

"Tara, you're hysterical. You can't see your girls like this. What you need is sleep. I can give you something to help you relax." Miriam pulled Tara's arm and led her to the living room. "Sit down. I'll be right back."

Miriam returned shortly with tea and a handful of white pellets. "Take these and drink the tea. You'll feel better in the morning—and we can discuss payment then."

Tara put the pellets in her mouth and drank the tea. She did need sleep. But even if she did, her life would still be a nightmare in the morning. Within minutes, her eyelids grew heavy. She leaned against the couch cushions, losing her battle against consciousness.

"*Mommy!*" a voice screamed.

Tara sat up.

"*Mommy, help!*" the voice screamed again.

Tara shot up. She needed guidance and ran to Miriam's bookshelf. Pulling out a book titled *Spiritual Warfare*, she opened it to the table of contents then chose a chapter titled, "Protecting Your Children."

As Tara read, everything made sense. She'd been confused, but it wasn't about her or Josh or even Louis. It was about her father's evil spirit. He had terrorized her when he was alive and she was a child, and now he was coming after her girls.

SOPHIA

"I'm so worried about Tara," Sophia said as she propped herself up on her elbow in bed. She rubbed her belly, the baby kicking fiercely.

Terrence adjusted his tie. "Tara? What about Josh? God, I feel awful."

"Her phone is going straight to voicemail, and I really want to make sure she's okay."

"Give me one reason why you should care about how she's doing."

Sophia held up three fingers. "Chelsea, Michelle, and Christine. They need their mom."

Terrence scoffed. "Maybe Tara should have thought about that before she started messing around behind Josh's back."

"But Terrence, you can't want me to forgive my dad after he cheated on my mom and left us for another woman, then turn around and bash Tara for doing the same thing," Sophia said.

Terrence sat on the bed. "I didn't want you to forgive your dad and act like nothing ever happened. But I did want to give you the opportunity to hear him out. Don't you think he's paid for what he's done?"

Sophia shrugged. "I don't know."

"Baby, I gotta get to the office. I love you. Good luck on your interview." Terrence leaned in for a kiss.

Sophia dodged his lips and pecked his cheek. He wasn't completely off the hook.

Terrence pulled up her shirt and kissed her stomach. "He wants my kisses," he teased.

After Terrence left, Sophia dialed Tara again, but it went to voicemail. She was utterly disappointed in Tara, but Sophia's love for her wasn't diminished. Then it dawned on her—she wasn't about to de-friend Tara because she'd cheated on Josh, but Sophia had practically disowned her father because of his indiscretion.

It was all too confusing. She still had her interview that afternoon and she needed to prepare, but she had to make sure Tara was all right first. Sophia dialed Tara's number one more time. After getting voicemail again, Sophia decided to get out of bed. She had to find her friend.

Sophia stepped off the elevator, and Corinne, who was usually all smiles, looked concerned.

Sophia smiled anyways. "Hi, Corinne. Is Tara here?"

Corinne looked around the lobby. "Yes."

"Well... can you buzz her and let her know I'm here?"

Corinne picked up the phone, said a few words, then put it down. Seconds later, Mariana hurried down the hall. She looked as if she had seen a ghost.

"Sophia, how'd you know that something's wrong with Tara?" Mariana said.

Sophia put her hand to her stomach, as if to protect the baby. "What do you mean?"

"She got to the office and looked like an absolute mess. Corinne and I asked her what was wrong, and she started mumbling about spirits and Josh and"—she lowered her voice—"some guy named Louis. We were just trying to talk some sense into her when she started screaming that we were all after her and locked herself in her office."

Sophia followed Mariana to Tara's office. A small crowd had gathered at the cubicle adjacent to it. Sophia couldn't hear any noise coming from Tara's office, so she tried the door handle and found it locked.

Mariana knocked on the door. "Tara, Sophia's here."

No answer.

Sophia knocked. "Tara, it's me. Can we talk for a moment?"

The door creaked open. "Just you," Tara said.

Incense wafted through the door as Sophia slipped in. She gasped. *What on earth?* A few candles flickered on the desk, wax carelessly accumulating beneath them. With a black Sharpie, Tara filled in what looked like a huge black bird on her forearm.

"Tara, what is that? What's going on?" Sophia asked, barely able to hear her words as her heartbeat pounded in her ears.

Tara wouldn't take her eyes off her arm. "It's a raven. I'm preparing," she said in an ominous tone.

"For what?" The look in Tara's eyes made Sophia want to run.

"There's a battle going on for my girls," Tara whispered. "I need to prepare to bring them into the light."

"What battle? You aren't making sense."

"I didn't expect you to get it! I'm the only one who can save them!" Tara threw down the Sharpie and grabbed her purse. "I need to fight this battle on my own."

She stormed out of the office. Sophia followed her, but with her pregnant belly, she couldn't move fast enough to keep up. When she did get downstairs, Tara's car peeled out of the parking garage.

Sophia pulled out her phone to call the police, but she didn't know where the girls' schools were or where Tara would go first. She called Josh, but he didn't answer. "Josh, Tara completely flipped out. I'm at her work. I think you should make sure the girls are okay. Call me when you get this."

Sophia dialed Terrence, and he answered immediately. "Terrence, I'm at Tara's work. She's completely flipped out, talking about a battle and the girls, and I don't know what to do next."

"Damn it, that doesn't sound good," Terrence said. "She probably just needs to talk to someone, like a professional."

"I think it's beyond talking to someone at this point. I don't know what to do."

"Maybe... no, never mind."

"What? I'll do anything," Sophia said.

"I was thinking maybe your dad knows a place that can help. He has connections all over the country."

"Oh. Hmm. Well, I guess I could call him now." She hung up with Terrence and dug her father's card out of her purse. Sophia swallowed her pride and slowly dialed the number. The phone rang, then he answered. "Dad, I need your help."

JOSH

Josh's head pounded. After searching all of Tara's stuff for some clue as to Louis's location, he'd given up. In his anger the night before, he'd ripped apart Tara's witch book, then he'd gotten drunk on a six-pack of Heineken and half a bottle of vodka before passing out on the couch.

He took out his phone and called his mom. "I'm outside. Can you just send out the girls?"

"Sure, Joshie, but is everything all right?"

"No, it's not. But right now I need to get the girls to school." Josh put on his sunglasses, silently cursing the bright sun.

Instead of the girls, Mom appeared at the door. "What on earth is going on?"

Josh waved dismissively. "I don't want to talk about it."

"You look terrible. Come inside. I'll take the girls to school while you relax."

"I'm fine, Mom," Josh said, shaking his head.

"No, you aren't, and I don't want the girls to see you so stressed. Now park, and once I'm gone, I want you to go inside the house."

Josh's head hurt too much for him to keep arguing. "Fine."

Once his mother and daughters had driven away, Josh went into his parents' house and sat on the couch. Though he turned on the television and put the volume up as high as it could go, all he heard were Tara's words—"I love you too, Louis." The noise mixed with the hangover gave him a piercing headache, but even that felt better than his heartbreak.

When his mother returned twenty minutes later with a clearly worried Teeni, Josh was drinking his third beer.

His mom shot him a disapproving look. "Joshie, get up and come with me. I'm going to turn down the TV and put on a show for Teeni."

Josh followed his mom to the guest room.

She closed the door behind them. "What happened?"

There was no point in mincing words, so Josh said, "Tara's been cheating on me."

His mom's jaw dropped. She covered her mouth with her hands. Josh's phone rang, and he looked at it.

"Is that her?" his mom asked.

"No, it's Sophia." Josh turned off his phone. "I lost it last night after I found out, and I went over to her house to confront Terrence. He knew about it and kept it from me. What the hell are friends for if they can't tell you something like that?"

"I know you're angry, but I'm sure he was doing what he thought was best."

"No, there's no excuse for him lying to me. I just can't believe

Tara would do this. We've been married for ten years. We have three daughters. What was she thinking?"

"I don't know, Joshie."

"Terrence saw them in Vegas. That was weeks ago. God knows how long she's been lying to me and sneaking around behind my back."

His mom fluffed the pillow. "I'm so sorry, but you have three daughters to take care of. You need to sober up and rest a little. I'll watch Teeni. You get some sleep."

Josh kicked off his shoes and lay on the bed.

━━━━◆◇◆━━━━

TARA

"*Tara.*"

Tara shook her head, trying to rid herself of the voice. She jogged through the parking lot of Chelsea's elementary school, hoping she wasn't too late. Her daughters were in danger.

She rang the metal bell on the desk. A second later, she rang it again.

The school secretary came to the front counter. "Mrs. Fisher, is everything all right?"

"*No.*"

"I'm fine. It's just that Chelsea… she has a doctor's appointment. I need to take her."

"I'll call for her now."

Tara paced the office.

"*Tara.*"

Tara jumped and looked around. No one was there.

Minutes later, Chelsea entered the office. "Hi, Mommy."

Tara swept Chelsea into her arms. "Oh, sweet cakes! Are you okay?"

"Yeah…"

"Good. Good. We need to go now," Tara said.

"Am I getting a shot?" Chelsea asked.

"No, why'd you ask that?"

Chelsea shrugged. "Then why am I going to the doctor? I'm not sick."

"Shh, shh, let's just go." Tara placed her hand on the small of Chelsea's back, leading her out of the office.

When they reached the car, Chelsea asked, "Is something going on, Mommy?"

Tara opened the back door. "Just get in the car."

Chelsea hesitated then climbed into the backseat.

"Put your seatbelt on. You need to be safe."

Tara clenched the wheel and sped to Michelle's preschool. She parked and jumped out of the car.

Chelsea slowly got out of the car with fear in her eyes. "Mommy, what's wrong?"

Tara was growing impatient with all of Chelsea's questions. "What do you mean?"

"We spent the night at Grandma and Grandpa's, and then you pick me up and say I'm going to the doctor's, but we're at Michelle's school."

Tara bent down and looked Chelsea in the eyes. "I can't explain right now. We need to make sure your sisters are safe."

"Safe? Daddy can help. Can we call him?"

"No! Let's just go get Michelle." Tara pulled Chelsea inside the preschool, and she only relaxed when she spotted Michelle coloring. "Michelle, time to go."

Michelle skipped toward Tara. "Hi, Mommy."

A lady wearing a blue smock approached Tara. "Can I help you?"

"Yes, I'm picking up Michelle early today. I'm her mother."

The lady looked at her watch. "Wow, you are early!"

"I'm her mother. I can pick her up whenever I like. Do you have a problem?" Tara snapped.

"No. Is everything all right though?" she asked.

"Fine." Tara grabbed Chelsea and Michelle's arms. Practically dragging the girls, she hurried out to the car.

Shifting into reverse, Tara checked her rearview mirror. Her dad's face stared back at her. She jumped and turned around.

Chelsea and Michelle looked at her.

"Are you okay, Mommy?" Chelsea asked.

"*Tara*," the voice said.

"Mommy?"

"*Tara.*"

Tara placed her hands over her ears. "I just need to get Teeni!"

She closed her eyes. An image of a wooden chair sideways on the ground and a pair of legs dangling a few feet above it flashed before her.

Tara opened her eyes, trying not to glance in the rearview at the girls' worried faces. She slammed on the gas. When she pulled into her driveway, she didn't understand why Josh's car wasn't there. Tara sprinted into the house, the girls following her.

"Teeni?" she screamed. She ran from room to room, but Teeni wasn't there.

She sat on the couch and noticed crumpled sheets of paper all over the coffee table and carpet. She picked up a balled paper, smoothed it out, and discovered it was a page from Miriam's book about spiritual warfare. Suddenly it clicked—her dad's spirit was sabotaging her.

She read the page in her hands. "Evil hovers in the dark, the enemy of light. Fire brings darkness to the light, the perfect purification."

She needed to purify the house.

She rushed to the bedroom. Stepping over the mess of clothes on the floor, she rummaged through her clothes in the closet. Finally she found the brown paper bag from Meta Waves. She ran back to the living room. With one fell swoop, she swept everything off the coffee table onto the floor. Turning the bag upside down, she spilled candles, matches, and an array of charms and healing elements onto the coffee table. One by one, she lit the candles.

A hand patted her shoulder, and she jumped.

"Mommy?" Chelsea said. "What are you doing?"

"I'm making everything safe for us, honey."

"*You'll never be safe,*" his voice said.

It wasn't enough. She needed a bigger purification. Tara ran to the glass door that led to the backyard. At the barbeque grill on the deck, she picked up the lighter fluid and charcoal. She needed something, anything that would burn. She placed the wood deck chairs in a circle, doused them with lighter fluid, and struck a match. She was going to win this battle even if she had to walk through fire to do it.

CHAPTER SEVENTEEN

GOING DOWN

Sophia

Sophia slammed the car door and hurried into Meta Waves. A bell jingled above the door.

"Blessings," a girl at the counter said.

"Is Miriam here?" Sophia asked.

"Yes, she's in her office. I can take you there."

"Please."

Sophia trailed the girl though the store. Though she had ventured through stores like this for fun or souvenirs, it concerned her that Tara seemed to be coming here for guidance.

The girl opened a door in the back. A lady, presumably Miriam, in a purple dress and wearing a crystal necklace sat on a low stool. She gestured for Sophia to come into her office. Sophia coughed as she inhaled the incense in the room.

Miriam narrowed her eyes at Sophia, her expression serious. "I can tell you are stuck between two paths. Would you like a reading?"

"No, I'm looking for my friend Tara."

Miriam's eyes widened. "She's not here."

Sophia wasn't sure why, but she sensed animosity. "Well, I'm really worried about her, and I know she's been seeing you."

"That woman has problems I want no part of." Miriam opened a drawer, pulled out a pad, and wrote on it. "Here, give this to her. I have work to do. So please...?" Miriam stood.

Sophia looked at the paper—a bill for services rendered. She glared at Miriam then rushed out of the office, through the store, and back to her car.

She called her dad again. "She wasn't there. I don't know what else to do."

"You can only do so much. Why don't you go home? She might show up there," her dad said.

"I'm scared for her."

"If it is as bad as it sounds, she might need to be hospitalized. Even if she doesn't need that, she does need help."

Sophia hated that things had come to this. "Yeah, I just don't know how to find her to get her help."

"Believe me, what you've described will be pretty obvious to others as well. I'm just worried about the possibility of her kids being involved. I'd like to drive up there."

"I couldn't ask you to do that." Not only was it a long way for her dad to come, but Sophia wasn't sure she wanted to see him.

"You aren't asking. I'm offering. I know I haven't been there for you in the past, but I want to start. I'd like to help your friend, Sophia. This sounds serious."

She sighed. "Okay."

"Okay. I'll hit the road soon and call you when I'm close. One more thing—if you need to, call 9-1-1. Keep everyone's safety in mind, especially yours and your baby's."

When Sophia got home, she was relieved to see Tara's car in the driveway. But her relief turned to worry when she opened her car door. The smell of smoke filled the air. It wasn't incense. It smelled like a campfire.

She covered her mouth with her arm, sure the smell wasn't good for the baby. She dashed to Tara's house. When she got near the door, someone screamed from inside. Banging on the door, she yelled Tara's name. There was no answer.

She ran to her house, following the scent. When she opened the gate to her backyard, the smell grew stronger. She looked over the fence. Huge orange flames engulfed a pile of wooden furniture in the middle of Tara's backyard, but there was no sign of Tara. Sophia ran inside her house and grabbed her landline phone.

"9-1-1. What's the emergency?" the operator asked.

"There's a fire in my neighbor's backyard. I think she's having a psychiatric emergency."

"We'll send help right over. I need to get some information from you."

Sophia gave the operator her name and address before hanging up. She knocked on Desiree's door then barged in.

Desiree looked up, wiping the sleep from her eyes. "What's wrong?"

"There's a fire in Tara's backyard. I don't know if it'll get out of control, but you should get up."

Desiree scurried out of bed. "What should we do?"

"I'm going over there."

"I'm coming with."

Sophia grabbed a cloth, wet it, then carried it with her. Back at Tara's, they banged on the door.

"Who is it?" a soft voice asked from inside.

Sophia and Desiree gasped, exchanging worried glances.

"It's Sophia. Open up."

"I can't open the door for strangers."

Sophia raised her voice. "Sweetie, I'm not a stranger. Now open up, please."

"Terrence said no."

"I know, but it's okay. Please!"

The door creaked open and smoke escaped the house, searching for freedom. Chelsea stood with her arm wrapped around Michelle, who was shaking, and tears lined both of their faces.

Sophia coughed and pulled the girls outside, hugging them. "Come talk with Desiree for a minute."

As Desiree led the girls to the sidewalk, Sophia hurried into the house. She covered her mouth and nose with the wet cloth and fanned the smoke away from her face with her free hand. The coffee table was covered with candles, so she drew a breath then blew as many out as she could. Movement in the backyard caught her eye. She went out and found Tara flinging clothes into a fire that was expanding by the minute.

"Tara, what on earth are you doing?" Sophia asked.

Tara turned around, a maniacal look on her face. "An evil spirit is attacking me and trying to get the girls. I must purify the house."

Sophia put her hand over her face. The heat from the fire stung her skin, and the black smoke made it hard for her to breathe. "Evil spirit? Tara—"

"Can't you hear them? They want me and the girls."

Sirens wailed in the distance.

"Calm down, okay? I'm just trying to help."

"I don't need help. Just leave!" Tara yelled.

The sirens grew louder.

"Come away from the fire. This is dangerous," Sophia said.

"You have no idea how dangerous this is. Our lives are at stake."

"Tara, your girls need you. Just come with me, please!"

A huge ember flew from the fire and landed on Tara. Her shirt caught fire. "He's got me. No!"

Sophia ran to the garden hose, turned it on, and doused Tara. Before she could turn the hose on the burning clothes and furniture, the sirens' blare grew so loud Sophia covered her ears and dropped the garden hose. Two firefighters charged into the backyard.

"Move back, move back," they instructed Tara and Sophia. "We need the hose."

Moments later, they returned dragging a huge hose and spewed water onto the fire. Five police officers surrounded Tara and Sophia.

Tara let out a bloodcurdling scream. "No, no, no, you're ruining everything. You're all evil! Get out of my house!" Tara charged at one of the police officers.

He grabbed her, twisting her arms behind her back, and put her facedown on the wooden deck.

"Don't hurt her! She needs psychiatric help!" Sophia said as the officer handcuffed Tara.

Another police officer pulled Tara to her feet.

Tara kicked violently. "Let go of me!" she screamed as they forced her through the house.

Sophia followed them to the front yard, where Desiree and the girls stood near the curb.

"Mommy! Mommy!" the girls cried.

As the policeman forced Tara into the back of a squad car, Sophia approached another officer. "Where are you taking her? What can I do to help?"

"I'm not sure exactly where they'll take her. It'll depend on the answers to a few questions. Are you all right? Do you need medical attention?"

She caressed her belly, thinking about all the smoke she'd inhaled. "I think I might. My head's feeling dizzy. Must be the smoke."

"The paramedics can take a look at you. They're on the way out here." The officer turned away and spoke into the walkie-talkie on his shoulder.

As the police car drove away, Sophia hoped they'd take Tara to a hospital and not jail. "Thank you."

⊷⊶⊷

JOSH

A loud knock woke Josh. He sat up and rubbed his eyes.

His mom popped her head in the room, her face twisted in worry. "Josh, get up, honey."

"What's wrong?" Josh asked.

"The preschool teacher just called me since I'm listed as an emergency contact and you weren't answering your phone. Tara went to the preschool and picked up Michelle. I don't know all the details, but they're concerned."

Josh stood and reached for his phone. He had eight missed calls and five text messages. Most of them were from Sophia, but the preschool's number was there too. He pressed the voicemail button, and the first was from Sophia.

"Josh, Tara completely flipped out," she said. "I'm at her work. I think you should make sure the girls are okay. Call me when you get this."

Josh's heart pounded. "Shit!"

"What is it?" his mom asked.

"Sophia left me a message earlier. She said Tara's completely flipped out."

"Call Sophia now."

Josh's hands trembled as he called Sophia. No answer. "Mom, I'm going home. Can you keep Teeni until I figure out what's going on?"

"Of course."

———————

Josh's stomach fell when he turned the corner onto his street. A fire truck, an ambulance, and three police cars were parked near his driveway. Yellow tape blocked off the entrance of his house. He parked and ran to the back of the ambulance, where Sophia sat, talking to two officers. Her face was as pale as if she'd seen a ghost.

"What happened? Where are Michelle and Chelsea?" he asked.

Sophia touched his arm. "Chelsea and Michelle are fine. They're at my place with Desiree."

Josh put his hands on his head. "Oh, thank God. What's going on?"

"Sir, do you live here?" the officer said.

"Yes. Yes, I do."

"What's your name?"

"Josh. Josh Fisher."

The officer wrote on his pad then looked up. "And what is your relationship to Tara Fisher?"

"She's my... wife." Josh looked around. "Where is she?"

"She's been detained."

"Why? What the hell is going on?"

"She set a fire in the backyard, and candles in the front room got out of control, so there was a small fire inside also," the officer said.

"But why?"

Sophia said, "Josh, we think she's having some type of psychiatric emergency."

"What does that mean?" Josh asked. "It's my fault. I should have been here."

Sophia put her hand on Josh's shoulder. "No, it's not your fault. But the girls are pretty shaken up. They've been asking for you."

Josh looked at the officer. "Can I go?"

"For now. We'll need to ask you some more questions later. The paramedics checked them out, but you should get them to the doctor's first thing tomorrow. They were inside for a while."

Josh ran to Sophia's house and found the girls sitting on the couch. Desiree was in Terrence's recliner, and Chelsea had her arm draped around Michelle's shoulder. A cartoon was on, but neither of the girls seemed to be watching it. Josh embraced his daughters.

"Did the police take Mommy to jail?" Michelle asked.

"Oh, no, sweetie. She wasn't feeling good, so they took her somewhere to get better."

"What's wrong with her?" Chelsea asked.

Josh wished he knew. But enough lies had been told. It was time for some truth. "I don't know, Chelsea. I just don't know."

CHAPTER EIGHTEEN

HOSPITAL

TARA

TARA TRIED TO SIT UP but couldn't. She squirmed, attempting to free her body. Thick brown leather straps tied her hands and ankles to the bed.

"*You failed. You're a failure,*" the voice said.

Tara shook her head. "No, no, no!"

The door swung open, and a man wearing blue scrubs ran toward her.

"Where am I?" Tara screamed. "I need to go! Help!"

The man lifted the hem of the white gown Tara wore and held out a needle.

"No, no, please," Tara pleaded.

The man inserted the tip of the needle into her thigh and depressed the plunger, then he left. A feeling like cool water flowed through her veins. She fought to stay awake, but her eyes closed.

A rustling noise woke Tara. She squinted, her eyes trying to adjust to the darkness. "Hello?"

A figure moved. "Hello, Tara."

How does this person know my name? "Where am I?"

The figure approached her. It was a heavyset African-American woman, her hair tied back in a braid. "You're at Silicon Valley Hospital."

"Why?" Tara asked.

"You can talk to your doctor later. She'll explain everything."

"Who are you? Where am I?"

"My name is Melissa. You're at Silicon Valley Hospital."

Though the woman had answered her questions, nothing made sense. "Why are you in here? What time is it?"

"I'm here to monitor you. It's three in the morning. Why don't you go back to sleep?"

"You don't need to monitor me," Tara said indignantly. "Where are my daughters?" The memory of terror in their eyes as she'd been forced into the police car created a huge ache in her heart. She had to see them and reassure them she was okay.

"I'm sure your daughters are fine. You need to rest."

Tara wiggled her wrists in the leather straps. "Can you take these off?"

"Only if you promise you won't hurt yourself."

"Why would I hurt myself?"

More movement, then a light pierced the darkness. Tara turned toward the light, and Melissa smiled as she walked toward Tara.

God, what is going on?

Melissa untied the restraint on Tara's right arm, then she went around the bed and untied the restraint on her left one. She did the same with the ankle restraints. Tara couldn't understand why they'd put the restraints on her in the first place. She had simply been trying to protect herself and her children.

"Try to get some rest," Melissa said.

The sun shone through the window, and Tara struggled to open her eyes. The room was completely empty save for the chair that Melissa sat on. *It wasn't a nightmare then.*

"Good morning," Melissa said. "How are you feeling?"

"I'm fine. I need to go home. I have work and my daughters. If I don't protect them, he'll get them!"

"Who is he, Tara?"

Tara didn't like Melissa's tone. "Never mind."

"It's eight forty-five, and breakfast is at nine. Why don't you try to get up?" Melissa rose from the chair.

Tara swung her legs to the left side of the bed. Her head felt as if it was swinging too. She put both feet on the ground and pushed off the bed with her right hand. Her legs felt as though they were filled with cement, so she reached for the bed again to steady herself. It took all her effort to walk the three feet to the bathroom.

Tara barely recognized her reflection. Her face was paper white; black bags sagged under her eyes. Her darker roots lined her tangled and oily hair. She didn't want to look at herself a moment longer.

"If you are feeling up to it, why don't we see about getting you breakfast?" Melissa said.

Tara needed to get to the bottom of what was going on. "I'm fine."

Tara and Melissa ventured into the hallway. At the end of the hall was a pay phone and a large window that overlooked the surrounding neighborhood.

A group of people of all ethnicities and ages were lined up at the opposite end of the hall. She padded toward them, but the weight of her body made her feel as if she were wading through water. At the other end of the hall was a large room with a television, tables, and chairs. A small glass window separated a nurses' station from the rest of the corridor. Tara looked around, trying to orient herself.

She tapped on the glass window at the nurses' station. "I was given a shot yesterday, and I feel terrible. When can I talk to the doctor?"

"Let me see your wrist," the nurse said.

Tara stuck out her left arm, surprised to see a wristband.

The nurse looked at it. "Your doctor is Dr. Phung."

"I need to see her now," Tara said.

"She'll be here between nine a.m. and four p.m."

"Between nine and four?" Tara asked, shocked. No one seemed to get it. "Look, I have to get to work. I have to make sure my daughters get to school. I cannot stay here. I need to talk to someone. I need to talk to someone now!"

She didn't add that she had to contact Josh. He no doubt hated her, but she'd force him to listen and she'd come clean about everything that had been happening with her dad's spirit. If she couldn't protect the girls, he had to.

"You need to calm down," the nurse said. "When the doctor gets here, you can talk to her then."

"What am I supposed to do now?" Tara asked.

The nurse rummaged through a few files then picked out one. "You're on the green sheet, so you have to eat your meal in the dayroom." The nurse pointed at the room with the television in it. "Eat something, relax, and wait."

Tara went to protest, but she barely had the energy to stand. She dragged her feet into the dayroom. A large white male wearing a hospital gown, a young Asian girl with her hair in pigtails, a forty-something Latino male with kneepads covering both knees, and a black woman with matted hair that looked like a beehive occupied the room. Tara didn't belong here. It was all a huge mistake.

Tara sat in a chair. A young man wearing a badge hanging from a string around his neck wheeled in a large metal cart carrying trays of food. He read names from a piece of paper on each tray. When he said Tara Fisher, she got up and took the tray he offered, but she had no desire to eat.

After opening the metal lid, she gagged from the smell of the reddish-brown mush with white lumps. She closed the lid and set the tray aside.

The man with the kneepads sat down next to Tara. "Yum, corned beef hash," he said before shoveling the mush from his tray into his mouth.

Tara threw the contents of her tray into the trash and placed the tray back on the metal cart.

"Finished already?" the cart attendant asked.

Tara didn't answer.

He flipped through papers on a clipboard then began writing. "I'm Matt, an MHT."

"What's that?" she asked.

"Mental health technician. I'm here to make sure everything goes well while you're here."

"Matt, I don't know where my kids are. I don't know why I'm in here."

"Just try to relax," Matt said.

That was enough. "Relax? Relax? How the hell am I supposed to

210

relax? I want to go home. I want to go home now!" Tara stormed out of the room.

She ran to the payphone at the end of the corridor then collapsed. She collected herself and picked up the phone. No dial tone. There was an exit door adjacent to the phone, so she pushed open the door, and alarms screeched. Tara covered her ears with her hands.

There was laughter, and his voice said, "*You'll never go home.*"

"No!" Tara screamed as she crouched in the corner.

Two men in white coats ran toward her.

"I just want to go home," she screamed as the men grabbed her arms and dragged her down the hall. "I just need to go home."

<hr/>

TERRENCE

"Would you like some tea?" Terrence asked Sophia.

"I'm fine."

Terrence placed his hands on her belly. Reassuring movement met his hands. He was relieved that in spite of all the craziness, the baby was okay. "You barely slept last night. Do you want to lie down for a little while?"

Sophia whispered, "I'm fine."

Terrence knew better.

Desiree pulled the handle on the recliner Sophia sat in. "At least put your feet up."

"It's Tara I'm worried about," Sophia said.

"I would be worried about her daughters. They must be freakin' traumatized," Desiree said.

Terrence nodded. "Yeah, they must be."

Sophia yawned. "I talked to Josh earlier. They're all staying at his parents' place. Just kind of unwinding."

Terrence winced when she said Josh's name. Josh wouldn't speak to Terrence even though Terrence had called him a dozen times. And Terrence couldn't blame him. Had it been a court of law, he would have been charged with aiding and abetting.

Desiree put her hands on her hips. "I've seen people trip out like that, like on acid or shrooms. But sometimes they don't come back."

"Let's not talk like that," Sophia said.

Darryl paced in their living room, his phone stuck to his ear. Under any other circumstance, having Sophia's father—the man she'd hated for the majority of her life—in their living room would have been strange. But since the world as Terrence knew it had turned upside down in the past twenty-four hours, anything seemed possible. Terrence was glad Darryl was there though, because Tara's breakdown was completely outside of Terrence's expertise. Darryl was friends with the psychiatrist at the hospital, and as Tara's next-of-kin, Josh had given the psychiatrist permission to discuss her condition with Darryl.

Darryl hung up and sat on the couch. "So it's not looking good."

"I knew it," Desiree said.

"Desiree, please," Sophia said. "What'd they say?"

"Basically what I expected. Based on the information you gave the police and the behavior Tara was exhibiting, her doctor believes Tara's experiencing psychosis," Darryl said.

"What does that mean?" Terrence asked as images of crazed killers came to mind.

"It means she's crazy," Desiree said.

Terrence was happy someone had said it and that he wasn't the only one thinking it.

"Desiree, it's not that simple." Darryl's tone was stern. "This is a serious medical condition."

"Well, what happened? What is psychosis?" Terrence asked.

"Psychosis is a break with reality. In that state, people can experience hallucinations, delusions, or catatonia, among other symptoms. It can happen when a person is under a lot of stress, isn't sleeping, or has taken some type of drug." Darryl looked at Sophia. "Does Tara take any drugs?"

"Who knows what she's been doing," Terrence said.

Sophia shot him an icy look. "Terrence, come on." Sophia said to Darryl, "No, I don't think so."

"Does she have a history of mental illness?" Darryl asked.

"I don't think so. She's never mentioned anything to me about it. When can I see her?"

"Whoa, whoa, whoa. Baby, you need to stay away from her. She damn near burned her house down, which could very well have burned our house down," Terrence said. "You put yourself and our little one in harm's way when you were trying to help her. Who knows what she'll do next?"

"Tara is one of my best friends. I'm not going to abandon her," Sophia said.

Terrence put his hand on Sophia's shoulder. "I'm not saying abandon—"

Sophia clasped Terrence's hands. "Then what are you saying? I just want to help, Terrence."

Terrence could appreciate Sophia trying to be a good friend, but his wife and baby took precedence.

"Visiting her is a terrible idea, Sophia," Desiree said.

"Terrence, Desiree, Tara shouldn't be looked down upon or ostracized. Like I said, this is a medical condition. She needs love and support just like anyone else would need if they were in a car accident or experienced some other tragic situation."

Sophia raised an eyebrow at Terrence.

Terrence tried to sound reasonable. "Love and support is one thing. Going to visit is something completely different. I don't want my wife or my baby anywhere around her."

"She just needs help. She's still Tara, and I know this must be horrible for her," Sophia said.

"Because I care for you and my baby's safety and well-being, I'm putting my foot down. No, I don't want you to go."

Sophia let go of Terrence's hand and struggled to her feet. Looking Terrence in the eye, she said, "You can't tell me what I can and can't do."

Darryl put his hands on Sophia's shoulders. "Sophia, why don't I go with you to the hospital? That way Terrence can rest assured that you and the baby will be fine."

"I think I can handle this," Sophia said bitterly.

"Please let him go with you," Terrence said.

"If it will make you feel better, then fine."

Sophia went to their bedroom.

Terrence followed her but paused at the door. She wouldn't listen to him anyways, so he went to the guest room they were changing into the nursery. They'd bought a dresser plus a chair for Sophia to sit in and nurse the baby, but they still had a lot more to buy.

He dialed Josh's number. Voicemail. "Damn it." He waited for the tone. "Hey, man. Just checking in. Look, I'm sorry. Hit me up when you get a chance. Later." He'd have to swing by Josh's parents' and have a face-to-face with him.

"Terrence?" Darryl called through the door. "Can I come in?"

"Sure." Terrence opened the door, offered Darryl the chair they'd bought for Sophia, and leaned against the wall.

Darryl sat. "This is going to be the baby's room?"

Terrence smiled. "Yeah. I can't wait to meet him or her. But Sophia and the baby could have really gotten hurt in the fire Tara set."

"I know. You must have been scared when you heard about what happened."

Terrence scoffed. "I'm not scared."

"No, of course not. But there are a lot of unknowns, and you're trying to protect Sophia. That's great. That's what makes you the husband you are."

At least someone understood him. "Then why can't Sophia see that?"

"She loves Tara. She's her friend. Over the decades I've been practicing psychiatry, I've seen that when a person has a mental breakdown, people around them can't cope. They disappear. And more than anything, they need the people they love in their life. They need their friends and family more than ever. I wouldn't put my daughter or grandbaby in harm's way. So trust me when I say that if Sophia visits Tara, she will be safe."

"Tara went straight-up crazy though."

Darryl shrugged. "It happens."

Terrence swallowed the lump in his throat. He cast his gaze down. "It's really my fault."

"Excuse me?" Darryl said.

"I knew Tara was having an affair. I saw her with the guy in Vegas. If I had just told Josh, none of this would have happened."

"This has nothing to do with you. A lot of different factors contribute to a psychotic episode."

"I feel so damn guilty. I let Josh down. And I can't feel bad for Tara. I get that she's Sophia's friend and Sophia wants to be there for her, but what was she thinking, cheating on Josh? Only idiots think they can have an affair without consequences."

Darryl looked away.

Damn. Terrence had put his foot in his mouth yet again. "I'm sorry, that didn't come out right."

"No, no, you're right. Adultery hurts everyone. I didn't expect to meet Laura and fall in love with her. But I'm sorry for all the hurt it caused everyone, especially Sophia. If I learned one thing, it's that your actions always catch up with you, one way or the other."

"Yeah, and that's why I feel so bad. Josh had the right to know."

"You did what you thought was right at the time. That's all you can ever do." Terrence shrugged. "I gotta get Josh to talk to me. I screwed up, but I gotta make it better." There was only one thing Josh wanted—to know the whereabouts of the man Tara had had the affair with. Terrence would have to figure it out and get the information to him.

JOSH

Josh stood in his parents' backyard, watching the colors in the sky change to a dark orange and purple as the sun set. A cold breeze rustled the leaves. The sound of footsteps made him turn. Hands in his pockets, Josh's dad walked toward him. Josh looked away. He didn't want to see that look on his dad's face. It was the same expression his dad had when Josh's dog had been killed by a car when Josh was ten.

"How are you, son?" his dad asked.

Josh shrugged. "I feel like I'm caught in one of those Lifetime movies Tara always used to watch. It's like, how can *this* be my life?"

"It's definitely different."

"My whole life came crashing down in one fell swoop. I don't know what I'm supposed to do now," Josh said.

"You just keep moving forward. This is a part of life. Tara's ill, but she'll get better."

Josh sucked in his breath. Sophia's dad had given him an update on Tara's condition, but it was still too hard to believe. Regardless of her health, she'd been lying and cheating for months. Nothing could make that hurt go away, and no one could make him feel sorry for her. "I don't give a damn about her getting better."

"You need to be focused on taking care of those girls. It's such a blessing that they're okay. You read in the newspaper from time to time about mothers with some type of sickness who end up harming their kids."

"You're right. They could have gotten hurt. I should've been there."

"But they weren't. Let's take things one day at a time. You can all stay here as long as you need to. You know, Mom and I fell on some pretty hard times ourselves."

Josh couldn't remember anything of this magnitude ever happening to them. "Oh, yeah?"

"You know, Mom doesn't like to talk about it, but we lost three babies before we had you. One was an early miscarriage, the second miscarried in the third trimester, and the third was stillborn. It just devastated us. Your mom wanted a baby more than anything else, and it just broke her heart to be so close and have that happen."

"I never knew that." Josh looked away when tears welled up in his dad's eyes.

"Like I said, Mom doesn't like talking about it. But after the stillbirth... well, your mom almost ended up in a place like Tara's in now."

The love Josh had for his daughters and how excited he and Tara had been during each pregnancy came to mind. "I can't even imagine."

"When we finally had you, it was like a miracle. Like God had opened up the heavens and handed us an angel. You were premature, so Mom was so scared that you weren't going to make it. She spoiled you rotten. But the point I'm trying to make is that you're going to get through this. Most people walking this earth have run into some type of tragedy and heartache. It's not what you're given that matters—it's the way you handle it."

"I have no idea how to handle it." Every moment was a battle against the emotions that threatened to overtake him. Josh had to fight for the sake of the girls.

"The answers will come. They will definitely come."

Josh loved and admired his dad, but in that moment, he didn't believe him.

His mom slid the glass door open. "Joshie, Terrence is here to talk to you."

Josh sucked in a breath. "Tell him to go home."

CHAPTER NINETEEN

VISITORS

TARA

TARA OPENED HER EYES WHEN keys jingled. Again, her wrists and ankles were in restraints. She lifted her head. Melissa's mouth was moving, but it was as if she were talking underwater and only bubbles were gurgling to the surface.

Melissa stood over Tara and spoke slowly. "Are you going to behave?"

"I'm... fine. I'll... be... fine," Tara managed to get out.

Melissa took her time untying the restraints, eyeing Tara suspiciously. Once they were off, Tara tried to sit up, but her head was spinning. She collapsed back down on the bed.

Melissa put her hand under Tara's back and helped her sit up. "It's the medication. You'll be a little slowed down, which is good. Try to stand."

Tara's eyelids hung low. She couldn't understand why the floor was moving. *Is this another trick they're pulling on me?*

Melissa moved Tara's legs so they hung over the side of the bed. Then she pulled Tara onto her feet. Tara stood momentarily then fell.

"Looks like that won't work. So plan B then." Melissa went out the door then came back with a wheelchair. "It's visiting time. All visitors are out in the hall."

Melissa hefted Tara onto the chair. Tara gripped the armrests as Melissa wheeled her out of the room. Tara closed her eyes, shielding them from the fluorescent lights.

"Tara," a voice said. "Tara?" But that time, it sounded different.

She opened her eyes. Sophia and a tall black man stood in front of her. *I must be dreaming.*

"What's wrong with her, Dad?" Sophia asked.

"It's just the medication. Tara, my name is Darryl. I'm Sophia's dad and a doctor. Can you open your eyes and focus on me?"

Tara opened her eyes. *Sophia hates her dad. It's a trick.* She shut her eyes tightly.

"Please, Tara. Open your eyes," Sophia said.

Tara struggled to open them again.

"That's it. Now just focus on me," the man said.

Tara's eyelids wanted to close, but she needed to get to the bottom of what was going on. She strained to keep them open. "Are you... real?"

"Yes, I'm real. So is Sophia. You're in the psychiatric ward at a hospital. They gave you medication, so things might seem a little confusing."

"Why... am I here?"

"You had a break with reality. Do you remember what happened yesterday?"

Tara closed her eyes. The burning heat from the fire, the smoke in her nose, and her fearful girls came to mind. "I remember... trying to purify everything. I failed. My girls... they're in danger."

A hand touched Tara's. "The girls are fine. They're with Josh," Sophia said.

"But he can't make my father's spirit go away. He'll go after them, like he went... after my mom and me. Ask Miriam. She'll... tell you."

"This may seem confusing," the man said. "But I want you to know that we're here for you."

"I just... want to go home. Can you take me... home?" Tara asked, unsure where home would be. Josh probably wouldn't allow her in their house.

"They placed you on a fifty-one-fifty hold, which means you can't leave right now. You need to stay here for at least seventy-two hours."

Tara covered her face with her hands. "I can't... do this."

"Tara?" Sophia said. "I'm your friend, and I'll always be here for you. We'll figure all this out together."

Tara closed her eyes. It was all too much.

When Tara opened her eyes, light streamed through the window. "Hello? Where am I?"

"You are still at Silicon Valley Hospital."

"Who are you?"

"Melissa."

"Don't you ever go home?"

Melissa laughed. "You must be feeling better."

Tara moved her wrists. They weren't tied down. She wiggled her feet. They were free. She eased onto her side and sat up. She lowered her feet to the ground. "What time is it?"

"Time for breakfast, so if you want to eat, go now."

Tara padded down the corridor to the nurses' station. "Can I make a call?"

"Let me see your wrist." Tara held out her wristband, and the nurse read it. She typed on her computer, presumably pulling up Tara's file. "Yes. What's the number?"

Tara had only memorized a few people's numbers since they were just stored in her cell phone, which she didn't have access to. Unfortunately, Sophia's wasn't one of them. But she knew Mariana's by heart, so she recited her number to the nurse and waited.

"This is Silicon Valley Hospital with a call from Tara Fisher," the nurse said. "Okay, thank you." The nurse put the phone down. "I'm sorry, but she didn't accept the call. Is there another number you'd like to call?"

As if the wind had been knocked out of Tara, tears welled in her eyes. She bit her lip. The only other number she knew was Josh's. "Can you call my husband? I'd love to speak to the girls."

The nurse gave her a pitying look. "Your husband's been clear that no calls are allowed to him or your daughters while you're here."

Tara sulked away. In the room next to the nurses' station were a handful of people. Some played cards, others talked, and a few watched television. Tara sat in one of the red plastic chairs.

The man wearing kneepads sat down next to her. "You look better."

Tara raised her eyebrows. "Excuse me?"

"I saw you yesterday morning, then they took you away kicking and screaming. Then they wheeled you past me during visiting hours, and you looked totally drugged up. But today you look better."

Tara narrowed her eyes at the man. "Are you stalking me?"

"Nah. But it's interesting to see new people come in."

"How long have you been here?" She wondered how long they held people in this place.

The man counted on his thick stubby fingers. Then he held up both hands. "Ten days. But this isn't my first stint here. Just checked in to make sure things didn't get out of hand like they have in the past."

"It's a mistake, me being in here."

"Yep, it always is," he said with a wink.

Tara stood and struggled back to her room. All her energy was gone. She crawled into bed. Hot tears soaked her pillow.

"*This is where you belong*," the voice said.

Tara shut her eyes and pressed her hands against her ears. She needed to figure out a way to get out of the hospital and fix the situation with Josh and the girls. She just had no idea how.

⬥⬥⬥

Sophia

Sophia's eyes weighed heavily, threatening to close. She couldn't sleep much, so she'd sneaked out of bed at four in the morning and had been having a movie marathon ever since. Halfway through *Waiting to Exhale*, she yawned, wishing she could drink some caffeine to combat the fatigue. In a weird way, witnessing Tara's affair was like reliving the trauma she'd been through with her own parents. She appreciated her dad helping but couldn't act as if years of bad blood didn't exist between them.

The doorbell rang. She got up, and Terrence jogged from their bedroom.

"I'll get it," he said.

"Morning," Darryl said after Terrence opened the door. "Did Sophia get any sleep last night?"

"I can hear you," Sophia yelled from the couch.

Terrence and Darryl came into the living room.

"Morning, Sophia," her dad said. "I wanted to check in. We have a lot to do today."

"Like what?" Sophia switched off the movie.

"Well, I spoke with Tara's doctor this morning, and we need to arrange a place for her to stay when she gets out. A safe place where someone can monitor her condition. Based on what you've said, I don't think her husband will welcome her home. Does she have family here?" her dad asked.

"Her mom lives in Sacramento. That's the only family I know of." Sophia took out her phone. "I'll text Josh and see if he has her contact information."

After a few minutes, Josh texted her back.

"He says her name is Karen Edwards."

Terrence retrieved his laptop from the office and typed away. "I think I found her."

He recited the number to Sophia, who dialed on her cell phone.

"Hello?" a voice answered.

"Yes, is this Karen Edwards?" Sophia asked.

"Yes, how may I help you?"

"My name is Sophia, and I'm Tara's friend... she's in the hospital."

Karen gasped. "Is she hurt? What happened? Where's Josh?"

"There's a lot to explain, but she's in a psychiatric hospital."

"Oh no... I prayed this would never happen."

"What?" Sophia asked.

"With her dad's history, I knew it was a possibility, but I hoped..."

"I don't understand," Sophia said. Tara had never mentioned her dad having a history of mental illness.

"Tara's father. He was schizophrenic."

Sophia's stomach dropped. *Sound normal, sound normal.* "Well, she's supposed to get out in a day or two, and she's going to need a place to stay. I don't know that she'll be able to return to her house."

"Tara can always come home. She knows that. She's just never wanted to after..."

"After what?"

"After her father killed himself. Poor girl, something no one should ever have to go through. I don't know if she'll want to come home, but she's always welcome."

"Okay." Sophia's hand shook as she lowered the phone to the table. She met Terrence and Darryl's inquisitive looks. "This could be worse than we imagined."

JOSH

Josh slammed his hand against the blaring clock radio. He groaned, shifting on the small couch in his living room. He couldn't bring himself to sleep in the bed he used to share with Tara. Staring at the clock, he tried to focus on the tasks at hand. He had to get up, get the girls ready for school, drop them off, pick them up, take care of Teeni during the day, cook dinner, then put them to bed. In other words, he had to keep living because the girls depended on him. But God did it hurt.

He stumbled down the hall. "Time to get up, Chelsea." He went to the next door. "Morning, Teeni. Morning, Michelle."

Michelle faced Josh without opening her eyes. "I ate the apple, and I can't wake up, Daddy."

Josh wasn't in the mood to play, but he planted a kiss on Michelle's cheek. "Did that work?"

Michelle opened her eyes. "You're not Prince Charming, Daddy."

"Well, Sleeping Beauty needs to go to school." Josh yawned and picked up Teeni from her bed.

She rubbed her eyes. "Where's Mommy?"

"She's still at the doctor's, Teeni," Josh said.

"Is she getting a shot? I always get a shot when I go to the doctor's. Is Mommy going to cry when she gets a shot?" Michelle asked.

"I don't know." Josh refused to have anything to do with Tara's condition, though his parents thought it was cold of him to refuse to visit her. They couldn't understand. Neither of them had betrayed the other the way Tara had betrayed him.

Michelle asked, "When's she coming home?"

Josh couldn't bring himself to say she wouldn't be coming home. "We'll talk about that later. Now let's just get ready for school."

After the girls were dressed, Josh poured the girls' cereal. While Teeni sang and Michelle chatted about the seven dwarfs, Chelsea's head hung low over her cereal bowl. A knock on the front door startled Josh. He hoped it wasn't Terrence or Sophia. He didn't want to see either of them. Peeking through the peephole, he let out a breath and opened the door.

"Morning, Joshie. Where are my little princesses?" his mom asked as she gave him a quick pat on the back then walked into the kitchen.

"What are you doing here, Mom?"

"I'm here to give you a break. I'll drop Chelsea and Michelle at school and take Teeni for the day. You can pick Chelsea up from school, then we can all have dinner together tonight."

"I can't let you do—"

"I insist. Looks like you need a shower and a shave."

Josh rubbed the stubble on his chin. "Fine," he said, though a shower and a shave would do nothing to make his life any easier.

After everyone left, Josh sat on the couch. Two-day-old sweat coated his body, but he didn't want to shower. He had slept less than three hours and could barely keep his eyes open, but he couldn't rest. And though the coffee table had been replaced and the burn mark on the carpet covered with a rug, the house still reminded him of Tara's breakdown, a memory he wished to forget. He needed to get out of there.

Speeding down the freeway, Josh hopped onto Highway 17 headed toward Santa Cruz. He rolled down the window and blasted the music, but nothing could break through his numbness.

Forty minutes later, he was at the beach. The wind whipped his skin as he headed to the shoreline. Seagulls circled the overcast sky, their cries mixing with the sound of the crashing waves. He shivered and zipped up his fleece jacket before he kicked off his shoes. His toes sank into the cold, wet sand. Bitterly cold water swept over his feet and woke him up.

As the reality of the situation hit him, his chest tightened. *How will this affect my daughters? Will Tara ever be normal again? Will she end up like the homeless people on the streets, talking to herself? Why did this happen? Why me? Why us?*

There were no answers.

The emotional pain was worse than the physical pain he'd experienced when he injured his back, and he needed something for it. He grabbed his shoes and ran back to his car, panting by the time he got there. When he checked his phone, there was a text from Terrence. For the first time in days, Josh smiled. Blasting the heat, he sped off.

Josh parked outside the tall building and flung the glass door open. It was full of people in suits and ties, and Josh didn't fit in with his soaking-wet jeans and sandy shoes. He didn't care. He ran up four flights of stairs then slowly climbed the remaining seven, wishing he'd taken the elevator. When he got to floor eleven, he threw open the door.

A receptionist gaped at him. "Can I help you?"

"I'm here to see an old buddy, Louis Steinman." The name tasted like poison as he wiped the sweat from his face with the back of his hand.

The receptionist picked up the phone and whispered into it.

Seconds later, a graying man at least a decade older than Josh appeared. A few inches taller than Josh, he had a thinner frame and beady gray eyes. Josh couldn't believe he was the bastard Tara had fallen for.

"Can I help you?" the man asked.

"You Louis?" Josh asked.

The man nodded, then realization flashed in his eyes. He stepped backward, and Josh lunged toward him. His fist hit Louis square in the nose, and the force of the blow knocked Louis onto the desk.

The receptionist screamed, "I'm calling the police!"

With one hand covering his nose, which spurted blood, Louis held up his other to her. "It's fine. He got what he came for."

Josh's hand, still sore from the wall he'd hit a few days earlier, throbbed as if it had caught fire. Though the man wasn't dead, his nose was most likely broken. It couldn't repair Josh's marriage, but a part of him had needed that. On the other hand, the last thing he needed was to be arrested. "Yeah, you're damn right I did."

TARA

"Visiting time," Melissa said. "Same people are here for you."

Tara sat up in bed. She ran her fingers through her hair as she left the room. Blinking back tears, she wrapped her arms around Sophia, who stood next to Darryl.

Sophia squeezed her tightly. "It's okay, Tara."

Tara couldn't control her tears, and her body was racked with sobs. She was so grateful to see a familiar face—something normal in a frighteningly crazy environment.

"Let's sit," Sophia said, gesturing to a red chair. "How are you feeling?"

"I'm ready to go home. I talked to my doctor earlier, and she said I can leave within the next day or so if I'm released to someone who will give me a place to stay and if I enroll in a partial hospitalization program," Tara said.

Sophia took Tara's hand. "I talked to your mother and—"

Tara narrowed her eyes at Sophia. "You what?"

"I spoke to your mother," Sophia repeated.

"What'd she tell you?" Tara had specifically told the hospital staff that they weren't to contact her mother, but that wouldn't matter now.

"She said she's willing to have you stay with her, and there's a good program at the hospital near her place."

Tara's heart pounded. "She chose him over me, you know? Did she tell you that? I can't go back."

Darryl shrugged. "They won't release you unless you have somewhere to go."

Though Sophia had retrieved their phone numbers from Tara's cell phone, neither Mariana nor Miriam were accepting her calls. Josh's mom had called to check on her, but she'd made it clear Josh wasn't willing to communicate with Tara.

"If I stay with her, when can I leave?" Tara asked.

"You could go as early as tomorrow if the doctor okays it," Darryl said.

"The doctor said I'll need to be further evaluated and educated on my condition—once they finally tell me what it is—medication management, that type of thing. Will this never end?"

"It will, but you've had a serious medical emergency. If you'd had a heart attack, you wouldn't expect to walk out of the hospital as if nothing had happened. The same applies here," Darryl said.

Tara exhaled. They were drugging her and locking her up with a bunch of crazy people for no reason, but she couldn't say that if she wanted to get out. She had to play along. "I need to think about going home with my mom. Thanks for coming."

She rose from the chair and hurried back to her room, where she threw herself on her bed. Though she didn't want to remember, all the memories came rushing back.

It had been a cold winter night during her sophomore year. Her mother hadn't shown up to pick her up from school, so Tara had had to walk for half an hour in the rain. She was fuming when she got home and saw her mother's car in the driveway. The inside of the house looked like a tornado had hit, but that wasn't an unusual sight. On her father's bad days—the days when he heard voices plotting to get him—he would go crazy and search the house for wiretaps, turning everything upside down until he finally gave up.

But that night, the house was eerily quiet, and neither of her parents seemed to be home. But because their cars were there, she searched the house. Tara finally went down to the basement, and there they were. Her father had tied her mother to a chair. Red welts were forming on her face, and dried blood was crusted on her nose. A gash on her mother's arm dripped blood.

She ran to her mother, but her father knocked Tara back. Her head struck the hard floor, and stars danced before her eyes.

"You can't have my soul!" he screamed at her.

"That's our daughter," her mother said as she wiggled frantically.

"It's just me, Dad," Tara cried. "It's Tara."

Her father covered his ears with his hands. Sweat dripped down his face, landing on Tara. The odor of alcohol filled her nostrils with his every breath. He picked up the kitchen knife that lay on the table, and she knew her life was over. She closed her eyes and held her breath.

But then his hot breath disappeared, and his footsteps pounded up the wooden stairs. She jumped when the basement door slammed. She opened one eye, then the other, and exhaled. Unsure how much time she had until he came back, she untied her mother. They ran up the stairs, fearing her father would return at any minute.

Realizing he'd left, her mother instructed Tara to pack as much as possible and fast. Tara ran to her room, grabbed whatever she could find, and threw it into a duffel bag. Minutes later, her mother told her it was time to leave.

When they arrived at Tara's aunt's house, Tara asked her mother, "You're staying too, right?"

"No, I'm going back home."

"But why? Look what he did to you. He could kill you! And I don't want to stay here by myself. I don't want you to leave me."

"Tara, you're fifteen and old enough to take care of yourself. You'll be fine here. But your father... he needs me. And I love him."

"I won't leave without you, Mom. If you don't stay, I won't either."

After fifteen minutes of arguing, Tara's mom wouldn't budge. She insisted she go home to her husband. Tara couldn't stand the thought of her mom going back alone, so they decided they'd both head back.

They called the police and notified them of her father's condition. Two officers waited outside their house when Tara got there. Tara followed the police inside and ran downstairs to the basement. As soon as she turned on the light, her father's corpse was illuminated, his neck bent at an unnatural angle while his body gently swayed.

After that, Tara willingly left her mother behind and moved into her aunt's house. Haunted by the incident, Tara fell into a depression so severe, she didn't think she'd come out. She'd never told Josh about any of it: her father's sudden "heart attack," why she'd left her mother's house, her depression, or even the therapy she went to once a week. It took her three years before she could even sleep alone without the bedroom light on.

As she lay in the darkness of the hospital room, she knew her past had finally caught up with her. Now her father wanted revenge. The final face-down with him was imminent.

CHAPTER TWENTY

BIG NEWS

TERRENCE

T ERRENCE SIPPED HIS COFFEE. HE hit Send, and the email with his monthly report disappeared from his inbox. Now that that was done, he drafted an email to Josh but left the subject line empty.

Josh, look, I messed up. I get that you're mad. But this is a hell of a situation to be in. You've been a good friend to me, and I just want to be there for you and the girls. Hit me up or come next door.—T.

He reread the email then sent it. He'd thought that Josh might have forgiven him after he'd located Louis with Corinne's help, but now he wondered what Josh had done with that address.

Leaning back in his chair, Terrence rubbed his eyes. His stomach ached from worry. The night before, when Sophia had come home from visiting Tara, her whole body trembled. This couldn't be good for Sophia or their baby. His next approach was the good-cop role, so he'd booked a reservation at Scott's Seafood for the evening. He planned on surprising her, reconnecting, and hopefully talking sense into her about getting some space from Tara.

He started to pull up another tab to look up movie listings, then he stopped. He had a new email from James McKay, the star college player he'd met with in Las Vegas. The player his entire career rested on right now. As he clicked on it, he held his breath. He read it then exhaled. Sip of coffee. Then another read. He had to make sure the words wouldn't change or evaporate into thin air. On the fourth read, it sank in. James McKay was going pro and wanted Terrence as his agent.

He dialed Sophia. When she didn't answer, he texted her. *I got BIG news. Call me ASAP!*

Terrence printed the email then raced down the hallway to Lance's office. "Lance, man, you aren't gonna believe this. James—James McKay—is going pro and—"

Lance jumped up. "He picked you! He picked you!"

Terrence shoved the email into Lance's hand. "Yeah, man!"

"I knew it! You did it, T."

"This is going to change everything! For me, for you, for the agency even."

Lance put his hands on Terrence's shoulders. "It's projected that McKay is going to be a lottery pick. Everything you've worked for is right at your fingertips."

Terrence couldn't believe his hard work had paid off finally. They would be able to keep the house and even take a vacation before the baby came. "I gotta try to call Sophia again."

Terrence hurried back to his office. He picked up the phone and dialed her again.

When she answered, she said, "Terrence, I'm on the phone with Tara's mom. We're trying to figure out the logistics of Tara moving in with her."

"Okay, but James just emailed me. He picked me as his agent."

A squeal erupted through the phone. "You did it! I'm so proud of you. I just need to finish talking to Tara's mom, then I'm calling back for a play-by-play. I love you."

"I love you too."

Terrence had never been so proud in his life. He made a quick call to James to confirm the news. As word spread through the office, coworkers gathered around his cubicle, high-fiving and making jokes.

After about ten minutes, his work phone buzzed. Jean's voice filled his office. "Someone named Desiree is at the front desk for you."

"Desiree? I'll be right there."

He hurried to the front desk, wondering what Desiree was doing at his office. Jean looked at him and raised her brows. He could understand her concern given Desiree's short black dress and knee-high boots.

"Hey, Jerry," Desiree said.

"What's up? Everything okay?" Terrence asked.

Jean cleared her throat.

"Oh, Jean, this is Sophia's sister," Terrence said.

Jean's face softened. "Oh, lovely. She didn't mention she was your sister."

"In-law," Desiree said. "Sister-in-law. Anyways, all this drama with Tara's been freaking me out, so I was doing a little retail therapy in the city. Then Sophia texted me that you landed James McKay. I had to stop by and treat you for lunch."

Terrence checked his wrist, surprised his watch read twelve. "Sure. I'll be back at one, Jean."

Terrence and Desiree headed out of the office, and a crisp breeze met them at the door.

Terrence pointed north. "Why don't we walk down to the best Philly cheesesteak spot in the city?"

"Okay, sure. But, like, how many calories do you think a sandwich has?"

Terrence laughed. "Don't even worry about that. You look great."

Terrence relayed the email and the subsequent conversation he'd had with James as they walked down the block. They entered a little deli that was packed to capacity. Terrence ordered sandwiches and sodas while Desiree grabbed two window seats.

Desiree smiled. "We needed good news after everything that happened to Tara. It's crazy what's going on with her, right?"

Terrence nodded. "Never in a million years would I have imagined any of this happening to us. It's like stuff you read about in the newspaper. Stuff that never happens to people you actually know."

"I've seen some crazy things with friends of friends trippin' out or whatever, but this is, like, the worst since there are kids involved."

"I wish Josh would talk to me. I miss the girls," Terrence said.

Desiree touched his hand. "It's going to take some time. He'll come around."

"You think?" Terrence wasn't so sure about that. He didn't want to invade Josh's personal space, and he didn't really have any other ideas to get him to forgive him.

"Yeah, he'll need to borrow some milk or something at some point.

Ooh, ooh, we could buy all the milk from the store and then he'll have to come around... literally."

Terrence chuckled. As they ate, Desiree's fingers moved at the speed of light on her phone.

"You're always on that thing," he said.

"Oh please, so are you."

"I check my work email, so I have an excuse. You wouldn't know about that though," he kidded.

Desiree frowned and hung her head.

"Don't say I said something wrong again." He was always saying something wrong these days.

"No, it's cool. I just sometimes wonder what I'm going to do with my life."

Terrence bit his sandwich. "Aren't you pursuing modeling and acting?" he asked through chews.

"Yeah, but come on, I'm not dumb. What's the percentage of people who actually make it?" Desiree sipped her diet soda.

"I don't know about that, but I know that only about three out of ten thousand boys playing high school basketball will be drafted into the NBA. That's like point-zero-three percent—"

"Aren't you supposed to be making me feel better?" Desiree joked.

"My point is that I work with that point-zero-three percent all the time. They exist. And if you want to make it, forget percentages and go for it."

"Thanks for saying that."

Terrence stared out the window. "It's kind of like meeting the person you're going to spend your life with. There're billions of people out there, and we're all waiting to find the one. Did you know me and Sophia met by an accident?"

Desiree leaned in. "No, what happened?"

"I hit her parked car. I didn't want to hit and run, so I left a note. We ended up meeting later to exchange insurance information. Sophia was just..." Terrence thought for a minute. "Beautiful. Classy. Cultured. In a non-weird way, she reminded me of my mom. So we chatted a little, and I found out that not only was she beautiful, but she was super smart, accomplished, and well-rounded."

"So the rest is history, right?" Desiree asked.

"Not at all. She walked out on me," Terrence said indignantly. "No plans for the future, no 'give me a call when you get a chance.' Just said she had to leave. Now, I wasn't used to that."

"And?" Desire asked.

"Well, I tried to brush off the whole incident, but I could not get her out of my head. I even Googled her, and she popped up on a couple of Cisco sites that talked about her volunteering on humanitarian trips. She seemed amazing. I called her and asked her out. But she said, no, she was too busy. So I had to launch an all-out campaign."

Desiree laughed. "You mean you became a stalker?"

"Hell yeah." Terrence chuckled as he recalled his efforts. "I called her a couple more times, sent her some friendly emails, hung around the shopping center where I'd first hit her car."

"What made her change her mind? I know how stubborn Sophia can be."

"She didn't tell you any of this?" he asked.

Desiree laughed. "Sophia talk to me? You must be thinking of a different woman."

"I sent her a resume with a cover letter stating why she should give me a chance, my qualifications. I said I wasn't asking for her hand in marriage, just the opportunity to get to know her."

"A love resume?" Desiree asked. "That's so sweet. So meeting her was a lucky break, literally."

Terrence shrugged. "That was about three years ago. I've found my one. And now we're going to become three. It's incredible. Anyways, enough about me. Can I ask you a question?"

"Shoot," she said.

"Besides shopping, what are you going to do with the money and the house?" He'd been dying to ask her that in the weeks she'd been living with them since her father passed.

Desiree shrugged. "I dunno. It still hasn't registered that my dad is gone, let alone that he left me money and a house. I'm in... shock."

"Yeah, I can understand that. But, Desiree, if you want to be a model and an actress, follow your dream. I know your mom and dad didn't necessarily love your career choice, but you have to live for you."

Terrence patted her hand. "You can have what you want, just believe in yourself."

Desiree held Terrence's hand and peered into his eyes. "Sometimes you want what you can't have though."

"A girl like you can have it all. Sophia and I are going to celebrate the big news tonight. Would you like to join us?"

Desiree beamed. "I'd love to."

CHAPTER TWENTY-ONE

HEADING HOME

TARA

MELISSA OPENED THE DOOR. "TARA, it's time to go. Your mother is here."

Tara didn't move away from the window. Though she couldn't last another day in the psych ward, she couldn't face moving in with her mom. In exchange for the police not pressing charges of child endangerment, Tara had agreed to only have supervised visits with the girls twice a week. Not being able to see them regularly would kill her.

"Or you can stay," Melissa said.

Tara grabbed her bag. Her mom was waiting in the long hall. She looked the same but older. A scrunchie tied her sandy-blond hair in a low ponytail falling below her shoulders. Her blue eyes were wet with tears.

"Ready?" her mother asked.

Tara shrugged. "I guess."

The ride to Sacramento took about two hours but stretched on forever as her mom tried to make small talk. As they got closer to Tara's mother's house, the house she had grown up in, a tight knot formed in Tara's stomach. The reality that she had lost everything sank in.

Tara's mom parked in front of a hardware store. "I need to stop and sign the papers for my FMLA leave."

"You work here?" Tara asked.

"It's a paycheck."

Tara's lips crept into a smile. *Perfect.* As her mom filled out the paperwork, Tara bought the only thing she needed.

When Tara's mom parked in front of her house, Tara's body froze. What she needed to do wouldn't be easy. After hesitantly stepping out of the car, she dragged her feet to the front door. She put one foot in the house, like testing the temperature in a bathtub. The house still smelled the same: a mix of Pine Sol, mold, and the vanilla air freshener her mother always had plugged into the wall.

"I fixed up your room," her mother said.

"I should have said this earlier, but I'm starving and I need a shower. Can you grab me something to eat?"

"Sure. What do you want?"

"Anything that isn't psych ward mush."

"Okay. I'm out of food. Wasn't sure what you ate these days, and I imagined we'd go grocery shopping together. I'll get something quick. I won't be long."

The house was stuck in a time warp with all her old pictures still hanging on the walls, stuffed animals lining the shelves, and the basement door. It was time. She had to confront the man who had caused her downfall. She needed to speak with her father.

After her mom had left, Tara stood in front of the basement door, trying to decide whether to fling it open or make it a slow unveiling. Her phone rang in the distance, but there was no one else she wanted to talk to. She put her hand on the cold metal doorknob. Then turned it. The door opened. She reached for the light switch and flicked it on. She hadn't been down there for over a decade, but she knew she had to go. She had to face him.

With each step, Tara repeated, "I'm coming, Dad."

Her phone rang again. When she lowered herself on the last step, she scanned the basement. Washing machine and dryer in the corner. A laundry basket half full of dirty white clothes. Beams crisscrossed the ceiling. A couple of boxes labeled "Christmas" sat on the opposite side of the floor. *Shit!* She had been so preoccupied with opening the door that she'd forgotten to bring her stuff.

She panted as she ran back up the stairs, her heart pounding harder with every step. Her phone rang again. She didn't even look at it. Nothing and no one could change her mind.

She went to her room and grabbed the rope she'd purchased from the hardware store. Then she dragged a wooden kitchen chair down to the basement.

Once the noose was assembled, she stood on the chair. She put the noose around her neck then kicked the chair away.

SOPHIA

Sophia shifted nervously in Maxine's office at Micro Analytics. She'd been there for over an hour, interviewing with Maxine first, then the CEO, then the sales team. They needed someone ASAP, one reason they'd agreed to reschedule the interview after Sophia had had to cancel her initial appointment due to Tara's emergency.

Though it was an independent contractor position, Sophia could prove herself and transition to full-time employee.

Though they'd celebrated the night before about Terrence landing James McKay, Sophia's uncertainty about her and her baby's finances and their future weren't lessened. After watching her mom end up with nothing after Carl's passing, and Tara losing everything she loved in such a short period of time, Sophia needed to have control over her life. She didn't want to have to rely on anyone—not even Terrence.

Maxine reentered the office with an easy smile and a sheet of paper. "Sophia, your resume and work history speak for themselves. Having you come in was a formality, though the team enjoyed meeting you. We'd love to have you join us, and I've printed out our official offer. I know you probably need to think it over, so please, take your time and let us know."

Sophia didn't have to think it over. She'd wanted a job for over a year. "I appreciate the offer, and I accept. I'm ready to start when you need me."

Sophia waved hesitantly as she entered her living room, where Terrence, her dad, and Desiree sat talking. "I got the job."

"Cool," Desiree said.

Terrence raised his eyebrows. "Really? Do they know you're almost seven months pregnant?"

"Yes. And don't act so surprised." She nudged him with her elbow.

"Well, I cooked a special dinner. And don't you two dare tell her what it is," Terrence said to Desiree and Darryl. "And congrats, baby." Terrence walked to the kitchen.

Sophia noticed Darryl's suitcase. "Are you leaving?"

"Yes. I was waiting to say good-bye to you." Sophia's dad picked up his suitcase.

Sophia ushered him to the front door. Half of her wanted her dad to stay and help navigate Tara's recovery, but the other half of her was glad he was going. "Thanks for coming."

He patted her on the back. "Congratulations on the job. And I'm really sorry about what's happened with Tara. But with a friend like you to help her, I have a feeling she's going to pull through it."

"I didn't want to ask this in front of anyone else, but do you think she'll ever be normal again?"

Sophia's dad squinted and looked up. "If she takes the medication and gets the right psychiatric help, then I'd say yes."

"What are the chances of that happening again?"

He put his hand on her shoulder. "The chances are that Tara will have another episode. But it doesn't have to be this severe or this dangerous. If she learns the symptoms and knows her triggers, she can manage her condition." As Sophia opened the front door, her dad cleared his throat. "What are the chances of this happening again? Me spending time with you."

This conversation was bound to happen sooner or later. "I've spent my life thinking you were a monster for leaving Mom. Now I see that things weren't so cut-and-dried. I ignored you trying to make things better over the years because I wanted you to hurt the way you hurt me."

"I'm so sorry—"

"I know you are. I finally understand that. But to answer your question"—Sophia shrugged—"I'm just not sure. I appreciate everything you've done, but I still have a lot to process."

Her dad hugged her tightly. "That's fair. I'm only a phone call away. You know that, right?"

"I do," Sophia said.

Sophia went to the kitchen table, sat, and closed her eyes. "Ready, and I'm starving."

A plate clanked onto the table. "Open up," Terrence said.

Sophia opened her mouth. A blend of curry and jasmine rice played on her tongue. "Mmm, Indian food. Our favorite." She rubbed her belly.

"Right again," Terrence said.

"Oh, I need to check on Tara. She's just getting to her mom's."

Terrence raised his eyebrows. "Right."

Sophia dialed Tara. The phone rang and rang then went to voicemail. Tara had promised Sophia she'd call her as soon as she stepped foot through the door. Sophia tried again, but still no answer.

Sophia shuddered. Even thinking about the things Tara had gone through growing up was mindboggling for her. Seeing what Tara was going through now broke Sophia's heart.

She called Tara once more. When Tara still didn't answer, a sick feeling settled in Sophia's stomach. She scrolled through her contact list and selected Karen's number.

"Hello?" Karen answered.

"Hi, Karen, it's Sophia. I hate to bother you, but Tara's not answering her phone, and I wanted to see how she's doing."

"We made it home. She's definitely down, but I think she's okay. She asked me to go out and grab her something to eat, so I'm just getting back home. You've been such a good friend. Why don't you hold on, and I'll put her on the phone. I'm sure she'll be happy to hear from you."

"Okay, thanks." Sophia couldn't imagine how hard it must be for Tara to be without the girls, Josh, and her home.

"Tara? Tara, Sophia's on the phone," Karen called. "Hmmm, that's strange. She doesn't seem to be here. Oh, wait. The basement door is open. Tara?"

A loud crash stung Sophia's ear.

"No, no, no!" Karen screamed.

TARA

Absolute darkness surrounded Tara. She fell down a hole, yet instead of a quick, stomach-dropping fall, it was a slow descent. It was cold. Frigid.

"Tara," her father's voice said. "I'm here."

Tara didn't open her eyes but her heart; then he was there. Sitting on the green couch in the living room, he thumbed through an old photo album. He looked like the pictures her mom had shown her from when her mother and father first met. His blond hair was still full. Tara couldn't detect a single crow's foot around his sparkling blue eyes. He was thinner too, but looked fit and wore a light-yellow collared shirt with blue jeans.

He stood and placed the open photo album on the wooden coffee table in front of the couch. "You wanted to speak with me?"

"Yes," Tara said, her voice quivering.

"Well, sit."

Tara stood still. All the hate and hurt and anger seemed to dissipate like steam when she saw him. He wasn't the monster she'd expected. He was the man her mother had fallen in love with.

"It's okay, Tara. I won't hurt you... again."

"You haunted me," Tara accused.

"No, no, that wasn't me. That was our worst enemy."

Tara didn't understand.

Her father tapped his head. "Our brain. Sometimes it turns against us."

He was trying to confuse her. "I'm not like you. There is no us," Tara said.

"How are you not like me? You lie, you cheat, you hurt everyone you love. How are we different?"

Her tears fell. "I didn't mean to—"

"You didn't mean to get caught? And once you did, once the shit hit the fan, you did exactly what I did. You forgot about everyone else and decided to check out. For good."

"Don't say that!" Tara screamed.

"Say what?" Her father put up his palms. "The truth? That you're just like me? I know you. I know us."

"I lost everything. I lost Josh. I lost my kids. I lost *it*. What was I supposed to do?"

"Your husband. Your kids. What about them... now? Did you think about how your actions would affect them?"

Tara couldn't speak. She had no defense.

"That's what we do," Tara's father continued. "We make it all about ourselves. As if bad things don't happen to good people all the time. Good people get cancer, kids get kidnapped, teenagers kill their friends drunk driving. The point is that you have had your personal tragedy. But instead of thinking about repairing what you did, you only thought about yourself. You ended it all. Congratulations, Tara. You did it." Her dad clapped sarcastically.

Tara's shoulders fell. "My life is over."

"So forget marriage, motherhood, friendship. Forget everyone but you. Give up! Take a seat on the couch and enjoy the rest of eternity. Here, look at this photo album. Agonize over everyone you left. Replay all your mistakes, because you gave up the one thing you had—the future."

Tara scoffed. "What future?"

"Tara, *your* future. Your ability to make amends, to recommit, to try again." Her dad's blue eyes focused on her.

Tara had made so many mistakes. "I just wish I could start over. I wish I could go back and change everything. I would be better to Josh. The affair would never happen."

"You can't go back, but you can go forward. Only forward. I wish I could, but I can't. You can. Go. Go and make it better. If I could, I would. I love you, Tara." Her dad placed his hand over his heart. "I will always love you."

"I want to go back," Tara said. "Please, I need to go back!"

"Tara! Tara!" Tara's mother screamed.

Tara fought to open her eyes as a vacuum-like sensation pulled her out of the blackness.

Tara's mom's arms engulfed her. "That's it, Tara. I'm here. Please don't do this."

241

Tara gagged violently, trying to get air into her lungs. "Mom?"

"Yes, Tara, I'm here."

"Help me."

PART THREE

CHAPTER TWENTY-TWO

CHECKING IN

Sophia

SOPHIA WADDLED INTO THE DOCTOR'S office for her weekly appointment and exchanged sympathetic glances with two other visibly pregnant women in the waiting room. She signed in before sitting down with a *Fit Pregnancy* magazine. *As if that wasn't an oxymoron.* She wiped sweat from her forehead. She loved late spring, when it was warming up but not too hot, and she was happy she would deliver before summer officially started.

After her name was called, she went back and stopped at the scale. "I don't even want to know how much I gained."

The assistant laughed. "I'll just write it down and not tell you."

Sophia stepped on the scale and closed her eyes. "I'm serious. Just write T-O-O much."

The assistant laughed again. "All done. Let's get you set in a room."

As Sophia waited for Dr. Smith, her phone vibrated. It was her daily call from her mom. "Hello, Mom."

"Thank God you answered."

"What's wrong?" Something was always wrong.

"I'm unraveling over here. Has Desiree said anything about the money? What about the house? My lawyer said she could kick me out. I can't be out on the street. I just can't—"

"Mom, it's okay. Nothing's changed since yesterday. She hasn't mentioned a word of any of it." There was a knock at the door. "I have to go. I'm at the doctor's, but I'll call you back."

"You need to keep me informed about Desiree!"

"Bye." Sophia hung up.

Dr. Smith entered the room. Her smile faded when she looked at Sophia. "What's the matter?"

Sophia rubbed her belly. "I'm fine. I was talking to my mother, and that can be somewhat... frustrating."

"I see. Other than that, how is everything?"

"I'm tired. I have to wake up every hour to pee all night long. And I'm huge. So great!"

Dr. Smith chuckled. "The third trimester can be challenging for some moms. You're thirty-six weeks, the last month, the home stretch, so every day, you're getting closer and closer to meeting your baby."

Sophia placed her hand on the huge watermelon that was her stomach. "I know. I can't wait to meet him or her. The nursery is just about ready. We've bought a few gender-neutral clothes, but we'll do more clothes shopping after he or she arrives."

Dr. Smith looked at the chart. "That's smart. And your chart looks great. How's work?"

Exhausted just thinking about it, she said, "The pace is 120 miles per hour. It's sales, so go, go, and go faster."

"Keep an eye on that. You don't want to overdo it." Dr. Smith patted Sophia's shoulder. "Have you thought about childcare after the baby is born?"

Sophia shrugged. "Thought about it, yes. Figured it out, no."

"This is a huge transition and a wonderful time in your life. Try to take a breath from time to time. Find the joy in pregnancy."

"Does eating Almond Joys count? Because I love those or anything chocolate actually," Sophia said.

Dr. Smith helped Sophia off the examining table. "Stay away from the Almond Joys."

Sophia checked her phone once she was in the car. She'd missed a call from work and had a voicemail announcing an emergency meeting being called to discuss layoffs in the company. Her heart thumped, and her breathing became labored. *Oh no.* Though she had a contract for six months, they could technically lay her off sooner. The last thing she could take was more bad news.

TARA

"Tara, let's start with you," Nicole said as she set her clipboard on her knee. "Say your name, a topic if you have one, and on a scale of one to ten—one being the absolute lousiest and ten being spectacular—rate your mood right now."

Tara's gaze wandered around the circle of nine other participants. It was her tenth week in the program, and the routine had become familiar and comforting. "I'm Tara, and on a scale of one to ten, my mood is a four. I just want to talk about my husband. It's his birthday today."

"Sure." Nicole wrote on her yellow pad. "Next."

"My name is Joan, my mood is a five, and I want to talk about going back to work," the woman next to Tara said.

Nicole nodded. "That's a good one, Joan. Thank you."

"My name is Matthew. My mood is a ten because I'm graduating from the program today. I don't have a topic," the twenty-year-old said.

Nicole, Tara, and most of the other participants clapped.

"Congratulations, Matthew," Nicole said.

Though Tara would graduate from the program on Friday, she lacked Matthew's enthusiasm. Graduating usually meant that the health insurance would no longer cover the program, not that the participants were somehow cured of all their mental ailments. That was certainly the case with Tara. Though she had literally come back from the brink of death after her mom untied the noose and called the ambulance that rushed Tara to the emergency room, she still had a long way to go to reintegrate into a "normal" life.

"My name's Felicia, and my mood is a three. I want to talk about coping with a diagnosis."

"Really good, Felicia," Nicole said.

Tara shuddered. The word diagnosis triggered memories of Tara's fifth visit with the psychiatrist assigned to her at the hospital.

The psychiatrist, a rotund woman in her early fifties, had spoken with a deep, soothing voice. "How are you doing in the program?"

Tara said, "I'm trying to do what I have to do..."

"Since we have reviewed your file and observed your behavior, I would like to discuss your diagnosis. Considering your family history and the events that occurred, I'm diagnosing you as Bipolar One."

A lump formed in Tara's throat, and though she tried to hold it in, the levee broke, and tears flooded her face. Though she'd definitely exhibited the symptoms and her father had had mental illness, officially being diagnosed was frightening.

"Mental illness is like any other illness. Sometimes people are diagnosed very young. But other times, let's say for example with heart disease, it doesn't present itself until later. Someone may have a family history of heart disease. If they eat an unhealthy diet and don't exercise, then they're more likely to develop heart disease themselves. In your case, since your father was schizophrenic, you had a predisposition to mental illness, and various factors like stress, not sleeping, and preexisting trauma triggered your episode. When you think back, can you think of other times when you've noticed shifts in your mood?" the psychiatrist asked.

Tara wiped away the tears sliding down her cheeks. She'd been severely depressed after her father's suicide. She'd had a brief episode after Michelle was born, which she chalked up to Baby Blues. Then after Josh's accident, she'd had to take off some time from work because of how sad she'd been.

Hearing that she had bipolar disorder was devastating. The rest of her life seemed bleak. She doubted she'd be able to have a normal life and would probably be in and out of hospitals and on medication for the rest of her life. The room spun.

"So my life's over," Tara said.

"I didn't say that," the psychiatrist said. "Many famous, creative, intellectual, and successful people have bipolar disorder. With the medications out there today, you can still live a healthy, productive life."

At the time, Tara couldn't really process the words coming out of the psychiatrist's mouth. Even now, it was hard for her to believe she had an illness that would affect the rest of her life. She had to take medication and constantly monitor her thoughts and mood. Shaking her head as if to clear out the bad memory, Tara took a deep breath and tried to focus on the other people talking.

"My name is Sarah. My mood is a six. I want to talk about divorce."

"Yes, Sarah, good topic," Nicole said. "Let's start with you. Go ahead."

Tara snickered. Did Nicole ever say, "That's the stupidest topic ever?"

"My divorce..." Sarah exhaled. "It's like death. I honestly don't know how to go on. What I dreamed of all my life, the fairy tale that was supposed to happen, has turned out to be a nightmare."

"It's natural to feel like that. Divorce is a huge transition," Nicole said.

"I feel like I got an F or something. I failed at being a wife." Sarah choked back tears. "I don't know who I am anymore."

"Oh, please." Felicia planted her hands on her round hips and had a combative look on her wrinkled face.

Uh oh. Tara braced herself. To say Felicia and empathy weren't friends was an understatement.

"Felicia, let's be considerate of others and their feelings," Nicole said.

"Let's be real. One out of two marriages end in divorce. Sarah's not alone. Only, like, two percent of Americans have bipolar. Do the math. Yeah, she has to join the other half of divorced Americans. But she's not bipolar"—Felicia pointed at her chest—"like I am now. She won't have to deal with an illness that's a source of shame and embarrassment she can never live down."

Tara didn't like Felicia's insensitivity toward Sarah, but she did understand Felicia's frustration. Bipolar had devastated Tara's life completely. On the other hand, the fear that she'd receive divorce papers from Josh weighed heavily on her also. Neither was easy.

"That's enough." Nicole raised her voice slightly. "Felicia, we're all entitled to our opinions, but I need to ask you to leave. You can come back after you've cooled down."

Felicia stood. "I don't want to be here anyways." She stormed out of the room.

Tara eyed Sarah, who was crying.

"She definitely didn't have her coffee this morning," Matthew said.

It was kind of Matthew to attempt a joke, but the mood had already been set. Seeing Felicia unleash on Sarah reminded Tara of doing the same to Josh. For the most part, she'd been oblivious to the emotional pain he had experienced as a result of his injury and losing his job. She'd only cared about how it affected her, not really empathizing with him.

"Sarah, I understand how you feel," Tara said. "You might not be bipolar, but you're suffering. I understand suffering."

"Exactly," Nicole said. "Sarah, do you have anything else you'd like to share?"

"No," Sarah said, her gaze cast to the ground.

Nicole turned to Tara. "Tara, you mentioned it's your husband's birthday. How does that make you feel?"

Tara shrugged. "He hates me. I haven't seen him for almost three months—the longest I've gone without seeing him or talking to him since we met when I was fifteen. I've tried to call him, but he just ignores me. His mom said he's still hurting. I'm hurting too, and sometimes it hurts so much I feel like I can't breathe. Being without him and my girls is the absolute worst thing that could have happened."

"You might have a strained relationship with your husband, but you still have your three daughters. That will never change," Nicole said.

"I can only see my daughters twice a week though. I drive down to San Jose and have two hours with them. They're kids, you know? Their lives are just going on without me in it. For all intents and purposes, I've lost them too." Tara picked up a tissue and dabbed her eyes.

"I hear you. Take it one day at a time. It won't always be like this," Nicole said.

"I know, I know. It's so unfair. I want my life back. I don't want to be here."

Nicole leaned forward. "Part of being here is coming to terms with reality. You were ill. Dangerous events occurred. It was serious."

Tara shrugged again.

"Tara, do you understand?" Nicole asked.

"I was having delusional thoughts and hallucinations. I set my backyard on fire. I attempted to hang myself. My girls could have..." Tara put her hands to her face and sobbed.

Nicole patted Tara's back. "I know it's hard."

Tara wiped her eyes. "It's absolutely horrific. I can't believe it happened to me. It's mortifying. And I don't blame Josh for hating me, but I can't lose him. I have to prove to him how sorry I am. That I can be better to him than I was before."

"You can't control your husband or if he forgives you. All you can do is get better." Nicole sat back in her chair. "One day at a time, Tara. One day at a time."

After the others had shared, they took a short break. In the restroom, Tara looked in the mirror. Her hair had reverted to its natural dirty-blond. She wore no makeup, and extra weight clung around her stomach and upper arms. Only three months ago, she had been hanging with Mariana, gossiping about the latest office drama, with her girls, and hanging with Louis in Las Vegas. Now she lived with her mom, spent eight hours a day exchanging sympathy stories with people in a hospital, and was on disability leave from work. Her life was pathetic. She was pathetic.

She returned to the session room, which was as boring as the sessions themselves—white walls, gray chairs, brown table with different literature on it about mental illness and support groups. Tara sat next to Joan, a short, plump woman with medium-length black hair. Joan had been in the group for about two weeks due to an episode of depression that had forced her to take time off work. The only way she could keep her job was to attend the program.

"Hi, Joan."

"I heard what you were saying about your husband," she said. "I went through a divorce about two years ago. I wanted to ask, do you still love him?"

"It took a lot for me to see it, but yes, I love him. He's the kindest man I know. He loves our daughters more than himself, and at one point, he treated me like a queen." Tara lowered her head. "But he hates me now."

"If you love him, fight for him. Even if you fail, at least you'll know you tried."

"You think?" Tara asked.

"Divorce seems easy, but it's one of the hardest things I've ever gone through." Joan put her hand to her heart. "It's like an open wound."

"The truth is that I never really thought about divorcing Josh. That's the problem. I wasn't thinking. I was just acting out. I asked his mom if he had plans to file for divorce, but she said that was a conversation Josh would have to have with me when he's ready."

"Call him," Joan said.

"But I told you—he hates me."

"You have to start somewhere, and wishing him a happy birthday is a good place. He'll know you remembered."

Joan had a point. Tara took a deep breath. She fished her phone from her purse then dialed.

JOSH

Josh opened the door to his parents' auto body shop. "Ladies first," he said to Michelle and Teeni as they skipped through the door.

His parents had called him that morning and said they needed to speak to him about something important. Josh hoped it wasn't bad news. He couldn't take any more, and he had something he needed to talk to them about. A clerk sat at the front counter.

"I'm here to see my parents," Josh said.

"They're expecting you in the break room," the clerk said.

Josh led the girls down the hall and knocked on the break room door.

"Come in," his dad called.

Josh opened the door.

"Surprise!" his parents and their staff of ten yelled before singing "Happy Birthday."

Josh forced a smile. As a single parent, he'd been so busy with their day-to-day routine that he had completely forgotten it was his birthday.

"Thanks," he said when the song ended.

His mom held up a white cake blazing with candles. "Make a wish, Joshie!"

He wanted to wish for the birthday genie to put his life back together. Probably not possible. He blew out the candles.

"Your dad and I want to take you and the girls out to dinner tonight. How does that sound?" his mom asked.

Josh shrugged. "Fine, I guess."

These days, he actually preferred the company of Jack Daniels. Jack was more of the strong, silent type, while people oozed pity for him. He didn't want to be pitied or asked how he was doing. While he was grateful Terrence had given him Louis's information, he wasn't ready to forgive Terrence yet. But without Terrence, he didn't have any friends to hang out with. That was fine though—he just wanted to be left alone.

Josh's dad tried to hand a piece of cake to Josh.

"No, thanks. I'm not hungry," Josh said.

"Cake, cake," Teeni yelled as she jumped up and reached for it.

"You've already lost fifteen pounds. Why don't you have some cake?" Josh's dad said, trying to force the plate on him.

Josh accepted the plate. "I'm good, Dad. But thanks. Here, Teeni." He handed it to her.

"Yes!" Teeni said.

His mom handed a piece to Michelle. "Go sit at the table, girls." She distributed cake to the staff members, who filed out of the room after receiving a plate, then she pulled Josh aside. "I'm worried about you. There's a lot on your plate right now, and you don't have many outlets."

Josh rolled his eyes. "I'm fine."

"Now excuse my French, but to steal from Steven Tyler, FINE stands for fucked-up, insecure, neurotic, and emotional. So yes, you are FINE, but I want you to be good. Great, even."

Josh put his hands over his ears. "Mom, please."

"Don't *please* me. I'm being honest. You deserve happiness."

Josh's dad approached him with another piece of cake. "Second chance for cake." He held the plate toward Josh. "Everything okay?"

"Everything was okay before Mom started dropping F-bombs," Josh said.

Josh's dad looked at his wife. "Honey?"

"Steven Tyler said it, not me. I'm just trying to help. Maybe you can get through to him," Josh's mom said before joining her granddaughters on the other side of the room.

"Josh, how've you been doing?" his dad asked.

Josh sighed. He couldn't lie to his dad. "Terrible. This isn't me. This isn't the life I want for me or the girls. I've been living off of credit cards and half of Tara's disability checks, and I'm basically a recluse. Dad, I need to ask you a question."

"Anything, son."

"Is that spot still open in production?"

Josh's dad patted him on the back. "It has your name on it."

"Thanks." Josh was surprised to find he meant it. His phone rang, and he pulled it from his pocket. His body grew hot, and he was sure he was turning red.

"Everything okay?" Josh's dad asked.

Josh held up the phone. "It's Tara."

TERRENCE

Terrence shut off his car's engine and leaned his head against the headrest. He stared at Josh's house. All the toys and bikes usually strewn across the lawn were gone. Dry yellow spots occupied what used to be lush grass. Terrence assumed Josh was too busy to bother with its upkeep, but he couldn't confirm that since Josh still wouldn't speak to him. And Terrence couldn't blame him.

After a short call with Sophia, he put his phone in his pocket. He'd left the office at four and sped home to surprise her with takeout. His coworker had told him about a new Mediterranean restaurant, and he was sure he'd finally stump Sophia's taste buds. But she'd just informed him that a last-minute business dinner with her team had been scheduled for seven o'clock. Since she'd probably go back to the office afterward, he figured she might not be home until nine or ten. *So much for dinner.*

Terrence missed the days before Sophia got her new job. She used to be happy to see him when he came home. They would pore over the details of his day and spend an exorbitant amount of time talking about their growing baby. Now she was usually so tired from work and the pregnancy that she spent most of her free time in bed and often spent the weekend with Tara in Sacramento.

Grabbing the food, he opened the car door, and the heat hit him. Just as he slipped the key through the lock, the front door opened.

"Jerry, guess what?" Desiree's eyes were wide and excited. She bounced up and down. "I got a gig!"

"Cool. What type and when?" he asked, happy he'd have his usual dinner companion even though Sophia wouldn't be home.

"It's a modeling gig. Tonight at six thirty in San Francisco."

Terrence put the food on the kitchen counter. "That's kind of late notice. How'd you get the gig?"

"I found it on Craigslist."

Terrence didn't want to dump a pail of water on Desiree's enthusiasm, but red flags were flying. "I don't really like the sound of that. You need to be careful with jobs off the Internet."

"It's fine, Jerry. I need to add to my resume. I need exposure."

"What kind of shoot is it?"

"It's for an Internet catalog—bathing suits."

Terrence narrowed his eyes. "Oh, hell no. That sounds like a really bad idea. I don't think you should go."

Desiree frowned. "Sometimes you act like you're my dad. Can't you just be happy for me?"

He wasn't anyone's dad… yet. He didn't have anything planned for the evening, and if Desiree insisted on going, he couldn't let her go by herself. "If you're set on going, I'll go with you."

"Really? You'd do that?" The excitement returned to Desiree's eyes.

Terrence shrugged. "Yeah."

Desiree jumped up and hugged Terrence. "You're the best. I'm going to finish getting ready. We need to leave in ten."

Terrence checked his watch. It was only five. They could go and be back before Sophia came home. He picked up his phone to call Sophia then put it down. She had said she was swamped at work, and since she was so caught up in it, she probably couldn't talk. He sent a quick text telling her he'd be home in a couple of hours, then he took off.

———— ✦❖✦ ————

"Are you sure this is the place?" Terrence asked as he surveyed the stonewashed concrete warehouse in San Francisco.

Desiree squinted. "There." She pointed at a number on the building. "Six-five-seven. This is it."

Terrence eyed Desiree. "This looks shady. I think we should go home."

"I need this," Desiree said desperately.

"Need?" Terrence raised his eyebrows. "I know we don't talk about it often, but your dad left you quite a sum of money. You're set."

"It's not about the money. This is what I want to do with my life. I have to start somewhere."

"All right." He believed in taking chances to reach goals and dreams, but if anything inside seemed off, he'd make sure they got out of there fast.

Desiree reapplied her red lipstick then got out of the car. She pulled down the tight cream dress that barely covered her bottom and plunged at the neckline. They hurried through the mostly deserted parking lot toward the warehouse. A metal chair propped open a side door. Inside, a sign that read "Big Time Productions" was tacked to the wall of the makeshift reception area.

A redheaded girl sat at the table below the sign. Terrence tried not to stare at her tattoo-covered arms or the large ring through her septum.

"Can I help you?" she asked.

"My name's Desiree Henderson. I'm one of the models for the shoot."

The girl stood. "Follow me. Ray will be doing the shoot." Terrence started walking, but the girl said, "Wait out here. We just need the model."

As Terrence waited in the makeshift lobby, he scanned his work emails on his phone. They were all about the big news that James McKay was about to enter the draft. Depending on how he did, Terrence's whole life could change.

"No," Desiree said from the other room.

Terrence stood.

"I'm not going to do that," she said louder.

Terrence searched the lobby for the redhead but didn't see her. He jogged toward Desiree's voice then entered a small room where a waterfall backdrop rested against the wall. His jaw dropped. Desiree sat on a prop boulder wearing a thong bikini bottom and a red string bikini top that barely covered her large breasts. Her curly hair fell down her shoulders and seemed to glisten under the lights. Dark eye shadow accentuated her light-brown eyes, and the red lipstick made her lips look plump and shiny.

A man cleared his throat. "Buddy, this is a private shoot."

Terrence focused on the two men in the room. One stood behind a camera on a tripod and had his long brown hair pulled into a ponytail, his chest hair sprouting out of his barely buttoned business shirt. The other man, short and stocky, held a clipboard and glared at Terrence.

Terrence puffed out his chest and strode toward the man. "I'm with the model. Desiree, you okay?"

"Yeah, but I'm done with this shoot, Ray." Irritation laced her words as Desiree climbed off the prop.

The man with the clipboard stepped toward Desiree. "I said take your swimsuit off."

Desiree glared at Ray. "You didn't say anything about nude shots in the ad. I'm not down with that."

"Look, honey, it cost me a lot of money to rent out this space. Now stop playing naive and take off your damn swimsuit," he demanded.

Terrence hurried toward Desiree, his gaze on Ray. "This shoot's over."

Ray slammed his hand against the clipboard. "This bitch is going to take the pictures, or she's going to pay me."

Oh, hell no. Terrence stopped inches in front of him. "Either get out of our way, or I call the police right now and report this scam of a business you're running."

The man behind the camera put his hand on Ray's shoulder. "Let her go. It ain't worth it."

Desiree's trembling hand grabbed Terrence's. "Come on."

Terrence's heart pounded as Desiree gathered her clothes and purse. They jogged past the reception area and through the propped-open door.

"I'm so sorry," Desiree said once they were in his car, pulling her dress over her head.

"Don't apologize. We need to get out of here." Terrence peeled out of the lot.

Desiree leaned her head against the window. "I'm such an idiot."

"You're not an idiot. But I did you a favor by coming here, so you owe me one."

Desiree leaned toward Terrence, anticipation in her eyes. "Anything."

"Never mention this to Sophia," Terrence said.

CHAPTER TWENTY-THREE

CONGRATULATIONS

TARA

"TARA, BREAKFAST IS READY," HER mom called from the kitchen. Lying in bed, staring at the ceiling, Tara said, "I'm not hungry."

Her girls and Josh occupied her thoughts. Of course he hadn't answered her call the day before. The program was teaching Tara to take responsibility for her actions and practice acceptance and realize that the fault for her behavior fell squarely on her own shoulders. She'd taken Josh and their marriage for granted, but she wouldn't make the same mistake again. Since she would soon be moving back to the area, she'd have to find a way to meet him in person.

She imagined Josh celebrating his birthday with the girls and his parents. She could almost hear their laughter and Teeni leading them in song, living their lives... without her. Based on her visits with the girls, they seemed to be fine without her. When she asked Eleanor how Josh was doing, Eleanor always said he was doing well. While Tara was glad that Josh was doing such a good job with their daughters, it seemed as if they didn't even miss her. But she missed everything: her husband, her children, her friends, her work, her life. Sometimes she even thought about Louis, but after he'd shown his true colors by dropping her effortlessly, she realized she'd risked everything for absolutely nothing.

Tara's mom entered her room. "You need to eat something and get to the hospital."

"Mom, I'm fat. The medication's made me gain over ten pounds. Skipping a meal would actually help."

"Food or no food, you need to get up and go."

Tara closed her eyes. "I know."

"What's wrong? Did something happen?" Tara's mom sat next to her.

"I tried to call Josh to wish him a happy birthday yesterday, but he didn't pick up."

Her mom patted her hand. "I'm sorry."

"I really messed up, Mom." Tara choked up. "I messed up everything."

"It's not your fault that you got sick."

Tara pounded the pillow. "But it *is* my fault that I had an affair."

"You made a mistake. Don't beat yourself, or the pillow, up." Her mom grinned.

"Not funny," Tara said, though it kind of was.

"You're still a good person. Josh knows that."

Tara sat up and looked her mother in the eye. "But I'm not. I'm not a good person. By being with Louis, I chose him over Josh the way you chose Dad over me."

Her mom's eyes turned watery. "I didn't choose your dad over you—"

"Yes, you did! He treated us like shit, and you stayed with him. He was absolutely crazy, and you didn't care."

"Of course I cared. But I loved your father, and it wasn't his fault he was sick any more than it's your fault you are." Tears crawled down her mom's face. "He wasn't always like that. He just got ill, and I wasn't going to leave him because of it."

"But you were going to just leave me at Auntie's." Tears filled Tara's eyes. "You said you loved him, but what about me?"

"I wanted you to stay with your aunt because I knew you were strong. I knew you'd be fine without me, maybe even better. But your father needed help. He needed *me*. I tried so hard, but I failed." Her mom hung her head. "I failed both of you."

Tara didn't want her mom to suffer any more than she had already. "You didn't fail, Mom. It's not your fault that he couldn't deal with being sick anymore. We make choices based on what we think is best, though we're not always right. And you saved my life. I haven't said it yet, but thank you."

Tara's mom wiped her eyes with her hands. "I've always loved you. Though I'm sorry for what brought you to my house, I'm grateful that we've had this time together. Now, you really should eat something and get going. You graduate from the program this week, so you're almost there."

Tara's mother left the room, her shoulders slightly hunched forward as if she'd been carrying a heavy burden all her life. Once her mother was gone, Tara lay back on the bed and stared at the ceiling. She had dug this hole she lived in. Every day, life kicked more dirt into it, threatening to bury her alive.

<hr/>

Without showering, Tara threw on some sweats and sped to the hospital. Nicole gave her a warm smile as Tara grabbed a seat in the circle of chairs.

"So, Carrie, it's your first day here. Tell us a little about what's going on with you," Nicole said.

Carrie appeared to be around Tara's age. She was pretty with deep-set blue eyes and light-brown hair that touched her shoulders. Tara leaned in a little, curious.

"I have bipolar disorder," Carrie started.

It surprised Tara over and over again how people who looked so totally "normal" had the illness that so frightened others.

"I had a pretty bad episode that I don't want to talk about in depth, but afterward, I was left with no job, no fiancé, and no money. So I decided to end it all." Carrie took a deep breath. "I drove to the American River, took all the pills I had in my medicine cabinet, left my car running, and clogged the tail pipe. That's the last thing I remember."

A lump formed in Tara's throat. She still couldn't believe she'd been in such a bad place that she'd actually tried to end her life. If she had succeeded, she would have absolutely devastated everyone, and she was thankful every day for another chance at life.

"How were you found?" Tara asked.

"A camper found me. I really feel like God saved my life. The camper called 9-1-1, and I was rushed to the hospital. Next thing I remember was getting my stomach pumped in the ER. I was in the hospital for a few days before I was released to the in-patient program here," Carrie finished.

Nicole wrote on her notepad. "We're certainly glad that you're here." She turned to Tara. "We're glad you made it too."

"Bad morning," Tara said.

Everyone in the circle nodded because they knew exactly what that was like.

"Would you like to check in?" Nicole asked Tara.

"My mood is so low it isn't on the chart. But I do want to talk about my kids."

"Go ahead," Nicole said.

Tara let out a loud breath. "Sometimes I feel like I can't breathe. Like my daughters are the air. I miss being around them, watching them dance, hearing them sing, and just their smells, their embraces. I don't know what to do. I never envisioned not having them with me."

"All your emotions are valid. But if you keep doing what you need to do, you'll gradually have more time with them," Nicole said.

Tara shrugged. "I guess. I wasn't thinking about how my actions would affect them. I took for granted that I had three beautiful, healthy daughters and a husband who loved me. I was so distracted that I missed out on what was important."

"Some people go their whole lives taking people for granted. Now you know how special they are to you," Nicole said.

"I do know that now." Tara shrugged. "I'm just trying to figure out how to convey that to them."

"Thank you for sharing. We're going to take a little break then start the medication management session," Nicole said.

Tara wandered over to the water cooler where Joan stood. "Hi, Joan. How are you?"

Joan looked up. "Hey, Tara. I'm nervous. I feel good here, but when I think about going back to work, even though I loved it, I feel like I'm suffocating."

"I don't even want to think about going back to work. I'm scheduled to return next Monday, but I'm absolutely dreading it."

"Why?"

"I lost it at work, and I don't know how to face everyone. I've talked to my boss a couple of times. He said my job is still there, but he doesn't seem thrilled about me returning. My coworkers won't talk to me, even though one of them was my best friend."

"They say you find out who your real friends are in times like these. Real friends will be there when you need them."

"That's true. My neighbor Sophia has proven to be one of the best friends I have. I'm so grateful for her."

"You're lucky then," Joan said.

Though she wouldn't call it luck, Tara did appreciate the people she still had in her life and the opportunity to make things better with her family.

JOSH

Josh left the pharmacy. Once inside his car, he grabbed a Xanax out of the bottle, popped it in his mouth, then started the engine. Though the pills took time to kick in, Josh somehow relaxed instantly. His mom had insisted she take the girls out while Josh visited daycare centers and decided which one to put Teeni in after he went to work at the auto body shop. He hadn't made a decision yet because he was nervous about leaving her with someone else all day.

He drove to his parents' house to pick up the girls. When he got there, his dad greeted him at the door.

"How were the girls?" Josh asked.

"They were angels like usual. Did you end up returning Tara's phone call?"

Josh lowered his voice. "Why on earth would I do that?"

"Because she's your wife," his dad said.

"That's just a title. It means nothing now," Josh said.

"I was at your wedding, Josh. You made a commitment to her. In sickness and in health, for better—"

"I'm done with this conversation." Josh stormed past his dad. "Girls, let's go."

As his heartbeat pounded in his ears, he refused to think about the source of his anger over his dad's comment. He knew if he dug deep enough, he'd have to admit there was an ounce of truth in what his father had said.

Teeni ran up holding a piece of paper. Wet rainbow-colored paint oozed down it. "Look, Daddy," she said with a proud expression.

"It's beautiful. Let's let it dry though." He turned to Michelle. "What'd you make, honey?"

Michelle held up a painting with various colored shapes. "See?"

"It's beautiful, Michelle," Josh said, though he had no idea what it was.

"I'm not Michelle, Daddy. I'm Rapunzel, and this is all my hair." She pointed at the picture. "Daddy, Daddy, do we see Mommy today?" She tugged on his shirt.

"Not today, sweetie," he said.

"I miss Mommy," Michelle whined. "When is she coming back to live with us?"

"She's not," Chelsea said.

Josh turned, surprised to see his eldest daughter sitting in the corner of the patio. Her arms were wrapped around her knees, hugging them to her chest.

"Excuse me?" Josh asked.

"What? It's true. Mom went crazy. She's not coming back," Chelsea said.

A lump formed in Josh's throat. "Where did you hear that Mom went crazy?"

Josh and his parents had been very careful to not use that word, nor tell the children about Tara's suicide attempt. Instead they'd said she'd been sick, and that made her act differently than her normal self.

"Everyone knows, Dad. And the kids at school make fun of me," Chelsea said.

Josh knelt down before Chelsea. "I'm so sorry, sweetie."

She stood, crossing her arms. "Whatever, I don't care. I just want to go home."

Michelle tugged on Josh's hand. "Mommy's crazy?"

Josh shook his head. "She's just Mommy. She's still just your mom." Chelsea stomped into the house, and Josh followed. "Can we talk for a second?"

"I don't want to talk."

"Look, I know it's hard for you not seeing your mom every day."

"I don't care," Chelsea said.

"You don't have to put on an act for me. This is hard for me too."

She looked into Josh's eyes. "It is?"

"Of course," Josh said.

"But you're mad at Mommy. You don't like her anymore."

Josh had to try to catch his breath, surprised at the depth of Chelsea's comprehension of the situation. "You know Mommy was sick. She did some things that were scary."

"Like the fire?" Chelsea whispered, as if it were a secret she didn't want anyone else to hear.

"That was part of it."

Chelsea hesitated then asked, "Are you going to get sick like that?"

Josh placed his hand on Chelsea's shoulder. "No, sweetie. I'm always going to be here for you."

"Will Mommy come home when she's better?"

"I don't know." Josh didn't want to crush her or her sisters. The girls were the only reason he hadn't filed for divorce yet, but every other part of him wanted absolutely nothing to do with Tara. He couldn't imagine ever being able to even look at Tara without seeing her betrayal. "For now, she's going to have her own place."

"And then what?" Chelsea asked.

"And then we'll see," Josh said, trying to appease his daughter.

"Will you at least call her? She seems so sad when we see her. Maybe tell her that you won't be mad forever." Chelsea's eyes pleaded with Josh.

"Okay, I will."

Chelsea stuck out her pinkie. "Promise?"

Josh hooked his pinkie around his daughter's. "Promise."

At a quarter until midnight, Josh lay on the couch, his seventh beer of the night moistening his hand. He clenched the can then took a long swig, the bitterness of the liquid matching his mood. Most nights he didn't fall asleep as much as eventually pass out. He was halfway there, but his conversation with Chelsea played in his head. He hated that kids teased her about Tara and that his daughters had to grow up without their mom. He was the one who had to see their empty faces every day, the way they still looked toward the door in the evening, hoping Tara would come home.

Josh chugged the beer. Groaning, he stood and swayed to the fridge. His head spun, but he needed another beer. He needed something to numb the pain that never left.

He opened a beer and took a sip, wondering what the hell he was going to do with himself. Though answers didn't come, one thing was sure—Tara didn't deserve to be let off the hook. Grabbing his phone, he struggled to see straight enough to dial her. He'd deleted her number from his phone, but he knew her number by heart, however broken his was.

At that time of night, he was sure his call would go to voicemail. He'd leave her a message telling her exactly what he thought of her. She deserved to have a recording reminding her of all the ways she'd fractured their family. The phone rang. Rang. Rang. Rang.

"Hello?" her tired voice said.

Josh froze.

"Josh, is that you?"

"I'm just returning your call. What do you want? Why do you keep calling me?"

Tara cleared her throat. "I've been calling to apologize."

Josh laughed. He couldn't believe her. "You act like your words mean anything at all."

"I deserve that. I've treated you terribly over the past year, and I'm sorry."

"You don't even really get it." Josh crushed the empty beer can. "You didn't just cheat on me. You could have killed my daughters, then you had the nerve to try to kill yourself. Do you know what that would have done to the girls? They would have never recovered."

"I was sick—"

"Bullshit! You're selfish. You only think of yourself. And congratulations, because now you have plenty of time to do just that." Josh hung up then slammed the phone on the counter. Though he had finally said his piece, nothing inside him felt better. He grabbed another beer, lay on the couch, and hoped darkness would fall.

———— ◦✄◦ ————

SOPHIA

Sophia was scanning her emails when her intercom buzzed. "Yes?"

"We need you in meeting room A," Maxine said.

"Be right there." Sophia placed her hands on her aching back as she walked down the hall to the meeting room. She opened the door, and her breath caught in her throat. "What's going on?"

"Welcome, Mama!" Maxine said.

Tears filled Sophia's eyes. She hated how emotional she was these days, but the sight of all her female coworkers and a meeting room decorated with balloons, streamers, and a huge table of presents touched her heart.

"Surprise," Terrence said, coming up to her.

"You planned this?" Sophia asked.

"Well, technically Tara came up with the idea. She insisted that since she couldn't be here, she'd buy all the decorations online. And since you're always at work, we thought this would be the perfect place to have it."

Sophia hugged Terrence tightly. "Thank you."

Terrence hugged her back. "Baby, you're the one who's been carrying our little guy for the past nine months. I should be thanking you."

"Or girl," Sophia corrected. "This is just so perfect. And there's cake!"

———— ◦✄◦ ————

Sophia lowered herself into her chair. She placed her hands on her huge stomach then caught sight of her watch. It was already seven thirty, and she had promised Terrence she would be home in time for dinner at six. But the baby shower had lasted two hours, and she was swamped. After the baby shower, she'd had an hour-long meeting with her director about her sales from the previous week, her current leads, and her forecast for next week. The meeting ended with the offer for a promotion to traveling sales associate for the western state affiliates. It felt too good to be true, but it was hers. She pulled out her phone and dialed Terrence. When it went to voicemail, she dialed Tara.

"Tara, thank you so much for everything you did for my baby shower. It was a really great surprise," Sophia said.

"Of course. You've been such a good friend to me. I'm just sorry I had to miss it. How are you?"

"I'm great. But... I have news," Sophia said.

"Okay, tell me if it's good or bad. I can't really take any bad news right now after how Josh unloaded on me last night."

Sophia twirled the phone's cord between her fingers. "You talked to Josh?"

"Yeah, but your news first. Good or bad?"

"Good. I was offered a promotion to become a traveling sales associate with a six-figure salary." Saying it sounded better than she imagined it would. "It'd give me and the baby the financial security I'd been longing for."

"Congratulations! But wouldn't that mean you'll be away from home more?"

"I'd have to hire a nanny, yeah." Sophia rubbed her stomach. "What do you think?"

"You have to decide what your priorities are. I know how important your career is, but you're also going to be a mother, and I know how hard it is to juggle motherhood and a full-time job. Believe me, money can buy presents, but it can't be a substitute for a parent."

Sophia sipped her bottled water. Tara often talked about how much she regretted not being around her daughters more. "How are you? How does it feel to almost be done with the program?"

"It's okay. I'm a little nervous about the move this weekend and starting back at the firm on Monday. I don't know how to act around everyone."

Sophia slammed down her bottle. "You were sick! If they can't understand that and show some sympathy, then they aren't even worth thinking about."

"Mariana was one of my best friends. Now she's acting like I'm some type of monster."

"I'm sorry. But I'm here, and I promise you I'm not going to go anywhere." Sophia meant it.

"I really appreciate that, Sophia."

Sophia glanced at her watch again. "I should be heading home, so let's talk tomorrow."

After hanging up, Sophia opened a new Microsoft Word document and typed a short letter officially accepting the position. She hit Print, put the paper in an envelope, and slipped the envelope into her purse. She was tired and ready to go home to her bed... and her husband.

———————— ⋙⋘ ————————

TARA

Tara tapped her foot nervously. It was her last meeting at the hospital, and she wasn't sure if she was ready to get on with the next stage of her life.

With a proud grin, Nicole said, "As Tara mentioned earlier, she's graduating today. We're proud of you, Tara. Do you have any last words for us?"

Tara looked around the circle. "It hasn't been easy, but this has been a safe place for me to process everything that's happened. Thank you."

"Remember to take everything one day at a time. It'll take you a while to get used to all the changes in your life, but you'll get there," Nicole said. "Does anyone have any last words for Tara?"

Joan said, "I've gotten to know you a little, and I want to wish you good luck. You're a fighter. I know you'll get back on track."

"Thanks, Joan."

Sarah raised her hand. "I've only been here a couple days, but I want to tell you to not give up. Like me, you've been given a second chance at life. Learn from your mistakes and grow to be a better person."

"Thanks, Sarah."

After talking to Josh, Tara understood that she needed to prove she was no longer the selfish person she'd been over the past year. She'd given up too easily, too many times. It was up to her to actively work on putting her life back together.

Felicia cleared her throat. "From what I've heard, you've been your worst enemy. You aren't all bad, and you aren't all good. You're human. Forgive yourself and move on."

"Felicia, that's the nicest thing you've said to me."

"It's the last thing I'll say to you too," Felicia said.

"In closing," Nicole said, "this program is a protective resting point for people on a difficult road. Caterpillars form a protective covering while they transform into butterflies, and Tara, you're ready to fly. In spite of what you may have done in the past, know that you are a beautiful person on the inside." Nicole clapped. "Have a great weekend, and I'll see everyone else on Monday."

As Tara drove to her mother's house, Nicole's words played in her mind. Tara had never thought that she was a beautiful person. Her past had left her bruised and battered, and she had always been scared that if Josh or anyone knew about her family history, they couldn't possibly love her. Now not only were all of her skeletons out of the closet, but she felt as if they were taunting her.

We told you they'd all leave.

<hr>

"Mom, I'm back," Tara called.

Tara's mother sat on the green couch in the living room, staring at a photo album with a crumpled tissue in her hand.

"What are you doing, Mom?"

"I'm thinking about your father."

Tara sat next to her. "Sometimes you have to close the book. Like you told me, you have to know when to let go." Ever since her suicide attempt, Tara had been at peace with her dad's memory and no longer haunted by him.

"I felt like I died along with him."

"But you didn't. I want you to live. I want you to be in your granddaughters' lives and my life."

"That would be wonderful." Tara's mom hugged her.

Tara stood. "I'm going to finish gathering my stuff."

Grabbing Tara's hand, her mom said, "I'm sorry this happened to you. It breaks my heart. Still, I'll be eternally grateful that we've had this time together."

"Me too."

Tara went to her room to pack her clothes. Tomorrow she would pick up the keys to the one-bedroom apartment she would be calling home. It wasn't fancy, but she was glad to be moving back to San Jose so her daughters could visit her when it got to that point. She'd told her mother to live, and that advice applied to her too. Whether or not she was successful at getting Josh to forgive her, life must go on.

CHAPTER TWENTY-FOUR

HOME SWEET HOME

TERRENCE

"BABY, COME ON ALREADY." TERRENCE gently tugged Sophia's arm.

Sophia struggled to roll over and turn her back to him. "I had to pee all night long and barely slept. I'm too tired to get up."

"I'm sorry, baby," Terrence said. "But it's almost noon, and we're supposed to go to the concert."

"Concert?" Sophia opened one eye.

"Yes, the one I mentioned weeks ago?"

Sophia extended her arm. "Okay, help me up."

Terrence placed his arm around Sophia and helped her to a sitting position. He kissed her belly. "Go change. The forecast says it's going to be another beautiful May day. Nothing but blue skies. The baby's going to love the music." It was a perfect kind of day to reconnect with Sophia since she'd been so busy.

Sophia grabbed her phone, and Terrence sighed. She didn't let that thing out of her sight for a minute.

"Shoot," Sophia said.

"What now?"

"Maxine's asking if I can come in today. I really should."

Terrence huffed. "We never spend time together. This was supposed to be a chance for us to chill."

"I know, but I'm still trying to prove myself. I'm sorry—"

"I never see you anymore unless I come to your office."

Sophia reached toward him. "I know. It's just..."

Terrence ignored her gesture. "Fine. Go."

He went into the nursery and adjusted the framed baby Noah's Ark picture hanging over the crib. He'd painted the room sea green the weekend before and still couldn't believe their baby would be joining them in a matter of weeks. He mumbled when Sophia said good-bye and left twenty minutes later, then he planted himself in his recliner in front of the television.

"Terrence, what's wrong?" Desiree asked when she entered the living room.

"How'd you know something's wrong?" he asked.

"Uh, I only see you every day. I know you by now."

Terrence chuckled. At least someone cared. "Sophia had to go in to work, so we're missing our concert."

"Hold that thought." Desiree ran down the hall.

"Perfect," Terrence said to no one. No one around there cared to give him the time of day.

Desiree returned ten minutes later, fully made-up, wearing a white summer dress. "Let's go. We're going to be late." She gave him a wink.

Terrence rose with a huge grin.

———— ◦✧◦ ————

They arrived at San Jose's downtown for an all-day concert with bands from all musical genres. Navigating through the sea of people, Terrence spotted an oasis of green grass underneath a large tree. Claiming the small patch, Desiree spread out their pale-blue beach blanket, and they both sat on its soft surface.

Desiree gathered her hair in her hands, peeling it off her sweaty back, and lifted her elbows above her head. "I love the heat, don't you?"

Terrence's body grew warm as he eyed Desiree's exposed skin. "Ice cream?" He needed to distract himself.

"Cool."

Terrence wove through hundreds of people buying merchandise, dancing to the music, and socializing with friends. Smoke from the barbecue grills clung to the air, mixing with the heat. The white tents sold chicken, hot dogs, hamburgers, and fries. At the end of the plaza, a tent sold ice cream. He bought two then strolled back to Desiree, enjoying the day and happy he didn't have to miss out because of Sophia's work.

"This is the best," Desiree said after her first lick.

Terrence tasted his again. She was right.

Over the next couple of hours, they shared the small patch of grass, listening to various bands, snacking, and joking. The crowd represented the diversity of the Bay Area—all ages, cultures, and nationalities gathered. A Prince lookalike, dressed in all purple, took the stage with his band. The intro for "Let's Go Crazy" blared from the speakers.

Desiree stood and pulled Terrence to his feet. "I love this song!"

She shimmied and shook to the beat, and Terrence couldn't help but join in with a two-step. The band had the whole crowd on their feet. As more people joined in, the dance space became crowded, and Desiree moved closer to Terrence until their bodies were pressed against each other. Whether it was from the heat or the physical contact, Terrence's temperature soared. Her soft, toned body felt good against his.

She leaned back into him. "I don't remember the last time I had this much fun."

"Me neither." His life had been so serious and tense lately, and he'd needed this reprieve.

"Thanks for bringing me. This probably would have been too much for Sophia anyways."

"Yeah, I'm glad you came," Terrence said. And he meant it more than anything.

TARA

Tara opened her apartment door. "Sophia!"

"Hey!" Sophia said, opening her arms. "I got off work early, so I'm here for the grand tour."

Tara hugged her friend, nervous to show Sophia around the hole-in-a-wall apartment that was all she could afford since half her pay was going to Josh and the girls. "It isn't really anything grand to see, but come on in. Here's the living room, and then my room, and a bathroom."

Sophia looked around. "Good. It's a start."

"What do you have there?" Tara motioned to the paper bags Sophia held.

"I brought some groceries, assuming you hadn't had the chance to shop yet."

Tara hugged Sophia. "You are so sweet and right."

After taking the bags from Sophia, Tara ushered her into the little kitchen where Tara unpacked the groceries. When she opened the second bag, tears formed. It was a bamboo plant.

"How did you know I love bamboo plants?" she asked.

"Josh mentioned it when I said I was going to help you get settled in."

"Josh? When did you talk to him?"

Sophia looked away. "We talk"—she shrugged—"sometimes."

"Like when? Why haven't you ever mentioned it to me?"

Sophia's voice softened. "I keep in touch with Josh to make sure he's doing okay. I knew if I told you, you'd want me to give you updates or ask me to ask him stuff, and I don't want to be in the middle. Terrence doesn't know either. Josh still won't speak to him."

"How is he?"

"He's hanging in there. It's not easy, but he's doing what he has to do."

"That's good." Tara sighed. "I hate what I did to him."

"You're human. At some point, you need to forgive yourself."

Tara cast her eyes down. "I don't feel like I can."

"Maybe you don't feel like that right now, but hopefully you'll see that punishing yourself isn't doing anyone any good. What's done is done."

Tara pulled a box of chamomile tea from the bag. "So I'm in the infirmary now?" It seemed like eons ago when she had been the one bringing over groceries for Sophia when she was on bed rest.

"It's soothing," Sophia said with a playful smile.

"So what did you decide about the promotion?"

"I'm going to turn in my letter accepting the position on Monday."

"And Terrence is okay with that?"

A worry line creased Sophia's forehead. "I'm still thinking of the best way to let him know."

Tara cocked an eyebrow. "I think you should tell him. We both know that secrets only lead to trouble."

Sophia placed her hands on her belly. "I know. But I need security. I love Terrence more than anything. He and our baby are the best things to ever happen to me. But experience has shown that the only person I can rely on is me. What if he decides to leave me? I mean, look what you did to—"

Tara's heart stopped. "You were going to say Josh, right?"

"I'm sorry. It's just that you had an affair right under his nose. Who's to say Terrence won't do that to me?"

Tara wanted to convince Sophia that Terrence would never do that, but when she'd married Josh, she never imagined she'd have an affair. Things happened, and maybe Sophia had a point. "I don't think Terrence will ever do that. But if taking the job makes you feel better, then do what you think is best. I'm here for you, and I'll help in any way I can."

Sophia hugged her. "Thank you. Now let's get to unpacking some of these boxes."

"That certainly sounds better than having chamomile tea," Tara said, grateful she had a friend like Sophia.

❦

TERRENCE

Terrence and Desiree danced into the house, singing and laughing.

"Oh, Sophia," Terrence said.

Sophia sat on the couch, a grimace on her face. "Where were you two?"

Terrence couldn't believe she had the nerve to look upset after she'd chosen to work on a weekend over spending time with him yet again. "Uh, the concert."

"You two went to the concert?" Sophia asked.

"Well, I wasn't going to waste the tickets." Terrence shrugged. "So yeah."

"Chill," Desiree said before going into the guest room.

Sophia glared at Terrence. "I think it's time we talk about Desiree making other living arrangements. I also wanted to tell you that—"

Desiree screamed. "I can't believe they did this!"

"Hold that thought." Terrence jogged into the guest room, where Desiree stared at her computer monitor. "What is it?"

Desiree pointed at the screen. "Look."

"Oh, shit!" Terrence put his hands to his head.

"What's wrong?" Sophia asked, popping her head in the doorway.

"Uh, nothing," Desiree said.

Sophia approached the computer, and her mouth dropped open. Terrence looked again, and the same picture was there—Desiree's face and a computer-generated image of her naked body.

Sophia put her hands on her hips. "Desiree, why on earth did you put naked pictures on the Internet?"

"That's not her. She wore a bikini at that shoot," Terrence said. *Damn it.* Sophia still didn't know about the shoot.

"The what? How do you know that?" Sophia's face twisted into a grimace.

"He went with me to make sure everything went smoothly. It's not a big deal," Desiree said.

"Shut up, Desiree. This is a big deal." Sophia turned her wrath toward Terrence. "Since when do you go with my sister to bikini photo shoots and forget to mention it to me?"

Terrence didn't want to upset Sophia further. "It's not like that—"

"So you two smoke weed, go to bikini photo shoots, concerts, and what else?"

Terrence didn't appreciate what Sophia was insinuating. "You don't need to go there."

"Why are you always so uptight?" Desiree said.

Sophia put her hands on her back. "You know what, maybe it's because I work my butt off and you just sit around doing nothing."

"I can go then," Desiree said.

Terrence didn't want any more drama or to see Desiree leave under these conditions. "Come on, now. Let's—"

"That'd be great. I'll get some air, you pack, and when I come back, you'll be gone," Sophia said to Desiree.

"Whatever," Desiree said.

Sophia stormed down the hall.

Terrence ran after her. "Baby, wait—"

"Shut up." Sophia grabbed her purse, flung the door open, and walked out.

"Shit," he said as Sophia drove away. Terrence sat on the couch, leaned his elbows on his knees, and rested his head in his hands.

Desiree stood before Terrence. "I'll leave, but what's the big deal about you coming to my shoot? Ever since I got here, it's like she's on you for everything. Smoking a little weed, doing something nice by arranging a dinner with her dad, worrying about her safety after Tara flipped out. No matter how big or small, all she does is get on your case."

Terrence sighed. Was Desiree right?

Desiree knelt and peered into his eyes. "I'm going to miss you, Jerry."

Before he knew it, Desiree's lips were on his. She slipped her tongue inside his mouth. Desiree's skin smelled like vanilla and was soft as a ripe peach. Her curly locks tickled his face. She tasted like cotton candy, while Sophia tasted like—

"Wait!" Terrence pulled away. "Desiree, we can't do this."

"You're right. We can't do this *here*. Let's go," she said.

"What? Where?"

"The DoubleTree. It'll be just you and me. No one has to know."

Terrence rose from the couch and went into his bedroom to collect himself. Then he went to Desiree's room, where she was packing her bags. "Let's go. I'll meet you there."

The corners of Desiree's lips turned up. "Okay."

Terrence scribbled a quick note for Sophia, then he rushed out the door.

When he got to the hotel, he met Desiree inside the lobby.

"One room, please," he said to the woman at the front counter.

"And do you need two double beds or one king?" the woman asked.

Terrence glanced at Desiree then looked the front desk person in the eye. "Just a king."

Desiree squeezed his hand. They took the elevator up to the fourth floor. He slid the key card into the lock. The light turned green, and the door clicked open.

"I'll be right back," Terrence said.

He left the room and went into the stairwell. How would he explain the kiss to Sophia? He had to tell her. He pulled out his phone and dialed her. It rang, but she didn't answer. "Sophia, it's Terrence. Look, something happened with Desiree earlier. She can't be in the house anymore. I'm at the DoubleTree, getting her a room, then I'll be right home. I love you."

Terrence hung up then headed back to Desiree's room. He'd say good-bye then put the whole mess behind him.

CHAPTER TWENTY-FIVE

WE ALL FALL DOWN

Sophia

"Please answer, please answer, please answer," Sophia whispered.

"Hello?" Tara said.

"Oh, thank God. You won't believe what just happened," Sophia cried.

"What? Are you okay? Is the baby all right?"

Sophia rubbed her belly, which was bombarded with tiny jabs. "I basically kicked Desiree out. She and Terrence went to a concert today and came back all happy and stuff, then I walked in on them looking at naked pictures of her on the computer, and then he told me he went with her to a bikini photo shoot."

"Concert? Naked pictures? Bikini photo shoot? I'm not getting it. What did Terrence say?"

Sophia's chest heaved. She had overreacted a bit. "Nothing. I'm just tired, and I have a weird feeling that something's going on with them."

"Where are you?" Tara asked.

Sophia gripped the steering wheel. "In my car. I told Desiree to pack and get out."

"If it's time for Desiree to go, then good. But at some point, you have to decide to trust Terrence. You can't keep putting up a wall between the two of you."

"But—"

"No buts. Go home. Hear him out. Give him a chance."

"Really?" That was not what Sophia had expected to hear when she called Tara.

"Really. Head back home. I'll stay on the phone with you."

Sophia didn't have many other options. She was nine months pregnant, exhausted, and just wanted to lie in her bed. "Okay."

Sophia made a U-turn. As she made a right onto her street, Desiree's car sped past. Sophia hit her brakes when Terrence left the house. She pulled over and turned off the headlights.

"Desiree just drove away, and Terrence is leaving now. Why the hell is Terrence following her?" Sophia asked Tara. "I'll call you back."

She made another U-turn and followed Terrence's car. He hopped onto the 101 Freeway, and Sophia's heartbeat sped up as she followed from two cars behind him. They exited at First Street. Her stomach dropped when Terrence turned into the Doubletree parking lot. She turned in after him. She wiped away tears as Terrence jogged into the hotel.

As she parked a few spaces away from his car, Sophia could hear her mother's voice saying, "What did you expect? I told you no man could be trusted. It was bound to happen."

Sophia held the key in the ignition, imagining herself going home, packing up her belongings, and leaving for good. Maybe she'd go to LA and raise the baby with her mom. If Terrence wanted Desiree, he could have her. That was what men did, after all. Find someone else. Break hearts. Disappoint.

She put the car in reverse and backed out of the space. But then a voice—her own voice—said, "Go confront Terrence—the man you love, the man you married, the man who fathered your baby. If nothing else, he should have to look you in the eye and be honest."

She closed her eyes, let out a breath, and parked. Her phone rang. It was Terrence, but she didn't answer. She strutted into the hotel and approached the lady at the front counter. "I need to know what room my husband just went into."

The lady's eyes ventured to Sophia's stomach then to Sophia's eyes.

"Tall, black, with another woman. Please. I just need to know," Sophia pleaded.

"Four twenty-five, but I never told you that, and use the elevator. The stairs are steep," the lady whispered.

"Thank you." Sophia took a deep breath and marched to the elevator.

On the fourth floor, she banged on their room door. It opened, and there stood Desiree, as naked as Eve before the fall.

Desiree sucked in a breath. "Sophia?"

"Where the hell is he?" Sophia yelled.

"He'll be right back. Sophia, go home. He wants me, not you. You can't always have it all, you know," Desiree said like a teacher explaining a lesson to a child.

Sophia glared at Desiree. "He doesn't want you." She forced herself to sound more confident than she was.

"Oh, really?" Desiree put her hands on her hips. "He kissed me. He'll be back any minute to make love to me. When's the last time he wanted to do that with you?"

Sophia dry-heaved. Bile rose in her throat, so she pushed Desiree aside and ran to the bathroom. Closing the door, she barely made it to the toilet before everything she'd eaten earlier came up. As she reached for the doorknob to leave, she heard the door to the hotel room close. She pressed her ear against the bathroom door.

"Terrence," Desiree said.

"Put some clothes on," Terrence said. "I just came back to say good-bye. I'm going home. We'll figure out later how you can get the rest of your stuff from my house. Stay here tonight."

"But, Terrence—"

"I love Sophia," he said. "She's my wife. Your sister. This is wrong on every level."

Sophia opened the bathroom door. "Terrence, what the hell is going on?"

Terrence's cheeks reddened. He looked at Desiree's naked body then at Sophia. "I can explain."

"Explain the fact that you kissed my sister and now she's standing naked with you in a hotel room?" Sophia yelled. Even though he'd just turned her down, why the hell was he even here with her?

Terrence put his hands on his head. "No, no, no, that's not how it is."

"Don't lie, Terrence," Desiree said. "You want me. You're just scared to tell her you don't want to be with her anymore. Life is too hard with her. She makes it that way. You can be with me. We could leave together."

"Is that true? You want to be with her?" Sophia needed to know the truth, whether it hurt or not.

"Absolutely not," Terrence said. "No—"

"Did you kiss her?" Sophia asked.

"No. She kissed me. I mean… shit!" Terrence said.

Sophia's mouth was dry. Her throat was closing up. She was sure she would suffocate. She had to get out of there. "I can't do this."

She brushed past Terrence and out of the door.

"Just wait, Sophia!" Terrence yelled.

Tears blurred her vision as she staggered down the hall. She banged on the elevator button.

"Please, Sophia, please," Terrence said as he grabbed her arm.

Sophia turned away from him. "Leave me alone!"

She didn't want to wait for the elevator. She needed to get away from Terrence. She hurried to the stairwell and opened the door.

"Sophia, come on. Let's talk about this," Terrence pleaded.

Sophia spun around. "Leave me alone!"

Without looking, she took a step and landed halfway on the step. She lost her balance and screamed as she fell.

❖

TERRENCE

Terrence ran down the stairs. "Call 9-1-1! Call 9-1-1!" he yelled, hoping someone in the hotel would hear him. When he reached Sophia, he found she was unconscious. He held her head. "Sophia, wake up. Please wake up!"

He reached under Sophia's legs to try to pick her up. A watery substance mixed with blood underneath her. He carried her out of the stairwell and into the elevator. When he stepped into the lobby, the front desk woman gasped.

"Please, call 9-1-1," he yelled.

The woman picked up the phone as he set Sophia on the lobby couch. Though her mouth moved, only his heart thumped in his ears. *I can't lose her. I can't lose them.*

The elevator doors opened, and Desiree emerged. "What happened? Terrence, what happened?" She knelt next to Sophia and gently shook her shoulder. "I'm so sorry. Wake up!"

A ringtone went off. He looked around. It ended then started back up again.

"Her phone," Desiree said and pulled it out of Sophia's purse. When she did that, a white envelope fell out of the purse.

Sirens blared.

"Go get them," he said to Desiree as he took the phone and picked up the envelope.

Desiree ran out the lobby doors, waving her arms. The ambulance screeched to a halt, and two paramedics rushed toward Terrence and Sophia with a gurney. One of the medics took her vitals while the other asked Terrence so many questions about her condition that he lost track of them all. Finally they lifted Sophia onto the stretcher, then they ran to the ambulance.

"Can I come?" Terrence asked, running after them.

"You can meet us at Valley Medical Hospital," one called over his shoulder.

Terrence ran back inside to gather Sophia's purse. The ringtone played again, and a picture of Tara appeared on the phone screen. He took a deep breath, helpless to do anything to help his wife or baby. "Tara?"

"Terrence, why are you answering Sophia's phone?"

Terrence could barely speak. "There's been an accident."

"What? My god, what happened? Where's Sophia?"

"The ambulance just took her to Valley Medical Hospital. I'm going to follow them there." Terrence ran out of the double doors.

"I'm coming now," Tara said before hanging up.

Terrence wiped away a tear and hurried to his car.

JOSH

Josh dragged the garbage bin to the sidewalk for collection. Desiree darted from her car to Terrence's house. As he rolled out the recycling bin, Desiree ran back to her car with luggage.

"Hi, there," he yelled.

Desiree stopped in her tracks. Her face was red and wet with tears. Though she stared in his direction, she looked right through him as if her mind was miles away.

"Everything okay?" he asked.

"There's been an accident. Sophia was taken to the hospital," Desiree said.

Josh froze. "Is she okay? Is the baby okay?"

"I don't think so," Desiree said before bursting into fresh tears.

"Are you going there now?"

"No, I'm going back to LA." Desiree ran back through the house's front door.

Something was definitely off, and Josh had a feeling that Desiree had had something to do with it. She'd been trouble since he first met her.

Josh hurried inside his house and called his mom. "Mom, I need you to babysit."

Josh sped to the hospital. First his work accident, then Tara's episode, and now this? His mom always said that God only gave people as much as they can handle, but how much could one person take? *Where's the silver lining? What's the important lesson to be learned? When will the good come from the bad?* From his viewpoint, life was bleak.

He parked then ran to the emergency room, where Terrence paced in the waiting room.

"How's Sophia? How's the baby?" Josh asked.

Terrence startled. "Josh? How'd you know?"

"I saw Desiree."

Terrence looked at his toes. "Did she tell you what happened?"

"Just that Sophia was in the hospital. She seemed upset and said she was going to LA. She was packing."

"Thank God." Terrence's face relaxed.

Josh gave Terrence a questioning look.

Terrence threw up his hands. "She kissed me. She had some crazy idea that I wanted to leave Sophia for her."

Josh raised his hand. "Whoa, whoa, whoa, what?"

"It's crazy. I mean, she's cool, and we had a good time together, but that was it."

"Okay, well, Sophia. What's going on with her?" Josh asked.

"She saw me and Desiree in a hotel room and—"

"Wait." Josh held up his hand again. "What? Why the hell were you in a hotel room with Sophia's sister?"

"Sophia had told her to leave, and I was going to put Desiree up in a hotel for the night." Terrence cradled his head in his hands.

Josh didn't buy the story, but he didn't want to push Terrence right now.

"Full disclosure, Tara's on her way here," Terrence said. "I talked to her and told her what happened."

Josh sucked in a breath. He wasn't ready to see her. "Have you seen her since… everything?"

"No. Sophia has though. Said Tara's really torn up over everything that happened."

Josh didn't believe it. "I think she's just upset that she got caught and lost her mind in the process."

"It must have been pretty bad for her to try to kill herself though. I couldn't believe that. Sophia rushed straight there to meet Tara's mom in the ER. She said Tara almost didn't make it."

Josh's anger returned. Everything Josh did revolved around his daughters, and he couldn't feel empathy for Tara when she hadn't even thought about them.

A doctor in scrubs walked through the door. His forehead was creased, and his gaze bounced around the waiting room. "Terrence Douglas?"

Terrence shouted, "That's me!"

"We need you now," the doctor said, gesturing to the doors.

"Okay." Terrence followed the doctor through the double doors.

Josh leaned his head against the hospital wall and closed his eyes, exhausted physically and mentally. Being a single parent, navigating the array of emotions that swept him up like a boat being knocked about in the ocean, and trying to figure out his future in an uncertain world was too much. *Please, God. Please just for once let it end up okay.*

"I'm here to see Sophia Douglas," a familiar voice said.

"Take a seat, please," the receptionist said.

"Okay, thank you."

Josh froze. He opened his eyes. It was Tara... kind of. She wasn't the bossy blond bombshell in tight clothes and high heels anymore. She wasn't the overly confident businesswoman who would have demanded to see Sophia's doctor immediately. But most surprisingly, she wasn't the crazed, scarlet-letter-A-wearing villain his mind had turned her into. Wearing a white blouse and jeans and carrying an extra ten pounds, she looked like a normal... person.

When Tara turned around, her eyes scanned the waiting room before locking on Josh. She slowly walked toward him and stopped two chairs away. "Can I sit?"

Josh shrugged.

Tara sat and stared at her hands. "Do you know anything about Sophia's condition?"

"No," Josh said. "They took Terrence back about fifteen minutes ago."

Tara cleared her throat. "I know I said this on the phone, but I need you to know that I'm sorry."

Josh usually bottled up his emotions, smiled when he was upset, ignored pain when he was hurting, but he couldn't be that guy around her anymore. "Sorry?"

"I know one word cannot possibly make up for what I did"—Tara shrugged—"but it's the only one I have right now."

"Tara, you ripped out my heart and crushed it!" Josh's body grew hot. "I lived as the nice guy—in our relationship, in our marriage—but not only did I finish last, you trampled over me to run into the arms of another man. So find a better word."

Tara looked away. "It was one of the worst mistakes of my life."

"Mistake? You call sleeping with another man over a period of months a mistake?"

"Nothing I say or do will change the fact that I hurt and betrayed you. I was so busy running from myself, my past, my parents. I was a head-on collision in the making. And I crashed. You might not believe this"—her voice cracked—"but my actions have created a prison that only I have to live in."

Josh glared at Tara. "I hope it's a life sentence."

Tara flinched as if his words were a whip that had struck her. "I deserve that."

Though the emergency room buzzed with activity, the silence between them reverberated in his ears. Josh had imagined this conversation hundreds of times: the things he would say to let her know how screwed up she was, the reasons why he would never forgive her, the problems the girls would face because of her actions. But in that moment, all those words seemed meaningless. Their only purpose was to make her feel horrible, and he could tell she already did. But the silence was more evidence that she wasn't the old Tara.

"I don't even know you," he said.

"Maybe I don't even know me. But I know you." Tara pointed at Josh. "I know the good-hearted, selfless, funny, loving person you are. Don't let me ruin that."

"You already have. How can I ever be that person again? How can I unlearn how cruel a person who's supposed to love you can be? How can I ever trust someone again?"

"I've learned that sometimes you have to let go of who you were in order to become who you can be."

The hospital doors swung open.

"Josh!" Terrence yelled, tears spilling down his face.

CHAPTER TWENTY-SIX

IT'S OVER

SOPHIA

SOPHIA OPENED HER EYES. A blinding white light surrounded her. It was too much. She closed her eyes.

"Sophia, it's okay. Don't be scared," a woman's voice said.

Struggling to open her eyes again, the same white light blinded her.

"There you go. Come on, Sophia."

"Is this heaven?" Sophia asked.

Quiet laughter filled the room. She recognized the laugh and turned slightly. Terrence stood over her, his face wet with tears. Then she remembered.

"My baby. How's my baby?" she whispered.

A cry pierced the room. *This can't be good.* She shut her eyes tightly, bracing herself for the blow. More crying. But the cry sounded like a... baby.

"Sophia, it's over. Open your eyes," Terrence said. "Look up."

A sheet separated her upper body from her lower half. Dr. Smith held a tiny baby around the sheet. "Here he is, Mom. He's perfect."

Sophia shook her head, confused.

"We did an emergency C-section," Dr. Smith said. "He's a little early, but he's going to be fine."

"He?" Sophia said.

"Yes, he's a boy!" Terrence said with a proud smile as if he'd landed the player of his dreams.

Sophia reached for the baby. Dr. Smith handed him to a nurse, who placed him on Sophia's chest. She cradled his soft, warm, squirming body, and tears came to her eyes. Sophia's mouth opened, but no words came out. He was perfect.

"Do you want to do the honors, Dad?" the nurse asked Terrence, holding out scissors.

"Sure." His hands trembled as he clipped the umbilical cord.

"We need to close the incision. Terrence, do you want to hold the baby?" Dr. Smith asked.

"Yes." Terrence rocked his son in his arms and bent toward him. "I'm your daddy."

A nurse approached Terrence. "Congratulations. We need to take the baby's measurements and run some tests, so I need to borrow him for a few minutes."

"All right." Terrence handed their baby to her. His eyes sparkled as he looked at Sophia. "Josh is waiting in the lobby. Can I go let him know everything is good?"

"Josh?" Sophia said. "What's he doing here?"

"I guess he ran into De—" Terrence's eyes darkened.

The events of the night rushed back to Sophia. The last thing she remembered was catching Desiree and Terrence in a hotel.

"Go ahead," Sophia said dryly. Then the reality hit her—Terrence's actions had caused her to miss the birth of her first child.

"Sophia, I'm—"

"Just go." She faced the wall. Once Terrence left the room, she looked at a nurse. "What happened?"

The nurse's eyes softened. "You took a spill down the stairs. Your water broke, and we had to operate to make sure the baby was safely delivered."

Sophia didn't even try to stop herself from crying. Though the lower half of her body was numb from the anesthesia, her body heaved with her sobs.

The nurse patted Sophia's arm. "It's all right."

"Nothing about this pregnancy has been easy. This is not how I planned to have my baby."

"I know it isn't ideal, but women have emergency C-sections all the time. Given the fall, you and your baby are in great shape." She squeezed Sophia's shoulder.

Great shape? Sophia disagreed. The events of her child's birth would forever be tainted with the image of Desiree's naked body in a hotel room with Terrence, like black paint thrown over the canvas of a masterpiece. Sophia didn't know how she'd be able to move forward with him.

TARA

Terrence burst through the emergency room doors. "Josh!"

Tara and Josh stood.

"What's wrong?" Josh asked.

Terrence did a double-take at Tara. "Nothing's wrong. I want you to come up and see the baby."

Tara squealed. "Oh my God, Sophia had the baby? How is she?"

"She's good. They did an emergency C-section, and she should be moving to another room soon." Terrence wiped his tears away with the back of his hand.

Tara breathed a sigh of relief. "Can I see her?"

"That's a good idea. She's pissed at me, and I can't blame her. When they say it's okay for her to have visitors, you can see how she's doing," Terrence said.

Josh patted Terrence's back. "Congratulations!"

"Look, Josh, you being here means a lot to me." Terrence turned to Tara. "You too, Tara. I'm really grateful."

Josh grinned from ear to ear. "That's what friends are for, right?"

"Friends?" Terrence asked. "I mean, after everything—"

"Yes, friends," Josh said.

Terrence smiled. "Right."

Tara trailed slightly behind Terrence and Josh as they walked through the white halls. Though it had only been months since she'd been there when Sophia had had complications in her first trimester, she felt as if she were in a different time and a different place, as though she had been transported to a completely foreign galaxy. She no longer had plans to go home to Josh, and Sophia would be leaving with a newborn.

While they waited in the maternity ward waiting room, Josh and Terrence caught up. Tara closed her eyes. Something about being in the same room as Josh made her feel better. His voice was like a lullaby. She had no idea how she had ever taken her husband for granted.

"You can see her now," a doctor said to Terrence.

"Her best friend's going to go in first. Tara?" Terrence handed Tara Sophia's purse.

Tara followed the doctor down the hall and into a room where Sophia rested in bed. A tiny swaddled baby rested against her chest.

Tara went to her. "He looks perfect. How are you?"

Sophia shrugged, tears in her eyes. "I'm fine, I guess."

"I have your purse. Can I get you anything else?" Tara asked.

"I want my mom. I'd like to call her," Sophia said.

Tara pulled up a chair next to Sophia's bed and gazed at the baby.

"I think he fell asleep. Do you want to hold him while I call her?" Sophia asked.

Tara brushed her hands against each other. "I'm a little rusty with newborns, but yes, I'd love too."

"I can't lift him because of the C-section, so can you pick him up?"

"Of course." Tara stood and picked up the baby, tears filling her eyes.

As Sophia spoke with her mom, Tara gazed at the baby. He had the sweetest face and a perfect button nose. Her heart broke for Sophia and what she'd gone through tonight, but Tara was beyond grateful that everyone was all right.

When Sophia ended the call, she raised her eyebrows at Tara. "She's heading here first thing in the morning. Apparently she doesn't want to drive so late."

"Okay, good. How are you feeling?"

"I don't know how to feel. Everything happened so fast." Sophia had a bruise on her forehead. Her wide eyes attested to the fact she was still in shock.

"I know how that feels." Tara cradled the newborn. She inhaled his aroma, like the scent of heaven radiating from him. "But in this moment, seeing your baby, I realize that some chapters have to end before a new story can start. It was scary and messy and unexpected, but your pregnancy had to end so your baby could be born. I know the circumstances weren't perfect, but don't let that overshadow the perfection of this baby. Forget everything that happened and start fresh now."

Tears slid down Sophia's cheeks. Her voice quivered as she said, "The worst-case scenario happened. I found Terrence with Desiree in a hotel room. She was naked. They had kissed—"

"I get that. The worst-case scenario happened. But I do not believe that Terrence was going to do anything with your sister. He's here. You're still here. Now your baby is here too. You need to talk to him. Hear him out. This is the 'after' that follows 'happily ever.'"

"You think I should talk to him?" Sophia asked.

"Absolutely. You look exhausted. Why don't I give you your baby, and you two can sleep?"

Sophia wiped away her tears. "Thanks, Tara."

Tara eased the baby into Sophia's arms and left the room. She couldn't force Josh to forgive her, but she at least needed to convince him that her apology was sincere.

Tara met Terrence and Josh in the waiting room.

"She's absolutely exhausted, and she and the baby are going to sleep," she told Terrence. "I don't know all the details, but you need to make it up to her."

Terrence ran his hand over his head. "I know."

"Would it be all right if I come back first thing in the morning?" Tara asked.

Terrence smiled. "Of course."

Josh yawned. "I'm going to take off too, but I know the girls will want to see the baby. Is it cool if we swing by tomorrow too?"

"I'd love the girls to come," Terrence said, giving Josh a hug.

Tara and Josh walked down the corridor.

"Josh, can we... talk for another minute?" Tara said.

Josh looked at his watch then at Tara. "For a minute."

They stepped to the side of the empty hall.

"I'm trying to make a clean start, so I have to be honest," she said. "I love you. I want you back. Not right now, maybe not even next year, but I want a chance to make it up to you. I want to show you I can be a better wife than I was before. Do you think you'd ever be able to forgive me?"

He glowered at her. "Why on earth should I? You know what, I'm going to go."

"I'm not the Madonna you once thought I was or the villain you think I am now. I'm somewhere in the middle. That's where we all are— somewhere in the middle. I messed up, but my life is nothing without you and the girls—without our family." Tara couldn't believe it'd taken all of this for her to realize that, but it was true.

Josh's chest heaved. "So it's all about you, right? I should feel sorry for you and act like nothing ever happened? I'm not allowed to be mad?"

"Of course you're allowed to be mad, and no, it's not all about me. But I'm the one who bailed when things got tough. I'm the one who has to earn forgiveness. I want to help you become who you can be. I want to raise our children with you. I don't want my mistakes to ruin you."

"They already have. I hate what you did to me. I hate what you did to our daughters. I hate what you did to us!"

A tear slid down Tara's face. "Me too, Josh. I hate me too."

"You're not listening," Josh yelled. "I didn't say that I hate *you*. I will always love you, but—"

"You still love me?" Those words were a lifeboat in an ocean as she'd been drowning.

He shrugged. "Unlike you, I never stopped."

"I never stopped loving you, Josh. I was confused and I made terrible choices, but I never stopped loving you. I'm proving to the courts that I'm taking my medication and staying healthy and safe. Let me visit with you. Let me show you that I mean what I say. I promise it will be different. I'll be honest about my whereabouts. Answer every call. I'll try anything you need to prove that I can be trusted again."

Josh checked his watch. "You've broken your promises before. I can't give you what you want now. It's late, and I'm exhausted. I'm going home."

As Josh left, Tara's hopes and dreams of reconciliation went with him.

SOPHIA

A soft kiss on the forehead roused Sophia. She opened her eyes to Terrence.

"Sorry to wake you. You looked so perfect sleeping here, and I wanted to give you and the little guy a kiss," he said.

Sophia patted the baby's back as he slept soundly on her chest, but she didn't answer Terrence. She didn't have words for him.

Terrence cleared his throat. "About earlier. The things Desiree said. I'm so sorry any of that happened."

"Well, what happened?" Sophia had never thought her own sister could betray her like that. And Terrence had played a part in it too. "You obviously led her to believe that you wanted her."

"It was all a terrible misunderstanding. I tried to tell you that in my voicemail."

Sophia looked up. "Voicemail?"

"Have you checked the message I left you?"

Sophia took out her phone. She played Terrence's voicemail, her heart softening with each word. "Is this—what you said—true?"

"Absolutely."

A tear slid down Sophia's cheek. She'd been so prepared for her marriage to be over. Even from the beginning, she'd always pictured it ending the way her parents' had. Maybe she'd had one foot out the door the whole time in anticipation of it. But as Tara had said, Terrence was still here. He still wanted to be with her. "You wouldn't leave me?"

Terrence grabbed Sophia's hand. "Never."

"I don't ever want to leave you either. You and our baby are everything," Sophia said. "Can you hand me the envelope in my purse? I need to tell you something."

Terrence retrieved the envelope and handed it to Sophia.

"Did you read this?" she asked.

"No. It's not my business."

Sophia took out the letter, tore it into pieces, then handed them to Terrence. "I was going to accept a job promotion as a traveling sales associate, but you two come first. I'm going to let Maxine know I'll take my maternity leave, then we'll decide what position is best for all of us moving forward—not just me."

Terrence kissed Sophia's forehead. "I'd love that."

Sophia chuckled softly. "It'll give me a chance to catch up on the movies I've neglected since I started working."

Terrence stroked Sophia's hair. "Whatever the future holds, we'll be together. I love you both so much."

"I love you too." Sophia closed her eyes and fell back to sleep.

⸺⸻◆⸻⸺

"That nurse swaddled my grandson too tight. I don't want his circulation cut off."

Sophia opened her eyes. Her mom cradled Sophia's baby in her arms, and Sophia's father looked over her mom's shoulder.

"Mom, when'd you get here?" Sophia asked with a yawn.

"I left the moment the sun came up. You know I wouldn't be anywhere else. Someone has to keep this hospital staff on their feet. What would the world do without grandmothers?" her mom said.

"Don't forget grandpas," her dad added. "Terrence called me, and I jetted down here."

"And friends. You have to have friends," Tara chimed in.

Love surrounded Sophia. Having her parents in the same room was next to miraculous, but then again, everything about her baby seemed miraculous. Her son was so perfect, and she had to consciously push away her guilt over not wanting him. The pregnancy she had terminated brought a pang to her heart as she wondered what that baby might have looked like. She would have had two children, siblings, and with that thought, her own sister came to mind.

"Desiree?" she asked.

Her mom stepped closer. "I haven't heard a word from her. And given Terrence's reaction when I mentioned her, I don't think I will."

Sophia didn't respond. Part of her hoped she'd never see her sister again either.

"Knock, knock." Terrence peeked his head into the room. "Everyone decent? We have special visitors."

"Come in," Sophia called.

Terrence walked in with Josh and the girls at his heels.

"Baby! Baby!" Teeni and Michelle yelled, running toward Sophia's mom.

Chelsea entered the room last, and her eyes lit up when she saw Tara. Tara opened her arms, and Chelsea rushed to her and nuzzled her head against Tara's stomach.

"Is it okay for these kids to be here, germs and all?" Sophia's mom asked as she walked away from the crowd and the jumping little girls.

"Mom!" Sophia said.

"It's true. You can look, but don't touch the baby, girls," Josh said. "We aren't staying long, but the girls couldn't wait to see the new addition."

"Bring him here so the girls can see him." Sophia held her arms toward her mother, but her mom didn't move. "Mother…"

Sophia's mom glanced at Michelle and Teeni and dragged her feet as she brought the baby to Sophia. Michelle and Teeni crowded around the bed.

"What's his name?" Michelle asked.

Terrence nodded as if to say, "Go ahead."

Sophia said, "Well, we gave this whole love, trust, marriage, and pregnancy thing a chance, and he's the result. So meet Chance Douglas."

"Perfect, that is just perfect," Sophia's dad said, squeezing her shoulder. "You and Terrence sure did well. I'm so proud of you two."

Josh kissed Chance's head. "We'll let you rest. We just wanted to pop our heads in. Girls, say bye."

"Bye-bye, baby," Teeni said as Michelle jumped up and gave Chance a kiss on the cheek.

"Come on, Mom," Chelsea said.

"You know the rules for now, sweetie," Tara said, patting Chelsea's back.

"But Dad has to pick out clothes for work. He's gonna work in the office, so he needs fancy clothes. You always help him shop," Chelsea said.

Tara raised her eyebrows at Josh. "Work?"

Josh shrugged. "Figured it was time to give it another shot. A lot has changed."

Tara nodded. "That's great, Josh. You'll do great."

Chelsea tugged Tara's hand. "Come on, Mom."

"Sweetie, I can't—"

"You know what?" Josh said. "Why don't you come with us? I thought about what you said last night. I can see that you're trying really hard, and I think I can try a little too."

Tara's eyes lit up as bright as a lighthouse guiding a ship back to shore. "Thank you." She gave Sophia's arm a squeeze. "I'll be back later."

"Okay, see you then," Sophia said.

The Fishers left the room: Josh first, Michelle and Teeni skipping behind, and Chelsea nearly attached to Tara's hip.

Terrence came to Sophia's bedside. "You think they might work it out?"

Sophia smiled. "After everything that has happened to all of us, if we're all still here, I think they have a fighting chance."

Author's Note

Dear Reader,

Though the events described in this book are fictional, many people have very real experiences with mental health problems. If you or someone you know is experiencing a situation that is potentially life-threatening, get immediate emergency assistance by calling 9-1-1, available twenty-four hours a day.

If you or someone you know is suicidal or in emotional distress, contact the National Suicide Prevention Lifeline 1-800-273-TALK (8255). Trained crisis workers are available to talk twenty-four hours a day, seven days a week.

To learn more about mental illness and to find support, the National Alliance on Mental Illness (NAMI) is a great resource. Visit www.NAMI.org or call their helpline, (800) 950-6264.

Sincerely,
Alessandra Harris

ACKNOWLEDGEMENTS

To my husband, thank you for teaching me what it means to love and be loved. Thank you to my wonderful children, who encourage me. I strive to be a better mom and person because of the four of you.

Mom, thank you for your unceasing prayers and the faith that you've given me. Dad and Maria, thank you for never tiring of sitting in your kitchen and poring over the details of this book for the past years and offering support and encouragement.

Lyz, my sister and first editor, you not only helped me believe I could actually write a book but also spent time helping me get the first drafts done.

To Marcel, Sonya, and Tavi: I couldn't ask for better family. To my best friends who have been there when it wasn't easy.

I'm appreciative of all the writers I've met over the years who've helped this book become what it is: Fred Wiehe and the writing class, San Jose Writers, and the group of ladies. And finally, all those at Red Adept Publishing: the acquisitions team, my editors—Alyssa and Cassie—and the proofreaders. You all have made my dream come true.

ABOUT THE AUTHOR

 Alessandra Harris loves drama... well, on the page, that is. As a writer of women's fiction, she delves into real-life issues without shying away from controversial topics.

After graduating from San Jose State, Alessandra volunteered as a contributing writer for CityFlight.com, a former online magazine geared toward the San Francisco Bay Area's African American Community. An avid reader of women's fiction, she transitioned to writing fiction with the help of writing instructors and critique groups.

Currently, Alessandra is the organizer of San Jose Writers, a diverse group of writers in the South Bay Area, California. At home, she enjoys spending time with her husband and four wonderful children.

Made in the USA
San Bernardino, CA
12 February 2020